Always never yours

Always never yours

EMILY WIBBERLEY

AUSTIN SIEGEMUND-BROKA

PENGUIN BOOKS

PENGUIN BOOKS
An imprint of Penguin Random House LLC
375 Hudson Street
New York, New York 10014

First published in the United States of America by Penguin Books,
an imprint of Penguin Random House LLC, 2018

LIBRARY OF CONGRESS CATALOGING-IN-PUBLICATION DATA
Names: Siegemund-Broka, Austin, author. | Wibberley, Emily, author.
Title: Always never yours / by Austin Siegemund-Broka and Emily Wibberley.
Description: New York, New York : Penguin Books, 2018. | Summary:
Between rehearsals for the school play and managing her divided family,
seventeen-year-old Megan meets aspiring playwright Owen Okita,
who agrees to help her attract the attention of a cute stagehand
in exchange for help writing his new script.
Identifiers: LCCN 2017058698| ISBN 9780451479846 (hardback)
Subjects: | CYAC: Dating (Social customs)—Fiction. | Theater—Fiction. |
Families—Fiction.
Classification: LCC PZ7.1.S535 Al 2018 | DDC [Fic]—dc23
LC record available at https://lccn.loc.gov/2017058698

ISBN 9780451479846

Printed in the United States of America

1 3 5 7 9 10 8 6 4 2

For our (respective) parents

Always never yours

ONE

ROMEO: *Is love a tender thing? It is too rough,*
Too rude, too boist'rous, and it pricks like thorn.

MERCUTIO: *If love be rough with you, be rough with love.*

I.iv.25–7

"ALL THE WORLD'S A STAGE . . ."

Brian Anderson's butchering the line. I listen for the posturing and borderline mania Shakespeare intended, but—nope. He's doing some sort of half English accent and throwing iambic pentameter out the window.

"How about we stop there for a second?" I interrupt, standing up and straightening my denim dress.

"Just once, Megan, could we get through the scene?" Brian groans.

I shoot him a look and walk into the middle of the "stage," which for today is the hill behind the drama room. Our drama teacher, Ms. Hewitt—who everyone calls Jody—sent us outside to rehearse whatever Shakespeare scene we wanted. And by "sent us," I mean kicked us out for being obnoxious. I picked the hill for our rehearsal space because I thought the pine trees nearby would evoke the forest in *As You Like It*.

Which was stupid, I now realize.

"I feel like we're not getting what's going on in the characters' heads," I say, ignoring Brian and speaking to the group. It's only the four of us out here in the middle of sixth period. Jeremy Handler wears a hopeless expression next to Brian while Courtney Greene texts disinterestedly. "Orlando"—I turn to Jeremy—"is fundamentally a nice guy. He only wants to steal from the Duke to help his friend. Now, Jacques—"

I falter. A glimpse of green catches my eye, a Stillmont High golf polo. Biceps I have to admire peek through the sleeves. A wave of brown hair, an ever-present smirk, and *wow* do I want to go over and flirt with Wyatt Rhodes.

He's twirling a hall pass, walking unhurriedly in the direction of the bathroom. He's chosen a good bathroom, I notice. Roomy, with plenty of privacy because it's not near the locker hall. Perfect for a brief make-out session. I could walk over, compliment his impressive upper arms, lead him into said bathroom—

Not right now. If there's *one* thing that could keep me from flirting, it's directing the hell out of Shakespeare.

"Now, Jacques," I repeat, regaining my directorial demeanor.

"Come on, Megan," Brian interjects. "This scene doesn't even count for our grade. Jody doesn't give a shit. She just wanted us out of the room. And you know everyone's distracted."

I'm opening my mouth to argue that every scene matters when I hear a voice. "Megan!"

I turn to find my best friend, Madeleine Hecht, jogging up the hill, her perfect red ponytail bouncing behind her, freckled cheeks flushed with excitement. "I just left the library," she continues, breathless—Madeleine volunteers in the textbook room during sixth period. "And when I walked past the drama room I saw Jody posting the cast list!"

Hearing that, my actors drop their scripts and disappear around the corner, obviously on their way to the bulletin board at the front of the Arts Center. Not suppressing a smile, I collect the scripts.

I'm a director, not an actress, so the cast list doesn't hold the same thrill and terror for me that it does for the rest of the class. But this year, I'll be making my Stillmont High stage debut in one of the smallest roles in *Romeo and Juliet*, the fall semester play. I'm guessing Lady Montague or Friar John.

I wouldn't be, except it's my dream to go to the Southern Oregon Theater Institute. It's the Juilliard of the west, with one of the best directing programs in the nation. For whatever reason, they require every drama student to have one acting credit on their résumé, a requirement I'm going to fulfill as painlessly as possible.

"Walk over with me?" I ask Madeleine.

"Duh." She quickly takes half the scripts off my stack, chronically unable to resist lending a hand.

Right then, Wyatt Rhodes emerges from the bathroom. I follow the lanky confidence of his walk, biting my lip. It's been six months since my last relationship. I'm due for my next boyfriend. Scratch that—*over*due.

"Wait here," I tell Madeleine.

"Megan—"

I ignore her, a boy-starved moth drawn to a polo-wearing flame. I'm grateful I spent the extra ten minutes brushing the inevitable knots out of my long brown hair this morning. I know I don't have Madeleine's effortless beauty, but I'm not *not* pretty. I guess I'm in the middle. I'm neither short nor long-legged. I have features not round, closer to round-*ish*. Mine isn't the body that comes with swearing off burgers or going running more often than every January 2.

Wyatt doesn't notice me, preoccupied with tossing his hall pass from hand to hand. I call out to him in a practiced and perfected come-hither voice.

"Hey, Wyatt." I gesture to his defined biceps. "Do the abs match the arms?"

Not my best work. I haven't flirted in too long. In fairness, it's kind of a high-school bucket-list item of mine to make out with a really, really nice six-pack, and the boy attached. Even in seven boyfriends, from athletes to drama kids, *nada*.

Wyatt grins broadly. I cannot believe I haven't hooked up with him yet. It's been obvious he's gorgeous for practically the entirety of high school, and this is far from the first time we've exchanged flirtations. He doesn't immediately come across as boyfriend material, but his hotness *must* bespeak a valuable interior. I can picture us now, having long, thoughtful conversations over cappuccinos . . .

"They do on the days I don't double up on breakfast burritos," Wyatt crows.

Okay, *short* conversations over cappuccinos.

"Today's one of those days," he continues. "But don't take my word for it." He eyes me invitingly, his voice unsurprised.

Not just because he's Wyatt Rhodes and he knows he's gorgeous, either. It's because I have a reputation for being boldfaced like this. Unabashed. Unreserved. It's no secret I've had seven boyfriends, and I'm not ashamed. Class Flirt is a title I've enjoyed every minute of cultivating.

I'm about to take Wyatt up on his offer when I feel a hand on my elbow. "Bye, Wyatt," I hear Madeleine yell pointedly. "We have to go to class." She drags me away from him, and in a low if not entirely unamused voice, she says, "What've we talked about, Megan? Wyatt Rhodes is on the no-flirt list." She considers a moment, adding, "He's number *one* on the no-flirt list."

"No, he's not," I reply. "Principal Stone is."

Madeleine gives an exasperated grumble. "Point taken. Wyatt's definitely number two. You put him on the list yourself, remember? After he asked in sophomore English what book Jane Eyre wrote?"

I nod grudgingly. "And there was the time he said *Furious Seven* was his favorite book on the yearbook survey."

"You're going to find a guy way better than Wyatt. Just give it time," she reassures me as we walk down the hill toward the Arts Center. "You don't think Tyler has any competition for Romeo, do you?"

Tyler Dunning is Madeleine's boyfriend. He headed off with a group of guys to rehearse *Macbeth* when Jody banished us.

"Of course not," I answer easily.

Tyler's a leading man in every respect. Tall, broad shouldered, with dark wavy hair—he's undeniably hot. He plays baseball in spring and still manages to score the lead in every theater production. Between his charisma and Madeleine's

5

universal likability, they're the total "it" couple of Stillmont High.

"Who'd you audition for?" Madeleine asks.

"Lady Montague."

She wrinkles her nose. "Who even is that?"

"Exactly." I grin. "She's the smallest role in the play."

I'm expecting the crowd packed in around the bulletin board when we turn the corner. What I'm not expecting is how everyone goes silent. I feel eyes on me and hear whispers start to spread.

"You guys aren't being weird at all," I mutter, trying to sound sarcastic despite my mounting nerves. I know this silence. It's the silence of the un-cast, the scrutinized walk to the gallows of your play prospects. For the first time, I feel what my classmates must whenever a cast list goes up. My pulse pounds, nerves thinning my breath. I envision apologetic emails from SOTI, halfhearted tours of other colleges in winter. Even though I'm not an actress, I need this part.

I step up to the list, my pulse pounding, and intently search the bottom of the sheet where the smaller roles will be listed. *Lady Montague* . . .

I trace my finger to the corresponding name. *Alyssa Sanchez.* My heart drops. Alyssa was the obvious favorite for Juliet. Jody's not messing around. This was brutal casting.

Reading up the list, I don't find my name. *Friar John, the Nurse* . . . Unbelievable. Even after I explained my situation to Jody, she still screwed me over.

Then I reach the top of the list.

TWO

PRINCE: *For never was a story of more woe*
Than this of Juliet and her Romeo.

V.iii.320–1

"THIS IS A MISTAKE, RIGHT?" IN SECONDS I've fought through the crowd and thrown open the door to Jody's office. *"Juliet?"*

I hear something clatter to the floor. Jody's office looks like a yard sale of mementos she's kept from every Stillmont production. There are playbills, props, and even pieces of sets stuffed onto the shelves. What looks like a brass doorknob rolls in front of me.

Jody stands up from her desk, her chunky turquoise necklace rattling. "You're not happy," she muses, studying me through her bright red glasses. They stand out even brighter against her gray hair. "I thought you'd be happy."

I feel a heaviness settle on my shoulders. A nervous pit opens in my stomach. "This isn't a misunderstanding?" I ask weakly. "It's not Anthony pulling a prank or, I don't know, a typo from an incompetent freshman you asked to print out the list?"

"No, the incompetence is all mine," Jody says, a hint of humor in her voice.

"I auditioned for Lady Montague, not the lead of the play!" I barely keep myself from exploding.

7

She raises an eyebrow, unsmiling. "Well, you got the lead," she says, her voice level.

"Why? I don't want it. Can't I be someone else? Anyone else?" I know I sound pleading.

"You're just nervous, Megan." Jody crosses her arms, but her tone has softened. "Yours was the only audition other than Anthony Jenson's that demonstrated a true understanding of the material. I've seen you direct Shakespeare before, I know you understand the play. You're Juliet, whether you like it or not."

"Jody, please." Now I'm definitely pleading. "You know I only auditioned because SOTI has an acting requirement. I've never acted in my life."

"It's a learning experience. I'm not expecting you to win a Tony," Jody says.

"Well, are you expecting *Romeo and Juliet* to be a comedy? No? Then—"

"Megan," she cuts me off sternly. "You auditioned for the play. You got Juliet. You can take it or leave it, but I've cast every other role."

I know I have no choice—Jody knows it, too. It's already the end of September. This production's my last chance for an acting credit before college applications are due in December.

"This is not going to go well for you." I sigh in exasperation, reaching for the door.

⚓

I've taken one step outside Jody's office when I run into something solid and flat.

"Whoa," I hear above me.

Of course. I step back to find Tyler grinning down from the imposing height of six foot whatever. "Hey, Juliet," he says, his deep voice working on me in ways I sincerely wish it didn't. "This could be awkward, huh?"

It hits me suddenly. Tyler's Romeo. And I'm Juliet.

I quickly recover. "Nothing could be more perfect than the two of us playing doomed lovers."

He laughs and turns to face Madeleine, who's come up beside him.

It's not a big deal, but Tyler and I dated last year. Now we don't. He's with Madeleine, but I'm not jealous or resentful. In a way, I was expecting it.

Honestly, hating acting isn't the only reason I don't want to play Juliet. The other reason is, I'm not a Juliet. I'm not the girl in the center of the stage at the end of a love story. I'm the girl before, the girl guys date right before they find their true love. Every one of my relationships ends exactly the same.

Take Tyler. He's the only guy I've ever felt myself close to falling in love with, and he dumped me six months ago to date my best friend. But I'm okay, really. Everyone knows Tyler and Madeleine are meant to be. Besides, I'm used to it.

It started when I was eleven. I'd just proclaimed to Lucy Regis my undying love for Ryan Reynolds with the intention to marry him. The next day we found out he'd married

Blake Lively. Not that that was a real example. Just an omen of things to come.

The first boy I kissed, in seventh grade, passed me a note in social studies the next day informing me he was going to ask Samantha Washington to the Hometown Fair. They've been together ever since. Freshman year, my first real boyfriend ended up cheating on me with the literal girl next door, who, it turned out, was Lucy Regis. They just celebrated their third anniversary.

It's happened time and time again. It's not a "curse" or something stupid like that—it's just more than a coincidence. And it's why I couldn't possibly get into the head of Juliet, western literature's icon of eternal love. If the world's a stage, like Shakespeare wrote, then I'm a supporting role. Or hidden in the wings.

"You're not going to steal my boyfriend, are you?" Madeleine teases, wrapping an arm around Tyler.

"No, that's your thing," I chide without thinking.

Madeleine's face immediately falls, and I'm afraid she's going to cry for the hundredth time. When Madeleine confessed to me her feelings for *my* then-boyfriend, it took two hours of hugs and reassurance before the guilty tears ended. It's not like they cheated—Madeleine's so ridiculously thoughtful that she told me before she even told him.

And it hurt. I won't pretend it didn't. But I knew the pattern. I knew what was going to happen with me and Tyler. And I understood I'd only get hurt worse trying to fight the inevitable. Better to let the relationship end before I fell for him for real.

I rush to put a hand on her arm. "It was just a dumb joke, Madeleine," I tell her. "You two are perfect."

She smiles, relieved, and leans into Tyler.

"You guys coming to the cast party?" Tyler asks.

"Where?" Cast parties are a Stillmont drama institution. Drama's sixth period, but rehearsal can extend until 5 or 6 in the evening. For every production, the cast and crew choose one location for post-rehearsal dinners and parties. I'm just hoping it's not Tyler's house.

"Verona, of course." He grins like this is amusing.

I groan. Stillmont's an hour from the Oregon Shakespeare Festival in Ashland. It's not a coincidence we're one of the strongest high-school drama programs in the state, probably the country. When I'm not being forced to play the most famous female role in theater, I feel pretty lucky to have a teacher like Jody, not to mention the departmental funding. Unfortunately, however, proximity to Ashland has its downsides. Namely, an inordinate amount of Shakespeare-themed establishments. Verona Pizza is one of the worst.

Tyler doesn't hear, or he pretends not to. He looks down at Madeleine. "I'll drive you home after."

"But I have—" she starts.

"I know," Tyler interrupts, tugging her ponytail affectionately. "Your sister's ballet recital. I'll have you home in time."

I roll my eyes. Watching them together was the quickest, if not necessarily easiest, way of extinguishing whatever lingering feelings I had for Tyler. Now when I look at him, I honestly can't imagine dating him—regardless of how his objective adherence to certain standards of male desirability might *occasionally* affect me.

They smile at each other for a moment, looking like the contented lovers in erectile-dysfunction ads.

I'd hate them if I weren't happy for them.

I walk to the restaurant while Tyler and Madeleine drive over together. Verona's just ten minutes from school—I'd probably go there every day if the place didn't repulse me. I'm hoping the easiest way to cure the cast's eagerness for Verona is a meal there followed by certain food poisoning.

In the parking lot, I glance up at the marquee, which today reads *To eat pizza or not to eat pizza? That is the question.* I shake my head. The Bard would be proud.

Inside, it's worse. The wood paneling of the booths gives way to kindergarten-quality murals of medieval towers and turrets, interposed awkwardly with out-of-context *Romeo and Juliet* quotes. *"What's in a name?"* is written in three different sizes over the soda machine, and I pass by *"Romeo, Romeo, where art thou, Romeo?"* over the door of the arcade. Yes, there's an arcade, and it's not even the correct quote. It's definitely *wherefore.*

The big booth in the back is packed with the usual theater crowd, but when I walk up, Anthony Jenson slides over to make room. He's holding a copy of the play, and when I sit down, he thumbs it open.

"This monologue is incredible," he says after a minute.

"Um, which?" I lean over. He's playing a lead, I'm certain of that. Ever since he transferred here freshman year, poached by Jody from a school district unwilling to cast a black actor in prominent roles, he's earned key parts in every production.

He glances up at me, mock-indignant. "You didn't check who I was playing?" He drops the script on the table in front of me. I read the open page. It's Mercutio's monologue about the fairy Queen Mab. "Everyone thinks Romeo's the best male role," he continues intently, "but Mercutio's way more challenging. He's got a long monologue, a death scene—" He breaks off suddenly. "What am I saying? I'm talking to Juliet!"

"Don't remind me," I grumble.

He eyes me sympathetically. "You'll be fine, Megan." He pats my shoulder. "In any case, it's a free trip to Ashland."

I blink. "Ashland?"

"The Shakespeare Festival—"

"I know what the Oregon Shakespeare Festival is," I cut him off. "What does it have to do with *our* play?"

"Nobody told you?" Anthony looks incredulous. "Stillmont got accepted to the high-school feature this year. We're performing *Romeo and Juliet* in Ashland in December."

A tightness takes hold of my chest. Jody just had to choose the most prestigious Shakespeare festival in the country to force me into the spotlight. "Learning experience, my ass," I mutter under my breath. I must look pale, because Anthony's watching me with an expression that's half concern, half distrust.

"You're going to be great. You *have* to be great. This production needs to stand out. Reps from Juilliard are going to be there, evaluating me—"

"I got it, Anthony!" I loudly interrupt. "I'm just nervous. I'll figure something out," I say.

Anthony's gone quiet. I glance over, guessing I'll find him with his head in his hands, weighing the devastation I'll wreak on his college chances.

But I notice he's no longer looking at me, and I follow his eye line—right to a blond and obnoxiously muscled busboy. He looks our age, but I definitely would have noticed someone like *him* at Stillmont. He must go to one of the private schools in the area.

"Oh my god," Anthony mutters, watching the busboy clear a table and head into the kitchen. I know what that look means. Like me, Anthony falls fast and falls often. The difference is, he falls hard. He believes every guy is the one, and he's devastated every time a relationship falls apart. Still, there's no use trying to stop him.

"Go," I say, standing up and letting him out of the booth. Wordlessly, he does.

I realize I'm left sitting next to a group of senior girls who I know all auditioned for Juliet. Alyssa Sanchez is looking at me like she wishes I would go full-Juliet and stab myself with a dagger right about now. Her entourage won't even make eye contact.

"I didn't audition for the part, you know," I say, hoping to defuse the tension. This kind of drama is yet another reason I prefer directing.

"Well, you got it," Alyssa replies icily.

"It's obviously going to be a disaster," I try to joke.

"Yes." She stands up. "It will."

A couple of her clique follow her out of the booth. I look around the room, feeling distinctly out of place—or out of context. I know everyone here from drama, where I watch and direct them, but never participate. Now I'm expected to act alongside them. I spot Tyler and Madeleine in the arcade, adorably tag-teaming a Whack-A-Mole game. Everyone else, I notice, is darting glances between Tyler and me. Between Romeo and Juliet.

Everyone except one boy, sitting by himself, writing feverishly in a notebook.

I recognize him as the new kid in drama this year. He's Asian, thin without looking underfed, with hair a little overdue for a haircut—which he's presently running his fingers through contemplatively—and wearing a well-fitting gray sweater. I'm not sure I've ever heard him talk, but he'd definitely be better company than Alyssa's minions giving me death glares. Without a second thought, I walk over and sit down in his empty booth.

"Owen Okita, right?" I remember his name from a class we had together once. Freshman math? I've seen him hanging out in the halls with Jordan Wood, the editor of the school paper who moved to Chicago this summer, but I've never really noticed him.

Owen blinks up at me.

"You weren't in drama last year," I continue.

"Don't I know it," he says, and his voice startles me. For a guy I've never heard speak, he sounds surprisingly sure of himself. "I'm completely out of my element."

"Who'd you audition for?" I ask, noticing he's fidgeting with his pen.

"I just wanted to play an extra. Instead, I'm Friar Lawrence. Like, I'm a character."

"Come on." I smile, relieved and sort of stunned to find someone else in my situation. "Friar Lawrence isn't an important character."

"Every character's important." He sounds slightly affronted.

I pause, curious. Owen signed up for drama in his senior year just to play an extra? "Well, why'd you audition, then?"

"*Romeo and Juliet*. It's, uh . . ." He looks embarrassed and drums his pen on the table. "It's my favorite play. When I saw drama was doing it I had to join, but I'm terrified on stage, and Friar Lawrence has a ton of lines."

I feel myself smile, respecting this boy who can admit to stage fright and appreciating *Romeo and Juliet*. "You think *you've* got it bad? Guess who I've got." I reach across the table and grab the pen out of his hand, putting an end to his nervous tapping. Owen's eyes follow it, his ears reddening.

"The Nurse?" he asks, stowing his hands under the table.

"The *Nurse*? Should I be offended?"

"I, sorry, I—" His ears flame brighter.

"Go higher," I instruct, enjoying how easy it is to fluster him.

Owen pauses. "Megan Harper," he says after a moment, like he's just recalled my name from the recesses of his memory.

I wonder if he remembers me from freshman math, too, or if he knows me for the reason everyone knows me—because I hang out with Madeleine and Tyler, homecoming queen- and king-to-be. I can practically see Owen connect my name to the cast list in his head. "You're Juliet . . ." He studies me. "And you're not excited."

"Nope." I return the pen in a gesture of goodwill.

"You must be the only girl in the history of high-school theater *not* thrilled to be Juliet."

"I don't think there's a girl alive who'd want to play Juliet opposite her ex," I reply.

His eyes widen. "Who's playing Romeo?"

Now it's my turn to be surprised. "You don't know?" I didn't think there was anyone left in Stillmont who hadn't heard in too much detail about Tyler and me breaking up. If he's unclear about my history, I guess he *does* remember me from freshman math.

"Uh. Should I?" Owen looks lost. I nod in Tyler's direction, and Owen's eyebrows shoot up once more.

"Seriously, I can't believe you haven't heard the story."

"My apologies for not being up-to-date on the drama-kid gossip," he says with a hint of a smile. I laugh, and his smile widens until it lights up his face. But before I can reply, Anthony's standing next to the booth.

"I got a job," he says, and without missing a beat, "Hey, Owen."

"You already have a job." I frown, looking up at Anthony. Then I notice the blond busboy collecting dishes across the room, and I realize what's happening here. "Anthony, tell me you didn't change career paths because you're hot on the busboy."

He rolls his eyes, but he's smiling. "Starbucks isn't a career path. And it's not for the busboy—it's for love. And the busboy has a name—Eric."

I'm about to complain about the loss of free Frappuccinos when my phone's alarm buzzes in my bag. "Shit," I say instead. I lost track of time. "I have to go."

"It's so early! You haven't even eaten!" Anthony protests. Then a moment later, his expression shifts. "Oh, right. It's five on Friday," he says, realizing.

I get up. "We'll talk about the busboy—"

"*Eric*," Anthony interrupts.

"—tomorrow," I finish, and give Owen a nod. "Talk to you later, Friar Lawrence."

I close the front door quietly when I get home. The house is silent, nothing short of a miracle these days. I head upstairs and hope my mom isn't frustrated. I'm a little late for our weekly video call.

Mom lives in Texas, where she moved when she and my dad divorced. When my dad divorced *her*, to be precise. I don't really understand why it happened. I know they married and had me when they were only twenty-three. People throw around things like *irreconcilable differences* and *too young* and *fell out of love*. I guess I don't really understand what it is to fall out of love. I *wouldn't* understand. I'm never given the chance.

But I remember the day my parents sat me down in the living room, my dad stony-faced and my mom trying to keep her composure, and told me it was over. The words *mutual decision* were repeated over and over. They began to ring false when Mom went to cry in the bathroom while Dad finished the conversation.

I didn't move with her to Texas because I couldn't pass up the Stillmont theater program, which she understood. I think it was good for her to get some distance from reminders of her ex-husband, me included. But I've spent every summer vacation at her condo in San Marcos since the split three years ago. While I could do without the 100-degree heat, it's nice helping out with the booth at the farmers' markets and fairs where she sells her jewelry.

I ease open the door to my room. It's a mess. Of course it's a mess. Three maxi dresses that didn't find their way to the closet are draped over my bedframe. It appears I launched a denim jacket at the green coat rack in the corner but missed, and it's heaped on the floor on top of my boots.

My laptop's buried under a tangle of jewelry—the remains of this morning's failed attempt to find a pair of earrings I'm pretty sure vanished in Tyler's couch. I sweep everything off and shove aside my wristband alarm clock. It was a "gift" from Dad, who was far too pleased with himself for thinking of it. I've worn industrial-strength earplugs at night since our house got noisier a year and a half ago but I have to wake up for school at 6, and the horrible wristband vibrates me awake.

I open FaceTime on my computer, taking a second to brush my fingers through my hair.

Mom's face appears on the screen. "Hey, I'm really sorry I'm late," I rush to say.

"If I expected you to be on time, I wouldn't be a very in-touch mother." She tucks a strand of wavy dark hair behind her ear. Mom has hair like mine, only much bigger. "What were you up to?"

"Just some unprotected sex with a guy I met on the Internet," I reply casually.

Mom blanches, then her expression flattens when she realizes I'm joking. "Don't terrify your mother, Megan. It's not nice."

Grinning, I continue. "I would've preferred unprotected sex with creepy Internet dude, honestly. I had to go to a cast party."

She studies me, confused. "For one of your scenes?"

"No," I groan. I explain about *Romeo and Juliet* and why I was forced to audition. "It turns out I'm . . . Juliet, or whatever."

Mom's eyebrows skyrocket. "You auditioned for a lead?"

"Of course I didn't! Jody's just being impossible. Believe me, I'd be anyone else if she'd let me."

Mom chuckles. "I'm just glad I wasn't in the dark about my daughter's newfound acting aspirations."

"No, there's nothing new with me," I say quietly.

Mom's watching me with something like concern when my bedroom door opens without warning.

"Megan, what did I—" My dad's voice comes through the door, followed by the rest of him. He stops when he catches sight of my mom. "Oh, right, sorry," he mutters, suddenly stiff. "Hi, Catherine," he says without stepping farther into my room. "How are you and Randall?"

"Fine," Mom replies in the pinched tone she always gets when talking to my dad. "How are you? And Rose?" she adds after a second.

"Tired." He gives what I think is supposed to be a smile, but it looks strained. "Rose is going to take leave soon."

"That's exciting." Mom nods.

Looking the opposite of excited to be having this conversation, Dad places his hand on the doorknob. "Well, I'll leave you guys to it. Megan, just keep the volume down."

I sigh, exasperated, and mumble about not being able to talk in my own bedroom.

Mom says gently after a moment, "You know, you're always welcome to move in with Randall and me."

I force a scoff. "And miss the opportunity to play Juliet opposite Tyler Dunning?"

Mom grimaces. "Oof, I'm sorry to hear that. But really," she continues, "if it's ever too chaotic there, we'd love to have you."

"Thanks, Mom," I say, softening, not wanting her generosity to go unacknowledged. She deserves a real answer. "It's just, I'm at the top of the drama program at Stillmont. I've built up my scene work here, I'm in charge of organizing the

21

Senior Scene Showcase, *Romeo and Juliet*'s even going to be featured in Ashland. I have to stay."

"Well . . . you can change your mind anytime," Mom says reluctantly. "What's this about Ashland, though?"

"It's nothing. Jody in her infinite wisdom put us up for a high-school feature at the Oregon Shakespeare Festival, and they took us," I say to the floor.

"That doesn't seem like nothing." Mom sounds excited. *Uh-oh.* "When is it? I'd love to come!"

"No, Mom, it's not a big deal, really," I hurriedly protest.

"Resistance is futile, Megan. If you won't tell me when it is, Dad will."

I'm rolling my eyes when from downstairs comes an ear-splitting wail.

"Sounds like you have to go," Mom speaks up over the screeching.

"What? You don't want to stick around? This will be going for the next twenty minutes," I say with half a grin, and she laughs. "I'll talk to you later, Mom."

I hang up and go downstairs. The source of the howling is sitting in her high chair in the kitchen. My nineteen-month-old half sister Erin is adorable, but she's got lungs that'd make her the envy of the spring musical cast. I stop in the doorway, wanting a final moment to myself.

My stepmom reaches for Erin. Rose is tall, blonde, and undeniably beautiful. If she looks like she just turned thirty, it's because she did. She and my dad have been married for two and a half years. I wasn't thrilled when I first met her. It was only months after the divorce, and I was still holding out childish hope my dad would change his mind and realize Mom really was his meant-to-be.

Rose ended that. When I learned my dad was dating a woman ten years younger, I had my doubts about his sincerity. I figured he was turning forty and having a midlife crisis, dating a pretty blonde who made him "feel young." He was a cliché.

Then I took one look at the two of them, and I finally understood what I didn't in two years witnessing my parents' crumbling marriage. He wasn't going through a midlife crisis. He wasn't chafing at the institution of marriage—he just wasn't in love with my mom. I saw the smile my dad gave Rose the day I met her, a smile I'd never remembered seeing on him, and I knew he could never really regret the divorce.

Because he'd fallen in love with Rose. It wasn't about her age, or about anything but the two of them together. He had become a cliché—only not the one I'd expected. He'd found his soulmate.

"Hey," Dad says from the stove, pointing a spatula at Rose. "I told you not to get up for anything." He glances back at her, his same adoring smile looking like a love-struck teenager's.

Rose also happens to be seven months pregnant.

She rolls her eyes but lays a hand on her stomach, her expression warming as she sits back down.

I should hate Rose. I should hate the very idea of her. Sometimes I even wish I did, but the truth is, I never have. It's not her fault my parents' relationship wasn't forever like I imagined. I don't blame her for my dad loving her in a way he never could my mom. Still, despite my inability to hate her, she and I are more like somewhat-awkward roommates than two people with the same last name.

Dad drops the spatula, wincing when Erin lets out a particularly shrill yell, and races to hand Erin her favorite stuffed elephant.

I give myself one more moment. I love Erin, and I don't dislike Rose, but it's hard sometimes. This is my senior year. I should be studying on weeknights and going to parties on Saturdays. Instead, I'm struggling to concentrate through my earplugs and babysitting. I should be figuring out my future and finding myself—instead, I'm figuring out a relationship with a new stepmother and finding baby food on my books.

It's not only that, though. What's hardest is watching my dad build a new life that I'm less a part of every day. Especially with Erin and the baby on the way, it's like they're just letting me live here for the year before I go to college. Before they have the family they want.

THREE

FRIAR LAWRENCE: *These violent delights have violent ends*
And in their triumph die, like fire and powder,
Which, as they kiss, consume.

II.vi.9–11

I RECOGNIZE HIS HAIR FROM A BLOCK behind him. Black, pushed in one direction like he's recently run his right hand through it a bunch. Which he probably has—I remember the way he fidgeted constantly in the Verona booth. As if when he's not writing in his notebook, his hands search incessantly for something to do.

Owen Okita walks by himself up to a corner, where a giant puddle's overtaken the curb, a remnant of yesterday's rainstorm. I spent the day watching and re-watching Olivia Hussey's performance in Zeffirelli's *Romeo and Juliet* for preparation, which only tightened the knots in my stomach. Today is Monday, the day of our first rehearsal.

I reach the stop sign and roll down my window in time to catch Owen crossing the street.

"Hey," I call. "You want a ride?" I'd welcome the conversation to keep my mind off the rehearsal.

He looks up, searching for the source of my voice. When

he finds me, his eyes a little surprised, he says, "I'm good. Thanks, though."

I wrinkle the corner of my mouth, putting on an offended pout. "I did shower, you know. I don't smell."

"That's not—" He shakes his head, cutting himself off. His eyebrows twitch in feigned inquisitiveness. "Do people often refuse rides with you because you smell?"

I can't help myself—I feel my eyes flit a little wider.

Owen looks satisfied when I have no reply. "I just like to walk," he explains. "It gives me time to think."

I shrug, recovering. "Your loss. For your information, I even used my coconut shower gel today. I smell *exceptional.*" I drive past him, catching in the rearview mirror how he blinks once or twice, then takes a step forward directly into the puddle. He glances down sharply as if he's just remembered it's there.

Madeleine's waiting for me in the parking lot when I pull in ten minutes later.

Even though she's beloved by everyone and could have her pick of best friends, from the cheer captain to the future valedictorian, Madeleine's chosen me. For whatever reason. I wouldn't even call her popular, except in the dictionary sense of the word. I'm liked well enough, but mostly people know me because they know her.

It's part of the reason I don't mind being known as the school flirt. Because then I'm *something.* Something other than just the girl who's friends with Madeleine.

When I reach her by the bike racks, she greets me with a gushing recap of her weekend. She spent Saturday running a bake sale for charity and Sunday indoors while it rained, building card houses and drinking hot chocolate with her sister and Tyler. Tyler never hung out with my family while we were together—not that Erin's fun unless you enjoy wiping runny noses and repeatedly cleaning everything within reach of her admittedly adorable arms. But Tyler and Madeleine's relationship is different. I guess when you have a relationship like that it turns even the boring things beautiful.

We walk into the locker hall, and I'm distracted immediately by Wyatt Rhodes, who's admiring his hair in a mirror he's hung up in his locker. It's the vainest thing I've ever seen.

But I can't blame him. I'm admiring him, too, and it's really unfair he needs a mirror to enjoy the view the rest of us have.

"Megan." Madeleine's voice breaks my concentration. From her gently stern expression, I know I'm caught.

"What if he's a great guy on the inside? We need to give people a chance," I implore weakly.

Madeleine grabs my elbow with her perfect peach nails. "Number two. On the list," she admonishes. She steers me past Wyatt. I don't restrain myself from stealing a final look over my shoulder. When we've rounded a corner, leaving Wyatt and his arms behind, Madeleine plants us in the middle of the hall. She pulls me by the shoulders to face her.

"We're going to the football game this week," she says with finality.

"What? *Why?*" I have zero interest whatsoever in organized sports, especially in the high-school context. Unless the uniform's a Speedo.

"Because then I'll know you're nowhere near Wyatt Rhodes on Friday night."

I grimace. "You're worse than my mom. What's wrong with a hookup, even when it's . . . you know, Wyatt?"

A group of junior girls I'm sure Madeleine's hardly ever spoken to wave enthusiastically. She smiles back before her eyes return to me. "Nothing's wrong with a hookup with Wyatt," she replies with accusatory innocence. "What you want isn't a hookup, Megan. It never is. You want a boyfriend, and you're looking in desperate places because you've been single longer than usual. But Wyatt Rhodes wouldn't make you happy. You know that."

I fall silent, unable to argue. Of course she's right. She's Madeleine.

"I won't go for Wyatt," I grudgingly promise. "But I'm *not* going to the football game," I declare. Madeleine gives me a wry smile.

"We'll talk," she says, tipping her head forward in a *this-conversation's-not-over* gesture. She turns down the hallway to her first-period class.

Heading for the doorway to mine, I catch a glimpse of Owen down the hall. His sweater's askew, probably because he had to rush to get to school on time. He's putting a pile of papers into his locker. One falls to the floor, and I recognize an issue of the school newspaper. He must have two or three copies. It occurs to me he's probably sending them to Jordan, figuring he might like to have a copy.

28

It must be hard, having your closest friend move to a different state in your senior year. Even though Madeleine gives annoyingly perfect advice, I can't imagine how adrift I'd feel if she moved away one day and left me here. I have a feeling Owen didn't just join drama because he's really into *Romeo and Juliet*. He's probably trying to find new friends. I make a mental note to invite him to sit with the drama kids at lunch.

He hurriedly grabs his things from his locker and races to a classroom door, only to pause right outside. As if he can't control himself, he pulls out his notebook and jots down a quick—I don't know what. Observation? Idea? Reminder? The Fibonacci sequence? For the flash of a moment, I wish I knew.

I reach for the door to my class, weighing Madeleine's words. She wasn't wrong—not only about Wyatt. I have been single for a while. I *do* want a boyfriend. If I survive today, I'm going to put real thought into finding someone I could care about and who could care about me.

Hours before the first *Romeo and Juliet* rehearsal, I want to vomit. Or disappear. Or both.

Instead, I try to pretend nothing's bothering me as I sit down in one of the circles of drama kids decamped on the hill outside the drama room for lunch. Everyone's here except Anthony, who without fail uses lunch to get ahead in his classes. I once tried hanging out with him until the librarian ejected me for complaining too loudly and too often about how boring geometry is.

I usually enjoy sitting with the rest of the drama kids, running lines and planning cast parties. Not today. I don't like the way everyone's eyes turn to me when I sit down.

"You must be, like, totally excited," Jenna Cho says, beaming at me from across the circle. Her enthusiasm's as infectious as a headache, and no less uncomfortable.

"I'm . . . Yeah, definitely excited," I halfheartedly reply. *Ugh.* If my acting's this stiff in rehearsal, this play is screwed.

I notice Alyssa eyeing me. "You know, I played Juliet in a summer production at the community theater downtown. I'd be *happy* to sit down with you and show you my notes." She forces a saccharine smile.

I smile back at her, just as insincere. "Thanks, but I've got it, Alyssa."

Jenna reaches forward to hand me the plate of cookies they've been passing around. "I mean, it shouldn't be challenging playing opposite Tyler." Her grin widens.

"It wouldn't be the first time sparks fly between a Romeo and a Juliet," Cate Dawson chimes in, eyebrows raised. "You two even have a history."

Of course that's the moment Madeleine happens to walk up, arm in arm with Tyler. I see her smile fade, and I know she heard Cate's comment. Even worse, I'm not oblivious enough to figure she's not already worried about it.

I have to defuse. "I'm the last person who could have sparks with Tyler. Been there, done that, right?"

The girls laugh, and Madeleine gives me a grateful smile.

"Yeah, creating chemistry with Megan," Tyler starts, looking around the circle like he's on stage. "This will be the truest test of my acting prowess yet." He flashes the crowd his most charming grin, and I remember *Hamlet*—"one may smile, and smile, and be a villain."

Just because I'm over Tyler doesn't mean his insults don't hurt.

The sting of Tyler's words hasn't faded by the end of the day. But when I get to drama, Owen's sitting outside the class-room, writing in his notebook. Again. Everyone else has gone inside, and I decide to enjoy a couple more Tyler-less minutes.

I stop in front of his feet. "Ready to sell some drugs to underage girls?"

Owen looks up, his dark eyes going wide. "What?"

"You know"—I nudge his shoe with my boot—"Friar Law-rence?"

He pauses, then asks with feigned seriousness, "You ready to pursue an inappropriate relationship with an overemo-tional teenager that'll end terribly for everyone involved?" His features harden into an inquisitive challenge, underwrit-ten with humor.

"Sounds like a typical Monday," I reply.

Now he smiles, and it's the same smile from Verona, the one that brightens his entire face. He gets up and holds the door open for me.

Where on an ordinary day the drama room's just chaos—

improv games breaking out in the front of the room while the choir crossovers belt show tunes by the piano—today there's order to the commotion. Most of the *Romeo and Juliet* cast sits in a circle of chairs in the middle of the room. The senior girls have gathered around Alyssa, who's reading from Juliet's death scene. Anthony paces in the back of the room, doing vocal warm-ups. I'm hit with a new rush of nausea, remembering what he said on Friday, how much this means to him.

Jody comes in a second after I sit down with Owen. "We're doing a read-through of the scene where Romeo and Juliet meet," she announces, and shoves a stack of scripts into Anthony's hands.

I notice Tyler, seated opposite me in the circle, smirking when he finds his place in the scene. Once Anthony's handed out all the scripts, Tyler stands up and starts right in. "O, she doth teach the torches to burn bright!"

I poorly restrain an eye-roll. In every read-through I've been to, the actors didn't get out of their seats. Tyler's just grandstanding. But even I have to concede he's delivering it perfectly. If this is the truest test of his acting prowess, he's acing it.

"Forswear it, sight, for I ne'er saw true beauty till this night," Tyler continues, his eyes burning into me.

"Either he *is* good," Owen mutters beside me, "or he means it."

"He's acting. Definitely acting," I whisper, crossing my arms and sinking into my seat. I'm dimly aware of the scene progressing for the next couple minutes, but all I can think about is my impending first line.

Like he knows he's screwing with me, Tyler saunters from his seat to mine and stops in front of me. "If I profane with my unworthiest hand this holy shrine, the gentle sin is this." He reaches for my hand, and I snatch it away on instinct.

Tyler's eyes narrow. Whatever Juliet's supposed to do in this moment, it's not that. I feel the whole class staring at me. Tyler repeats the line, reaching for my hand once more. I force myself to let him take it. But when he leans down to brush his lips across my knuckles, I flinch and rip my hand from his. I hear Anthony groan.

"*Megan*," Tyler whispers in a sigh of frustration.

I look at Jody. "It's a read-through, not a rehearsal. Can't we just read from our chairs?" I nod pointedly at Tyler's, which is empty.

"Don't be difficult," Jody says, hardly glancing up from her script.

"Fine," I murmur, even though it's not. "Um, could you go again?" I ask Tyler.

He takes a deep breath and delivers the line, impeccably concealing his irritation. I close my eyes as he takes my hand, but I know I'm not covering my grimace when I feel his breath on my skin. He's leaning down. I should bite my tongue, push myself to be Juliet.

But I can't. I jerk back for the third time, and Tyler's jaw tightens.

Wait, I realize, *this could work.*

"Good pilgrim," I begin, heaping sarcasm on the line before he can restart the scene. Tyler looks startled to hear me actually reading my part, and I hear the room holding its breath. "You do wrong your hand too much, which mannerly devotion shows in this"—I transform Juliet's lines from demure and cautious to combative and superior—"for saints have hands that pilgrims' hands do touch, and palm to palm is holy palmer's kiss."

Jody's gone still, pen pressed to her lips. But Tyler steps into the new dynamic without missing a beat. His delivers his lines flawlessly, making Romeo work twice as hard to impress my unimpressed Juliet.

"Saints do not move, though grant for prayers' sake," I say, sneering.

"Then move not while my prayer's effect I take." Tyler leans forward, lips puckered, and I dramatically turn my head to offer him my cheek.

I hear snickers around me, and Tyler and I banter the next couple lines. When I apply an extra dose of sarcasm to Juliet's final remark—"You kiss by th' book"—everyone laughs.

I feel my shoulders straighten. Everyone's eyes are still on me, but for the first time I don't feel the need to step out of the spotlight or deflect with a joke. Tyler bounds off to exchange lines with Jenna, the Nurse, and I'm left reflecting. If there was one thing I wasn't expecting from this rehearsal, it was to not hate every second of it.

The door opens in the middle of the scene, and a stagehand walks in holding a box of props. I'm following along with the dialogue when something tumbles from the box and loudly hits the floor. I glance up at the moment the stagehand bends down, and suddenly it's not just *a stagehand* picking up what he dropped.

It's a veritable hipster Adonis. I recognize his face, I just don't remember it being this, well—hot. It takes me a second to connect this stunning figure to Billy Caine, the scrawny stage manager I talked to a couple of times when I directed *Twelfth Night* last year. He's changed his hair to a slicked-back undercut, and from the way his black V-neck stretches across his chest, he looks like he went to the gym once or twice over the summer.

I realize the room's gone silent. Owen clears his throat next to me, and I remember—Juliet has more lines. I glance down at the page, but my brain won't form words out of the letters.

I splutter what I remember of Juliet's next line, "What is yond gentleman?" *What indeed?*

"That's enough," Jody interrupts, standing up and walking into the middle of the circle.

She's right. I've completely lost our momentum, not to mention how I reinterpreted the character in a huge, spur-of-the-moment decision. Jody pauses, gathering her thoughts, and I prepare for the worst.

"Megan . . . I like what you brought to Juliet's dialogue with Romeo," she finally says, and I let out a breath I hadn't realized I was holding. "But," she continues before I get too relaxed, "you lost focus, and the whole room felt it."

I hear a couple chuckles. *Great.* I guess it's not just my acting I have to worry about. It's my propensity to get distracted whenever a hot guy enters the room.

"I'm sorry," I get out.

Jody waves a heavily ringed hand. "Let's go again."

FOUR

ROMEO: *There is no world without Verona walls*
But purgatory, torture, hell itself.

I FIND ANTHONY OUTSIDE THE DRAMA ROOM when rehearsal's over. I want nothing more than to get out of Juliet's head, even if I have to eat terrible pizza in a historically inaccurate restaurant. I didn't embarrass myself further following the Billy Caine incident, but I wasn't exactly a Juliet to die for.

"You're walking to Verona for your shift, right?" I elbow Anthony playfully. "I'm totally rehearsed-out."

"I don't know what you're complaining about," he says indignantly. "I spent three hours memorizing my Queen Mab monologue, and we didn't even do my scene today!"

"Um, you didn't have to suffer the lips of Tyler Dunning," I reply.

Anthony raises his eyebrow. "I don't know about *suffer . . .*"
I swat his shoulder. "Yeah, I'm going to Verona," he says after he's pinned my hand. "But you sure you don't want to stick around?" He nods somewhere behind me, and I turn to follow his gaze—to Billy Caine talking intently to Owen.

36

"You noticed?" I ask dryly.

"Megan. Everyone noticed. I think William Shakespeare himself felt it in the grave." Now he elbows me. "It's about time for your next torrid whirlwind romance."

I take a second to study Billy's skinny jeans. "I'll meet you at Verona in twenty minutes."

I drift over to where Billy and Owen are talking and overhear a snippet of their conversation. It sounds like they're discussing poetry. Billy's praising the "forest imagery" but says the internal rhymes need work.

"I love it when guys talk internal rhyme," I remark, walking up next to them. "Hi, Owen. Hey, Billy." I smile.

Owen cuts in. "Uh, it's *Will* now."

Billy rolls his eyes, and I look from him to Owen. "I feel like I'm missing something."

"It's not a big deal," Billy—Will—says. "I just decided I prefer to go by Will."

Yes. Yes. We prefer Will. Everything about him works together perfectly. The blond hair, the fitted clothes, the elegant, understated name. I think I just might die.

"Cool," I say instead.

Will unleashes a dazzling smile. "Hey, I really liked your original interpretation of Juliet. You nailed that scene."

"Well"—I try to sound nonchalant—"I had to make her interesting somehow. It's hard for me to relate to someone so coy and hard to get." I see Owen's eyebrows shoot up, but I'm focused on Will's growing smile.

"It could be worse. You could be trying to get a guy to fall in love with you while pretending to be a man." He crosses his arms, daring me to get the reference.

"*Twelfth Night*—or *As You Like It*. Yeah, I guess it's better than having my hands cut off by two lunatic brothers," I say, playing along.

Will raises an eyebrow. "I like *Titus Andronicus*! You know, it definitely beats having to get it on with a donkey."

"Well, Tyler *is* an ass," I mutter under my breath, knowing he's referring to *A Midsummer Night's Dream*.

"This is really cute," Owen interjects, "but, Will, did you want to give me your notes on the lyrics?"

"Lyrics?" I turn to Owen. I would be annoyed he interrupted my boldfaced flirting if I weren't intrigued.

"Owen writes lyrics for my band," Will says with the studied casualness of a guy who practices telling girls he's in a band.

My eyes widen. "*You're* in a band?" I ask Owen. Will I could believe, but shy Owen . . . ?

His ears go red. "I'm not. I just write the lyrics."

"I didn't know you were a writer." It would explain the ever-present pen and notebook.

"Are you kidding?" Will says, and I look back at him. With his debonair smile and incredible hair, I can't believe I ever looked away. "This kid does nothing *but* write. I can barely get through a conversation without him jotting down an idea for one of his plays."

"Will, the lyrics?" Owen holds out his hand, visibly uncomfortable.

Will hands Owen a folded sheet of paper from his pocket, and I go into conversational desperation mode. I'm not inclined to let Will leave before I procure a phone number. "Hey, you guys want to go to Verona for some undercooked pizza?"

"Alas," Will says, "I have to go over a scene diagram with Jody. But I'll see you Wednesday."

"What's happening Wednesday?" Not that it matters.

"It's the first run of your balcony scene. I'm head of the stage crew, so I have to be there. But besides"—he smiles a smile it's hard to believe occurs in nature—"I wouldn't miss it."

I wrinkle my nose. "You don't want to see—"

"Yes. I do." He looks me right in the eyes, and I swear my knees might give way. I guess I *won't* brainstorm boyfriend prospects tonight. Will could be exactly what I'm looking for. Even if I have to run the balcony scene a thousand times, suddenly Wednesday can't come soon enough.

Will walks off, treating me to a new perspective on his hotness.

"So, uh . . . pizza?" Owen's voice returns me to earth.

It takes me a second to realize I invited him, too. "Uh, yeah. Let's go."

The shortest walk from school to Verona is through the woods. It's not like Stillmont is encircled by trees—it's more like they intersperse the town, encroaching in surprising stretches. I like walking in the woods. I'm not one for Transcendentalist poetry and Bon Iver and stuff, but I've come to crave the quiet. Especially since Erin arrived.

I lead Owen onto a faintly defined path over the thick roots. "I didn't know you and Will were friends," I say.

"We're not," Owen replies, then corrects himself. "Well, we're not good friends. I'm friends with Jordan, and he was friends with Jordan. But now Jordan lives in Chicago, and he was—"

"The friend-glue," I finish the sentence. I know exactly what he's talking about. I've tried hanging out with Anthony's Math Olympiad friends while he wasn't present, and it did not go well. They glared when I confused the titles of *Star Trek: The Next Generation* and *Star Wars: A New Hope*.

"That's . . . exactly what it is," Owen says thoughtfully and with amusement. "But yeah, Will and I, we're friend-*ly*. I write him lyrics, and he gives me songwriting credit on their nonexistent recordings."

I grin. "He seems . . . different," I venture. "What's his deal?"

"Different?" I hear a nearly imperceptible edge in Owen's voice. As much I love the changes in Will, Owen evidently doesn't. "*Billy* went to a songwriting camp this summer. It was Will who returned. He kind of redefined himself."

I pause, hitching my bag up on my shoulder. "He got really hot."

Owen laughs shortly. "Well, don't tell him. He's been insufferable since he got back."

"I very much intend to tell him!" I glance over my shoulder to find Owen eyeing me skeptically.

"You're going to go for this guy after one conversation

swapping Shakespeare jokes and staring into each other's eyes?"

"Duh. I just said he was hot."

I turn back to the path and hear Owen laugh behind me. "I guess if it's love, one conversation's all you need. You'll make a fine Juliet yet."

"Love?" I snort, kicking a rock off the path. "When did I say love? I just think it'd be fun. I'm not really the love-at-first-sight, long-walks-on-the-beach, balcony-scene type." Not that I wouldn't be that type, if I believed those things weren't just a beautiful fiction. I want them just like everybody else. I'm just not holding my breath.

"What do you mean?" Owen sounds genuinely interested.

I don't usually talk about my unique pattern of breakups, but there's something about Owen that has me feeling like he'd understand. "Remember what I told you about Tyler? He dumped me for my best friend, Madeleine, and now they're, like, the perfect couple. The thing is, that's not the first time a guy's left me for the real deal. It's a perfect trend—everyone I date, it's right before they find exactly what they're looking for."

Owen is silent for a moment. I don't look back, worrying he's deciding I'm paranoid and self-pitying. But he only sounds sympathetic when he says, "Getting dumped sucks."

"I'm not dumped," I reply quickly, defensiveness creeping into my voice. "Guys don't leave me because of *me*. It's not like I scare them off," I add, needing to make this clear. "I'm just . . . the girl before."

"You're Rosaline," Owen says, and I stop. He's standing in

the middle of the path, hands in his pockets, looking out into the woods like he's lost in thought.

"The girl Romeo leaves for Juliet? That's not the most flattering comparison," I mutter. But in my head I know it fits.

He looks at me then, no longer contemplating—he's seeing me, giving me his full attention. I realize it's something I've never had from him in the past couple of days since we started talking. Whenever I've encountered Owen, he's been half-focused on his notebook or lost in thought.

He shakes his head. "I think Rosaline's really interesting. She's an underexplored part of the play. In a lot of ways, her story's probably more interesting than Juliet's. Or at least I think so."

The earnestness in his voice and the way he's looking at me have me turning back to the trail. I can't help feeling like he's seeing me for something I'm not. "First you say I'll make a fine Juliet, now I'm Rosaline"—I laugh, trying to bring the conversation back to casual—"I better be careful. If I keep talking, I'll turn into Tybalt."

I wait for Owen's reply. When I don't hear his footsteps behind me, I turn back around. He's climbed onto a rock and is holding his phone up toward the treetops in the universal human display of looking for cell service.

"Why do you need reception?" I ask. "We're five minutes from the restaurant."

"Cosima wants to FaceTime me," he says matter-of-factly.

"Cosima?" I stifle a laugh at Owen's woodland acrobatics.

"My girlfriend."

Owen has a girlfriend? *Interesting.* "What kind of name is that?" I ask, genuinely curious.

"It's Italian," he says, clambering down from his rock to find a new spot. "Like, she lives in Italy. We're in such different time zones, we have to video chat every chance we get."

An *Italian* girlfriend? Owen is full of surprises. I do a little mental math. "Isn't it like the middle of the night there?"

"Yeah, it's late." He's now standing between two giant pines. His expression even, he waves his phone with deliberate, unhurried movements. For someone who stopped suddenly to climb onto a boulder, he seems decidedly untroubled by his lack of success. "I'm trying to catch her before she goes to bed, but there's no service."

"We *are* in the middle of the forest," I point out unhelpfully. When Owen says nothing, I go on. "Well, I want pizza. Say *ciao* to Cosima, your Italian girlfriend who lives in Italy." Before I continue down the path, I catch the hint of a smile on Owen's lips.

In Verona, I find Jenna Cho and a couple of noblewomen from today's scene sitting in a booth by the soda fountain. Mercifully, Tyler and Alyssa are nowhere to be found. I could use a break from his smugness and her constant judgment. I slide into a seat as Anthony sidles up to take our orders.

"Wow, Anthony." I try not to laugh. "You look ravishing."

He's wearing a T-shirt printed to resemble a medieval tunic, and there's a Robin Hood–esque hat two sizes too small perched on his tight black curls. It's hideous, and wonderful.

"Megan, nothing you say can take this away from me," he says defiantly. He searches the room behind me. "Hey, where's Billy?"

"It's Will now," I correct. "He's not coming, but Owen's on his way. He's talking to his girlfriend right now."

"Cosima?" Jenna asks, something knowing in her smile. The rest of the table chuckles.

I feel like I'm missing the joke. "Yeah, why?"

"You know she's not real, right?" Courtney Greene answers with a conspiratorial smirk. "Owen's totally making her up. There's no proof."

Anthony clears his throat. "I have other tables, you guys. Would you like to, you know, order?" He pulls a quill out of his pocket. Unable to contain myself, I burst out laughing. We order a couple Benvolio's Banquets (pepperoni, sausage, and peppers, in what feels like a reach of textual interpretation), and Anthony gives me a final chastising look.

Owen shows up a few minutes later, looking out of sorts. He slides into the booth opposite me. Unhesitatingly, I smile and ask, "How was Cosima?"

"Blurry," he grumbles. The group exchanges glances. I know Owen notices because he turns to Jenna wearily. "You seriously don't still think she isn't real, do you?"

"There's no proof," Courtney repeats.

"Is this normal cast behavior?" Owen asks me, half-jokingly exasperated. "They've been interrogating me since my *first*

44

day of drama about my real"—he levels Courtney a look—"genuinely human girlfriend."

"Better get used to it," I reply resolutely. The corners of his mouth curve upward. "Does she have a Facebook?" I try to give him a chance. I pull out my phone and open the app.

Owen frowns like he's heard the question before. "Cosima thinks social media's frivolous," he mutters.

Now I have to smile. "Awfully convenient." But before he can reply, I see I have an unread email. The subject line reads, "Your upcoming Southern Oregon Theater Institute interview!" I lose track of the Cosima discussion as my eyes scan the email. I've put off dwelling on the interview, but now it's in a couple days, and I'm having trouble thinking about anything else. The churning in my stomach only worsens when Anthony drops off the greasy pizzas.

"Hey, um, Megan," I hear him say quietly beside me. "Could I talk to you for a second?"

Eager for the distraction, I jump up and follow him to the salad bar—overwhelmingly the least crowded part of the restaurant. "What? Do you need me to go get you a change of clothes?" I ask when we've stopped.

Anthony cocks his head, not amused. "I'll have you know, I intend to wear this to your wedding. And your second wedding. And your third wedding."

I cross my arms, holding back a smile. "That's okay. It's the fifth wedding I have a good feeling about."

He laughs. "But really"—he drops his voice—"I need your wise counsel."

"Is it about boys?"

"Of course."

"Then you've come to the right place." I lean into the counter. "What's up?"

"Eric invited me to a party," Anthony explains. "But I'm not sure if the invitation was casual or potentially something more."

"Well, do you even know if Eric—" I break off when I notice the hostess walk by leading a family of five to a table. Anthony's hardly in the closet—everyone at school definitely knows he's gay. He just might not want his personal life publicized to his coworkers and random neighborhood families. "Do you know if Eric . . ." I try again, "enjoys sausage pizza?" I finish, wincing, and Anthony's eyes widen.

"That was *bad*," he admonishes.

"I know." I grimace. "But . . . does he?"

Anthony takes a deep breath, like he needs to prepare for what he's about to say. "I don't know, Megan. I've never seen him . . . order it. But I don't know if he enjoys it in private. If it were served to him, he might partake." Anthony rolls his eyes, halfway to a grin. "I just want to know what this kind of invitation means to guys. Is it definitely casual? Definitely a date?"

"It depends," I start. "Both have happened to me. When Charlie invited me to Courtney's birthday, I knew it was a date because he'd pursued me pretty obsessively for weeks before. When I went to a movie with Chris, I didn't really know. You know how Chris is. He barely has facial expressions. When Dean—"

"You're no help." Anthony sighs, frustrated, then looks behind me. "Hey, Okita, come over here for a second."

I turn to find Owen standing at the salad bar, understandably dissatisfied with the pizza. He squares his shoulders uneasily, uncomfortable to be singled out.

"I need a straight guy's perspective," Anthony continues. "The guy I like invited me to a party. Is it date, or is it just something straight guys do?"

Owen immediately turns endearingly thoughtful. His eyebrows go up, his eyes searching the room, bright like twin light bulbs. "I'll need to weigh several factors," he says finally. "How friendly is he? Did he invite other coworkers? What was his tone like?"

"Eric's not very social with people here," Anthony says, and I can hear him struggling to suppress the excitement in his voice. "I don't think he invited anyone else."

"This sounds good," I offer.

Anthony's excitement finally breaks through. "Good like, I should wear the navy blazer?"

"Whoa." I put a hand on his arm. "I think it's a bit early for the navy blazer."

"I wore it on our second date," Anthony fires back. "Remember? I cooked us carne asada—I seem to recall it going pretty well."

It did, I remember. It was the first time I really made out with a guy, and the last time Anthony made out with a girl. His cooking is legendary. It might be literally impossible for a guy Anthony's interested in—or girl, in the case of yours truly—to have his homemade carne asada and not fall for him. "You're right," I say. "That was an excellent date."

I notice Owen's startled expression. He's looking between Anthony and me, slowly putting the pieces together. He squints skeptically. "Wait, you . . . you guys dated?"

"It was years ago," I explain, watching Anthony, who looks lightly amused. "It was before Anthony admitted his love for sausage pizza." Anthony bursts out laughing, collapsing onto the salad counter.

"Wow." Owen's watching me intently again, like he did in the woods. There's endless depth to his dark eyes. "What you were telling me earlier, it's real."

"Oh, it's real," I say.

"We agree, then," Anthony announces, ignoring Owen and me. He pushes himself off the counter. "Blazer it is." The lady sitting in the booth behind him coughs pointedly, looking in our direction. "Shit," Anthony mutters, glancing over his shoulder. "I have, like, three tables I should be waiting on." He darts off, pulling out his ballpoint quill.

I walk with Owen back to the booth and sit down, taking out my phone to confirm the interview. Just reopening the email brings on a new wave of anxiety. I'm not the greatest student—I don't have a 4.0 and a résumé full of extracurriculars. I'm not like Madeleine, with her AP tests and her volunteer work, or Tyler, who's had recruiting scouts at his baseball games since sophomore year.

The only thing I *really* care about at school is directing, and when I think about college or the future, SOTI is pretty much everything. I wouldn't be doing *Romeo and Juliet* if it weren't. I know my directing credits put me up there with the best of applicants, but the interview is something else entirely—I'm not the most polished or poised conversation-alist.

"Who're you texting?" Cate Dawson's voice interrupts my typing, and she winks when I look up.

"I bet it's Tyler." Courtney smiles suggestively.

"It's definitely Sexy Stagehand Will," Jenna chimes in.

"I'm not *always* texting a guy. I have real shit, too," I snap before I can stop myself. The table goes quiet, and I immediately feel bad. It's not like they said anything mean, and I do talk about guys constantly. I just wish they hadn't assumed.

I feel like everyone's waiting for me to elaborate, but I've never been one to talk about real-life things like college or the future. It's easier to be the Megan they expect me to be, to bear my disappointments in private. "I'll be texting Will *later*," I say, putting on a grin.

I watch them exchange glances, still too uncomfortable to laugh. I drop my eyes to my phone and try to pretend I don't notice their silence.

"What if I organize a group FaceTime with Cosima? Will you believe me then?" Owen interjects. The group's eyes light up. I release a relieved breath, glad the conversation's moved on. Not unaware Owen's brought back up a topic he dislikes in order to spare me, I gratefully give him a quick smile, then hit SEND on the email.

FIVE

JULIET: *It is an honor that I dream not of.*

I.iii.71

STILLMONT HIGH IS NOT A BIG PLACE. There's one main building, a gym in the back—one of my favorite places because PE's practically a flirting free-for-all—and an Arts Center that houses the drama room and a much cleaner orchestra room. Pines dot the quads in between the buildings, which aren't large. There's not a lot of ground to cover.

Paradoxically, the school gives us seven minutes to get from class to class. *Seven minutes.* That's enough time to hook up in the band closet, or to hit up the vending machine, eat your snack, then hit up the vending machine again and still make it to class. I spend most passing periods consoling Madeleine about her AP workload or, recently, hearing about the latest chapter in the ongoing romance of her and Tyler.

Today, we've taken a leisurely stroll to the second-floor bathroom. The only other girl in here leaves, and from outside the stall I hear Madeleine clear her throat. "Can I talk to you about something?" she asks, her voice unusually shy.

I'm mid-pee. "Uh." I fumble for the toilet paper. "Yeah."

"It's about Tyler and . . . sex," she says haltingly.

"I . . ." I can hardly restrain my laughter. "I might need a moment, Madeleine. To pull my pants up."

"Right. Of course." I practically hear her blush.

Once I've opened the stall door and stepped up to the sink, I turn to her. "Okay, hit me."

Her face grows brighter. "Tyler's planning something for this weekend. He wouldn't tell me what. But I'm getting, you know, that vibe from him." Her freckles have disappeared under the red in her cheeks.

I nod sagely. "The vibe." I wait for Madeleine to elaborate, but when she doesn't, I search her uncertain expression. "You've gotten the vibe before, though, right?"

"That's kind of the problem," she says quietly.

"Wait." I turn off the faucet as it dawns on me. "You two haven't had sex yet?"

"We've done other things," Madeleine rushes to say, like I've accused her of a crime. "And there's been a couple times when it seemed like he wanted more, but no, we haven't done it yet. I wanted to . . ."

She looks at me expectantly. I wait blankly for her to continue before I realize what she's saying.

"You haven't had sex because of *me*?" I splutter. She's just staring at me, growing redder. "You know," I continue more gently, "you don't need my permission to have sex with your own boyfriend."

"But it's a little weird. The last person Tyler had sex with is you," she points out.

"Don't think about that." I lay a hand on her arm. "Really, it doesn't bother me."

"I'm glad, but it's not that. . . . Well, it's not only that." She looks into the mirror, avoiding my eyes. "I just sometimes feel a little intimidated."

I raise my eyebrows. "Intimidated? Tyler can get the job done, but he's nothing to be intimidated by."

Madeleine gives me half a smile. "Watch it, that's my boyfriend you're talking about." But her voice drops when she continues. "No, it's not Tyler I'm intimidated by . . ."

I wait, uncomprehending. What she's suggesting—it's, well, it's crazy. "By *me*?" I get out. The idea that Madeleine, with her striking auburn hair and green eyes and her fairy-tale romance, could ever be intimidated by someone like me is laughable. It's not like the times Tyler and I did it were anything but a couple of virgins figuring things out together. It's a proven law of the universe that I'm not the girl who guys remember.

"Well, yeah," she says with a shrug. "What you and Tyler had, it was spontaneous, exciting, romantic. You were the kind of couple everyone watched. You burned bright—"

"And burned out," I interject.

"When you were together, what you had was passionate," Madeleine argues, sounding a little desperate. "I'm just afraid that after you, I won't be enough."

"Madeleine." I grab her hand and force her to look at me. "Tyler's into you now. You're just building this up."

"I hope." She still looks unconvinced. "But you and Tyler were each other's firsts. I can't compete with that."

"Firsts? What does that matter?" It's not like I chose Tyler to be my first because I thought he'd be "the one." I just knew

I felt something with him I hadn't with boyfriends before. I liked Tyler, and I guess I knew I could fall in love with him. I wanted to be closer to him. I'd hardly believed I'd found my soulmate—at Stillmont High, no less—but I wanted the physical aspects of the relationship. There's something about having that emotional connection made physical, the romantic rendered real, that's unique and impossibly enticing. Even though I knew the relationship would end, I felt in those moments of togetherness I could finally step out of the wings and into the center of our stage.

But none of that has to do with Tyler's position in the line of boyfriends with whom I'll one day have sex. He was my first because he was special—not special because he was my first.

"There's nothing extraordinary about Tyler being my first. Trust me," I tell Madeleine.

"Not to you, maybe," she says, looking at the floor.

But to Tyler? I'm caught off guard. If it had meant that much to him, we wouldn't have broken up. But I'm not going to tell Madeleine that. Still, some smaller voice in me wonders why Madeleine would believe otherwise unless Tyler said something.

The bell rings, and it takes me a second to realize we've somehow used up the entire passing period. Madeleine looks panicked—I'm certain she's never been late to class ever. I'd have to laugh if I weren't still reeling from what she just said.

But I don't want her to leave worried about my history with Tyler. "You and Tyler are perfect for each other, and you're going to have a perfect first time," I manage as Madeleine hurries to pick up her bag. "Speaking as the former authority on Tyler Dunning's sex life," I go on jokingly, "I have all the confidence in the world that you'll blow his mind."

"Thanks, Megan, really," she breathlessly says over her shoulder, and runs toward class. I follow her out, my mind lingering on what she said before.

It's not like I still have feelings for Tyler or even want him back. It's just unexpectedly nice to know what he and I had hasn't been entirely forgotten, even if he'll be giving a night of tender, fumbling, teenage love to my best friend this weekend.

Yet unfortunately, I'm the one in bed with Tyler after school.

In a prop bed, specifically. With the entire cast watching us. We're in the drama room, the plastic chairs arranged in rows in front of the open space we're using for a stage.

The bed's not even Juliet's, either. It's a leftover from the spring musical, *Rent*, and it's completely period-inappropriate —black and wrought-iron and unmistakably '90s. Will hasn't finished any of the set pieces, although I've taken every opportunity to admire his after-school shirtless construction process.

We're rehearsing Act III Scene v, the one where Romeo and Juliet wake up together after their own night of tender, (probably) fumbling, teenage love. We're both lying on our sides, Tyler behind me, pressed a little too tightly to my hips. The closeness combined with his Romeo eyes isn't helping me forget Madeleine's words from earlier. Not in a good way—it's just uncomfortable.

"Whenever you're ready," Jody tells us from the front row of seats.

Before I can start the scene, I feel Tyler brush my hair behind my ear. Then he kisses me on the temple. I jerk and nearly bust him in the lip.

"Good, Tyler," Jody calls. "I liked that."

I rush through my lines, knowing the sooner I finish the scene, the sooner I can get out of this bed. "Wilt thou be gone? It is not yet near day. It was the nightingale, and not the lark, that pierced the fearful hollow of thine ear. Nightly she sings on yond pomegranate tree—"

Jody interrupts me. "Juliet's trying to get Romeo to come back to bed. You sound like he couldn't leave fast enough." She's pursing her lips in a bit of a smile, like she knows just how true her appraisal is. Some of the cast laughs in the audience, and I catch Alyssa rolling her eyes in frustration.

"Well, I . . ." I start, searching for some interpretive explanation to defend my discomfort. "I'd like to play Juliet feistier. You know, modernize her." Honestly, if I were directing, I'd be into the approach.

Jody nods, considering. "Okay, but you still have to make the scene work," she says. "Go from the top."

I close my eyes and take a deep breath, trying to find my inner Juliet. When I open them, Tyler's gazing down at me with a teasingly longing look. "Wilt thou be gone!" I snap, knowing I'm throwing the scene out the window. But I just can't handle Tyler. His expression changes, and the amorous

Romeo fades from his features. He's just Tyler, irritated with his ex-girlfriend.

I sit up and face Jody. "Okay, I know that was too much, but—"

"Megan," she cuts me off. "Feisty Juliet works well for when she meets Romeo. It doesn't work here. We have to believe Juliet is so in love with Romeo she would die for him." I notice Alyssa watching me from the audience, smug. "You need to spend some time with the play," Jody continues. "Really learn how to get into Juliet's head."

I give Jody a look saying, *you knew this would happen.* "Okay," I reply even though I know it's impossible. The best I can hope for is faking it. But it doesn't matter if I pull this off, I remind myself. I'm not an actress, I'm not meant for the spotlight. I just have to get my acting credit and get through this play.

SIX

ROMEO: *Can I go forward when my heart is here?*

Turn back, dull earth, and find thy center out.

II.i.1–2

THE HOUSE IS A MESS WHEN I get home.

With rehearsal over, I can finally push Juliet out of my mind and focus on something important. I rush up to my room, where I throw on the most professional outfit I own— a tan dress I never wear in my daily life and a blazer I borrowed from Rose's closet. Trying to quell my nerves, I bound back downstairs.

I have to leave in ten minutes for my SOTI interview. But first, I search under piles of Dad's paperwork and Erin's sticky toys in the kitchen. I printed my arts résumé before school, and I know I left it on the kitchen counter, which I guess experienced a natural disaster in the last eight hours. I push aside one of Erin's arts and crafts projects and clumsily stick my hand into a glob of glitter glue. Even though it'd definitely make my application stand out, I'm going to have to have some stern words with my baby sister if she's turned my résumé into her latest sparkly impressionistic work.

My eyes fall on what's underneath Erin's finger-painting, and I stop.

It's a real estate magazine. But not one of the Oregon ones I've seen in some of my friends' houses—it's full of listings in New York.

I pick it up, dazed. *Why would my dad and Rose have a magazine of homes in New York?* But the moment the question forms in my head, I know the answer, and suddenly my worries about the interview feel distant.

"If you're looking for your résumé, I moved it to the table by the door." I hardly hear Rose's voice from the couch. She's taken to lying down for quick naps in the middle of the day.

I don't bother to thank her because I'm already climbing the stairs, magazine in hand. I check Dad's bedroom first. His desk is empty except for the stack of budgets for the middle school where he's vice principal. The obvious next stop is just down the hall. I hear his hushed voice reading *Runaway Bunny* as I push open the door to Erin's room.

"Dad." I try to pack urgency into my low whisper, noticing Erin nodding off in her crib.

Dad gives me an admonishing look and tiptoes out of the room. Only after he's quietly closed the door does he turn to me, still holding *Runaway Bunny*. "I just got her down, Megan. This better be important."

"We're moving to New York?" I hold up the magazine. "When were you going to tell me?"

The guilt that flashes in his eyes confirms what some part of me was still hoping wasn't true. "Nothing is final yet," he says after a moment. It doesn't matter how gentle and even his tone is, I can barely meet his eyes. He hid a life-changing family decision from me.

I try very hard to control the volume of my voice. "But you're looking at houses."

"With the baby coming and Erin growing up, we're going to need more space." He's speaking with the patience I've heard him use on overwrought seventh graders.

"So you're looking in *New York*?"

"Rose wants to be closer to her parents while the kids are young." I hear irritation creep into his tone.

"You weren't going to *tell* me we're moving to New York in—I don't know when?" I realize I've crumpled the magazine in my hand. "You expect me to just pack up my bags and move across the country with no warning whatsoever?"

His expressions shifts. Suddenly, he looks surprised, even a little apologetic. "Oh, no, Megan. None of this is happening until you're done with high school and settled in college."

Just like that it makes sense. It's not about us moving to New York. It's about *them* moving to New York.

In a way, it's the natural progression of what's been happening for the past three years. First my dad got remarried, then he had Erin and started a new family. Now they're going to leave the town where he raised me and start over somewhere else, finally closing the book on the last remaining chapter of my dad's former family.

I open my mouth to protest, and then I realize I just want out of this conversation. "I have to go to my interview," I mutter. "You know, so I can get into college and have somewhere to go when the rest of you move." I shove the crumpled magazine at him and fly down the stairs before he can call me back.

"Good luck," Rose wishes weakly as I run out the door.

Trying to force the conversation from my head, I get into my car and crank up the volume on the stereo, even though I'm in no mood for the Mumford & Sons CD well-intentioned Madeleine burned for me.

I drive to the Redwood Highway for the first time in months. The clouds hang low and heavy in the sky, and the rain patters my windows insistently—it's a constant presence this time of year. I don't get out of Stillmont often, because there's not much to do outside town. The all-ages club on Route 46 straight-up sucks, and I hardly ever drag Madeleine to concerts in Ashland. Her indie-folk playlists tend not to overlap with my Ramones and Nirvana.

The only other reason I have to take the highway up through the hundred-foot redwoods is SOTI. Specifically, the June and December Mainstage Productions. It hurt the first few times I went by myself after my mom moved. We used to go as a family before the divorce, but without my mom to persuade my dad to come, I weighed whether I wanted to go on my own. In the end, I decided the opportunity to watch the best student theater in Oregon was too important to pass up. I've gone to every production in the past three years, from *Othello* to *Chicago*.

Which is how I know the hour-long drive through the

forest by heart. With nothing but the trees to look at, my mind returns to the picture-perfect homes in the real-estate catalog, and I reach for my phone without a second thought to call Madeleine and tell her everything over speaker phone. She's the perfect listener—she doesn't sugarcoat or force advice on me, she just lets me talk. It helps a little, the way it always has.

When we hang up, the redwoods have given way to the strip malls and college-town shops of Ashland. I park in the visitor parking lot outside SOTI's geometric concrete buildings and take a moment to try to dispel the twin discouragements of rehearsal and my fight with Dad. *Not* how I want to feel before the most important interview of my life.

I'm not like most SOTI students, who go there because they love theater. I'm the opposite—I love theater because of SOTI. Before I cared or even knew I lived near one of the best drama schools in the country, I was being dragged to Mainstage Productions twice a year. I complained every time, but whenever I glumly questioned why we had to go, Mom would explain theater was important to our family. She loved to tell the story of how she and Dad fell in love when they both were stagehands in a college production of *My Fair Lady*.

I never cared about that until eighth grade, when everything changed. I could feel my family falling apart around me—every morning beginning with a whispered fight and every night ending with my dad sleeping on the couch. I know now that when Mom announced we were going to *A Midsummer Night's Dream*, it was a final effort to rekindle what they'd lost. It didn't work, obviously, but when the curtain closed, I realized I hadn't felt my family fracturing for three magical hours. My dad held my mom's hand, and at intermission they even laughed while trying to explain the story to thirteen-year-old me.

I didn't realize it until that *Midsummer Night's Dream* performance, but theater was never just an outing for my family. It was a time when we were a unit. No matter how briefly, no matter how ugly things were when we got home. There's something about theater, an immediacy that brings stories to life in a way nothing can tarnish. You can put down a book or pause a movie, but a play is breathing right in front of you—it refuses to be stopped. It's why I joined drama freshman year, and it's what I've held on to ever since.

I pull up a campus map on my phone and head toward the directing department. My interview is in Professor Salsbury's office, which looks like it's next to a black box theater, a small performance space with only a couple of rows of chairs and without a backstage. Once I step inside the building, I glance into the theater, where a couple students are putting blocking tape on the floor.

I hear them swapping notes on scenic interpretation in theater shorthand, and for a moment I feel like I'm exactly where I belong. It doesn't matter where my parents live. *This* is everything I need. This will be my home.

Feeling a rush of confidence, I knock on Professor Salsbury's door and walk in when he calls, "It's open!"

He's sitting at his desk, poring over a play. His rumpled gray oxford looks like he slept in it, and he doesn't seem much older than a student himself. "Hey, Megan, it's great to meet you!" he says with disarming enthusiasm.

"Uh, yeah, uh, thank you for having me." I take a seat opposite his desk. "I brought a résumé, if you want to have a look . . . ?"

"Prepared!" He reaches for the paper in my hand, his eyes lighting up. "I like that." He studies it for a moment, and I feel myself relax at his approving expression. "You've directed an impressive diversity of material. For someone your age, especially," he continues. "I notice you've met the lighting and set design requirements—great experiences to have."

"They were," I jump in. "They really helped me decide how to direct *Twelfth Night*."

He nods, briefly glancing up at me. His eyes return to the page. "You've done a musical—*West Side Story*, a favorite of mine—and a couple of experimental pieces, but it looks like a lot of your work has been in Shakespeare."

"He's the best," I say. "Really original opinion, I know."

He laughs and sets the résumé down. Then he looks me right in the eye. "So why directing, Megan?"

I'm ready for this question. "Because theater feels like home. It's the one place where I'm part of something that can bring people together or transport them," I finish decisively.

"It's clear you love theater." He studies me, his voice growing more serious. "But I want to know why you're a director."

"I'm really not a natural actor," I say. "I never feel comfortable or genuine or creative when I have an audience."

Salsbury gives me a gentle smile. "Well, you'll have to get

used to it to some degree. We do have an acting requirement, which I see you haven't fulfilled yet."

"Not to worry," I reply lightly. "I'm getting through it."

"Getting through it is one thing." His smile falters. "The requirement is there for a reason. Uncomfortable though it is to have an audience, learning how to inhabit a role will give you a deeper understanding of the emotions you'll need to bring out in every scene. It'll make you a better director. Even Shakespeare probably learned a thing or two from performing in his own plays."

My stomach sinks. Not just because Salsbury's eyeing me with a new uncertainty—because I know he's right. It seemed easy to brush off Jody's criticism in rehearsal and tell myself I don't care. But if I want to be a real director, I can't dismiss performing on stage just because it makes me uncomfortable.

"You wouldn't happen to be in Stillmont's *Romeo and Juliet*, would you?" His question surprises me. The professors here don't seriously keep tabs on every local high-school production, do they?

My hands start to sweat, and I fold them in my lap. "I'm, um . . ." *No point in hiding it.* "I'm Juliet."

Salsbury's eyes light up once more. "Well, I'm looking forward to seeing your performance."

"You—what?" I stutter.

"In December," he answers. "You know, the high-school feature at the Oregon Shakespeare Festival. A group of faculty members and I go every year."

Of course. Of. Course.

Just when I thought the Juliet situation couldn't possibly get worse. It was enough to play a lead in front of Jody, my entire school, and the ardent Shakespeare enthusiasts who attend the festival. Now I have to go on stage knowing I'm being evaluated by the faculty of my dream university. I remember Anthony telling me Juilliard people would be there, critiquing him, but acting is what Anthony's good at. It's what he's spent countless hours perfecting. I'm going to look ridiculous, and everyone there from SOTI will be watching.

I force a smile. "I . . . look forward to seeing you there," I manage.

SEVEN

CHORUS: *Now old desire doth in his deathbed lie,*
And young affection gapes to be his heir.
That fair for which love groaned for and would die,
With tender Juliet matched, is now not fair.

II.prologue.1–4

WHEN I WALK INTO REHEARSAL ON MONDAY, I notice the *Rent* bed's nowhere in sight. *Thank god.* The front of the room isn't set for a scene, and I know that can only mean one thing— Jody's doing a one-on-one with someone who has a monologue. I just hope it's not me. She comes out of her office, and I begin involuntarily fidgeting while the rest of the class files in. She watches silently until everyone's in their seats and the bell rings.

"Anthony," she calls, and I feel my shoulders sag in relief. "It's monologue time." Anthony fist-pumps in his seat, obviously excited for an hour of uninterrupted work on his part. "The rest of you," she continues, "pair up, work on memorizing."

My relief turns to irritation. Anthony would've been my partner. Without him, I search the room for a replacement. Everyone's pairing off. I notice Tyler looking at me with an inquisitive eyebrow raised. There's a certain logic to Romeo and Juliet working together, I know. But after Friday's bed-room scene and Madeleine's confusing intimations about Ty-ler's and my first time, I want space from him even more than usual.

I pointedly look elsewhere, and my eyes lock on to a fa-miliar crop of black hair. Owen is talking to Alyssa. Before she can get her claws into him, I dart over and grab him by the sleeve. "I need you . . ." I say into his ear, pushing him forward.

He turns, his startled expression—his default, I've come to understand—returning, one long eyebrow curving up-ward questioningly. "Common sense dictates your partner's over there." He nods in Tyler's direction. "You know, Romeo?"

I make a face. "*Romeo* and Juliet? No, no, no," I scoff. "Friar Lawrence and Juliet, now *they* have a lot to work with."

Owen cracks up. He looks over his shoulder, where Tyler's dramatically proffering his hand to a group of sophomore girls. "He *is* being particularly obnoxious today."

We walk out into the hallway and toward the auditorium. Jody demands silence for her one-on-one rehearsals, and while we'd normally take the chance to rehearse outside, it's raining today. So instead, we're headed to the theater, which offers enough space for pairs to rehearse in corners of the room without overhearing each other's every word.

Still, the cavernous space sometimes echoes irritatingly. When the door swings shut behind us, I steer Owen down the aisle to the stage. "You want to run lines on stage?" He sounds incredulous.

"Of course not." I open the door to the left of the front

row. "We're going backstage. I have a key to the green room. It's quiet in there."

I lead him up the darkened staircase, through the empty wings, and to the locked room behind the stage. Owen follows me, his footfalls softly crunching on the cheap carpet of the stairs. I figure he's studying the cast-and-crew photos lining the wall from productions before my time. I know them by heart—2001's *Beauty and the Beast*, 2005's *Grease*, 2014's *Much Ado About Nothing*. I remember being crestfallen to learn they'd done *Much Ado* right before I started high school.

We reach the upper level. What passes for a green room at Stillmont is more of a hallway. It's long and narrow, with only a single couch covered in dubious stains.

Owen looks around when I close the door. "If Will comes by and you guys start making eyes at each other again, I'm out of here. This is way too intimate a setting." He drops onto the couch.

"If Will comes by, I'd *want* you out." I shrug. "The things we could do on this couch . . ."

Owen winces with exaggerated disgust. "Way more imagery than I wanted."

I collapse next to him. "If only it was more than imagery. It's not like he's made a move or anything," I say with more frustration than I intend to show.

I know he notices from the way his expression softens. "Don't read into it. Will . . . is new-hot."

I wrinkle my nose. "He's what?"

"You know, like new-money." Owen gestures in the air, his

knees jutting far over the edge of the couch. "Will's new-hot," he says. "He doesn't know the etiquette for these situations."

I raise an eyebrow. "These situations?"

"Like . . ." I catch him blushing. "Having a girl, um, interested in him."

"Interested would be putting it mildly," I declare. "You're his friend. Feel free to nudge him in my direction, or, you know, shove him forcibly," I say half-jokingly, pulling out my script and opening it to Act V. "You want to run your scene with Friar John?"

"Want would be putting it generously." His lips curl faintly, and I let out a laugh. *He's quick on his feet*, I find myself thinking, not for the first time. "But yeah, I guess," he adds.

I open to Scene ii and say loudly and clearly, "Holy Franciscan Friar, brother, ho!" Owen jerks back, and I point at the page. "No, really, that's Friar John's line."

He glances down. "Right." He looks up, trying not to read from the script. He swallows uncomfortably. "This same should be the voice of Friar John. Welcome"—his eyes flit to the page—"from Mantua," he finishes.

"That doesn't count," I cut in. "You haven't even started memorizing, have you?"

"I haven't had a lot of time," he grumbles, agitatedly bouncing his knee once or twice. "I had a breakthrough on my next play, and I spent the weekend outlining."

Curious, I set the script down. "Wait, really? Can I see it?"

"No!" he blurts out, then looks uncomfortable. "It's just, it's nowhere near ready," he says, rubbing his neck.

"What's it about?" I haven't exactly met very many teenage playwrights, and I guess I want to know what Owen Okita in particular writes about.

Owen turns his deepest-ever shade of red. "I got inspired by the conversation we had last week, actually."

"Wow." I put a hand on my chest, jokingly flattered. "I've always wanted to be immortalized in drama."

He smiles slightly. "It's about Rosaline. From *Romeo and Juliet*," he continues. "There's, like, nothing about her in the play, but in Shakespeare's Verona, she could have a life and a story of her own. She could be more than an early piece in someone else's love story."

His words deflate me. I'm a little more disappointed than I'd like to admit that this is the inspiration Owen drew from me. "Rosaline's story isn't as interesting as Juliet's," I say softly. "That's kind of the whole point."

"It could be interesting." Owen sounds defensive, and I don't blame him. I *did* just diss his play. "But I've been having trouble getting into Rosaline's head."

"Hence the weekend of not memorizing your lines," I say.

He shrugs. "There's just not that much about her in *Romeo and Juliet*, and it's hard to get into the mindset of this minor character who's left in a strange position from the events of the play." He folds the spine of the script in his lap, his thumb stained dark blue with ink. "I have to find her direction. Is she heartbroken? Or maybe she's embittered and pleased with Romeo's death."

"Or she knows fate won't give her some star-crossed love, and she's trying to convince herself it's a good thing." The

70

thought leaps to my lips before I know where it comes from. Hoping Owen doesn't read something more into my comment, I stand up sharply.

He only nods carefully. "That's really good," he says, his eyes going distant. He looks like he's in a different world, or just in his head. It's the look I saw in the woods and in the restaurant at the cast party—and on his sharp features it's entirely flattering.

Someone knocks on the green room door, and Owen blinks. I feel an unfamiliar disappointment when that faraway look disappears from his face. I drag myself to the door, hoping it's not Jody or someone else coming to yell at us—we're not actually supposed to be in the green room unsupervised.

Instead, I find Madeleine on the other side of the door, fussing with the strings on her Stillmont High sweatshirt and wearing a nervous, giddy smile. "Hey, Madeleine. Everyone doesn't know we're back here, right?" I quickly check behind her.

"What?" She looks thrown. "No, Tyler told me you guys were in the auditorium, and I figured you'd be in here . . ." She pauses, visibly uncomfortable. "Can I talk to you for a minute?"

"Yeah." I open the door wider. "What's up?"

"Um." She peers behind me to Owen sitting on the couch. "*Just* you?"

"Right. Of course," I say, remembering our talk in the bathroom and realizing exactly what's on her mind. I step into the wings and shut the green room door behind me. "This wouldn't have anything to do with the *extraordinarily* good mood Tyler's in today, would it?" I ask as Madeleine leads me out of Owen's earshot.

She turns to me with a tentative smile. "We had sex."

"You had sex this weekend and waited until the end of the school day to tell me? I demand details in reparations." I cross my arms with mock-sternness.

She chews her lip. "Really? I'd understand if—"

"Madeleine, stop," I tell her, dropping my arms to my sides and meeting her eyes. "I'm your best friend. I want to know as much as you want to share." Her smile returns, tingeing her cheeks light pink. "Was it perfect?" I press.

"He had it all planned out," she begins hesitantly, her voice wavering with excitement. Her words come more easily as she continues. "He drove us up to the cabin—you know, the one his family owns by the lake. He cooked dinner for the two of us, and he even had a bottle of his parents' champagne. Then when the sun went down, we went skinny-dipping. It was beautiful, there were stars and everything, like a movie or a postcard or something. And when we went inside . . ." Madeleine leaves the sentence unfinished.

I'm silent for a moment, because what I'm visualizing isn't a lake and a thousand stars. It's the couch in Tyler's basement, the sounds of the *Twelfth Night* cast party echoing down from upstairs. I enjoyed that experience with Tyler, feeling close to a guy I cared about, and feeling for once like *I* was important. Like *I* was the lead in a love story. But neither Tyler nor I imagined it to be this big, life-changing thing. And the décor, the timing—it wasn't exactly an experience someone would write poetry about.

Of course Madeleine had the perfect night. I'm *glad* it was perfect. I am. While Madeleine's watched me date a nearly constant stream of guys, I've watched her spend all her free time studying and volunteering and *not* having a boyfriend, and meanwhile becoming this incredible, beautiful person. It's nice to see her finally have the boyfriend piece, too.

"I told you you had nothing to worry about," I say finally.

"I guess." She tucks a loose curl behind her ear, smiling softly at her feet. "Anyway, I should get back to the library. I just wanted to tell you in person."

"I'm glad you did," I say, but an unexpected pit opens in my stomach. I walk her to the stairs. "Skinny-dipping under the stars at a beautiful lakeside cabin," I add, forcing a smile. "You give us mere mortals hope that true love is possible."

She laughs. "It is, Megan." She grins and practically bounds down the stairs.

I stand in the hallway, her words echoing in the small space. *It is.* I don't know why her confidence upsets me. Or why hearing about Madeleine's perfect night feels like a lump of lead under my lungs. I knew this was coming, and I wasn't lying when I told her I was fine with it. But I can hear the words Madeleine didn't say. Tyler gave her a night he never gave me because what they have is more real, more worthwhile than what we had. In his head, our night is forgotten, obliterated by something better.

Which it should be, I remind myself. They love each other.

But I guess I liked the idea that Tyler's and my first time meant something to him—that for one boyfriend I was worth remembering. Instead I'm realizing, however close I felt to the center of Tyler's and my stage, I was far off. Far from important. Far from extraordinary.

I try to push the feeling away. I open the door to the green room and find Owen reading lines under his breath. I remember what he was saying about Rosaline, how she doesn't have to be just a precursor to someone else's happy ending.

Madeleine and Tyler are perfect together—they're Romeo and Juliet without the tragedy. I've known their relationship was unique since the first time they sat together at lunch as a couple. Madeleine laughed at something Tyler said, and his eyes lit up like he'd never heard something so lovely before. It reminded me of the way my dad smiled at Rose. There are some things a person can't get in the way of.

But I'm not going to be just a bystander to their epic romance. I don't want Tyler, but I do want to be wanted.

"I need your help with Will." I interrupt Owen's reading and sit down next to him.

His head pops up. "Okay, first, you just made me lose my place," he says, sounding exasperated, but he shuts his book and gives me his attention. "Second, you don't need my help. You're doing fine on your own."

"No, I'm not," I admit. I've watched Will build sets after school three times, and still he hasn't said one word to me since we met. "What you were just telling me about Will being new-hot, that's the kind of insight I need. I don't know a lot about him, about what to expect, how to read him, what he's interested in. I like him," I say. "And I don't want to screw it up. You're his friend—you could help."

Owen doesn't say anything for a moment. He begins tapping his pen on his knee, and it takes everything in me to resist grabbing it out of his hand. "It could get uncomfortable if Will figures out I'm trying to set him up with someone," he finally replies.

I smile slightly, hopefully not enough for him to notice, because his answer wasn't a no. He knows I'm right.

He moves to drumming his pen on his notebook, and I realize how I can convince him. "I'll help you with your play." It comes out sounding like a statement, not an offer.

His pen stops, and he looks at me with curiosity, or hesitation. "I'm not really looking for a cowriter," he says gently.

"Not a cowriter." I shake my head. "I'll help you figure out Rosaline's character. You said you were having trouble getting into her head. Think about it. I *am* Rosaline." Owen blinks, his contemplative look returning. "You liked the idea I had about Rosaline convincing herself not to want what Romeo and Juliet had. I can give you more of that. I know what it's like to watch your ex fall for someone they'd die for, over and over," I go on. "I could tell you about first dates, last dates, breakups—oh, the breakups."

He's tempted, I can tell by the spark in his eyes. But he only asks, "Wouldn't that be kind of weird? Interviewing you about your romantic history?" His ears turn pink.

"It wouldn't be weird for me. I'm not embarrassed by it," I say with a shrug. But by the blush spreading to Owen's cheeks, I know it's not me he's worried about. I'm going to enjoy scandalizing him if he agrees. "Besides," I continue, "you said the play was inspired by me. You're a writer, Owen. How can you refuse the chance to get real, deep emotional insight into a character? That's what I'll give you," I finish triumphantly.

He thinks for a long second. I watch the wheels turning behind his dark eyes.

I stick out my hand. "Do we have a deal?"

When he puts his hand in mine, it's without a trace of hesitation. His fingers wrap all the way around my hand, and his palm is surprisingly rough. "Deal," he says.

"I am *not* going to regret this," I say, and withdraw my hand.

He narrows his eyes. "You . . . Don't you mean *I'm* not going to regret this?"

"Yeah, that too. But I *know* I'm not going to regret it," I reply, and Owen grins, a bit bashful. "What can I do?" I ask, ready to get down to business. "Do you want to start with my first boyfriend? My post-breakup ritual, what?"

He drops his *Romeo and Juliet* script in my lap. "You can read for Friar John. Jody's going to kick me out if I don't have something memorized by the end of the day."

EIGHT

ROMEO: *. . . all these woes shall serve*
For sweet discourses in our times to come.

III.v.52–3

OWEN LIVES ONLY TEN MINUTES FROM ME. Unlike my street, his is hemmed in by trees, and I think I see a trailhead down the block when I get out of the car. His house is a single story, and there's no car in the driveway. The lawn is brown, the leaves in dry piles by the sidewalk.

I knock on the door, and Owen opens it almost immediately. "Hey," he says with a smile.

"Wow." I peer past him into the living room. "Your house is *clean*." I hardly remember what a clean house looks like. I found some dried macaroni on my bag the other day.

"Is it?" He shrugs, but he looks a little pleased. "It's because my family's out right now."

He leads me down the hallway. The walls are sparsely decorated, only a couple of framed pictures of Owen and what must be his younger brother. Next to them hangs an enormous black-and-white photograph of a boyishly handsome Asian man in a seventies-style suit. I pause in front of it. "Is this your dad?" I ask.

Owen glances over his shoulder, puzzlement momentarily written in his brows. His eyes find the photograph, and his mouth twitches with contained laughter. "My mom *wishes* that were my dad. That's Yûjirô Ishihara," he says. "My mom grew up in Kyoto, and when she was a teenager, he was pretty much the biggest star in Japan. She was obsessed. *Is* obsessed," he adds, "even though he died thirty years ago."

"Damn. Your mom's a legit fangirl." I take a closer look, considering Yûjirô's eyebrows and jawline. "I get it, though."

"Great," Owen grumbles, pushing open the door to his room. "Not you, too." I follow him, grinning to his back.

The first thing I notice about Owen's room is the movie posters that line the walls. But they're not movies I know—half the titles are in French, and most of them feature surreal imagery I can't begin to decipher. "Whoa," I say, and look back at Owen, who's noticed my survey of the room.

"I have a bit of a thing for French cinema," he says casually.

"Oh? I hadn't noticed," I deadpan. "But seriously, how do these fit in with Shakespeare and Eugene O'Neill?"

He gives me a crooked grin and brushes his hand through his hair. "I'm a complicated man, Megan."

I step farther into the room. "English theater, French movies, *Italian* girlfriend . . ." I search for photos of Cosima on his cluttered dresser, his conspicuously clean desk, and his windowsill storing a set of encyclopedias. "She's not going to interrupt us on FaceTime, is she?"

"No, she already went to bed," he says, his voice neutral.

"*Of course* she did," I tease. I walk over to his desk and start opening drawers, finding only impressive stacks of note-books in each.

"Excuse me," I hear behind me. "What exactly are you do-ing with my personal possessions?"

I glance over my shoulder to find Owen leaning against the wall, his arms folded across his chest. He pushes him-self off the wall waist-first and crosses the room to shut the drawer I'm perusing.

"Looking for a picture of Cosima," I answer like it's obvi-ous. "She doesn't think being photographed is frivolous, too, does she?"

"No," Owen replies coolly. "I just don't have any pictures of her, is all."

"Where did you guys meet?" I ask, undeterred. I turn to the bookshelves by his bed. A small framed photo of Owen and Jordan from middle school sits between a beautiful hardcover of *The Great Gatsby* and a collection of Emily Dickinson poems.

"It was a summer theater program in New York." He sounds a little defensive. I can't see his face because I've walked be-hind him, but I'm certain he's blushing.

"Well, what's she like?" I press him.

"She's from a little outside Bologna. She writes dark, ex-perimental suburban stuff. Like David Mamet from Italy. Her parents are local politicians."

"You totally didn't answer my question."

He turns to face me, tilting his head and looking confused. "Yes, I did."

"No, what's she *like*?" I repeat. "You told me what she writes and where she lives, not who she is. If you're going to invent a girlfriend, you should flesh her out a little more." It's not that I definitely believe he made her up, it's just that I enjoy getting a rise out of him. "For someone who writes plays, Owen, you really should have a better command of character."

He frowns and raises an eyebrow at me. "She's social, she has a lot of friends. And a sarcastic sense of humor. Better?"

I grin. "Getting there," I toss back. "I'm still not convinced."

"Do you want help with Will or not?" he asks loudly. Without waiting for my answer he continues. "I thought we were here to work on my play."

"Fine," I say with a dramatic sigh, then take a seat on his bed and recline on his pillows. "Ask me anything."

Owen rolls his eyes at my posture before sitting down in his desk chair. He pulls a notebook from the top drawer, and suddenly his whole demeanor changes. His shoulders drop, he sits up straighter and fixes his eyes on me. I wait for him to ask about my thoughts on love or my feelings about myself, the kinds of things I'd imagine a playwright would want to know.

"How far do you and your boyfriends typically go? Like, sexually?" he clarifies.

My mouth drops open for a second, both at the question and at Owen's unexpected composure. Not about to let him think he's scandalized me, I give him a lazy grin. "You get right to it."

I expect Owen to blanch, but he doesn't. "It's important to the play."

"Well, if it's for the play." I smother a smirk. If he wants detail, it's detail he'll get. "Tyler was my first. We only did it a couple times, mostly on the couch in his basement in the middle of cast parties, with everyone upstairs." I ignore the lingering bite of comparing those memories with Madeleine's recent account, instead preoccupying myself with hoping I'll catch Owen's ears going red.

When he only continues writing, I deflate a little. I'll have to work harder. Which won't be a problem given the detail I could provide. "I wouldn't say it was amazing, but there *was* a reason we did it more than once . . ." I say suggestively, frowning when Owen only nods. I'm used to hushed laughter and gossip-glittering eyes when I provide details of my escapades—the consolation prize for their early, inevitable ends. Owen is . . . resisting. It's unexpected, and I'm uncertain what to make of it.

"I'm trying to get an idea of what Rosaline might feel if she'd slept with Romeo before the whole Juliet thing." His eyes remain fixed on his notebook. His hand moves with practiced speed, his pen in precise jolts. "Do you feel differently about Tyler than your other exes?"

"Not really." I shrug. "I did *plenty* with other guys."

For the first time, Owen's shoulders stiffen. I grin. *Everyone* has a sex-awkwardness pressure point, even young Shakespeare over here. I go on. "I went to third base with Chris behind the gym after homecoming sophomore year. Only hands were involved with Charlie because his mom was always coming home at inopportune times. Obviously nothing with Anthony—oh, third base with Dean, which took freaking forever. I had to—"

"That—that's enough, thanks," he cuts me off, completely crimson.

"Ha! *Finally*," I explode.

He looks up. "You were trying to make me uncomfortable?"

"Well, a little, yeah." I eye him playfully.

He lifts his pen, looking like he wants to say something, until he finally does. "Is this . . . how you are?"

"Is what how I am?"

"This, you know . . . forward. Provocative." I know it's not a criticism, or a joke. He watches me, his mouth a neutral line, his eyes searching. He really wants to know.

I laugh harshly. "I've earned the right. When you've had as many relationships as I have, you learn to find the humor in . . ." I reach for the right word.

"Heartbreak," Owen says.

"That's a bit more poetic than I would have gone with, but basically." He says nothing, and I pounce on the opportunity to change the subject. "Besides, teasing you is too much fun to resist." I reach toward the chair and pat him on the knee. "You're just so . . . sweet."

He shakes off my hand. "No, I'm not," he huffs.

He's looking at the floor, and I feel a sting of remorse. Owen *is* sweet. He's been nothing but kind to me, and I just turned that into something he feels self-conscious about. "You're right. I'm sorry."

"I have other questions, you know." Owen recovers his composure, returning to his notebook. "If you're ready to answer them like a mature human being." He flashes me a brief smile.

"Okaaaaay . . ." I drag out the syllables, relieved I'm forgiven.

"Does how far you go with a guy affect your feelings in the breakup?"

I pause a second. He deserves a thoughtful answer this time. "The sex doesn't matter, per se. But if I've been with a guy long enough to have done things with him, I'm used to having him in my life, and it's worse when we break up. Even then, though, when I see him with someone else and they're perfect in every way he and I weren't, it's hard to stay upset."

Owen stops writing. "I would think it'd be the opposite— that it would hurt worse."

"Not when you're expecting it. My relationships end for something bigger. In the end, it's comforting."

He gives me a long look, like he's waiting for me to elaborate, or to burst into tears or something. I don't know what he's thinking. When I do none of the above, he makes a couple more notes. "Do you believe in true love?" he asks out of nowhere.

"True love?" I scoff, not meeting his unfaltering eye contact. I don't know why the question throws me. Maybe it's the way he asked it, like true love is common and obvious enough to be brought up as easily as the weather. "I told you. I'm not really the romantic, love-at-first-sight type," I answer.

"You also said Tyler and Madeleine are perfect together."

"So?" I reply a little hotly.

"So," he repeats, his tone measured, "if two people are perfect for each other, it suggests their connection is better than others. Deeper, truer."

"True love exists, like, in the world." I gesture vaguely to the air around me. I've witnessed true love too often to think otherwise. What Madeleine and Tyler have is true. Same with my dad and Rose. "But I'm certainly not holding out hope for it myself."

"Hmm," Owen muses, his eyes sparkling. He leans back, clearly confident about whatever he's going to say next. "It's interesting you think that."

"Think that? I *know* it. It's my own feelings." My skin itches down my arms. I roll my shoulders, trying to loosen the sudden tension in my back.

"And yet, when one relationship ends, you jump easily into another."

"Which, as the entire student body can tell you, means I'm flirtatious and boy-crazy. Two things I'm not ashamed of, by the way," I add, chin up.

"Of course." He nods quickly. "I'm not saying you should be. I just wonder why, if you're *only* flirtatious and boy-crazy, you go from relationship to relationship instead of hookup to hookup." His eyes bore into mine again.

I blink. I haven't known Owen very long, and somehow he's seen into the quietest, smallest corner of my heart. It's a wish I don't let out very often. Not everyone finds someone perfect for them. Or if they do, sometimes that person doesn't think *you're* perfect for *them*. My mom's lingering affection for my dad showed me that.

"I thought this was supposed to be play brainstorming, not psychotherapy or something."

Owen puts down his pen, his expression growing gentle.

"You're right. You've given me a lot of great stuff to work with."

The silence hangs in the air. I don't know what to do next. I guess I'm here to ask about Will, but would it be weird if I did? Or would it be weirder if I didn't? Would that just show I'm more rattled than I'd like to admit? I wish I could think of something to dispel the tension.

"Not amazing, huh?" Owen asks suddenly, and I'm thankful he's smiling. "Tyler, I mean."

I feel a grin spreading across my face. "His final performance didn't exactly live up to the acclaimed early previews."

Owen lets out a quick laugh. "Not a long run then?"

"Closed in minutes. Hoping Will lasts longer . . ." I raise an eyebrow.

"That's Sexy Stagehand Will to you," Owen says seriously.

"Of course." I lean forward. "Your turn. What's up with Sexy Stagehand Will? What's taking him so long? It's been days of me giving him my best bedroom eyes—and not like shitty, twin-bed bedroom eyes," I add. "Like four-poster, silk-draped, chateau bedroom eyes."

"Bedroom eyes?" Owen cocks his head skeptically. "Is that a thing?"

On the bed, I lean a little closer and look up at him through smoldering, half-lidded eyes.

"Ah," he says almost immediately. "Well, Will's not used to this kind of thing. He wouldn't make a move unless he knows you're interested."

"I'm not just going to march up to him in the middle of school or rehearsal and plant one on him. Not if he might not be into it. I do have *some* dignity."

"What if it's not at school?" Owen muses. "Will's band is playing a house party this weekend. It'll give you guys a chance to find some privacy."

Yes. In front of a crowd is one thing, but if I can get him alone, I'd definitely make a move. "Perfect," I say. "Sounds like I'll have a new boyfriend by Monday."

Owen looks at me curiously. I can read the question in his eyes.

I sigh with impatience, and maybe a little something else. "I told you, I'm not holding out hope for love. I like Will. I want Will to be my boyfriend. Even if I hope *someday, something* like . . . true love"—I almost can't get the words out—"is possible for me, I'm expecting nothing from him other than our relationship falling apart just like the rest."

"You're certain it'll fall apart," Owen asks, "and still you're eager to start a new relationship?" There's nothing judgmental in his tone.

It's not like I haven't asked myself the very same question. "What else can I do? Otherwise I'll just be watching everyone else." I get up off the bed and pick up my bag by his door. He's still watching me with the scrutiny of his interview, even though he's put his notebook down on his desk. "Besides," I add, throwing my bag over my shoulder, "it'll be fun while it lasts."

NINE

JULIET: *Give me my Romeo, and when I shall die,*
Take him and cut him out in little stars,
And he will make the face of heaven so fine
That all the world will be in love with night
And pay no worship to the garish sun.

III.ii.23–7

EVER SINCE MY DAD TOLD ME ABOUT the move, just being home puts me in a bad mood. I've spent afternoons this week doing homework in the drama room or, when Jody goes home for the night, in the corner booth in Verona eating half-baked pizza and watching Anthony watch Eric. But on Friday night, I'm home early to talk to Mom.

I head downstairs to hydrate before the party. I'm in luck—Dad's at a school board meeting, and the house is quiet. In the kitchen I walk past Erin in her high chair contemplating the universe over a tiny bowl of applesauce. When I grab a bottle of water and close the fridge, something splatters on the wall next to me. I spin to find Erin regarding me, pink plastic spoon in hand and a big grin on her face. She lets out a giggle, and I notice there's applesauce in her ear.

I sigh. "Rose?" I call. There's no answer. Seeing no other choice, I turn back to Erin. "You can't go around looking like that," I chide. Gingerly, I scoop her out of her high chair, careful to avoid the applesauce sliding down her cheek. She shrieks in delight.

I leave the water running while I wet a paper towel and wipe down Erin's face. Clearly thinking this is the best thing in the world, Erin flings her hand through the stream, splashing water on the halter dress I've chosen to catch Will's eye. I put my hand on my hip and adopt an indignant tone. "You did *not* just do that." I flick a drop of water at her in return, and she explodes into giggles.

"Megan?" I hear Rose from the hall before she steps into the kitchen, her eyes jumping from me to Erin. "Sorry, I walked away for a second to pee for the twentieth time today." She smiles. "You two look like you're having fun."

I was. But when Rose lays a hand on her swollen stomach, I'm reminded of why my dad's moving across the country. "You left her with applesauce. I had to clean her up," I tell Rose, working to keep my voice unemotional.

"Thanks, Megan," she says gently as she walks forward to pick up Erin. "Erin would thank you, too, if only she could pronounce your name," Rose adds, smiling. "The hard *G*, you know?"

I only shrug before I head upstairs.

When I get on FaceTime with Mom five minutes late—as usual—I must still look out of sorts, because she immediately studies me, concerned. "What's wrong?"

"Did you know Dad and Rose are planning to move to New York?" I blurt out.

Mom looks taken aback, but she quickly recovers. "They . . . haven't told me about that, no."

"Well, they're looking at houses," I charge on. "I only found out because they left a real-estate catalog in the kitchen."

I watch her fuss with the mug of tea she's holding, one I realize I don't recognize. It wasn't one of the things she packed into cardboard boxes before she left Oregon, and her marriage, to find a new home in Texas. I've never known how that felt to her, but now I'm beginning to understand. I'm beginning to know the disconnection from home she must've felt, even though I'm staying put in Oregon for college—hopefully—and she moved halfway across the country.

I blamed her the night they told me she was moving. I didn't understand why she'd decided to leave. When I caught her hours later forlornly staring at the family photos in the hall, I realized she hadn't. Not really.

"Megan, I'm sure they were going to tell you," Mom says softly. "You know your father. He never lets anyone into his plans until he's figured the details out himself."

"Yeah. I guess," I mutter.

"If this bothers you, you should talk to your dad." Her voice is still sympathetic, but there's a patented Mom firmness to it. "He'd want to know you're upset."

"Why bother? It's not like they'd listen to my opinion."

Mom says nothing for a second, her eyes flitting downward. I know we're both remembering some of the worst fights of her and Dad's final months together. Shouting matches about Dad's tendency to make decisions for the whole family without listening to her, or even talking to her. There's a motorcycle in the garage to prove it.

"You know, New York might not be the worst," she says with a hesitant smile. "You could go to shows in the city when you're home from school."

She's trying, like she must've when she unpacked in her new home. She must've searched for what was exciting and worth looking forward to where she'd be living. Not wanting to worry her, I nod.

"You *could* come to Texas," she adds in a quietly hopeful voice.

"Maybe," I say. I don't tell her moving to Texas wouldn't fix the real problems. It wouldn't keep my dad and Rose from building a new life without me. It wouldn't keep them from erasing the only home I've ever known, consigning my child-hood memories to the past.

"How's the play going?" Mom asks, and I know she's trying to distract me.

"It's going okay," I mumble. "We're mostly just working on memorizing. I haven't done a lot of real performing yet."

She sets down her tea, a worrisome gleam in her eye. "Well . . . Randall and I have gotten tickets to come to the Ashland showcase."

Shit. "Wow," I say instead. "Sounds great, Mom."

"It'll be Randall's first trip to Oregon," she goes on excitedly. "I was thinking the three of us could go to the lake. I finally get to show him where you grew up, and I know

Randall's looking forward to spending more time with you."

"That—would be really nice," I get out.

Mom cranes her neck to look behind her. "He's in the other room if you have time for a quick hello."

"Um, sorry. I have a party to get to. How about next time?"

"A party?" Her eyebrows lift. "You'll tell me about the new boyfriend tomorrow, I expect?"

I roll my eyes. "There's no boyfriend." *Yet.*

Mom gives me a look that says she knows better. "Be careful, Megan."

"Bye, Mom," I say loudly before I disconnect.

I shut the computer and put on my burgundy lipstick in front of the mirror. The thought of both parents and their significant others in Stillmont puts me on edge. It's hard to watch Mom and Randall next to Dad and Rose, the perfect couple Mom and her boyfriend will never be. Mom met Randall online after two years of blind dates and setups in Texas. Dad met Rose months after the divorce. They were married within the year, and with their second kid on the way, they still have Friday date nights and can't keep their hands off each other.

Because of course Dad bounced back. It's easier to be the one letting go.

I park at the end of Derek Denton's driveway, an impossibly long path to where his house perches on a bluff. Cars are parked the whole way up like it's Coachella and not a high-school house party. It's dark here, without streetlights among the trees. This is one of the priciest neighborhoods in southern Oregon, and I can see why. When I look up there's nothing but treetops and endless stars.

It takes ten minutes to walk up to the door, though my heels are partly to blame. It's a chilly October night, and I gratefully pull my jacket tight. When I get inside, I'm surprised I don't recognize everyone here. Stillmont is a small school, and I've only been to a couple of parties where the invites reached into other towns nearby, but Derek's living room is filled with people I've never seen before. The house is even bigger than it looked from the outside, with a wide oak staircase up to an indoor balcony where a group of girls lean on the railing, nodding along to the music. I look over the heads of the already inebriated crowd to the double doors that open onto an illuminated azure pool, where a few brave souls have jumped in despite the weather.

But next to the pool I spot what I'm looking for, a cleared space with a drum kit and a couple of amps. Setting up a microphone in front of the drums is the tall, leather-jacketed, gorgeous reason I'm here tonight.

I plunge into the crowd, stepping past the coffee table where Jeremy Handler is presently passed out. Courtney Greene shoves a red Solo cup in my direction. "I'm good!" I yell, not to be deterred.

"Megan!" someone shouts in my ear, and I turn. There are only a couple of voices that could stop me right now, and one of them is Anthony's, especially when I know tonight's the night he's supposed to be out with Eric. He looks no less surprised to see me than I am him.

"Wait." I recover first. "Wasn't Eric's party—" Then I realize. "*This* is the party Eric invited you to?"

"Yeah," he says. I notice he's wearing one of his best outfits—his caramel chinos and the iconic navy blazer over an oxford with the top two buttons undone. "What are you doing here? I didn't know you were coming out tonight."

I throw a glance toward the makeshift stage where Will's now tuning a guitar. *Be still my heart.*

"I see." Anthony nods slowly.

"How's it going with you?" I search the crowd. "Where's Eric?"

Anthony seizes my arm. "It's going *great*. Eric picked me up, and we drove over here together. Which means he's driving me home." He gives me a smile I recognize from years of being front row to his flirtations. "High hopes for the night."

Behind him, I catch sight of Eric in a neon frat tank, holding up two Solo cups and heading our way. Anthony grins, and I gently shove him in Eric's direction. The screech of an amp cuts through the shitty dance music inside, and I take it as my cue to press on to the back door.

Finally, I reach the stage. "Will!" I shout from a couple feet away, trying to sound like I'm surprised to run into him— not like he's my single objective for the night and hopefully the next couple months.

"Megan, hey!" Will faces me, looking genuinely surprised. "I didn't know you'd be coming." He sets his guitar down and gives me a grin that has me rethinking the whole privacy premise of tonight.

"This house is crazy, right?" I nonchalantly toss my hair. "I heard there's a path to a bluff with an incredible view."

"Really?" He looks interested, and my stomach somersaults. He crouches down next to an amp to plug something in. "Give me a—"

"Hey, Will!" The voice comes from what must be one of Will's bandmates, who's standing on the other end of the stage. "The PA's broken again. I've tried plugging shit in everywhere and—nothing. We need that stagehand magic."

Will sighs, frustrated, and looks at me apologetically. "I have to—" he starts.

"No worries," I cut him off, hoping he doesn't hear my disappointment. "The show must go on. I'm looking forward to it."

His devastating grin returns. "Find me after, okay?"

"Definitely." Like he has to tell me. Even though it physically hurts to pull myself away, I retreat into the crowd growing on the edge of the stage.

Will must be a genius with PAs, because it's only five minutes later that he steps up to the mic while the rest of the band take to their instruments behind him. Without introduction, Will counts them off and strikes the first chord. He's incredible. I am dead. They're playing a kind of alternative punk that I'd probably enjoy even without the hot singer.

I try to move up, but I'm blocked by Dean Singh, my ex from two years ago. He's dancing overeagerly with Amanda

Cohen, whom he left me for when she transferred to our school three months into our relationship. I watch him smash a sloppy kiss on her lips in front of me.

I hesitate, wrestling with the warring desires to get a better view and to avoid Dean. I didn't exactly exit the relationship gracefully. I wasn't completely used to being dumped yet, and I let Dean know I was pissed. There might have been defiling of his locker involved. We haven't spoken since, and I'm not looking to break the streak. In a moment of panic, I spin and search for a new vantage point to watch the band. My eyes find Anthony on the outdoor balcony.

I quickly go inside and step over a worrisome bikini top on my way up the stairs. It's less crowded up here with everyone on the dance floor. When I walk out onto the balcony, Anthony's draped on the railing, his eyes fixed on the crowd below. Immediately, I know something's wrong. In no typical party would Anthony be by himself while everyone else is having fun.

"What's up, Anthony?" I hesitantly ask when I reach the railing.

He wordlessly points to the edge of the dance floor, where I glimpse a flash of neon. Eric.

He's dancing—with a girl, the sort of girl someone like Eric would be expected to attract. Bleach-blonde hair, tall, curvaceous.

"They could just be friends," I say, watching the girl press her butt into Eric's front. "Besides, you said things were going great. I bet it's nothing."

Anthony turns to me, his eyes combative. "Does she *look*

like just a friend?" He nods to where Eric's now running his hands down the girl's sides.

I have to admit, it doesn't look good. A guy in a Saint Margaret's School lacrosse jersey walks past Eric and thumps him on the back. That's where Eric goes to school, I have to guess. He exchanges bro-nods with the lacrosse guy, then returns to his concentrated grinding.

"I don't get it," Anthony mutters. "I really felt like we connected in the car."

"I'm sure you—" I hear my name shouted up from the lower level. Anthony and I both turn, startled, to peer over the railing.

Owen's standing under the balcony. He must be the only person in the entire party not dancing or watching the band. He's wearing a gray sweater and black jeans, and even though I know I've seen the outfit before, it looks somehow better tonight. When our eyes meet, he grins.

"What're you doing up there?" he calls.

I gesture in the direction of Will and the band, who've finished their first song to drunken cheers. "Better view!" I shout.

"How Juliet of you." Owen nods at the balcony, his grin widening. I have no choice but to roll my eyes. Beside me Anthony groans, and I glance to Eric—whose hands have risen perilously close to Blondie's chest.

Anthony's head drops into his hands. But he jerks upright when I take him by both shoulders and spin him to look me in the eye. "Anthony," I say urgently. "This?" I gesture to him crumpled on the railing. "Isn't how you get guys interested.

Especially not when you're wearing the blazer and button-down you *know* leave people breathless." He gives me a weak smile. "Pull yourself together. Get down there," I continue. "Talk to him. Dance with him."

My monologue doesn't exactly leave Anthony looking like a virile sex god, but some of the despondency's gone out of his expression. He straightens his blazer and walks inside, and I lean over the balcony's edge.

"Owen," I shout. "This is ridiculous. Come up here."

Will counts off the second song, and I take special note of the way he pushes his slightly sweaty hair out of his eyes. Sometime between the hair push and Will gripping the mic with both hands in a way that makes me wish it were my face, Owen comes out onto the balcony.

"Did you bring a date?" I ask him when he joins me by the railing.

He frowns, but I can tell he's trying to hide a smile. "No, Megan. I didn't bring a date. I have a girlfriend."

"Oh, *right*. I keep forgetting."

He scrutinizes me for a second. "Is there . . . applesauce in your hair?"

"What?" I quickly try to hide my head from Owen and grab my hair, mortified when I feel something sticky. "It was—a crazy pregame," I mutter, furiously trying to brush it out.

Owen turns back to the band. It feels like he's giving me a moment to collect myself, and I'm grateful. "They sound okay tonight," he says.

"They sound *amazing*. They're probably the best band I've ever heard."

"You mean seen," he says with the hint of a smile.

"Seen, heard . . . What's the difference?"

Owen laughs. "Remind me to take you to a real concert sometime."

It's a tossed-off comment, but for a moment my mind lingers on the idea of Owen Okita taking me to concerts, to other places on nights out . . . But I lose my train of thought when I hear Will sing, *"Come on, baby, touch me and feel me burning for you!"*

I can't stop listening. Hot lead singer notwithstanding, they *are* good. *"You're a fire in the night, crimson in the trees,"* Will sings. *"If you do nothing else for me, baby, burn me down, please."*

"Wow . . . Will, these lyrics, it's working for me," I say in a low voice.

Owen rubs the back of his neck, looking uncomfortable.

"Wait." I grab his arm. "Owen. Did *you* write these?"

The blood rushes from his face. "Yes, I did."

"No wonder you're with your fair Cosima if she inspires lyrics like these. A few weeks of theater camp and you two really got down to business."

He shakes his head sharply. "The lyrics weren't inspired by anything. I was just trying to channel Neruda's love poetry in a modern context. It was a poetical exercise."

I raise an eyebrow. "Is that what the kids are calling it these days?"

"I swear," he insists. "They're completely innocent."

"*Sure*, Owen."

I feel my phone buzz. Pulling it out of my purse, I find a text from Anthony. **YOU NEED TO COME DOWN HERE**, it reads. Anthony texts entirely in capitals. When I asked him why, years ago, he told me "the world won't wait for men who write in lowercase."

y, I send back.

I WANT TO DANCE WITH ERIC. TOO SCARED. NEED BACKUP.

I look down into the crowd and spot Anthony awkwardly hovering near Eric and the girl. I notice the Saint Margaret's lacrosse boys have moved away from the dance floor to the keg by the doors. Smiling, I stow my phone and grab Owen's arm again. "Come on," I command. "We've got to go dance."

He looks startled. I swear, one of these days that expression's going to stick. "Us? Now?"

"It's a group thing. For Anthony." I walk backward while tugging him toward the door. "It's nothing to make Cosima jealous."

Owen breaks into a grin. "So you admit she's real?"

"You're impossible." I roll my eyes, leading him down the stairs. "Come on, lover boy."

I keep hold of his arm as we make our way through our drunken classmates. The crowd hasn't thinned out, and I'm nearly elbowed in the face by a couple baseball guys I recognize from Tyler's games. I let go of Owen when we reach Anthony, who's worked up the courage to move closer to Eric. Luckily, Eric and the blonde have separated long enough for us to join them and form a lopsided dance circle.

I reach for Anthony's hand and playfully grind up on him, and he places his hands on my hips. Anthony's a good dancer once he's been loosened up.

As soon as the blonde walks off to join the group of girls beckoning her over, I nudge Anthony in Eric's direction and face Owen, who's making a good effort at dancing. I watch him bob his head for a couple beats before I take his hands and dance lazily with my fingers entwined in his. I feel him hesitate for a second, but then I exaggeratedly flip my hair, and he relaxes, grinning.

When the band starts a faster number, Owen cranes his neck to look over my shoulder. Following his eyes, I turn and catch sight of Anthony and Eric swaying near each other, holding hands below their waists.

I whip to face Owen. "Oh my god," I mouth. He nods slowly, eyebrows arched. I laugh and pull him closer, our bodies just barely touching. He stiffens, but still he doesn't pull away. By the time the song ends, he's gripping my hands tightly and we move faster in rhythm through the next couple songs.

"That's our set. Thanks, Stillmont," I hear Will's voice coming over the mic. "You've been a beautiful audience."

I step back from Owen and wipe the sweat from my forehead, catching my breath. He gives me a shy smile, a smile in which I see a different Owen than the one hunched over his notebook in Verona. An Owen willing to follow me onto a dance floor and match my every move with one of his own. Just when I think I have him figured out, he keeps finding ways to surprise me.

The thought hangs in my head for only a moment because,

out of the corner of my eye, I glimpse the blonde girl from earlier heading our way, followed by two Saint Margaret boys. Eric drops Anthony's hand—and while Anthony watches in stunned silence, Eric grabs the girl and presses his lips to hers, folding her into a shameless kiss.

I lock eyes with Anthony.

Horror, heartbreak, and anger collide on his face. I open my mouth, trying to think of something to say—of what I could possibly say—but he's storming off before I've even gotten his name out. The crowd's breaking up, staggering back into the house. I push aside exhausted couples clinging to each other on the patio, following Anthony.

I finally reach him by the pool, but he holds up a hand. "Please, Megan," he says in a low, uneven voice. "I just need to be alone right now."

"Let me drive you home at least," I say, because it's the only thing I have to offer.

"No, go back inside. Find Will. I'll be fine, really. I'll get a ride with Jenna." He irons a little of the waver out of his voice.

I stand there and watch him slowly walk into the house with everyone else, wondering if I'd be a shittier friend to let him leave or try to follow. Before I've decided, Owen steps up beside me.

"Is he okay?" Owen asks.

"Not really. But Anthony's tough."

He nods. "Well, I wanted to catch you because the band's packing up. Now's your shot with Will."

He's right. I'm here for a reason, and I can't leave without trying. I look to the stage, where Will's drummer and guitarist are hauling equipment toward an open van parked in the back. But Will's caught in a circle of girls near the mic stand, each of them leaning in a little closer than what could be considered friendly. I'm not surprised to find Alyssa's among them.

Part of me irrationally hopes he'll look for me over the heads of his new groupies. But of course he doesn't.

"Are you going?" Owen sounds expectant.

I gesture to the girls encircling Will. "I'm not interested in playing that game." And I definitely don't want to stick around and watch him notice someone else. "I'll just wait until everyone's leaving and talk to him then."

With nothing better to do, I follow Owen into the enormous, trashed living room, where inexplicably he begins picking up beer cans and Solo cups and throwing them into the black Hefty bag taped to the wall. Feeling guilty next to Mr. Party Samaritan, I grab a towel and wipe up a salsa spill on the chip table.

"You're his friend. What has Will said about me?" I ask after a couple minutes.

Owen drops a can into the trash bag, then stops, seemingly weighing his words. "He said you're hot in a deep way."

I straighten up. "What does *that* mean? No, wait, it doesn't matter. It sounds promising." I take a seat on the stairs and smile to myself, until curiosity gets the better of me. "But what does that mean?"

Owen laughs at my change of heart. He leans on the banister, his eyes becoming contemplative. His words come slowly at first, but they gather momentum while he speaks. "It means you're, like, this unafraid force of being. You know exactly who you want to be, and you never pretend to be someone you're not. It's inspiring. Being around you—" He looks up sharply, then shakes his head. "This trash bag's going to break," he says abruptly, tying off the bag beside him, eyes averted from mine. "Would you hand me another?" He points to the box of bags on the table.

Judging from the limp outline of the one he's tying shut, it's nowhere near full. But I grab a new bag anyway.

I hand it to him, saying nothing. I don't know what *to* say. Owen tapes the new bag to the wall, then straightens his sweater like he's desperately searching for a distraction. I feel something I hardly recognize—a blush rising in my cheeks.

No one's ever said anything like that to me. I've never thought of myself as a force of . . . anything.

"No wonder you write the lyrics," I say lightly before the silence gets too awkward.

Owen's laugh sounds relieved, but he stuffs his hands into his pockets.

"Will didn't say all that, did he?" My voice comes out soft, and at first I think he didn't hear me over the music pounding through the walls. No one's turned the iPod off even though the party's dying down.

"Not exactly," Owen says after a long moment. He glances sideways, and I want to ask him what he was going to say next, before he cut himself off to ask for the trash bag, when I hear someone's footsteps coming from the now nearly empty patio.

"Hey," Will says when he sees us.

"Good set tonight." Owen sounds casual, none of the gentle sincerity of a couple seconds ago lingering in his voice. "I should head home," he continues, tossing a pointed look in my direction. I know he's purposefully giving me time with Will. "I'll see you guys for rehearsal on Monday."

He leaves us by the stairs. I waste no time in getting up and smoothing my dress. Without saying a word, we drift back outside. There's a certain charge in the air, like we both know where this is headed.

Will pauses under the strings of small, dim lights strung over the patio. "I looked for you after the show, but I couldn't find you."

"I knew you were getting mobbed." I shrug, not wanting to think about Alyssa and the groupies right now. "Hot lead singer and whatnot."

He laughs, his voice rough and raspy from an hour of singing, and I wish we'd skipped the small talk. "You get right to the point. I like that," he says, eyeing me like he's wishing the same thing.

I'm leaning forward to kiss him when there's a horrible retching sound next to us. We both startle back to find Jeremy Handler, head between his knees, spewing an acrid beige outpouring onto the grass. "Wow . . ." Will mumbles.

"Yeah. We have to find a better place for this."

"What was it you said about a bluff with a view?" he asks, a smile returning to his eyes.

"*Yes.*" I grab his hand. "Perfect."

The path begins behind the pool, and it's startling how quickly the backyard full of beer cans—and now vomit—disappears on our way up. Hardly a five-minute walk up the trail, it feels like Will and I have stepped into a starlit night completely our own. I lead him to the rocky edge of the bluff. The view is unbelievable, sweeping over the sparse lights of Stillmont and the moon reflected in Hudson Lake.

"I don't want to be the kind of guy who fishes for compliments," Will speaks up after a moment of looking out on the view, "but what'd you think of the band?"

I grin and face him, my hand still in his. "I think you're a great vocalist," I say not untruthfully. I take a step closer. "And Sexy Stagehand Will is an understatement."

His eyebrows nearly reach his hairline. "Is that what people call me?"

I close the distance between us. "Certain people," I say in a hushed voice. Then my lips are on his. He stills and pulls back after a second, looking at me questioningly. "You said you liked that I got right to the point," I whisper. "This was the point, wasn't it?"

Will's uncertainty fades, replaced by something that stops my breath. "Yes. It definitely was."

For a single heartbeat, I look into Will's eyes and wonder if I'm doing this right. If I shouldn't slow down and get to know him before beginning this. The whisper of an idea slips into my mind. *Maybe I shouldn't begin every relationship with the expectation it'll end. Maybe it could last if—* I bury the thought.

I don't have time to waste. I'm going to enjoy every second I have with Will before it's over.

He pulls me in this time and kisses me hard. Even though we're a long way from the ocean, it feels like waves crashing.

I glance in the mirror once I've gotten back in my car, and *holy shit, is my hair messed up*. It's fifteen minutes past my curfew, but there's someone I have to text before I go home and have my phone taken away for the weekend. I haven't texted Owen before, but we exchanged numbers after our first play-brainstorming session.

went gr8. Thx ur the best, I send him with a kissy emoji.
Who is this? he replies.
u didnt put my # in ur phone??? megan, I shoot back.
It's a couple moments before my phone buzzes again.

Forgive me for not recognizing you through the grammar of a sixth grader from 2001. Is this how you write everything, or are you very drunk?

Smiling to myself, I return, **NOT drunk. who do U usually text w/? david foster wallace?**

David Foster Wallace is dead, Megan. I WISH I texted with David Foster Wallace.

I find I'm grinning wider.

back 2 point: Will!!! (RIP david foster wallace)

My phone buzzes seconds after I've hit SEND.

Punctuation! Like rain in the desert!

keep it in ur pants, Owen, I fire back.
I watch the typing bubble for a half minute before I re-ceive his reply.

**I'm happy for you about Will. I hope you still want
advice, though, because my play's nowhere near done.**

I know this is probably just Owen being a Serious Writer, but still I'm touched he wants to hang out. I send back, **dnt worry, Im not going anywhere.**

TEN

JULIET: *O, swear not by the moon, th' inconstant moon,*

That monthly changes in her circled orb,

Lest that thy love prove likewise variable.

II.ii.114–6

WILL'S WAITING FOR ME OUTSIDE ENGLISH WHEN lunch begins. I wasn't expecting him, and I beam when I notice him leaning on the lockers. It's nearly been a week, and we haven't had the conversation where we "define the relationship." But it doesn't matter if we're dating, or hooking up, or just friends with benefits, even if it's only PG for now. Whatever we are, I'm enjoying it.

He reaches for my hand as we walk down the hallway. Momentarily surprised, I jerk to face him. "Handholding? I'll take it," I say coyly. In the past couple days, we've jumped straight to the more physical, more private forms of contact, skipping over the simple stuff like holding hands.

"I'm not moving too fast, right?" He flashes me his irresistible smile.

I play along. "I don't know, Will. It's bold of you."

"Megan Harper talking to *me* about being bold?" He releases my hand and spins to walk backward facing me.

I laugh. "I haven't a clue what you're implying."

"Oh really?" He cocks an eyebrow. "Even with what happened yesterday after rehearsal?"

My stomach clenches deliciously at the memory of a Grade-A make-out session in the green room, complete with a costume rack knocked over and a shattered prop lamp.

"You raise an excellent point," I concede. Still thinking about yesterday, I grab his hand and stop him outside the art closet. His eyes light up. Wasting no time, he follows me inside and closes the door.

Twenty-two minutes later, I straighten my skirt and step out into the hall. Will places a hand low on my back, and we head to the quad. We find Tyler and Madeleine, Owen, Jenna, and a few juniors I know on the hill outside the drama room. Without warning, Will sweeps his arm behind my back, dips me slightly, and kisses me. With tongue.

When he pulls back, he's grinning. "Too bold?"

I place a hand on his chest. "It's Megan Harper you're talking to, remember?"

He laughs and follows it up with a quick kiss. "I'll see you after rehearsal."

"You better," I warn. I sit down between Madeleine and Jenna, my eyes on Will as he walks into the Arts Center.

"Where's Will going?" Madeleine asks next to me. I notice she looks genuinely disappointed. One of the things I love about her is, not only does she comfort me through every breakup, but she's excited every time I date someone new—no matter how often that is.

"He had to finish some set design." I give her a fake pouty look, which she returns.

"You mean we *don't* get to watch you make out for the rest of lunch?" Owen dryly laments. "How will we survive?"

I grab one of Madeleine's celery sticks and chuck it at Owen. He catches it to his chest and promptly eats it. Madeleine, looking mildly indignant, moves her celery farther from me. "Have you guys talked about it yet?" she asks. "You and Will? Walking you from class, that looked like boyfriend stuff."

I shrug. "Not yet. We're taking it slow."

I hear a low chuckle from Tyler, and I'm surprised to notice Owen shoot him a look, his expression hardening. "What did *that* mean?" Owen asks flatly.

Tyler glances between Madeleine and me, recognizing the indelicate position he's put himself in. "I've just never known Megan to take it slow," he finally says haltingly.

I hardly have time to be offended before Madeleine puts a hand on my knee. "With a guy who looks like Will, I know *I* wouldn't." It's a remark aimed to irritate Tyler, and from the way he stiffens and crosses his arms, I know it worked. "What's he like?" she continues in a gossipy tone.

"He's funny, and he's confident . . ." I begin, only too happy to brag about my new boy-*whatever*. "And he's the best kisser *ever*." I don't look at Tyler, but he knows I'm talking to him.

"Sounds like this one might last out the month," he sneers.

Madeleine whacks his shoulder, staring daggers at him.

It's sweet of her, but the damage is done. It's one thing for me to joke about my short-lived romances—it's something else for people like Tyler to think *I'm* the flighty one in my relationships. I might enjoy the flings, the fooling around, the green-room make-outs, but I'm never the one to keep them from developing into meaningful relationships. I get up to leave, no longer in the mood to talk about Will, and catch sight of Owen watching Tyler furiously.

I throw my bag onto my shoulder. "Don't be a dick," I overhear Madeleine hiss. I ponder where exactly I'm going to go, but the bell rings, deciding for me.

"Why, that same pale hard-hearted wench, that Rosaline, torments him so that he will sure run mad."

Anthony's strutting across the small stage in the drama room, delivering his lines with his characteristic panache. I'm sitting in the front row, next to Owen, the play open on my lap in a feeble effort to look like I'm memorizing my lines. Tyler's a couple of rows behind me, obnoxiously rehearsing for a group of enraptured sophomores, but I'm trying not to dwell on what he said during lunch. Instead, I'm determined to sort out something else bothering me.

Anthony's been avoiding me since the party. Every day, he rushes out of rehearsal before I have the chance to talk to him, and he hasn't replied to a single one of my texts. I have no idea why. I know he's hurt about Eric, but it feels like he's upset with me, too.

"Farewell, lady, lady, lady." Anthony says his final line, and Jody waves him off stage, dismissing him. I sit up straighter and try to catch his eye. It works—for a moment. But then his eyes dart from mine, and he ducks out the side door.

"We'll do Act Two Scene three next," Jody declares, breaking my concentration. It's not one of mine, but even though I'm dying to follow Anthony, I can't leave until Jody dismisses me. Owen gets up and walks to the front of the room, where Tyler's waiting on stage. I realize it's a Friar Lawrence scene, and immediately I feel for Owen. Every week, he's the only person who gets more nervous than I do on stage.

Today, something's different.

Owen's script doesn't shake in his hands, and he's not fidgeting with his sweater the way I know he sometimes does. *Good for him*, I think to myself. I remember dancing with him at the party—when Owen dives into something, he's kind of inspiring.

I pull out my phone. I'll have to redouble my efforts with Anthony. I work on composing yet another hopeless text, but it's next to impossible when I don't know why he's dodging me.

"What a change is here!" I jerk my head up, surprised by the unusual fire in Owen's voice. "Is Rosaline, that thou didst love so dear, so soon forsaken? Young men's love then lies not truly in their hearts, but in their eyes." Owen's face is red, not in embarrassment this time, but in what looks like genuine anger.

He's really busting Romeo's balls, I think before Jody waves her hand and steps onto the stage. Even when Owen drops his script to his side, he's glaring at Romeo. Or maybe it's Tyler.

"Tell me about your interpretation here, Owen," Jody says, pen to her lips. "Why did you read Friar Lawrence that way?"

"Romeo's a jerk, honestly," Owen grimly replies. "Friar Lawrence criticizes him for being thoughtless and disloyal to the girl he was in love with two days ago, and he's right."

Jody considers for a moment. "That's a good reading, but Friar Lawrence is a friar, a man of the cloth. He wouldn't come on quite that strong." Owen grudgingly nods, and Jody tells them to take it from the top.

They begin the scene again, and I watch closer this time, intrigued now. Owen tempers his voice, but I know him well enough to detect the concealed anger in his rigid posture and his clenched jaw. *He's pissed at Tyler . . . for what he said today*, I realize. *For me.* I feel a rush of gratitude. Even if I'm only doing this play for an acting credit, I'm glad it's brought Owen and me together.

Out of the corner of my eye, I notice Will stop in front of the window in the drama room door. He makes no move to come in, and I consider incurring Jody's wrath to cross the stage and drag him in here. Then he laughs, and I realize he's talking to someone. He takes a step to the side, revealing Alyssa right at the moment she's not-so-casually reaching out to touch his arm.

"Wast thou with Rosaline?" I hear Owen say from the stage.

"With Rosaline, my ghostly Father? No. I have forgot that name and that name's woe," Tyler replies.

It's happening again, I realize, watching Alyssa laugh uncomfortably close to Will. He and I didn't even get to define our relationship before it began falling apart. First the groupies at Derek's party, now this. I wish I could ignore it and return to my script, but for some masochistic reason, my eyes linger on them in the hall.

Whatever Will and I are, we won't be much longer.

I walk out of rehearsal an hour later determined to find Will. He never came inside, and even though we'd planned to meet afterward, he's not waiting in the hall like he was yesterday. Figuring he might be working on the set in the woodshop, I round the corner and nearly collide with a red-haired someone.

"Megan," Madeleine says, and places a hand on my shoulder to steady me. "Hey, I'm sorry about lunch today." I hear guilt in her voice.

"Oh, uh—it's fine, really. Have you seen Will?" I move to step past her. Tyler and lunch feel distant now, and it's not like what he said is Madeleine's fault.

But Madeleine doesn't release my shoulder. "No, it's not fine. What he said was *not* okay. I have half a mind to break up with him for it."

That stops me. I'm not Tyler's biggest fan, but I wouldn't want to come between him and Madeleine. I look right into her contrite expression. "You guys can't break up. You're perfect together," I say gently.

Her eyes soften. "It doesn't give him the right to dump on my best friend. I'm going to talk to him."

"Only if you want to. Owen already laid into him during rehearsal. Don't feel like you have to withhold sex from him or something."

I'm expecting her widened eyes and scandalized smile. "Megan!"

"Never mind," I tease, "I know you couldn't hold out for long anyway." She tries to swat me, but I dodge and spin out of her reach to continue down the hall. "I have to find Will," I call over my shoulder.

"Hey, what are you doing the Saturday after next?" I hear behind me.

I turn to face her. "I don't know. Why?"

"I'm organizing a tree-planting day," she begins. Madeleine's not content to restrict her volunteerism to school days. Since sophomore year, she's spent weekends working with something called the Oregon Forester Society, planting trees and holding Earth Day fairs. The sick thing is, I don't even think she does it for college. I think she *enjoys* it. "I wondered if you wanted to come and hang out?" she continues. "I know I've spent a lot of time with Tyler, and I miss you. It'll be time for just us."

"And some freshly planted trees," I shoot back with a grin.

"It'll be fun! Promise."

Madeleine's never invited me to one of her community service projects, probably because she rightly knows digging holes in the forest isn't my thing. But time with my best friend is. "Of course I'll go."

I turn to continue my search for Will, but then I pause. I'll see him tomorrow. Besides, the idea of finding him in the woodshop or pulling him into the art closet suddenly doesn't seem quite so important.

ELEVEN

FRIAR LAWRENCE: *They stumble that run fast.*

II.iii.101

I'M UPSTAIRS IN MY ROOM A WEEK later, thrilled to be working on a script that's not *Romeo and Juliet*, when Dad comes in without knocking.

He sits down on the bed. "What's that you're reading?" He sounds like he's uncomfortable, which would make two of us.

I could give him the long answer. I'd tell him I'm planning the blocking for Act I Scene xi of *Death of a Salesman* for the drama department's Senior Showcase in November. I'm in charge of the whole event this year after three years of directing scenes for it despite not being a senior—I won the esteem of the upperclassmen when I directed the freshmen drama production of *The Crucible*, and I've been invited into the Showcase ever since. This year, I couldn't co-direct the winter production with Jody—because I'm the lead—so I'm especially eager to work on the Showcase.

But I know Dad's not here because he's genuinely interested. I give him the short answer. *"Death of a Salesman."*

"I hope Tyler Dunning's not playing Willy Loman," Dad grumbles sarcastically.

"What, you're not a fan of Tyler's work?"

"I had enough of Tyler's acting when he promised to bring you home by ten on Halloween," he replies with the hint of a smile. I can't suppress one of my own. Sometimes Dad's funny even when I don't want him to be.

"That *was* one of his finer performances."

Maybe he *did* come in here just to talk. I look up from the book, waiting for his reply. But his eyes have shifted to somewhere near the bottom of my coat rack, and the humor of a couple seconds ago dissipates.

"There's something I wanted to talk to you about," he says.

Great. The line that begins every unpleasant conversation with a parent.

"Rose and I have continued to make some inquiries into homes outside New York City," he goes on, "and we've narrowed it down to a few."

"Cool," I reply flatly.

"We have to fly out and look at the houses with a realtor." He sounds unfazed by what I thought was a pretty obvious display of disinterest. "This weekend."

"What?" I hear my voice go up. "*This* weekend? I thought the move wasn't happening until I went to college. Or is there something else you haven't told me?"

"It's not happening until then." Dad puts a hand on my knee, as if *that'll* make everything better. "But we have to visit soon because I don't want Rose to travel too close to her due date."

"Of course," I mutter.

"While we're gone, you and Erin will stay at Aunt Charlotte's."

I sit up in surprise, letting my book fall shut. "Why do *I* have to stay with Charlotte? It's far from school, and I'm seventeen years old, Dad. I'm not going to burn the house down."

"Megan . . ." He rubs a crease in his forehead.

"What?" I snap. "Next year you'll be in New York, and I'll be here on my own anyway. We should just get used to it now."

He glances up at me. He's silent for a moment, and I think I see a shadow of hurt in his eyes. Or maybe he's just tired of arguing with me. It's hard to tell.

When he does speak, I'm glad he's not using his patronizing middle-school-principal voice. "You're calling me every night," he says softly.

"Text. I'll *text* you."

He gets up and walks to the door, and I think he's going to leave without saying anything else. But he stops and turns back, smiling slightly. "Please try to text like a fully functioning adult. If I suspect you've been drinking, Charlotte's coming over."

"Whatever you say," I mumble, in no mood to joke. I pick up my copy of *Death of a Salesman* and wait for him to leave.

Today, I decide when I get to school the next morning, *is the day I force Anthony to talk to me.*

I don't want to think about the conversation with my dad or the upcoming trip, and I'm hoping to distract myself. I send Anthony one more text from the parking lot, which he doesn't answer, and when I go to find him in the library at lunch, he's nowhere to be found, like he knew I'd look for him here. In rehearsal, I'm too busy sucking at Juliet's death scene to keep an eye on him, and he slips out before I stab myself on stage for the hundredth time today.

I have no choice but to drive over to Verona after rehearsal. I park in the gravel lot under the marquee, which today declares, *A pizza by any other name would taste as gr8.*

The jukebox is playing Dire Straits's "Romeo and Juliet." This is too much. But before I can dig out a nickel to change it to something non-Shakespearean, a clamor from the corner booth distracts me. I glance over to see Anthony pouring orange soda for ten eight-year-olds in soccer uniforms, half of whom are standing on the booth.

"Anthony," I say from the jukebox. His eyes find mine, and he blinks. Without a word, he sets down the last drink and darts directly toward the kitchen.

But he's too slow. I intercept him by the soda machine and block his path. "Why're you hiding from me?"

"I'm busy, Megan. I'm on my shift." He steps past me with some impressive footwork.

I follow him into the kitchen. It's a slow-moving hubbub of white-aproned employees placing pizza pans in the ovens and dishes into the dishwasher. "I think it's because of the Eric thing," I tell him over the noise.

He pales, a horrified expression crossing his face, and I know exactly why. Eric's washing dishes at the sink, potentially within earshot. Anthony fixes me with a glare and grabs me by the arm, pulling me to the other end of the kitchen and into the ingredients locker. Only once I'm inside, leaning against a wire shelf stocked with bags of flour, does he let go of my arm.

"I don't want to talk about it, okay? Not with him, not with you," he says urgently. But what catches me is the tremor in his expression. He doesn't look angry—he looks nervous.

"Have you even asked him where you guys stand since the party?" I lower my voice.

"Why bother?" he fires back. "I saw enough."

His shoulders sag. He sounds like he's given up. It's nothing new—Anthony's always burying his feelings at the first sign of something falling apart. But I know he really likes Eric. He's just too insecure to fight for what he wants, which means he needs me to do it for him.

"Stay here," I tell him. Leaving the ingredients locker, I walk directly to the sink.

"Eric," I say over the running water. He turns, plate in hand, but he doesn't exactly look surprised that I'm in the kitchen, where I'm definitely not supposed to be. It's like he watched Anthony and me walk into the kitchen. Like he's aware of Anthony's whereabouts, like he keeps track of him. It's what I do when someone I like is nearby.

"What's the deal with you and that girl from the party?" I ask abruptly.

His eyes widen for a split second, then he resumes scrubbing the plate, and his voice is casual when he replies. "You mean Melissa? She's . . . a friend. I go to Saint Margaret's, and she goes to our sister school. I know her from school dances and stuff. I don't know—we hooked up." He's playing it cool. If I weren't a director, I wouldn't know he's acting.

"Are you guys, like, a thing now?"

For a brief moment, I think I see his eyes flit to somewhere behind me—to the ingredients locker. "It was nothing serious," he says slowly, his eyes returning to mine.

"Do you *want* it to be a thing?" I press him.

Now I know he glances to where Anthony's waiting. But then he shrugs. "She's not really my type, but who knows?" he says coolly. "I wasn't expecting to hook up with her that night. I only knew about the party because I overheard a couple of Stillmont guys who came in here talking about it. I didn't figure people from *my* school would be there."

He fixes me with an indicative glance, and what he's really saying fits into place in my head.

I remember how he danced with Melissa every time the Saint Margaret's guys were nearby, and how he danced with Anthony only when they weren't. He's not out to his school. He did invite Anthony with a purpose, but it was ruined when people he knew showed up.

I nod, hoping my expression tells him I understand. Wordlessly, Eric peels off his gloves and takes a water pitcher out into the restaurant.

I return to Anthony, who's exactly where I left him, hanging out with the flour and canned tomatoes. "It's safe to come out now," I tell him. Expressionless, he walks out into the kitchen and picks up an order of breadsticks off the counter. "But you should know," I continue, "Eric's not dating Melissa, he said she's not his type, *and* he looked at you twice. I think he got cold feet at the party because he's in the closet. If I were you, I'd ask him out on a more private date."

But Anthony doesn't meet my eyes. "Thanks, Megan. I have work."

He goes into the dining room, and I'm left in the kitchen, confused and a little hurt. I just served up the guy Anthony likes for him with a side of breadsticks. Instead of going for it, Anthony chose to walk away. Brusquely, I shove open the door in the back of the kitchen and kick the gravel as I walk to my car.

I'm getting out my keys when I hear Anthony call my name. He's still wearing his frilly hat, which only makes me laugh a little inside because whatever fear was in his eyes earlier has disappeared. Now he's angry.

"This is why I was avoiding you." He strides toward me but halts suddenly in the middle of the parking lot, like he doesn't want to come too close. "I knew you'd do something like this. You can*not* keep interfering with my relationships. I know *you* come into any hint of a romantic situation guns blazing, but I'm not like you. I can't just rush into things."

I'm in no mood to be lectured. "Why not? You like him. I think he likes you, but you'll never know until you try."

"He's had every opportunity to talk to me," Anthony

replies darkly, "to explain what you're only guessing. If he wants this, he would've come to me."

"It doesn't work that way," I almost yell. "It'd be nice if it did, but getting the boyfriend you want is hard work. You can't expect anything to happen if you don't make a move. If you want him, do something about it." I know I struck a nerve because his expression clouds over. "Don't be afraid of this," I go on, gentler. "The only way this definitely doesn't work is if you do nothing."

He stays silent. I've done my best. "I have to go home," I say, pulling out my keys.

I get in the car and twist the key in the ignition. With the windows rolled up, I barely hear the muffled, "Did he really look at me twice?"

I roll down my window. "Forlornly." I nod.

"I guess . . ." He puts his hands in his pockets. "I could invite him over for carne asada."

My lips begin to form a smile. *"What?"*

Anthony returns the hint of a grin and nods in the direction of Verona.

"Break a leg," I tell him.

When I pull onto the highway, for once I'm grateful for Dad and Rose's trip to New York, because I know what I'm going to do tomorrow night. I'm taking my own advice.

TWELVE

ROMEO: *Thou canst not teach me to forget.*

I.i.246

I WORKED HARD ON THIS OUTFIT.

I hunted for nearly an hour in my closet for a dress, but nothing felt quite right. It was only when I got the brilliant idea to take apart the bridesmaid dress from Dad and Rose's wedding that I found the perfect thing—a pale pink shift with lacy detailing in the neckline. It hits me mid-thigh, and I've paired it with studded black ankle boots and feather earrings to keep from looking too girly.

Because tonight, I have a plan. Will's coming over, and we're going to have sex for the first time. I'm not going to wait around for him to define our relationship. I want to enjoy every part of whatever this is with him while I can, and though I haven't fallen for him yet—though our relationship's much younger than Tyler's and mine was—I'm not letting that get in my way. Why would I? I'm practically an adult. I'm a non-virgin, a sex-having person. This relationship's quickly expiring under a ticking clock named Alyssa, and I want to feel that closeness with Will. So what if I have to rush a few steps?

By eight, I'm downstairs in my bronze eye shadow doing what every girl dreams of on a Friday night—reading *Romeo and Juliet* on the couch. Dad and Rose went to the airport this morning, Erin's at my aunt's, and I have the house to myself.

I roll my eyes at Juliet's latest oversentimental proclamation. *This bud of love, by summer's ripening breath, may prove a beauteous flower when next we meet.* The play's a terrible distraction while I wait.

The doorbell rescues me from Juliet's pining. I leap off the couch, then take a second to rearrange my hair. When I reach the door, I know I look amazing. I pull it open, and Will stands before me.

Never mind. He just redefined amazing.

He's wearing a faded denim jacket over a plain white V-neck, and he's cuffed his tight black pants above his Timberland boots. He rests his hands lightly in his pockets, and it takes everything in me not to attack him right there on the doorstep.

"Hey," he says, and my pulse pounds. "I thought you might need a break from *Romeo and Juliet*"—he holds up a copy of *Shakespeare in Love*—"with some Romeo and Juliet."

I laugh and shut the door behind him. "Two sexy Williams in one night? I think I'm blushing."

He raises an incredulous eyebrow. "I've *never* seen you blush."

"Then you're not trying hard enough," I say over my shoulder, walking farther into the living room. I reach the stairs and look back to find he's sitting on the couch. Instead of following me. *Owen was right, he is clueless.* I remind myself he's probably never done this before. "Oh," I say nonchalantly, "I thought we'd watch on my laptop upstairs."

"Why?" Will looks puzzled. "We've got the bigger screen down here."

Oh my god. "I thought we'd watch on my bed," I clarify with a meaningful look.

It takes him a second, but then the light goes on in his eyes and he jumps off the couch. "Oh. Yeah. Of course. Good thinking. *Great* thinking."

Finally! Smiling to myself, I lead him upstairs. He's quiet the whole way. As I'm putting the movie into my laptop, I notice he's standing aimlessly in the middle of the room. Hands back in his pockets, he meanders over to my bookcase—on the opposite side of the room from my bed.

"That's from *The Crucible*," I say, nodding to the cast photo on the shelf he's studying. "Freshman spring. It's the first show I ever assistant-directed."

"I remember," he says, his back still to me. "I was in the crew."

"No way." I put the laptop down, surprised I don't remember him and never noticed him in the photo. I walk over to the shelf beside him. Searching the photo, the first thing I notice is Tyler in the middle of the group, putting on his not-yet-perfected Tyler Dunning grin. There's Anthony, a couple of rows behind him, his hair grown into something resembling an Afro and his arm around me. We were dating at the time. I lean in and inspect the back rows, and—

"*No,*" I gasp. Because there's Will—or Billy, actually—rail-thin and with the awkwardly stringy hair of freshman boys everywhere.

"Don't say a word," Will says through his teeth.

I round on him teasingly. "But your *hair.*" It's a sharp contrast from the perfect, gelled sweep of blond hair he's presently running his hand through.

He steps back from the bookcase, a flush of red rising up his neck. "I know, I know," he mutters. "It's the reason I've never had a girlfriend."

I wait for the "until now," but it doesn't come. Will continues to look at the other shelves in my room, and I'm left once again wondering what he considers me. I told myself it didn't matter if I'm his girlfriend or just his hookup buddy, but I kind of want to know. Before I get the chance to ask, he turns back to me, the confident glint back in his eyes.

"Not everyone can be like you," he says, nodding to the photo. "Beautiful then, too."

His words push the question from my mind. We're obviously on the same page, because he wraps an arm around my waist and pulls me to his lips. The kiss somehow feels different, charged with both of our expectations. For the first time, it's the first step to something else.

Breaking off, I lead him to the bed and slide off his jacket, my lips still stinging. I lightly push him onto the mattress and close my laptop on my desk. "I don't think we'll need the pretense," I say, kicking off my boots and climbing on top of him.

"We wouldn't have watched much anyway," he breathes before I grab him and kiss him again.

His hands slide down to my waist, and I feel his fingers pressing into the small of my back. I run my hands down his chest when he moves to kiss my neck, his hand inching up the hem of my dress. Then I'm pulling off his shirt. Then I'm lifting my arms over my head, and my dress hits the floor. Then his fingers glide up my back.

Then my phone buzzes.

"Shit." I jump off the bed. The phone vibrates a couple more times, and I know Dad's upset. The rule was me texting him, not him texting me. "Give me a second," I tell Will. "I forgot to do something."

Dad's sent exactly the same text three times—**Where are you, Megan?**—and then an accusatory line of question marks.

im home, I shoot back.

I set down the phone and start to climb back into Will's lap. Just as we're picking up where we left off, my phone rattles from my desk once more. I sigh angrily and scramble off Will again. "Sorry . . ."

It takes me a second to make sense of what my dad's sent. The first message reads, **What do you think?** and below it are three images too small to discern on my phone's lock screen. I slide it open, and my heart plummets.

Three photos, each a different angle of a badly lit sidewalk view of a house. *Chesapeake Lane*, reads the sign on the street corner.

What do I think? Like it matters what the house looks like.

Whatever house they choose, it'll be a perfectly nice place for Erin and the baby to grow up, and for me to stop by on holidays to sleep uncomfortably in an impersonal spare bedroom.

looks fine, I send back.

I toss my phone not gently onto my desk and turn back to Will, eager to put Chesapeake Lane out of my mind. I crash into him again, and he's pulling me closer, and I'm reaching for my bra. But I can't bring myself to do what I wanted to. He's sitting underneath me, and he's gorgeous, but I feel hollow.

He's noticed my hesitation and caught the look on my face. "What is it?" he asks.

"It's nothing," I say, because there's no reason to tell him more.

I clamber off him and pick up my dress off the floor. I'm pulling it over my head when I hear him say, "Wait, what?"

"I'm sorry," I say in a flat, unconvincing voice. "I'm just not in the mood right now."

"Okay . . ." He sounds skeptical, even indignant. I watch him get dressed. "Guess we'll do this another time."

If he even wants another time, a familiar voice says in the back of my head. With the way Alyssa's been acting around him, and how I just totally screwed tonight up, I'd understand if he didn't want to give me a second chance.

He walks out of my room, and I don't bother seeing him to the front door. I pause uncertainly in the middle of my room, wishing I could have ignored my dad and just focused on Will.

But even now, I find myself staring at the photo Will and I were looking at minutes earlier. I survey the plays on my bookshelves, the coat rack in the corner, the playbills pinned to my bulletin board. In a matter of months, everything will be packed into cardboard boxes and shipped to New York, and the room I grew up in will be empty.

I collapse onto my bed, where a hard corner digs into my back. I reach under me and pull out the DVD case of *Shakespeare in Love*.

My plans for the night come back in an uncomfortable rush. I feel unsteady. And I know it's not only because of the impending New York thing. I run a hand through my hair impulsively, trying to iron the tremble from my fingertips. What was I doing with Will? What felt promising and exhilarating and *right* an hour ago feels upside down now.

I thought I could do this. I thought our relationship status wouldn't make a difference. I thought I could have sex with Will right now and capture the connection, the closeness that I'm desperate for—a little too desperate, I guess. Part of me wonders if I didn't know deep down it wouldn't work.

Part of me wonders if the texts from Dad weren't the only reason I stopped things.

I'm glad Will and I didn't go further, I decide. But everything's in limbo now. My relationship's not a relationship. My home won't be for much longer. Everything's lurching out of reach, and I'm in territory I don't recognize.

I force myself upright. I can't look at Will's DVD right now. I can't be reminded of how tonight could have gone, and how fractured we left things. I shove *Shakespeare in Love* into a drawer and out of my mind.

Owen's on my doorstep the next morning.

When I woke up after three hours of fitful sleep, I threw on the first things I found in my room. Now I've parked myself on the couch in the living room once more, and I'm reading the same scene of *Romeo and Juliet* I was last night. It still sounds ridiculous, and while I'm finally beginning to memorize the lines, it's not helping me to picture myself saying them on stage at Ashland.

I open the door to find Owen wearing a dark blue button-down with his hair neatly combed, and for a moment I regret my old jeans and hole-ridden The Clash T-shirt.

He holds up a crisp white paper bag, beaming. "I brought coffee and bagels."

"Oh. Wow, thanks," I say, stepping aside to let him in. We'd planned a couple days ago that he'd come over this morning for our second play/Will-information session. What we hadn't planned on was him bringing me breakfast.

He turns to give me a knowing smile. "I figure you probably had a late night."

He means Will. "Something like that," I say.

I grab a couple of plates from the kitchen and set them out in the living room. But when I look up at Owen, I see his eyes flit into the kitchen, and a strange combination of expressions crosses his face. "Does a baby live here?" he asks abruptly.

I follow his gaze to Erin's high chair, which, I realize, Will probably didn't even notice. "Oh, yeah. But she's at my aunt's."

Owen looks pale. "Whose . . . baby is it?" he ventures gently.

"Oh my *god*," I explode. "You do *not* think I had Tyler Dunning's love-baby." It's too ridiculous for me to be offended, honestly.

He looks briefly relieved, until he winces in obvious mortification. "I'm— I didn't—" he stutters.

I have to laugh. "Erin's my half sister," I explain. "My dad and my stepmom's kid."

He nods understandingly. "I have a ten-year-old brother. You can hardly go five feet in my house without stepping on a LEGO." He winces again.

"I was in your house." I take a sip of the still-too-hot coffee. "There wasn't a LEGO in sight."

"Yeah, because I cleaned for two hours before you got there."

He says it casually, like it's something he'd do for anyone. And who knows? He might. Still, it's sweet. I almost tell him that, and then I remember it didn't exactly go over well last time I called him sweet. "Hey, I'd trade LEGO for applesauce in my hair any day," I say instead.

His eyes widen. "It *was* applesauce!"

I nod grimly.

Owen sets the bagels down on the coffee table in the living room. I reach in and grab a cinnamon raisin. He takes the other and drops into the armchair next to the couch. "You probably don't need my help, what with last night," he preempts me, crossing a foot onto his knee. He's dashed lines of familiar blue ink on the white rubber edges of his Converse. "Will told me when you invited him over yesterday."

I don't reply right away, spreading cream cheese on my bagel. "He didn't text you afterward, I guess."

Owen's eyebrows go up. "Guys don't really do that, Megan."

"Do what? Text?"

"No . . ." he says slowly, looking a little amused. "Text about . . . certain topics."

"My mistake." I return a faint smile. "Well, I kind of hoped he'd texted you. Things ended . . . weird."

Owen frowns, concern creasing his forehead. "Weird like he didn't want to?"

"Owen. Please."

He goes red. "I— Of course, he wanted to," he stutters.

Wait, what? Was that Owen calling me hot? Or hook-up-with-able, or whatever? Part of me wants to press him on the subject further, but I'm not sure if Owen's the type to handle my flirtatiousness. He might think I'm genuinely coming onto him. "He did want to," I say, "and we did, or started to. Then when we . . . didn't, he seemed kind of pissed, and I don't know where we stand now."

Owen's blush hasn't entirely faded, but his voice is even when he tells me, "Will's not pissed. He's a better guy than that. What happened?" He clears his throat, and the blush comes raging back. "I mean, why didn't you guys do it?"

"I got a text from my dad." The words come out before I've even thought about how I'm bringing up my family. But once they're out there, I realize how much I do want to talk about it with someone. Before I know it, I'm telling him more. About the hookup, about the photos from my dad. About New York.

"You're moving?" Owen sounds startled.

"*They* are," I quickly reply, "when I graduate. Rose, my stepmom, is pregnant again and wants to raise her kids in New York."

He nods, considering for a long second. For someone who's only really known me a few weeks, he looks unexpectedly relieved to hear I'm not going anywhere. "I can see why that would kill the mood," he finally says.

I let out a rueful laugh. "Yeah."

"Did you tell Will all of that?" Owen watches me as he takes a hesitant sip of his coffee.

"I wasn't sure if I should. I mean, that's the other thing. He said something about never having a girlfriend, and it sounded like he didn't think of me that way. I didn't want to, like, unload my personal shit on him if he doesn't see us as having that kind of relationship."

"I have to say," Owen begins, "if you just shut down a hookup without an explanation, I'd understand if Will was a little confused. Remember, he's pretty inexperienced. I don't know how many conversations with girls he's even had. It might not occur to him to ask what's wrong."

He has a point. Will's so gorgeous, it's easy to forget that everything's new to him. "I guess," I tell Owen. If Will's that inexperienced, he might not even know how to bring up the

135

question of a relationship with me. "What do *you* think? Do you think he considers me his girlfriend? Has he said anything?"

He takes another sip of coffee, clearly stalling. "I don't . . . know, Megan," he says delicately, or uncomfortably.

"Well, could you please ask?"

He gives me an uncomprehending look. "Yeah, in the midst of our next slumber party, after the pillow fight. When we're exchanging our deepest, most tender secrets over a flashlight, I'll be sure to bring you up."

"That'd be great, Owen. Thanks," I say dryly.

"I was just—"

"*I know.*" I roll my eyes. "Just, the next time you talk to him about Cosima, bring the conversation around to Will and me."

"Evidently I'm not saying this right," Owen says with forced patience. "The conversations you're imagining, they don't happen. Especially between . . . me and Will. We're not that close. No friend-glue, remember?"

"*Please, Owen,*" I implore, batting my eyelashes and knowing damn well it'll work.

He sighs, dropping his head back over the chair. When he returns his eyes to me, I can tell he's hiding a smile. "Fine. For you."

"That wasn't so hard, was it?" I stand to collect our dishes. "Now, what do you want to know for your play?" I call over my shoulder as I carry the plates into the kitchen. *Wow*, I catch myself realizing, *I'm glad Owen didn't look past the high chair.* The kitchen is a mess, and not just an Erin mess. There's the box

136

of microwave macaroni I left out from yesterday's dinner, a pile of Rose's paralegal paperwork on the counter, and a piece of scratch paper from the Trig assignment I didn't finish next to the toaster. Mental note—clean the house before the next time Owen comes over.

He's taken his notebook out by the time I walk back into the living room. "I'm working on Rosaline's relationships with characters other than Romeo," he says while reviewing his notes. "Would she have known Mercutio or Tybalt or Romeo's family?" He looks up from his notebook, fixing his eyes on me. "I was even toying with the idea she might've known Juliet."

I know where he's going with this. "You want to talk about me and Madeleine."

"Why are you friends with her?" he blurts.

I guess I'm not the only one who gets right to the point. Still, the transparent way he said it makes me laugh. "What's not to like?"

"Stealing your boyfriend."

"It's more complicated than that," I say. "We've been friends forever. She moved to Stillmont a month before the end of freshman year, right around when my dad remarried. Even though she hardly knew me, she immediately invited me to stay over while my dad was on his honeymoon. She spent twenty hours with me in the hospital while Erin was being born, she baked brownies for me every day I missed my mom, she's come to every one of my shows, she's been there for me after every breakup—"

"Except for one," Owen interrupts.

"It's not like she decided to steal my boyfriend." I shrug.

He looks skeptical. "Well . . ."

"She fell in love with a guy who I *happened* to be dating, and he fell in love with her. I didn't exactly imagine kids and a white picket fence with Tyler Dunning, and you can't help who you fall in love with."

"I suppose not," he says softly, his eyes averted almost pointedly, as if he wants them anywhere but on me.

I go on, feeling like it's important I defend Madeleine. "When she realized she had feelings for Tyler, she told me. They both did. It's not like I didn't see it coming. Tyler has his faults, but he treated me decently, better than Romeo did Rosaline."

Owen determinedly taps his pen on his knee. "There's really no bad blood between you and Madeleine? The whole best-friend thing isn't some passive-aggressive act?"

"Wow. Devious, Owen." I give him a half smile. "No, everyone figures that. But I'm honestly happy for my best friend. Love is inconvenient sometimes. I mean, *you* know. It's probably not ideal to have a girlfriend in Italy."

Owen's stopped writing. He's staring down at the notebook, and he's got that contemplative look I'm realizing I quite like. "Yeah," he says. "It's inconvenient."

"How often do you guys even talk? What with her strict bedtime—"

"She doesn't have a strict bedtime," Owen cuts in. "It's just the nine-hour time difference."

"Whatever. It doesn't look like cross-continent FaceTime is the easiest thing in the world, either."

"We talk every weekend," Owen says grandly, like this is something to be proud of.

I make sure to look aghast. "Every *weekend*? What about the other *five* days of the week? Already we're only talking about phone sex here, I don't know how you—"

"Oh my god, Megan." He hangs his head in his hands.

"What?" I say, laughing. "I tell you everything about Will and me!" My face hurts from grinning. Which . . . is unexpected, after last night.

"Not because I ask about it!" Owen fires back, but he's definitely on the verge of laughing himself.

"Wait, *do* you guys have phone sex?" I drop my voice seriously.

"You have no idea." He quirks an eyebrow, and he's almost got me convinced, until he doubles over laughing.

"You actually *can* act!" I say, enjoying the way his hair has gotten ruffled.

He catches his breath. "What were we doing here again?" he asks with a rhetorical air, pen to his lips. "Oh yeah, helping me on my play."

"Fine . . ." I hold my hands up in surrender. "Ask away, Shakespeare."

By Sunday night, I've surprised myself in two ways. I've memorized Juliet's long scene with the Nurse, even the monologue and my cues from Romeo, and honestly . . . I'm proud. It's the first time working on *Romeo and Juliet* that I

139

feel like I've accomplished something. Even if I can't pull off a convincing Juliet performance, at least I won't lose my shit and forget my lines in front of a huge audience.

I'm in the kitchen, reading the balcony scene over a dinner of macaroni—which I remembered to return to the cupboard this time—when I hear my phone vibrate on the table.

I glance down at the screen. Anthony's texted, **NEXT FRIDAY NIGHT. YOU'RE COMING OVER.**

I take a bite and type with one hand, anthony, if i didnt kno sum things id think u were propositioning me

CARNE ASADA. ERIC, he replies. Immediately, I drop my fork and snatch my phone off the table.

omg omg omg omg, I send back.

Either Anthony's in a hurry or he expected my enthusiasm, because he replies simply, **BRING A CASUAL DATE. WANT EVERYTHING TO BE CHILL.**

roger, I confirm.

Anthony's typing bubble reappears, and a second later I receive, **UM WHO'S ROGER??**

meant yes!! I send, then follow up with, ugh id never date a "roger," def not a sexy name

BEG TO DIFFER, Anthony replies.

Smiling, I send him, what happened w eric??? call me

SORRY. SHIFT STARTING.

I open the NEW MESSAGE window, but before I type Will's name, I hesitate. Inviting him to be my "chill date" would

140

kind of implicitly dismiss the questions I still have concerning yesterday. If only Owen could've shed some light on things between my possibly-boyfriend-but-who-knows and me.

I just have to talk to Will in person, I decide. Tomorrow I'll find him between classes.

I poke my fork into my macaroni container only to discover it's empty, so I walk to the other side of the kitchen and drop it in the trash. The echo of plastic on plastic is surprisingly loud.

It's stupid, but it makes me feel lonely. The house feels stiflingly empty. I thought I'd be relieved to have peace and quiet with Erin out of the house—I had epic plans for today of napping on the couch and blasting music in my room—but I'm surprised to find the solitude is starting to bother me. I even slept with my industrial-strength earplugs in because I felt weird without them.

I study *Romeo and Juliet* for two hours before I hear keys in the front door and my heart does an unfamiliar leap. Not bothering to play the cool, independent teenager, I jump up to meet my family at the door. The first face I find is Erin's. She's held over my dad's shoulder, eye-level with me, and she breaks into a tiny-toothed smile when she sees me.

"Menan!" she squeals.

Rose, walking in behind my dad with a hand on her stomach, notices Erin's delight. "Looks like somebody missed her sister."

Somebodies, I think. I lift Erin off Dad's shoulder, and he immediately turns back to get the luggage out of the car. Erin

reaches for one of my earrings, and I coo to her uncomprehending grin, "Let's try to go twenty-four hours without getting your food in my hair, okay?"

"How was your weekend?" Rose asks from the doorway.

"Good. Quiet," I say. But she's looking at me like she wants
to hear more, and I feel unexpectedly grateful after a day of
nothing but texting by way of social interaction. "It's nice to
have everyone home," I add.

Dad walks back through the door, wheeling two suitcases
behind him. He briefly smiles at the sight of me with Erin,
but when his eyes land on Rose, a look of horror crosses his
face. "You weren't supposed to carry anything!"

"Oh, come on," she says, smiling and shrugging the small
diaper bag off her shoulder. "It's nothing."

But Dad's halfway to her by the time she says it. He
quickly seizes the diaper bag and kisses her on the temple.

"Henry," she chastises like she's exasperated, but the blush
coloring her cheeks gives her away. She meets my eyes when
Dad's walked out of the room. "He's ridiculous sometimes,"
she says, fighting a smile and losing.

"Just sometimes?" I ask, half-sarcastic, and Rose chuckles.

"Did you eat? Or can I make you something?" Rose quickly
returns to mom mode.

I set Erin down in her playpen. "I'm good. But thanks," I
reply, wishing now I hadn't already had dinner.

I head up the stairs to my room while Dad unpacks and
Rose watches Erin. I plug my headphones back into my
computer—Erin will be going to bed soon, and my dad's
strict about hearing music from my room after nine—but

it doesn't bother me. For a moment, I'm just happy to have everyone back home.

Until I remember why they left in the first place. I've always assumed I'd go to college near home, near my family. I'd pictured coming home on weekends, being there for Erin's milestones and the new baby growing up. If they're in New York and I'm at SOTI, none of that will happen. I'll visit them for Christmas and summer, and that's it. It's not just the house I'm going to lose when they move, not just my childhood bedroom. It's the thought of this family, however new it is, being nearby.

THIRTEEN

ROMEO: *Why then, O brawling love, O loving hate,*

O anything of nothing first create!

I.i.181–2

I DON'T GET THE CHANCE TO TALK to Will until Wednesday. He hasn't met me between classes this week, which isn't a good omen for the conversation I'm hoping to have. I couldn't at lunch due to a forgotten Gov exam I had to study for, and when I walk into the drama room, I notice the stage crew is nowhere to be found.

Rehearsal is demoralizing. Whatever confidence I had from memorizing the monologue flies out the window when Jody criticizes my "level of enthusiasm" in Act II, Scene vi. Apparently, I didn't sound convincing in my portrayal of a thirteen-year-old eager to marry the boy she met a week ago. So it's not in the best of spirits that I walk down to the parking lot after school to find Will.

I round the corner and, for a moment, every one of my worries vanishes. Because there's Will, shirtless, nailing together the pieces of a wooden staircase. Now I'm *certain* he's hit the gym over the summer. My mouth goes dry, which is a good thing, because what jumps into my mind is a joke about how big of a tool he's working with.

But when I walk over to him, I say only, "Hey."

"Megan, hey." He straightens up and grabs his shirt from the stairs, wiping the sweat from his forehead. "How was rehearsal?" he asks like he's searching for something to say.

"It was fine." I sound no less stiff. "I just, uh— I wanted to apologize for what happened Friday. I hope you know it wasn't you."

He looks surprised. "Oh, it's . . . all right," he finally says.

"Is it? Because we haven't talked or texted since then."

"It's fine, really. I've just been busy." He nods to the sets behind him. "Besides, it kind of seems like you have other stuff on your mind." I can't tell if his tone is concerned or frustrated.

"I did, but . . ." I take a breath, remembering Owen's advice. "I figured I should probably tell you what was going on with me."

"You don't have to do that," he says quickly.

"Oh." Well, now I'm really confused. Is he trying to be considerate, or does he not care? "Yeah, it's whatever," I say, trying to sound like it is indeed *whatever*.

He nods, then smiles. "So do you want to see the balcony set I'm—" he starts, but he's interrupted by the ding of a text from his pocket. Before I can reply, he pulls his phone out and glances at the screen. "Shit. I told Alyssa we would figure out a time when I could help her memorize lines."

"Alyssa?" It's on the tip of my tongue to point out that Alyssa hasn't missed a chance to remind everyone how well she knows *Romeo and Juliet*. She doesn't need help.

Will's phone starts to ring. "Yeah. And now she's calling me. I'm sorry, Megan." He sounds genuinely apologetic.

"It's cool. We'll just talk later," I say, but he's already picking up the phone.

With nothing else to do, I walk toward my car. The parking lot is carpeted in pine needles. I take out my phone, weighing my options. I need a date for Anthony's carne asada, but this conversation's only made me more reluctant to invite Will.

I get in the car and open a message to Owen. **U busy fri nite? Need platonic date 4 carne asada**

I smile when Owen's reply comes in before I've even turned on the car. **I love carne asada. I'm in.**

Owen's waiting under the giant fir tree that towers over his house when I pull up on Friday. Instantly, I notice what he's wearing—a dark blue button-down, slacks, and leather shoes with just the right amount of scuff.

"Whoa." I nod to his outfit. "It's not a real date."

"Of course it's not, Megan." He furrows his brow quizzically and gets in the car. "Wait, why do you say . . . ?" He smiles wryly at me. "Are you saying I look nice?"

"Nicer than I'd want *my* boyfriend to on a not-date with another girl." I turn around in Owen's driveway.

"Sounds like you're implying something, but I don't really know why when I could say the same thing about you." He gestures to my close-fitting, black velvet dress.

"Touché." Part of me is glad he noticed, the part that chose

146

this dress wondering what he'd say. Not that I'm the kind of girl who'd go for a guy with a girlfriend—not that Owen's the kind of guy I'd go for in the first place—but I won't say I don't enjoy a little harmless flirting with him. "Seriously though, thanks for coming with me tonight," I say as we're passing Verona on our way to the other side of town.

"No problem. But, why exactly did you invite me? Why does carne asada require a platonic date?" He's idly tapping on the armrest, and I know it's because he doesn't have his pen in his hand.

I realize he signed on for tonight without hesitation, without me even explaining the plan. "Remember Eric, the guy from the party? Anthony wants to have him over for carne asada. It's Anthony's best move. It always works."

Owen raises his eyebrow. "What exactly do you mean by 'works'?"

"Let's just say, when he used it on me, we only got fifteen minutes into *West Side Story* before I decided there were things I'd rather do. Anthony, now that I'm thinking about it, probably just wanted to watch the movie," I say, considering.

Owen laughs. "Sounds like Anthony should just have Eric over alone then."

"Anthony's afraid Eric won't be into it. He wants me there in case Eric comes over not wanting tonight to be romantic, and I *guess* there's the possibility Eric's not gay. But if he is, and if things do go well, Anthony doesn't want to have unintentionally created a group-hang vibe. That's why he wants me to have a platonic date. It could be a casual hang, but it could also be a double date."

"Wow, complicated." Owen looks impressed, then thinks for a minute. "What if it *does* turn into a double date? What are we supposed to do?"

"Sex on the table sound good to you?" I promptly reply, unable to restrain myself.

We've pulled into Anthony's driveway—and thank god, because I burst out laughing when I see Owen's face. His eyes are blown wide, like he's very earnestly trying to figure out if I'm joking. "Jesus, Owen. I was kidding. We'll FaceTime Cosima or something. It'll be fine."

Eric's not here yet. Ours is the only car in front of Anthony's house. Anthony told me his parents are at an engagement party for one of his twenty-two cousins. I lead Owen up to the front door, positive he's blushing a shade previously unknown to man. He's silent, and, feeling guilty, I figure I must have gone too far with that sex-on-the-table comment. I should probably ease up on him.

I knock on the door, hearing Anthony's go-to cooking music, the Black Eyed Peas, from inside. While we're waiting, Owen leans on the wall in front of me. "Cosima went to bed hours ago. We'll have to think of something *better* to do," he says slowly.

There's a suggestive look in his eyes, and I feel my jaw drop open. I know I'm joking when I flirt, but Owen?

He breaks into a grin. "Jesus, Megan. I was kidding." His voice is playful, and he shakes his head. "Your face, I swear. I never thought I'd see Megan Harper stunned into silence."

Anthony opens the door, and Owen walks in past him, leaving me impressed and even a little disappointed. He obviously was thinking of that comeback the whole walk up the driveway, and I find myself half wishing it wasn't just a comeback. Which then has me thoroughly wondering why I'd wish that, even fractionally. This is Owen.

We're overtaken by the smell of chili and lime inside. Anthony rushes back to the grill, and I follow him and Owen in, passing Anthony's mom's intimidating crucifix in the hallway. Mrs. Jenson is Mexican and was raised Catholic, though on Sundays she goes to the gospel services at Anthony's dad's Baptist church.

"This is a bad idea," Anthony mutters behind the grill. "He doesn't like me—"

"Shut up. You look amazing," I reassure him. He does, too. "The vest, the rolled-up sleeves, the hair . . . it's really working for you." He meets my eyes and lets out a breath, looking like he's regained some of his confidence.

Then the doorbell rings. Anthony's panic returns, and he thrusts the grilling tongs he's holding into Owen's hands. While Owen, surprised, steps behind the grill, Anthony takes a hesitant couple of paces toward the door.

I stop him and reach for his apron. "Here." I untie it, pull it over his head, and push his curls back into place. He gives me a grateful look, and I lightly shove him in the direction of the door.

When I join Owen by the grill, he's deftly turning over the strips of beef. I guess he notices me studying him, because he shrugs. "I cook sometimes," he says simply.

I hear the front door open and glance over at Anthony. Eric walks in, and it's clear he's come from some practice or game. He's wearing a green and white jersey with ROGERS written on the back. I grin. *Of course Anthony thinks Roger is a sexy name.* He and Eric exchange quick heys before Eric tilts his head in the direction of the kitchen. "Smells awesome. I'm pumped for some carne asada."

I watch Anthony to gauge his reaction. "Yeah, man. It'll be . . . tight," he says, wincing. I wince with him. He's trying, but the nerdy thespian in him can't pull off bro-talk.

They head onto the deck outside the kitchen, and the four of us congregate awkwardly around the grill. "Hey, Eric," I say, mostly to break the silence. "You remember Owen from the party, right?"

Anthony's obviously just recalled that Owen's presently cooking dinner and darts over to take back the tongs.

"Yeah," Eric says. "What's up?"

"Nothing much," Owen starts. "Good to see you again," he adds like he's trying to keep the conversation going. Eric nods, and the silence returns. I try to think of everything I know about Eric, searching for possible conversation topics. *Busboy, possibly gay, not into Melissa from the party* . . . and that's it. Not exactly the greatest pre-dinner topics.

Eric fortunately saves us. He glances toward the table, then calls to Anthony, "Could I help with anything?"

"Drinks," Anthony gets out. "There's soda in the garage you could go grab." He sounds as relieved as I feel to have something to say.

I make a split-second decision. "I'll show you where," I say, leading Eric into the living room and toward the garage.

We find a couple two-liter bottles of root beer on the wire

shelves next to a bicycle hanging on hooks from the ceiling. While Eric's hefting the bottles down, I nervously wait by the door, weighing my words. I have no idea how to broach this topic.

"You know, whatever might happen tonight, Owen and I won't say a word to anyone," I blurt, and immediately I wince, regretting how presumptuous and insensitive that came out. What if I've crossed into territory he didn't want to tread? I wonder for a horrible moment if I'm completely wrong about him and I've misinterpreted his comments, his interactions with Anthony.

Eric falters, hand on one bottle, then gradually places it on the floor. "I appreciate that, Megan," he says finally. "There are things about me I wouldn't want my all-boys, Catholic school to know."

I nod, relieved. "Which, by the way," I venture with half a smile, leaning an elbow on the shelves, "an all-boys school? That's got to be either a dream come true for you, or a complete nightmare."

Eric laughs, his posture relaxing a little. "It's a nightmare, trust me. I've never really . . ." his voice grows quieter, heavier. "I've never had the chance to do this before."

I stand up straighter. The comment catches me, and it takes me a moment to figure out why. I can't imagine going to Eric's school, balancing everything he has to every day, and I know I'd be eager to experience this side of myself if I were in his position. But Anthony's not just some boy-shaped experience to be had. I won't let him be used or get hurt. "If you're only interested in Anthony because you've never had a boyfriend," I begin, "and he's an easy secret to keep from your friends—"

Eric cuts me off. "It's not that," he says decisively. "It's about him."

I permit him a smile. "Well, then I have to give you the obligatory best-friend speech," I go on. "Anthony's serious when it comes to relationships, and he's been hurt before. He really likes you." Eric's expression softens. "Don't screw this up," I finish.

I pick up the root beer and walk out without waiting for him to reply.

"Dinner's about ready," Anthony calls when I'm back in the kitchen. "Everyone should sit, and I'll bring it out."

We head to the round dinner table where I've helped Anthony memorize countless monologues and cues over the years. Anthony follows with the sizzling platter of carne asada.

Nobody's saying a word. Owen, next to me, is giving an inordinate amount of attention to pouring his root beer. Anthony appears to be dutifully avoiding Eric's eyes, while Eric looks at me imploringly.

I don't understand what's going on here. I've given Anthony plenty of encouragement to go for Eric, and I just straight-up told Eric how Anthony feels. What else could they *possibly* be waiting for?

I glance at Eric and notice he's wearing a lacrosse jersey, like the guys at Derek's party. Trying to jumpstart the conversation, I ask, "What, uh, lacrosse position do you play?"

"I'm a midfielder," he answers unhelpfully.

I try to catch Anthony's eye to signal that this is where he should jump into the conversation. But he's only determinedly stuffing strips of steak into a tortilla. Unbelievable. I look back at Eric, struggling to recollect even the first thing I know about lacrosse. I'm pretty sure there's a ball but . . .

"This is crazy good, man," Eric says to Anthony through his first mouthful.

Anthony looks up—*thank god*—and gives Eric a stilted smile. I know he's thrown by the level of jock-bro that Eric's exuding. Otherwise he would never go catatonic like this under pressure.

"My brother plays lacrosse—" Owen says suddenly, and I could kiss him.

Wait, did I just think that? I blink. Obviously I didn't mean literally.

"—but he's ten, so when I say 'plays lacrosse' I really mean he hits me with his stick." Eric cracks up, and before I get the chance to shoot Owen a grateful look, he and Eric are having a full-on conversation about the great sport of lacrosse. While they're occupied, I nudge Anthony's foot under the table with a get-your-head-in-the-game glance.

"Hey," Eric says suddenly, interrupting his conversation with Owen, "looks like we're out of salsa."

Anthony blinks, his eyes flitting to the jar of his mom's homemade salsa on the counter, then back to the table. "Oh, um," Anthony stammers. "I'll get it." He starts to stand.

"Let me," Eric says. But as he gets out of his seat, my eyes go wide because in one innocuous motion Eric's placed his hand over Anthony's. I watch Anthony straighten like there's an electric current running through him.

When Eric's back is turned, I find Anthony's eyes. Where there was defeat just seconds ago, now there's the kind of exhilarated determination I've only seen when he's walking off stage after nailing a performance. "Oh my god," he mouths at me. Eric returns with the refilled bowl, and I watch Anthony expectantly, waiting for his next move.

I don't even know how it happens. But the next moment, I feel Owen's hand in my hair. I jerk to face him as he withdraws his hand, removing—a clump of guacamole. The only possible explanation is I was so focused on Anthony, I absentmindedly ran a dirty hand through my hair.

"First applesauce, now guacamole." Owen grins, wiping his fingers on his napkin. "Your baby sister's not here to blame this time."

"Are you saying I'm messy, Owen?" I pull a scandalized expression.

"I didn't say it. You did," he replies.

I open my mouth with a comeback, but Eric preempts me. "You guys are cute," he says. "How long have you been dating?"

It takes a moment for me to realize he means me.

And Owen.

Me and Owen.

I look at Owen, and it's impossible to read his expression. Somewhere between bemusement and indignation, probably.

I don't know what Eric finds cute about Owen pulling guacamole out of my hair, but I'm thrown. "We're, uh . . ." I begin, not sure what Anthony wants me to say, or what Owen wants me to say. He was supposed to be my flex date for the night, but I wasn't anticipating actually having to lie about our relationship status.

"Oh, my mistake," Eric quickly amends, picking up on my hesitation. "I thought this was a double date."

It's not a second later that Anthony blurts, "They've been together for a month!"

I cut Anthony a glance, but I have to smile. It's one thing for me to lie about dating Owen, but if someone else does it for me, I guess I'll just *have* to play along. I spare Owen an apologetic look before I lay my hand on his. He stares down at it like it's radioactive, but he doesn't move. His hand is warm under mine.

"We met at auditions for our school's *Romeo and Juliet* production," I tell Eric, then fix my eyes lovingly on Owen. Weeks of playing Juliet have given me an aptitude for playing the doting girlfriend, it turns out. Owen looks like a deer in the headlights. "I promised myself I wouldn't date within the cast, but Owen was unrelenting." I catch Owen roll his eyes. "He even wrote lyrics about me for his friend's band, and let me tell you, they were . . . steamy."

Owen turns to me, and there's a spark in his eyes. "It's pretty impossible to resist Megan. She's an *outstanding* actress."

I bite my cheek to keep from laughing. "Eventually I

stopped objecting. He makes a really hot friar." I stare at him, daring him to keep the act going, and he stares back at me, undoubtedly considering his next line.

"Is this the play you're in?"

I've been so preoccupied with Owen, I didn't notice how Eric's eyes have shifted to Anthony.

"I have a role, yes," Anthony says smoothly.

"He's being modest," I cut in. "He's the best actor at Stillmont. He has a huge part—you should see his monologue."

"I'd like to." Eric's voice softens.

"I could give you a preview . . ." Anthony offers. When he's on, his flirting game is downright inspiring.

"Right now?" Eric smiles. "At the table? In the middle of dinner?"

"In private," Anthony says simply, and I have to restrain myself from giving him a standing ovation.

Eric pauses, and I know he's enticed by the invite. "I'd like that. But I'd like to see the real thing, too."

I'm pretty certain everyone's picked up on the definite charge in the room by now. I spring out of my seat and grab Anthony's plate. "Let me clear the table," I quickly offer. "Anthony, this was incredible, per usual. Owen and I have the dishes covered since you cooked."

Of course, it's not like I needed to say anything. Anthony and Eric are halfway to the hall by the time I've finished speaking.

I carry the plates to the sink and turn on the faucet. Owen comes up next to me with a couple more dishes. He hands them to me, then stops beside the sink, like he's trying to decide whether to say something. "A really hot friar?" he finally asks way too nonchalantly.

I shake a spoon at him, splashing water on his face. "I didn't know I was impossible to resist, either."

Owen swats me with a towel, grinning. "Yes you did, Megan." I laugh, noticing how he didn't deny it.

Only once we've finished the dishes do I realize we haven't heard anything from down the hallway in a suspiciously long time—no, a promisingly long time. Like he's just read my mind, Owen glances in the direction Anthony led Eric. "What do you think is going on in there?" he asks softly.

"How about you go check?"

He whirls, eyes wide. "No. No way."

"Fine." I shrug. "You wait here." I throw my towel at his face and tiptoe down the hall. Anthony's bedroom is on the left, next to a very realistic portrait of Jesus. I only know where his room is from the study sessions where he helped me not fail my finals—definitely not from when we were dating. His door is ajar, spilling light into the darkened hallway. First I see one pair of knees jutting off of Anthony's bed, then I adjust my angle to get a better view of . . . Anthony and Eric kissing to their hearts' content.

I feel a rush of vindication. I linger only long enough to see Anthony push Eric down onto the bed. Quietly, I return to the kitchen, where Owen's waiting. I beam at him. "They're totally making out," I whisper, and start cleaning off the counters, looking for dessert. I know Anthony made something.

"This is kind of weird. We're just going to hang out here while they . . . uh . . . while things progress?" Owen stands stiffly to the side.

I move a giant bag of flour to reveal a golden apple pie. "Uh, yeah," I say over my shoulder. "I'm not going to let this pie get cold." I pass Owen on my way into the living room and notice his skeptical look. "Anthony's fine with us having pie *while things progress*," I promise. "Believe me. I've done this before."

I drop onto the couch and hold a fork out to Owen while digging into the center of the pie, not bothering to slice it. I think it's my moan of pie-induced ecstasy that persuades Owen to grab the fork and sit down next to me.

"Howv da play gumpf?" I ask through a mouthful.

"What?" Owen studies me.

I swallow. "How's the play going? Can I read it?"

He shakes his head with surprising vehemence. "It's nowhere near ready. I'm still deep in outlining."

"*Outlining?* I've given you so much material."

He stabs the pie with a little less enthusiasm. "I haven't had a lot of time."

"Because of *Romeo and Juliet*?"

"Yeah, and home stuff." He doesn't lift his fork, and it remains in the center of the pie. "You know, picking up my brother, making him dinner, helping him with his homework."

There's something serious in his eyes, his squared shoulders. I set my fork down. "You do a lot for your brother," I say after a second.

Owen shrugs. "It's not so bad. It's my mom who works night shifts and two jobs."

He falls silent, but I don't want to interrupt in case he's going to say more. Besides, I wouldn't know how to respond. I wish I did—I'm even a little embarrassed I don't—but while I've bared family problems to him, I've never heard his. Instead, I poke at the pie.

He does go on. "My dad walked out on us the year my brother was born. My mom works really hard to make things possible for us, like the theater camp I did last summer—it wasn't cheap. It's nothing to take care of Sam in return."

"I had no idea," I say, hearing how inadequate it sounds.

He gives me a quick smile. "Yeah, I'm not exactly the over-sharing type. I'm more comfortable writing in my notebook than talking to most people."

"You don't seem to have a problem talking to me." I nudge his shoulder with mine.

"You're not most people."

He's looking at me intently, and there's a hum in the air I wasn't expecting. One I don't know what to do with. I look down. "No," I say, trying to sound undisturbed, "I'm loud, sarcastic, boy-crazy—"

"—thoughtful, perceptive, witty," Owen finishes. He doesn't look away, and I lift my gaze to meet his. The truth is, I could say the same thing about him. He's quiet and patient enough for me to talk while he listens, and yet he keeps surprising me by making me laugh. I nearly do tell him. Instead, in the silence that follows his comment, I inch closer to him on the couch and take his hand, entwining my fingers with his.

Owen doesn't move. I watch him look down at our hands and then up at me. There's possibility in his eyes. I lean forward, but before I reach him, he quietly says, "You like Will."

I pull back just a bit. I definitely felt like Owen wanted this. Why would he bring up Will? I tell him what I haven't wanted to admit before now is the truth. "It's not going to happen with Will."

He blinks. "What? Why?"

"It's run its course. Trust me. I've been here before. I know what happens next."

"But you still like him." His eyes are guarded.

I drop his hand. What brought us this close on the couch was how easily I felt I could like Owen one day. I could use him to get over Will or even fall for him for real, even though I know he's right—in this moment, I do still like Will. "Yeah," I say bitterly, "like that ever means anything."

"Why do you do that?" I'm surprised to hear he sounds accusing.

"What?"

"You sell yourself short," he says, softer this time. "You give up. It's what you're doing with Juliet and the play. I think you did it with your and Tyler's relationship, too. If you like Will, then don't write it off. I know you, Megan. Don't undervalue yourself."

His speech momentarily stuns me. It's charged with conviction, and the words linger in the air while I search for what to say.

It's on the tip of my tongue to point out that even if I like Will, I can't force him to like me, when Anthony's door

160

bangs open. Eric storms down the hall, his hair disheveled. He startles when he sees us and stops for a moment. "It was good to see you guys," he mutters distractedly. "I've got to go." Before we have time to react, he throws open the front door, and he's gone.

Anthony trails into the room, looking dazed. I'm on my feet and rushing to his side. "What happened? It looked like it was going great," I say, realizing a second late I just let it slip I'd spied on them.

If he notices, he doesn't care. "It was. Everything was perfect," he says emptily. "And then his dad called, and he got weird and distant and just left."

"Was there a family emergency or something?" I ask.

"Of course there wasn't a family emergency," he snaps, finally whipping his gaze to me. "This was just a terrible idea."

"A terrible idea? You just hooked up with the guy you've been obsessed with."

"Which is everything I could have hoped for, right?" he fires back. "It doesn't matter he's obviously in the closet with no intention of having a relationship with me—or that he's definitely never going to talk to me again." He's yelling now, and there are tears in his eyes. "Because it's enough I got to hook up with him, right? It might be for you, Megan. But not for me."

I fumble for words. "I didn't mean . . . I'm not— You don't have the first clue what's *enough* for me," I fire back, finding my voice. "Or how much I did to help you. If it wasn't for me, you wouldn't have had what you did have. Which wasn't nothing."

"I didn't ask for your help. Whatever you did, whatever you said to him—you pushed him. You pushed us both. Not everyone wants to take things at your pace. Relationships aren't a race against the clock." I flinch, but Anthony blazes on. "I've never even had a real boyfriend. I thought Eric would be different. I thought he got me. It's hard enough meeting guys in high school. It's not like I've got endless relationships and hookups around the corner to console myself with—hard though it might be for *you* to understand."

"That's not fair," I say, stung.

"Not fair?" He steps closer to me, and I can see he's shaking. "Not fair is having to move schools because you're too black and too gay to get lead roles. Not fair is dreading every school trip because you know no guy wants to be your roommate. Not fair is worrying every time you flirt with a guy if he's going to laugh in your face."

His words have me looking past the malice in his voice. Anthony hardly ever talks about this stuff, but I'm not unaware of the toll it takes on him. And I know tonight meant a lot to him. Of course he's heartbroken. "I'm sorry. I think you'll have another chance with Eric," I say gently.

"I know you do. You don't get it. It's easy to tell yourself everything is going to be okay when really, inside, you've already resigned yourself to failure."

I feel tears of hot anger in my eyes. I don't have the words to deny what Anthony's saying. Maybe I am resigned, and maybe it's unhealthy. But right now, I don't know how not to be.

"Fuck this." I hear my voice waver. "I'm trying to be here for you. I'm trying to help. But forget it. You don't want to talk. You only want to take your ruined night out on me."

Grabbing my bag, I remember Owen behind me. "Come on, Owen," I tell him, walking to the door. I think I catch him give Anthony an apologetic glance before I follow in Eric's footsteps.

We drive home in silence, wrapped in too many layers of things left unsaid. Owen's not meeting my eyes, and we exchange muted good-byes when I drop him off in front of his house.

The windows of my house are dark when I pull into the driveway. I walk in the front door, past the remnants of what looks like a family craft night, and up to my room. It takes everything I have not to slam the door behind me. It's not just thoughts of Anthony and Owen that torment me. It's something more selfish, too—that I teared up in front of them, and I'm not the kind of girl who cries.

I don't even bother turning on the lights. I head straight for my bed. But once I've buried myself under the covers, I can't sleep. I dwell on the words Anthony flung at me. He said things a person shouldn't say to a friend even when angry.

Nevertheless, they rang painfully true. Anthony might be right. I've always thought my relationships give up on me.

It's easier, in a way. They're out of my control—comfortably predictable. Inevitability has become my coping mechanism.

Except what if it's become more than that? The question comes with a queasy rush. What if somewhere along the way, a coping mechanism became a chain around my neck, pulling me in directions I didn't want to go? I'm beginning to feel like whatever happens to my relationships, my negativity can't be helping. What if they don't give up on me—what if I give up on them?

I turn over to face the wall, fighting to calm my racing thoughts. This time of night, fresh from what happened with Anthony, is not the time to fray the edges of those questions, hard though I'm finding it to force them down.

There's one thing I do need to do tonight. I have no business going for a guy who has a girlfriend while I have feelings for someone else, no matter how thoughtful, perceptive, and witty he is. I reach for my phone on my nightstand and type out a text to Owen.

sry for earlier. b4 anthony

He doesn't reply, and I can't help remembering how quickly he did when I invited him to Anthony's. He could just be putting his brother to bed, I tell myself. I try to let it go, but twenty minutes go by and I'm still awake, still worrying I lost two friends in one night.

i hope i didnt mess stuff up btwn us, I type before I can stop myself, then a second later I add, **ur a good friend**. I hit SEND.

This time, it's only a couple minutes before his reply comes.

You're a good friend too. You don't need to
apologize . . .

I feel myself let out a relieved breath. Then I receive a second text.

I get it. I know I'm a really hot friar.

I laugh, hurting a little less. I send him my reply.

the hawtest. can't wait to c u in ur frock

FOURTEEN

JULIET: *Was ever book containing such vile matter*

So fairly bound? O, that deceit should dwell

In such a gorgeous palace!

III.ii.89–91

IT'S DAWN, AND I'M DRIVING UP THE dirt road to where Madeleine texted me to find her for tree planting. It's thickly forested on both sides, and my mom's old Volkswagen skips over the loose rocks. I crest the hill, and spreading out below me is the horizon painted pink by the rising sun.

It's beautiful. And I hate it.

I take one hand off the wheel to rub sleep out of my eyes. Only for Madeleine would I get up at five in the morning on a Saturday and venture into nature. I spot her car on the side of the road, where she told me it would be, and pull in behind it.

Walking into the woods, I pull my scarf over my very messy ponytail. October's giving way to November, and it is *cold*. In the crisp morning light my breath is depressingly visible. I hear rustling up ahead, and voices drift to me a second later. I can't believe Madeleine actually convinced other people to come to this.

When I enter a clearing in the forest, I find a handful of volunteers working with shovels, among them Madeleine, whose head is bent over the hole she's digging. She looks better than anyone has the right to at this ungodly hour in the middle of the forest, wearing a blue bandana with perfect carelessness over her tidy bun and a baggy Windbreaker that somehow still flatters her frame. She doesn't notice when I come up next to her.

"You know," I say, and Madeleine's head pops up, "this is awesome. Whenever I look into the woods, what I find my-self thinking is, *needs more trees.*"

She rolls her eyes. Grinning, she grabs the small sapling beside the hole and drops it in. "They're to replace the foliage lost when a couple of drunken idiots on a camping trip started a fire." Now that she mentions it, the ground here does look ashy. "Besides," she continues, patting the dirt around her tree, "it looks great for college."

She straightens up and produces a trowel from her back pocket. Holding it out to me, she gives me an expectant look. *Is she serious?*

I pull a fake pout.

She's not amused. One eyebrow arches, and she waves the trowel in the air, flinging dirt at me.

"Okay, okay," I grumble. We walk to the next sapling, a few feet over. Following Madeleine's lead, I kneel and shove my trowel into the earth, no idea what I'm doing. Far away, I hear the chattering of some indiscernible woodland creature. Madeleine, however, knows exactly what she's doing, and she confidently removes a shovelful of dirt in one even motion.

"Doesn't it ever get tiring being perfect?" I ask, watching her.

I meant it half-jokingly, but she wrinkles her nose. "Perfect?"

"I mean, saving the forests, volunteering at the library, perfect GPA, perfect boyfriend. It's a lot to keep up. Don't you ever just want to screw something up?" I got two hours of sleep after somehow ruining one of my closest friendships, and here Madeleine is, saving the planet.

She stops digging and stabs her shovel into the ground. "What's with you today? You're snarkier than normal."

I shrug. She's not wrong. With last night weighing on me, of course I'm snarkier than normal. "This is just me at six a.m.," I mumble. I feel her scrutinizing me, but after a second she resumes digging with a little more force than before.

"Do you think I give up too easily?" I ask abruptly. The thought's been burning in my head since Owen and I talked on Anthony's couch. Madeleine's been my friend for a lot longer than Owen. She'd have perspective he doesn't.

She straightens up once more, this time pausing with one foot planted on her shovel. "Give up on what?"

"On everything. You know . . ." I hesitate, reconsidering. It's not *everything*, really. I haven't given up on SOTI, haven't given up on Anthony or Madeleine herself, even when we fight. "On relationships," I finish.

"This is about Will," Madeleine says knowingly.

"Yeah, Will, and everyone, I guess," I go on. "I've had a ton of boyfriends, but I've never been in a relationship longer than four months." I'd never thought anything of it before, but pondering Owen's words in bed at 2 a.m., it began to depress me.

"Well, you shouldn't waste your time when a relationship's not working." She pulls off her bandana and wipes her face with it.

"But what if I'm too quick to think a relationship's not working? I was ready to give up on Will after one awkward night and seeing Alyssa flirt with him. Which, you know, Alyssa flirts with everyone. Everything."

Madeleine doesn't laugh. She puts a hand on her hip. "Why are we talking about this?" She sounds slightly exasperated. God forbid I disturb her community-service time.

"I don't know. Just looking back, it feels like I was too quick to . . . write some of them off." I'm using Owen's exact phrasing, I realize.

"But . . . Tyler was different," she says slowly.

I point my trowel into the soil and shovel out more dirt. The motion comes easier this time, like I'm finding a rhythm. It feels good, even. "I guess. I mean—" I stop myself, realizing who I'm talking to. "It's not like I want him back," I quickly reassure her. "It's just, maybe I let things fall apart with Tyler and with my other boyfriends, too."

From the look on her face, I know my reassurance didn't work. Blood has started to color her alabaster cheeks in uneven splotches, and her downturned mouth is twitching. Her eyes are narrowed and fixed on me. It's a look reserved for instances like unfair grades and jocks pushing the yearbook staff into lockers.

"It wouldn't have made a difference with Tyler, okay?" she says quietly.

I shake my head. "I just mean hypothetically. What if it would have—"

"We were together before you even broke up," she nearly shouts.

My mouth drops open, my trowel into the dirt.

"You . . . *What?*"

"He kissed me the closing night of *Twelfth Night.*"

I stand there, blinking in the brightening day, my thoughts chasing each other in circles. I remember the closing night of *Twelfth Night*, the final cast party of the season at Tyler's house. It was one of the rare instances of Anthony getting drunk, and Jenna and I watched him recite a version of Hamlet's soliloquy. *To beer or not to beer.*

I remember how Tyler and I had had sex for the first time just weeks earlier, and we would go on to break up about a month later. I remember them both coming over to my house a few weeks after the breakup, asking if it was okay with me for them to date and promising they'd done nothing together at that point.

I remember believing them.

All the anger drains out of Madeleine's face. Her eyes fill with tears, her face goes pale, and she rubs the bridge of her nose. I can't believe she has the nerve to drop this on me and then cry about it. Wanting *me* to take care of *her.*

"I shouldn't have said that," she says weakly, her voice pinched.

"No, you *should* have said it six months ago." I can't even look at her.

"I know. I'm *so* sorry, Megan. I should have," she blurts out through her tears, but there's exasperation or even frustration behind her remorse. "I know things have been weird between us, it's why I wanted today to—"

"I *defended* you," I cut her off. "Everyone thought you and Tyler cheated, and I played the best friend because I trusted you. You told me nothing had happened while we were still dating."

"I know, I know." Tears are streaming down her face, and a couple volunteers' heads have turned in our direction. "Please, let's go to my car, let me explain . . ."

Some of my anger has ebbed away. I take a step toward her, my instinct kicking in to forgive and be there for her. But before I reach out to her, I remember what Owen told me. *Don't undervalue yourself.* I shouldn't sweep my hurt under the rug so Madeleine doesn't have to feel bad. My feelings matter, too. I'm tired of pretending they don't.

I turn on my heel and walk back to my car, leaving Madeleine to her tears.

I wake up to six missed calls from Madeleine after sleeping for the rest of the morning. I delete the voicemails without listening to them.

Surprisingly, I feel good about how I handled the fight.

Not about the reason for the fight, obviously—I feel really betrayed. I honestly believed my best friend when she promised she hadn't hooked up with my boyfriend behind my back. Even if they are the perfect couple, what they did fucking sucks. But I'm genuinely proud that I stood up for myself and didn't just let something go instead of meeting it head-on.

Which has me thinking about Will.

Yeah, Alyssa flirtatiously touched his arm and wanted to "read lines" with him—the oldest trick in the book. But it was just a week ago he was in my room telling me I'm beautiful. I'm done waiting for him to drop some hint about how he sees our relationship. I'm going to find out.

I grab my phone off my desk. **u busy?** I text him.

Not right now. Why? he replies.

I text him a location and, **30 min!!!** And I don't let myself worry about whether he'll be there.

Thirty minutes later, the bell chimes on the front door of the place I told him to meet me. Will's head of immaculately slicked hair appears in the doorway. His eyes flit over the shelves, and I signal to him with a wave from my small table in the back.

He sits down across from me, looking quizzical. I push the almond blueberry coffee cake I ordered toward him. "You want something to drink?" I ask.

He stares down at the cake, then looks up at me, lightly amused. "What's happening here?"

I take a deep breath. "A date." I turn one of the forks so it faces him. "Coffee cake?"

"A date," he repeats, reaching for the fork. He doesn't look entirely convinced.

I begin reciting the speech I prepared in my head on the drive over. "I feel like we've been off ever since the night we hooked up at my house. I have a tendency to rush things, but I don't want to do that anymore. Which, I guess, means I'm not ready to have sex with you"—I pause—"yet. It's definitely a yet." Will smiles. Encouraged, I continue. "I like you. I want to be with you. I want to date."

He puts down the fork. For a horrible moment, every doubt I've had about this plan floods my mind. *He's not interested. He likes Alyssa. I came on way too strong. He wants to have sex now.* And worst of all, *Owen was wrong—I don't give up too easily. People give up on me.*

Instead of saying any of those things, Will puts his hand over mine on the table. "I . . . have to tell you, I was a little intimidated when we started hooking up. Everyone knows you're hot, and funny, and talented. It was hard to measure up to."

I blink. I didn't know "everyone" thought that. To the rest of the school, I thought I was just Madeleine's flirty friend. Madeleine's perpetually dumped friend.

Will goes on. "I didn't know how to handle it, but I want to be with you, too, Megan," he says with a growing smile.

Muscles I didn't realize were tensed relax, and I feel unbelievably relieved. But I'm not done yet. It's now or never. "Okay, then I want a straight answer," I say. "Boyfriend?"

Will nods once, definite and unmistakable. "Boyfriend."

"Well," I say, beaming, "great."

"I guess that makes this our first date. And we are . . ." He looks around the room. "Where, exactly?"

I let my eyes wander over the familiar surroundings. In the front of the shop, antique books, foreign titles, and bestsellers vie for space on wooden shelves that look on the verge of collapse. Posters of long-dead literary figures curl away from the walls over the register. A spindly staircase in the center of the room winds up to an alcove overcrowded with Shakespeare paraphernalia. The smell of what must be the strongest espresso in Oregon wafts from the coffee counter in the back, where Will and I are sitting. It's dimly lit, dusty, and perfect.

"It's Birnam Wood Books," I tell him. "I first came here to annotate *Macbeth* for a scene workshop. I found it because of the reference. Ever since, it's been pretty much my favorite spot."

Will sniffs the air. "Kind of musty."

"It's great, isn't it?"

He takes a bite of the coffee cake and shrugs. "It's definitely the first time I've gone on a date to a bookstore. But then," he adds, almost like an afterthought, "it's the first time I've gone on a date." It's not as if I'm surprised, but it's sort of endearing to hear him admit it. "How's *Romeo and Juliet* going? I notice the balcony scene's on the schedule again this week."

"Don't remind me." The last rehearsal went terribly. I'm hopeless on the lines where Juliet declares her love for Romeo, no matter how much emotion Tyler puts into it or how often Jody stops us to repeat it. "Right now, I'm more focused on the Senior Showcase and the scene I'm directing," I say.

"But that's one scene," Will says slowly.

"I'm *directing* one scene," I quickly counter. "I'm organizing the entire showcase."

"I just don't get why you'd focus on that." His tone's light, but underneath it there's something nearly judgmental. "*Romeo and Juliet*'s going to Ashland. Come on," he says, the grin I once found dazzling losing a little of its luster, "you're the lead in a professional-level performance. That's way bigger than Stillmont's Senior Showcase."

I shrug, trying not to be annoyed that he doesn't get it, or offended by the way he said *Senior Showcase*. "It's my senior year. I've been a part of the showcase since I started high school. I want it to be perfect, you know?" Will nods, but his eyes remain skeptical like, no, he doesn't know. "Besides, I'm not going to let the showcase interfere with Ashland."

"Do you have a cast yet?" he asks after a second, and I'm relieved he's taking an interest.

"No, why?" I raise an eyebrow flirtatiously. "You interested?"

"I might be," he says slowly. "If I'm promised special attention from the director."

"I think that could be arranged."

He grins. Then without warning, he takes my hand and pulls me toward the front of the shop. "A first date merits a first gift. Don't you think?" he asks over his shoulder.

Butterflies I haven't felt in a while flutter in my chest. "You don't have to," I half protest, enjoying Will's affection if a bit thrown by the gesture.

"I insist," he says unhesitatingly. He doesn't slow his steps, and I follow him.

Near the front, I find my eyes drifting to the shelf of leather-bound notebooks on one side of the door. I admired them the past couple times I was here, and—

"This." Will holds up a black bracelet. "This is perfect."

Oh. "It's beautiful," I'm quick to say.

He gives me a pleased smile. When he places it on the glass counter by the register, I notice there's a word engraved on the inside. Or—a name.

"Ophelia?" I ask.

Will hands a twenty to the cashier while turning to me. "Yeah!" he says enthusiastically. "Isn't *Hamlet* the best? Or, like, definitely"—he holds up a hand, correcting himself— "*one* of the best."

He takes the bracelet out of its packaging and hands it to me. I slip it on with a grateful smile, choosing to overlook that Ophelia does nothing for the entire play except obsess over her boyfriend until she goes crazy. And it gives me a quiet, familiar thrill. I appreciate Will's eagerness, his affection, and what it represents—togetherness. It doesn't matter what the bracelet says. It's a gift from my boyfriend.

FIFTEEN

MERCUTIO: *A plague o´ both your houses!*

III.i.111

DESPITE THE SUCCESS OF WILL'S AND MY date, I get to school on Monday in not exactly the greatest of moods. When I went home on Saturday, two hours and one torrid make-out session in the Shakespeare section later, I overheard my dad on the phone. It was on speaker, and I only stuck around long enough to figure out he and Rose were talking to a realtor whom they'd hired to appraise the house. To put a price tag on seventeen years of homemade dinners, birthday parties, fights, tears, and memories.

For the first time ever, I stopped myself before instinctively texting Madeleine. There's a part of me, a very big part, that wanted to tell her what I'd overheard. But then I remembered that I'm not talking to her. That she's not the friend I thought she was.

I ignore her during English and pass her without looking at her between classes. Eventually, I notice Anthony's giving me the same treatment. But I have Will to distract me, a task he accomplishes with impressive tongue work, and the day goes pretty much okay. Until lunch.

I walk to the hill outside the drama room, knowing Madeleine's going to be there. I'm not going to talk to her. Not a chance. But I've decided I won't be the one to run from her. She's not going to steal my boyfriend *and* my lunch spot.

I march right into the middle of the group and sit down next to Owen. I can feel Madeleine looking imploringly at me. "Hey, Megan," she pleads. "Can we talk? I tried calling you this weekend."

Without looking at her, I unwrap the chicken-salad sandwich Rose insisted on packing for me. "There's a reason I didn't pick up." Not wanting this conversation to go any further, I pointedly turn to Kasey Markowitz, the junior who played Olivia in *Twelfth Night*. "Kasey, I know you're a junior, but I want you to sign up for my senior scene. I'm doing a gender-flipped Happy Loman, and I think you'd be great."

She flushes, obviously flattered, but Madeleine interrupts.

"You're seriously just ignoring me right now?" Her tone's gone from pleading to pissed.

I finally whip my head in her direction. "I'm sorry, I'm not in the mood to talk to my former best friend who was screwing around with my boyfriend behind my back." Next to her, Tyler's eyes widen, and I briefly wonder if she even told him that I know.

Everyone falls silent, and Madeleine's cheeks ignite. Hurriedly, she drops her Thermos into her bag and gets to her feet, smoothing her skirt with trembling hands. Tyler tosses me an apologetic look. "I have to . . ." He gestures in her direction. "I'm sorry, Megan," he says before leaving to follow Madeleine. I don't know if he's apologizing for walking away from the conversation or for betraying me while we were dating. Either way, I'm not ready to deal with how furious I am with Tyler.

Everyone gradually resumes their conversations, occasionally stealing glances in my direction. Everyone except Owen, who leans into me. "I'm getting the sense something . . . changed since we talked about Tyler and Madeleine."

Seriously? Now? "Get your notebook out, Owen. I've got some *great* material for you," I snap.

He jerks back. "What? No." He sounds stunned, even hurt. "I'm not trying to get material. I'm trying to be your friend."

I feel a stab of guilt. Of course Owen's just trying to be my friend. It's what he's been doing since the day we met. I exhale. "It turns out I was an idiot for not believing what *everyone* told me. Madeleine let it slip this weekend she and Tyler hooked up a month before he and I broke up."

"That . . ." Owen reaches for words. "Definitely sucks."

"I'm not surprised on Tyler's end, honestly. But Madeleine . . . She's the one person I couldn't believe would do that to me." I stare at the ground and absently rip out blades of grass. "The messed-up thing is, part of me wants to pretend it didn't happen. There's more stuff going on with my dad, and I wish I could talk to her, have her sleep over, like we did when my parents were splitting up."

He nods. "What are you going to do?" he asks evenly.

"Do? I'm not the one who has to *do* anything. I want her to . . . I don't know. Figure out a way to make it right."

"She will," Owen says without hesitation.

I shoot him an incredulous look. "How do you know?"

He glances down like he's considering the question. "I don't," he admits. "But she will if she's the kind of friend worth having."

I don't know what to say to that. I want to believe Madeleine's the kind of friend who would want to fix things between us. And I do believe it. I'd forgive her if she showed me that I mean more to her than how she treated me.

I feel my stomach sink. I'm not the only one who deserves to feel that way. Anthony means more to me than the way I've been rushing him, too. He should take his relationship— or flirtation, or whatever it is—with Eric at whatever pace he wants.

"You know," Owen says, and I realize he's been waiting patiently during my lengthy introspection, "I'm not Madeleine— sleepovers with me might be a bit weird—but I'm here for you if you need."

I look up into his dark, thoughtful eyes. "Sleepovers with you wouldn't be *weird*, Owen . . . unless you're into 'weird.'" I wink. Before he begins to blush, I lower my voice and say sincerely, "But really, thanks."

I have Trig after lunch. Outside Mr. Patton's door, I decide I'm going to skip class. I know it'll be boring, and besides, I have urgent business. I turn and walk against hallway traffic until I reach the science wing, where I wait for the next fifteen minutes after the bell rings and the hallway empties.

When Ms. Howell leaves the AP Physics room, I hover by

the bathroom door and try to look like I have total permission to be here. I know where Howell's headed. I had Intro
Physics with her last year, and without fail she goes to the
parking lot for a smoke break fifteen minutes into each of her
afternoon classes.

I slip into the room behind her. It's a scene of utter chaos.
The AP students are armed with fluorescent purple Nerf
crossbows. Foam darts fly across the room trailed by students
with measuring tapes and notebooks. A dart hits me in the
back of the head, and I hear a whiny voice complain that I'm
interrupting the data-collection process.

I don't bother to apologize. I'm here for one reason, and
he's in the back of the room.

Anthony's head is bent over his notebook. He doesn't look
up when I lean on the counter next to him. "I'm in the middle
of class, Megan," he says flatly.

"I know. It'll only take a second."

He drags his eyes from his paper and glares at me. "What,
you haven't messed with my life enough already?"

I flinch. "I'm sorry," I hurriedly continue, knowing I won't
have long before he shuts me out again. "I shouldn't have
rushed you. You were right, even though you said some shit
that really hurt."

Anthony looks away, but he doesn't ignore me. "Why are
you here, Megan?"

"I want to be a good friend. The kind of friend worth having. You've been a good friend to me, and I want to make
things right." I take a deep breath. "I'm sorry I forced you to
take things faster than you wanted to."

"It's not just about being sorry," he replies immediately, his voice harsh. "You don't understand how not like you I am. I know you wanted to help, but you never bothered to consider what kind of help or encouragement or friendship *I* wanted. I don't have your no-holds-barred attitude toward relationships, and I never will. You're fearless, and that's awesome," he goes on, something somber entering his eyes. "But it's painful and honestly frustrating when you push me to date the way you do."

"I understand," I reply. "Or I'm trying to understand. I'm going to keep trying, if you'll let me. To be fair, though, I didn't exactly force you and Eric into your bedroom together," I point out, and Anthony's eyes flicker. "You're hardly timid when it comes to guys. But I know I went about this wrong," I rush to add. "I'm sorry I screwed everything up with Eric. I won't intrude in your relationships from now on. Promise."

His expression begins to soften. "You didn't screw everything up," he says gently. "It's my fault, and Eric's, not yours. I'm sorry, too. I took some low blows at your relationship history, and I didn't mean what I said."

I smile tentatively. "They weren't entirely undeserved, but thanks. I'm not going to tell you what to do, but you know, I'm here for you."

"I want to hit pause on the Eric situation," he says after a long second. I know from his hunched shoulders and the waver in his voice that it's not something he's pleased to admit.

"I understand," I say quickly.

"But for the record," he continues, beginning to smile, "the *entire* night wasn't terrible."

"No night with your unbelievable carne asada could be."

He laughs. "Stuff with Eric . . . wasn't the worst."

"It didn't look it."

Anthony's eyes slowly widen with realization. "You did *not*."

I give him a close-lipped smile. "Just for a second."

He shakes his head admonishingly, but he's grinning. "Well, watching you and Owen concoct your fake relationship story . . . It was *almost* the highlight of the night." He fixes me with an indicative stare. "You know, you two would actually make a cute couple."

I say nothing. I won't pretend the thought's never flitted through my head, but he's . . . Owen. No way would a guy who's never without his notebook, whose current relationship consists of blurry video chats twice a week, who's quiet and reserved, go for someone who's brash and forward like me. No. I'd be better off sticking to guys who want to get to the point. Guys like Will.

Instead of saying all that to Anthony, I seize the crossbow from the counter and shoot a dart into his chest. He rolls his eyes. "Why are you even talking to me?" I ask with joking indignation. "You're in the middle of class."

SIXTEEN

JULIET: *O Romeo, Romeo, wherefore art thou Romeo?*

II.ii.36

"DENY THY FATHER AND REFUSE THY NAME, or, if thou wilt not, be but sworn my love—"

"Nope!" Jody's voice rings sharply to where I'm standing on the balcony set. It's the first day of rehearsal with the half-painted wooden structure Will built—a single-story tower with a staircase down the back and a trellis with plastic ivy winding up the front. I think Jody expected performing on the set would awaken my inner Juliet. No such luck.

I hear Tyler sigh from the stage below. I don't blame him, really. It's the sixth time Jody's interrupted us before we've even finished the scene. On the other hand, I'm not exactly overflowing with sympathy for Tyler Dunning at the moment. It's been a week since Madeleine's confession, and I haven't forgiven either one of them. Not even close.

Jody climbs onto the stage. "This isn't working," she says, her eyes on me. "I know you're trying to find the softer Juliet, Megan, but it's not coming through. No one is buying this romance."

"It's partly my fault," Tyler butts in before I have the chance to reply. He glances over at me pityingly, and I feel my blood heat with anger. He's got some nerve, implying my performance is falling apart because of personal stuff between him and me. It's not just patronizing, it's wrong.

"I feel like I'm playing Romeo's opening lines too comedic," Tyler continues. "It's probably throwing Megan off."

Wow. Even worse. Tyler never criticizes his own work. He must think I'm on the verge of having a meltdown in the middle of rehearsal over something he did to me half a year ago.

Jody rubs her eyes. "No, Tyler, it's not just on you," she mutters. Putting her glasses back on, she looks from Tyler to me. "I think the two of you need to take a couple minutes to talk through the scene dynamics. Regroup backstage, and we'll pick up in five."

I literally would rather change a thousand of Erin's diapers. Clenching my script, I head down the narrow stairs. Tyler's waiting for me backstage, rubbing his neck, looking uncharacteristically nervous.

"Jody's on the warpath today. I actually think the scene's going pretty well," he says in a rush and way too casually.

I stare at him hard. "Why are you doing that? First you try to take the fall. Now it's Jody's fault? I can handle getting critiqued."

"I guess I feel bad." He shuffles his feet uncomfortably. "You know, for my part in what happened. I never meant to cheat on you."

Is he for real? "Oh, well, if you never *meant* to, then it's fine."

He pulls a remorseful expression—one I've seen too

many times on stage. "I'm trying to apologize, Megan."

"Then I should fall over myself forgiving you, right? What you did was shitty, and I'm not just going to be cool with it because you feel bad." I hear Anthony hurling insults at Jason Mitchum on the other side of the curtain, rehearsing Mercutio and Tybalt's fight sequence. At least everyone's not just listening to Tyler and me.

"Huh." He rubs his jaw. "I didn't think you had it in you."

I narrow my eyes. "What?"

"You just never seem to really care about, well, anything."

I blink a couple times, his words setting in. First Anthony telling me I'm resigned to failure, now Tyler thinking there's nothing I care about? Is *that* who everyone thinks I am? Just a girl who flits through life without trying, without hurting, without caring about anything except the next guy?

"Well, I do care," I fire back. And I want to prove it. I glance down at the script in my hand. "Right now I care about figuring out this scene."

He stares at me disbelievingly for a moment, then scoffs. "I don't know what to tell you, because honestly I'm killing it out there while my Juliet can't even be bothered to look impressed at my flawless intonation. You have no idea the nights I've spent perfecting iambic pentameter—"

"Tyler, shut up for a second." Surprisingly, he does, and I realize in an unexpected rush of inspiration what's wrong with the scene. "This is exactly the problem. If you read the lines, Juliet is not impressed by Romeo's wordiness. But there's a point in the scene where something has to change, because by the end Juliet's professing her love to him. I feel like we haven't figured out that point." I notice Tyler's actually listening. "We need a moment where something softens her—where she falls head over heels."

"What do you propose?" he asks.

"We need something genuine, where Romeo's words get out of the way."

He nods slowly, but his eyes are bright, and I can tell he's with me. "Something physical?" he offers.

"Exactly." I'm liking this interpretation. I only need to figure out how to fit it into the script. Looking past Tyler, my eyes catch the wooden stairs leading up to the balcony. I nod toward the set, the idea coming together in my head. "This is what we're going to do. My genius boyfriend built the set so you can climb the trellis."

Tyler starts to grin.

I find the page in my script and point. "Here."

"Deny thy father and refuse thy name, or, if thou wilt not, be but sworn my love, and I'll no longer be a Capulet." I'm back on the balcony, doing my utmost to look like a teenage girl in the throes of irresponsible love.

This time, I'm not just trudging through the lines. I'm excited, and it's making the dialogue come easier, more naturally. When Juliet asks, *Wherefore art thou Romeo?* into the night, she's not flush with passion, not yet. It's more like she's trying the feeling out.

"What's Montague? It is nor hand, nor foot," I continue

reciting, "nor arm, nor face, nor any other part belonging to a man." I allow Juliet a smirk, knowing what part she has in mind. "That which we call a rose by any other name would smell as sweet."

When I finish my speech, Romeo leaps out of the bushes, and I immediately turn Juliet skeptical. I'm downright stand-offish by the time she proclaims, "I have no joy of this contract tonight. It is too rash, too unadvised, too sudden, too like the lightning, which doth cease to be ere one can say 'it lightens.'" I'm *enjoying* delivering the lines, capturing the inflection. It's almost better than watching actors navigate their lines when I'm directing.

"O, wilt thou leave me so unsatisfied?" Tyler moans, and the rest of the cast laughs from the audience.

I haughtily raise my chin and ask him challengingly, "What satisfaction canst thou have tonight?"

I catch Tyler's eye. He's turned toward me, and the audience can't see his face when he flashes me a quick grin. I hold my breath as he executes a running leap onto the trellis. In two graceful steps, he's scaled up to my level, and out of the corner of my eye I notice Jody lean forward in what I hope is interest.

"Th' exchange of thy love's faithful vow for mine," Tyler utters in a stage whisper.

Then for the first time in six months, Tyler Dunning's lips meet mine. I give Juliet a moment of stunned recoil before I melt into the kiss. He smells the way I remember, but it's not weird like I expected it to be. I don't feel like Megan Harper kissing her cheating ex. I feel like Juliet falling in love.

Maybe it's because I'm getting better at getting into character. Or maybe it's because he's not kissing me like Tyler Dunning, not reaching for my bra and parting my lips with too much tongue. He's kissing me like I imagine Romeo would, his hands remaining on the balcony while he gently presses his lips to mine.

"I gave thee mine before thou didst request it, and yet I would it were to give again," I breathe when he pulls back.

"Okay"—Jody's voice cuts between us—"stop there."

I turn to where she's standing. Every ounce of excitement I just felt for the scene drains out of me, and doubt rushes in. The cast is hushed like I've never heard them during notes— except for Alyssa, who's whispering in Courtney's ear and sneering at me. I search Jody's expression for any indication of what's coming, whether she's going to tell us to rethink the scene again or whether I'm finally kicked out of the role for good. I figure it's one of the two.

But it's not me she speaks to first. "Tyler, what could have possibly compelled you to climb the set and kiss your costar?" I hear nervous laughter from the audience. "Last time I checked, that wasn't in the script or the blocking we discussed. When I told you to step through the scene in private, I didn't mean come up with an entirely new, entirely dangerous staging."

"It was Megan's idea," Tyler says unhesitatingly, jumping off the trellis. *Well, so much for trying to take the fall for me.*

Jody turns her attention to me. "You're an actor here, Megan. Not a director. You need to remember your role." It's an agonizing few moments before she continues, like she's torturing me on purpose. "But . . . I'm impressed," she finally says with a slight smile. "That's the Juliet I've been waiting for."

I breathe a sigh of relief without entirely meaning to, hearing Owen's words in my head. *Don't undervalue yourself.*

"Me too," I reply.

I walk out of rehearsal half an hour later, still grinning stupidly from nailing the scene, and go directly to the bulletin board in the front of the Arts Center. The campus is quiet this time in the afternoon, the sun beginning to dip below the trees and paint the pavement. There's only a scattering of cars left in the parking lot, those belonging to the cast and the athletes here for afternoon practices.

Today was the deadline to sign up for the Senior Showcase scenes, and while I really should head home—Dad told me if I was late to dinner one more time there would be ill-defined "consequences"—I have to know who signed up. The exhilaration of the showcase beginning to come together, combined with the *Romeo and Juliet* rehearsal, is nearly enough for me to forget how messed up things are with Madeleine.

I fold back the open-mic night poster on the bulletin board to find the flier I printed out with *Death of a Salesman* at the top. I left four lines for the four actors I need. I'll sort out who plays who later. The first name I spot is Tyler's. Yeah, he'll be a perfect Willy Loman. Sorry, Dad.

I read down to *Kasey Markowitz,* who I'm glad took my advice and signed up, and *Jenna Cho*, written in her exaggerat-edly loopy handwriting.

Then at the bottom of the list, *Owen Okita*.

He's written his name in the deep blue ink I recognize from the endless scrawl in his notebook. I feel my chest warm with gratitude. He didn't even tell me he'd be signing up, and I wonder why stage-shy Owen would volunteer before it oc-curs to me, of course he would. He's a good friend like that.

But the feeling only lasts a moment because I realize there's one name unaccounted for, one I was really hoping to see. Will made it sound like he wanted to sign up.

The door to the drama room swings open, and Owen walks out, backpack slung over his shoulder and notebook in his hand. "Owen!" I shout. "You signed up for my scene!"

He spins to face me, his eyes finding mine. "You're right. I did," he says, looking amused. "I wanted to experience Megan Harper directing firsthand."

"Was that before or after you watched me *direct* an actor into kissing me?" I had to. I can't help it.

But Owen doesn't blush this time. Instead, he rolls his eyes. "Before, Megan. Cosima, remember?"

"Come on, Owen. If it's on stage, it doesn't count."

"Good to know," he says, and I swear there's a sparkle in his eyes. He comes up to read over my shoulder. "Who else is on there? I didn't really check before, I was in a rush."

"Tyler, obviously . . ." I say under my breath. I'm hyper-conscious of Owen behind me, his face next to mine.

He takes a step back, and he's frowning when I turn to face him. "Why's that obvious?" he asks.

"Well, it's just, my scenes have a reputation for stealing the show . . ." I know how full of myself that sounds, but whatever. It's the truth.

Owen grins. "Right. Obviously." But he must notice I don't return his smile, because quickly his face turns concerned. "Hey, what's up? You seem upset."

"It's stupid, but I thought Will would sign up," I mutter. It's not Owen's problem, I realize as I tell him. I pull out my phone and write a message to Will.

senior scene signups?? I send, and look up at Owen.

"*Death of a Salesman* doesn't feel like Will's kind of thing," he ventures.

"I guess," I reply. A second later, my phone vibrates. I glance down and read Will's text.

Shit, I forgot!! I'll make it up to you later? ;)

"He forgot," I say emptily, returning my phone to my pocket. Owen bites his lip like he's trying to figure out what to say. Before he does, my phone starts vibrating repeatedly. "Someone's calling me," I say, pulling my phone back out.

"Is it Will?"

I check the screen. "Uh, no," I say, surprised. "It's my mom's boyfriend. I guess I should answer."

"Oh, of course." He nods. "I'll talk to you later."

I start to raise the phone to my ear, but watching Owen push open the Arts Center door, I call after him. "Hey." I hold up the signup sheet. "Thanks. You'll make a perfect Biff Loman."

He breaks into a wide smile before he turns and leaves me to my phone call.

I hit ANSWER. "Hey, Randall," I say.

On the other end, I hear a clattering sound and then Randall's voice. "Megan, hi! I'm not getting you at a bad time, I hope?" He sounds surprised, like he wasn't certain I'd pick up. "Your mom told me you have rehearsals after school, and I didn't know if you'd be done, and there's the time difference—"

"It's not a bad time," I cut him off.

In the background, I hear an unexpectedly loud voice. "Randall, buddy! We need you! Epps just bowled spare number two. We need the Strike Master."

I have to smile. *The Strike Master?* "Are you at a bowling alley?" I ask Randall.

"I'm, oh, I'm sorry," he stutters. "I, the team I'm on, we're in the second bracket of a regional tourney. I ducked out a bit early. I wanted a quick word with you."

"Okay . . ." I've never been able to figure out how to talk to Randall. I don't know how my mom does it. Honestly, Randall's kind of an incongruity in the life of my mom, the former experimental visual artist who never fails to meet my sarcasm with some of her own. Randall is an accountant and painfully awkward. When I met him, he was wearing toe-shoes—those goofy shoes that look like gloves for your feet, which he wore around the house even though I'm fairly certain they're meant for running—and he excessively complimented everything my mom cooked that first night like he was afraid she'd kick him out if he didn't. He keeps unveiling odd new hobbies, first pottery and now this. How does my mom go to bed next to a guy who spends weeknights in regional bowling tournaments?

"What's up?" I ask when he says nothing.

"I'll be in Stillmont in a couple weeks," he says a little too loudly. "I hoped you might be available to get coffee?"

"Yeah. Um. Okay." I don't know why Mom didn't ask me herself. Then a worrisome thought occurs to me. "Wait, is Mom coming with you?"

"No! I'm, uh, no, it's a business trip," he clarifies. "I'm only going to be in Oregon for a day or two, but I'd kick myself if I didn't spend time with my—with you. But your mom's very excited to be coming in December for the festival!"

"Right . . ." If this phone call's any indication, a one-on-one coffee date with Randall is going to redefine stilted small talk. But I should give him the benefit of the doubt. He's nice, and he must make my mom happy somehow. "Okay, yeah," I say with more conviction. "Text me when you're in town, and we'll figure it out."

"Perfect! I'll—I'll just text you," Randall exclaims like the idea had never occurred to him.

"Cool." I'm about to hang up. But instead I add, "Break a leg. You know, with the tournament."

"Thanks for the *warning*, Mom."

It's Friday, 5:13 p.m. In the grainy FaceTime window on

my computer, Mom's eyebrows go up. "Warning?" she chides with half a frown. "You need a *warning* before you talk to Randall? I never got a warning when I'd come home to find the newest boyfriend making out with my daughter on the couch. I get to have a love life, too, Megan."

Damn, Mom. "I didn't mean it like that," I say, chagrined. "Like, what do we even have in common? It's going to be so awkward!"

"You have me in common!"

I roll my eyes. "Not exactly the subject I want to discuss with my mom's boyfriend. I guess I'll have to brush up on my professional bowling news if I'm going to have something to say to the Strike Master."

"Be nice to the poor man," Mom orders, not amused. "He's not used to talking to seventeen-year-old girls."

"I should hope not." I adopt a scandalized tone, and Mom laughs. There's a knock on the door, and per usual, Dad infuriatingly walks in without waiting for my permission.

"Hi, Catherine." He nods to the computer, and instantly my anger dissipates. I'm struck by how congenial he sounds. There's none of the tension or reserve that typically characterizes my parents' conversations.

"I hope I'm not too early?" Dad asks.

"No, now's fine," Mom replies, and I whip to face her.

"Fine for what?" I look between them, trying to figure out what could possibly compel my mom and dad to talk in my bedroom like old friends.

They exchange a look, and I know whatever this is about,

it's something serious. "We wanted to discuss something with you," Dad says in his vice-principal's-office voice, sitting down on my bed.

"*We?*" I repeat.

He goes on, making more eye contact than I'm used to. "Rose and I put in an offer on the house in New York, and it looks like the seller's going to accept."

Without a word to Dad, I turn to Mom. "You knew and didn't tell me?" I don't try to hide the hurt in my voice.

She meets my eyes unwaveringly. "We wanted to have the conversation with you together." Her voice is even, but there's something placating in it, like she's trying to urge me to take this in stride.

Not going to happen. "What else have you decided in these conversations I didn't know were happening?" I ask bitterly.

"Megan, we're grown people who have a daughter together. Occasionally, we talk," she replies.

No, you don't, I think to myself, knowing better than to say it out loud. How many times have they told me to check with each other about who'll pay for my summer programs and plane tickets, to convey happy birthdays, to figure out separating their iCals and the family iTunes library? *Now* they're talking again?

"There's something else we've discussed, actually," Dad says next to me, his eyes shifting back to my mom. "Catherine, you want to, uh . . . ?"

"Your father and I have talked quite a bit more lately," Mom says gently, "and what with your festival, Randall and I have decided we're going to extend our visit a couple weeks. We'd like to be there for the birth of your sister."

I suck in a breath. Already the idea of a couple of dinners with both my parents and their respective significant others had me nervous. But this? Watching my dad be the perfect loving spouse to Rose and father to the new baby? Waiting for my mom to finally realize just how little she—or I— belong in Dad's new family?

"Sounds . . . weird," I say. It's the understatement of the century.

The corners of Mom's lips begin to curl, and there's a knowing gleam in Dad's eyes, like they're sharing a joke. It's the kind of look I remember from years ago, when they were always stealing glances they thought I couldn't see after I'd pushed them to their parenting limits. It's almost too painful to watch.

"Maybe a little." It's Mom who speaks up. "But it's exciting. For you, for your father. . . . And while your dad's in the hospital with Rose, it'll be a chance for you and me to hang out. Do mother-daughter things."

"With everyone here? It's still weird." I won't look at either of them.

"We'll get to spend time together, the seven of us," Dad chimes in.

The seven of us. It sounds impossibly strange. Erin's birth was jarring enough, but with every new step my dad takes, his family gets further and further from me. And while I enjoy every Friday-night video chat with my mom, I can't deny that she's changing, too, that I understand less and less about this person who takes pottery classes and dates someone like

Randall. It doesn't feel like seven of us. It feels like four and two, and me fitting nowhere in the middle.

I'm spared having to reply because there's a huge clatter from downstairs followed by a tiny voice bellowing, *"Noo-noos!"* It's Erin-speak for noodles.

"That didn't sound good," Mom says, a smile in her voice.

"Erin's taken to throwing her dishes. I have to go clean Spaghetti-O's off the wall. Third time this week." Dad heaves himself off the bed with a resigned sigh, then glances at my mom in the FaceTime window. "I'm looking forward to having you guys in town. It'll be a chance to welcome in the new shape of our family."

He lays a hand on my shoulder before leaving the room, and even though I didn't think it possible, my heart plummets even lower. I don't let it show on my face because I know Mom's still watching me, still hoping her efforts to make this sound positive might have worked.

But I hate the feeling of a "new shape" of my family. To me, that shape feels like the pieces of *my* family broken apart, held together only by memories everyone's trying to forget.

Everyone except me.

SEVENTEEN

> **JULIET:** *I should have been more strange, I must confess,*
>
> *But that thou overheard'st ere I was ware*
>
> *My true-love passion.*

II.ii.107–9

I LOVE SHAKESPEARE, BUT I'VE HAD JULIET'S dialogue and cues running through my head for a month now, and it's a breath of fresh air to rehearse a scene without the words *anon* or *forsooth*.

"Give my best to Bill Oliver—he may remember me," Tyler says in the voice of a defeated Willy Loman, ending the scene I chose for my piece in the Senior Showcase. He gazes wistfully into the distance like he's looking into the past, and then his shoulders relax. He and the other three members of my cast turn to me from the drama room stage, waiting for directions.

It's been two weeks of Senior Scene preparations. Two busy weeks. Outside of *Romeo and Juliet* rehearsals, I've worked every night on directing my scene *and* organizing the entire event. I've had to rehearse my actors, book the auditorium, arrange the ads for the programs, figure out the lighting with the theater-tech kids, and keep the other directors on schedule for the performance.

Honestly, I love it.

Checking on everyone's scenes isn't too hard, and it's fun seeing what they're working on. Anthony's doing Samuel L. Jackson's final monologue from *Pulp Fiction*, which includes a level of profanity I had to push the teachers to permit. Brian Anderson, I'll grudgingly admit, is doing a pretty nice job directing and starring in a scene from *Rosencrantz and Guildenstern Are Dead*. The only possible problem is Courtney, who's putting on something from *Cats*. Why. Just why.

With the showcase at the end of the week, I'm pleased with the progress on my own scene. Today's rehearsal went well. My instincts were right in casting Kasey, and I have a hunch that after seeing her performance, Jody will give her the lead in the fall play next year. Tyler's obviously stepped into the role like he was born to play Willy, and he and Jenna pair really well. Even Owen's holding his own—and I have a feeling he'll cut a nice figure in a 1940s suit.

"Perfect, guys," I yell from the back of the room. "See you all tomorrow."

They shuffle off the stage while I walk forward to collect the few props we're working with. I reach down to pick up a briefcase Tyler's knocked over, and out of the corner of my eye I notice Madeleine hovering by the door. I figure she's waiting for Tyler, and I take an extra-long time returning to my seat and packing my bag, busying myself in the hope she'll leave before I have to pass her. I know Madeleine feels horrible, and I don't enjoy that she's suffering, but I'm not ready to face her. I can't help the hurt I feel whenever I think of what she confessed to me.

"Megan?" I hear her voice right behind me, and I fumble the pen I was stuffing into my bag.

I straighten up, glancing around the room to find everyone else gone except Owen. He's standing near the back door, watching me warily. I silently plead with him not to leave me here to deal with this conversation on my own. Not answering Madeleine, I brush past her and head for the door.

She's undeterred. "Can we talk?" she says to my back.

"I'm busy right now," I get out. I hear her footsteps trailing after mine, and I realize if I go to my car right now, she'll just follow me. Madeleine is nothing if not persistent. Time to take action.

Instead of going to the door, I course-correct toward the stage. "Owen," I say urgently, coming up with a bullshit theatrical criticism on the spot: "We need to—rethink Biff's emotional progression in the end of the scene."

Owen, whom I internally thank for waiting by the door this whole time, hesitates uncertainly. I give him a pointed look and glance at Madeleine. His face softens as he understands. "Yeah, do you want me to run the lines, and you can tell me where it goes wrong?" he asks, dropping his bag and walking to the stage.

"That'd be great," I practically sigh in relief.

Madeleine rolls her eyes, understanding what's going on here. I should've known I'm not a good enough actress to sell this excuse. "Please? It'll only take a second," she begs while Owen climbs onto the stage, looking thoroughly uncomfortable.

I ignore her. "Whenever you're ready, Owen."

"He did like me. Always liked—" he begins before Madeleine cuts him off.

"Enough, Megan." She walks up to the stage. "This is so typically you. Something goes wrong, and you're ready to move on like our friendship was never important to you." The sudden fire in her voice stops me. It's not something I hear often from poised, polished Madeleine. Not something anyone hears often. "I'm your best friend," she continues, "and I made a mistake."

"Forgetting to return a library book is a mistake," I scoff. "And yeah, you were my best friend, but—Owen, where do you think you're going?" He's inching toward the side door, trying to escape. He turns back, his expression pained.

"I'm *still* your best friend," Madeleine returns. "I'm still the girl who was there for you when your stepmom moved in, who pulled all-nighters blocking scenes with you in your room, who picked you up from a hundred rehearsals when you didn't have a car. You remember when you asked me if being perfect was exhausting?" She pauses, but she doesn't sound like she's waiting for an answer. Her anger has faded, and her eyes fill with tears. "Well, now you know I'm not. What's exhausting is having to look like I am, having to live up to everyone's expectations. Sometimes I feel like if even one person figures out the truth, I'll—disappear. I know lying to you was worse than kissing Tyler, but I couldn't tell you. I couldn't watch the person who means the most to me realize I'm not who she thought I was."

I say nothing, weighing her words. I want to forgive

her because it's obvious how terrible she feels, and I'm no stranger to forgiving people who've hurt me. I really liked Anthony, but I forgave him for dating me when he knew he had a thing for guys. He wasn't out and wanted to keep up appearances, and I sympathized with his situation. I even forgave Tyler for dumping me for my best friend, and I guess I've already forgiven him again for cheating on me.

But Madeleine hurt me worse than any boyfriend, because almost every boyfriend isn't supposed to be forever. Madeleine and I were.

She wipes her eyes, her 4.0-GPA, after-school-volunteer composure returning. "That's what I wanted to say. If it's worth anything, I'm sorry and I miss you."

With that, she walks toward the door.

Owen shifts uncomfortably on his feet. I watch his eyes flit from me to her and back.

I don't want to give up on Madeleine. I don't know if she's made this right or not—I don't know if she could ever make this right—but sometimes not giving up on somebody means forgiving them even when it feels like the hardest thing in the world. If I want Madeleine and me to be forever, I can't let her leave feeling like her apology was worth nothing.

"Wait," I call after her.

She stops just short of the door. Slowly she turns, her eyes expectant but guarded, like she's not daring to hope. I walk off the stage to where she's standing, and despite how she's crossed her arms, I step forward and wrap her in a hug. She stiffens, startled for a second, before wriggling her arms free and hugging me back.

"I get it," I say over her shoulder. "You could never disappear." She hugs me tighter, and I hear her sniffle. I hold her for a minute longer until her breathing comes more evenly. "You even had the perfect apology, stupid," I add with a chuckle.

I feel her laugh into my shoulder.

Madeleine and I take a detour to the bathroom so we don't look like emotional wrecks when we get home. She's a renowned ugly crier, a reputation earned amid the A-minus-in-AP-Euro debacle of sophomore year. I'm not faring much better, my mascara streaking black lines down my face like I'm in an emo music video.

We part ways in the hallway after we've put ourselves together. Walking back to the drama room, I run into Owen, who's coming out the door in the opposite direction.

"Owen!" I say, surprised. "You're still here."

"Uh, yeah. You left your stuff in there." He holds up my bag and jacket.

"Thanks. You didn't have to wait for me." I take my things from his outstretched hand. "You want to go get pizza? I was going to drop in on Anthony."

"That depends." Owen grins. "Do you have a tearful reconciliation with him scheduled for today, too?"

I laugh. "Nope, I got that one done a couple weeks ago." We walk toward the front of the Arts Center, and I pull out my phone. "I'll text Will. He should come, too. I know how much you love to watch us flirt."

"It's practically an extracurricular activity," Owen returns, giving me a sideways glance. "I could probably put it on my college applications by now."

I roll my eyes. When I begin typing the message, he reaches over and covers the screen with his hand.

"Please," he says with mock desperation. "Call him. By the time he deciphers your mangled stream of abbreviations and dropped punctuation, we'll be there."

"Will understands me just fine," I say indignantly, shoving him lightly. But the idea of getting Will on the phone does sound good. I hit the CALL icon, pointedly ignoring Owen's triumphant smirk. It's a couple rings before Will picks up.

"Oh. Hey, Megan?" Will's voice sounds distracted.

"Hey. Owen and I are going to Verona. Meet us there in fifteen?" Owen holds the door for me, and we walk out into the quad.

"Now?" Will says in my ear. "I'm, um, kind of busy. I have to run some errands for set crew."

"It's seven at night, Will," I say more softly.

"Yeah, we're really behind." I think I hear his voice take on a bit of a defensive edge.

I want to be the cool girlfriend who doesn't mind stuff like this, who doesn't blink when her boyfriend has other plans, who doesn't overanalyze whether he's avoiding her. But I can't hide how much the brush-off deflates me. "You've been kind of busy a lot lately," I hear myself say.

He exhales over the line. "I know. I'm sorry. We'll do something this weekend," he promises. "Once the showcase is over."

I hear the sincerity in his tone, and the idea of a real date this weekend replaces my worry about his reluctance tonight. I glance at Owen walking beside me. "Okay. I'm going to make Owen help me come up with something awesome for us to do."

Owen looks back at me, his eyes wide and horrified. "I am *not* helping Will get laid."

I cover the mic on the bottom of my phone. "What about *me*?" I ask Owen, batting my eyes. "Will you help me get laid?" His ears redden, and he speeds into the parking lot a couple steps ahead of me.

"Huh?" Will's voice pulls me back to the phone. "Uh. Yeah. Okay. I'll talk to you tomorrow."

"Sounds good." I drop my phone into my bag and catch up to Owen. It's night, and the parking lot's single light casts the pavement in orange. "Meet you over there," I half shout to him in the fog now rolling through the trees.

"Or you could give me a ride?" He's stopped next to the light pole.

The moment he says it, I notice mine is the only car in the school lot. "Yeah, of course." I remember the time I saw him walking to school and he refused the ride I offered him. "Do you walk every day?" I contemplate the distances. From Owen's house to mine and mine to school . . . "Isn't your house, like, four miles from here?" I open my car door.

He goes to the passenger door and gets in next to me.

206

"Yeah, my mom usually needs the car. One of her jobs is on one end of town, the other on . . . the other." He shrugs. "I do like the time to think. It's why I don't take the bus."

Impressed and feeling very lucky for my old Volkswagen, I say nothing. We pull out of the parking lot and drive the rest of the way in silence. Past a certain time of day, the roads in Stillmont get eerily quiet. There aren't many restaurants in town, and most people eat at home, which is why there's not much of a dinner rush—and why we end up at places like Verona Pizza when we do dine out.

Shall I compare thee to a $4.99 breadsticks platter? reads the sign lit on a backdrop of the forest when we pull up.

Inside, Anthony catches sight of Owen and me and escorts us to one of the booths lining the far wall. We pass Eric wiping a table, and I tap Anthony on the shoulder from behind. "Hey, how's—" I catch myself before I say his name. "Nope, not going to mention you-know-who."

"Voldemort?" Owen asks, grinning unhelpfully.

"Knock it off, Owen." I smack him on the shoulder, and we take our seats on opposite sides of the booth.

Anthony smiles at me. "It's okay." Glancing over his shoulder in Eric's direction, he drops his voice. "He's been giving me weird looks today, actually." I stay silent but raise my eyebrows knowingly. Catching the look and rolling his eyes, Anthony says, "I have to get your drinks."

I turn to Owen, who's been watching our conversation with writerly interest. "Okay, date ideas," I say, opening the Notes app on my phone. "Let's go."

"Do we have to?" he groans.

"Please, Owen? I need your help." I smile at him coquettishly.

"*My* help? Girlfriend who lives in Italy, remember?" His brow rises with wry incredulity. "I don't exactly have dating experience. And definitely none in Stillmont."

Okay, he has a point. Anthony drops off two Sprites, then leaves before we have the chance to order. "But you know Will," I say to Owen, taking a sip of flat soda. *Fuck this place. Really.*

"Yet somehow I've never taken Will out on a date," he replies, sounding amused.

"Come on. If Cosima suddenly came to town, where would be the first place you'd take her? Besides your bedroom, of course." I try for my usual provocative nonchalance. But to my genuine surprise, the joke tastes bitter on my tongue. The idea of some beautiful, foreign girl in Owen's bedroom isn't exactly hilarious.

Owen, however, doesn't seem fazed. His eyes have gone distant while he considers. "I'd take her to Birnam Wood Books," he announces after a second.

I flush despite myself. "I love that place!"

Owen's eyes find mine, and I can tell he's pleased. "But it's not Will's thing."

"Oh." I push aside my disappointment. *I* thought he liked it. "What about the old movie theater downtown?"

"The Constantine?" he says immediately.

"Do you think he'd like that?"

He pauses and finally shakes his head. "I tried to convince

him to go once to a Jean-Luc Godard screening, but he wasn't into it."

"Well, what *does* he like?" I ask, exasperated. "Paintball? Thai food? Strip clubs? Please let it not be strip clubs."

"Concerts?" Owen sounds like he's guessing. "He's mentioned the all-ages club on Route 46. You know, the one where college students pretend they're DJs on the weekend."

I wince. "I hate that place. Why is this so hard?" I open the Internet on my phone and search "best date spots in Stillmont." Before the page loads, Anthony swings by and drops a tray of pizza on our table. Or—*pizzas*. There's a whole pie's worth of slices on the platter, but each appears to have come from the remnants of a different table's meal.

"What the hell is this?" I ask, pushing apart two of the obviously disparate slices with a tentative finger.

"It looks like free pizza." Anthony shoots me a reproving look. Owen swallows a smile.

"From *other people's tables*?"

Owen reaches for a slice. "It looks delicious." He piles enthusiasm on the word. I watch in horror as he takes a bite of what I vaguely recognize was once a Benvolio's Banquet.

Anthony glances at me as if to say *told you so* before he walks away, presumably to check on his other tables. Since I'm definitely going nowhere near the undoubtedly plague-ridden pizza, I pick up my phone to find that the search results have loaded. I tap the top one, which looks promising. It's a list of "Ten Places to Date in Stillmont" from the *Josephine County Courier*.

"Owen, come over here." I slide to make room on my side of the booth.

He doesn't move. "But I'm eating," he protests through a mouthful.

"Well, bring your reject pizza with you." I pat the seat next to me. With an exasperated grunt I know he doesn't mean, Owen carries his plate and pizza with him, and sits down next to me. His elbow brushes mine, and just like that I'm very aware of how short this bench is. It's probably meant to hold nine-year-olds.

I scroll down the list, feeling him looking over my shoulder. Birnam Wood Books, the Constantine, and the club on Route 46 go by. With Stillmont's size, I guess I shouldn't be surprised there's not a ton of places for this sort of thing.

Owen stops me in the middle of one final halfhearted scroll, his hand grazing mine. "I've been there," he says, setting his pizza down and pointing to an entry called Bishop's Peak.

"Where's there?" I study the photo. It's of a campground on a mountain overlooking a forest. The view is ridiculous, honestly. Judging by how much higher it is than the dense greenery below it, it must take hours to hike there.

"It's the end of this trail," he says, his shoulder pressing against mine. "It's beautiful and quiet. It would be the perfect place to take someone if you want to be alone with them."

I tilt my head to look at him. "It sounds like you're speaking from experience." I raise an eyebrow.

He laughs, and I realize I feel him shaking all down the

length of my side. "No, I was just there to write. I definitely did not get lucky up there."

"Well, we should do something about that." It's out of my mouth before I fully realize what it sounds like I'm implying. Owen stiffens.

But he's not the only one. The flirtatious stuff I say is always designed to put guys on edge and intrigue them, to make them think about me in a way they might not have. But this time, it backfired. *This* time, I'm unable to think about anything but where my skin touches Owen's below my sleeve. My face gets hot, and I realize I'm blushing at my own joke.

I feel an unfamiliar urge to put distance between the two of us, but I'm penned in by the wall. Instead, I settle for clearing the air. "It sounds like it would be a great date spot," I say haltingly. I uncomfortably rub the Ophelia bracelet from Will.

"It's where I'd take you," Owen replies quickly. Realizing what he's said, he stutters, "I mean, where I'd—where'd you—where Will should take you."

Well, now we've both gone and said way too much. I have to smile. Nudging his shoulder, I watch his ears go that delightful, familiar shade of red. "You and I *should* go there." His eyes widen. "To brainstorm for your play," I add with a wink.

I lean farther into him, and it feels like giving in to how much I like the sound of the things we've suggested. I don't exactly know why, but I'm drawn to Owen. I probably have been for a while. I guess the reason my flirtatious joke backfired is that it wasn't a joke at all.

Except I have a boyfriend. Having to remind myself of that is as unexpected as everything else tonight. In all of my relationships, I'm never the one to forget her commitment.

Will. I want to go to Bishop's Peak with Will. I'm going there with Will.

Owen's face is still close to mine, our shoulders still pressed tightly together. And when I lift my gaze to meet his, I find him watching me with inevitability in his eyes, like he knows exactly what I was close to doing because he's been waiting for it.

Which is why I blurt out, "I need to pee."

He pulls back, looking confused. "Oh," he says.

"So I need to get out," I say heatedly, beginning to step over him. My lingering confusion has given way to frustration with myself, frustration about not knowing what I want. Or worse, worrying that I might know exactly what I want.

"Oh." He stumbles out of the booth. "Were you just going to climb over me?"

I slide down and straighten up. "You say that like it'd be a bad thing," I say, stepping past him, attempting to force my voice into its old flirty flippancy. I don't think it works. Not wanting to hear Owen's reply, I dart in the direction of the bathroom, nearly colliding with a group of middle-school girls.

I barrel through the swinging door. Like every other inch of this restaurant, the bathroom's walls are covered in Shakespeare verses. I face the mirror and ignore them, the way I always do.

I turn on the faucet and splash cold water on my face.

"This is ridiculous," I tell myself out loud in the mirror. *I do not like Owen Okita. He's a great friend, but he's not my type. Tyler, Dean, Will, they're my type. Owen's bookish, quiet, and constantly preoccupied with his journal,* I remind myself.

Okay, he's kind of cute, with his startled smile and the way his ears redden every time I—

"Stop," I order myself. "I have a boyfriend." He's overcommitted, but my boyfriend nonetheless. Owen has an imaginary girlfriend. We're friends. Nothing else.

I turn and head for the stall. But one word written in several places jumps out at me from the quotes on the wall. "LOVE is merely a madness." "I know no ways to mince it in LOVE, but directly to say, 'I LOVE you.'" "LOVE comforteth like sunshine after rain." "The course of true LOVE never did run smooth." Whoever bothered to paint them there used obnoxiously iridescent colors everywhere they wrote *love*.

I slam the stall door behind me.

As I'm about to sit down, I hear the bathroom door open and close, followed by a low voice asking, "Megan?"

"*Eric?*" I nearly stumble. That could have been tragic.

"I—I know," he rushes to reply. "This is bad."

"Why— What are you doing in here?" Why does this keep happening? Why do people get the impression cornering me in a stall is a good time to start a conversation? I pull up my pants.

"It's about Anthony." Eric walks farther into the bathroom. Grudgingly, I unlock the stall and step out to face him. "I didn't want him to overhear. He's pissed, isn't he?" he asks nervously. I open my mouth to answer, but he continues. "Of course he is. He probably hates me. You probably hate me, too. I promise I wasn't using Anthony because I can keep him a secret. I don't *want* to keep him a secret, it's just— My dad called. He wanted to know where I was. I think he guessed, and— He doesn't— And Anthony— He's, you know—"

I interrupt him. "Eric, I feel like you should be saying this to"—I glance toward the door—"someone else?"

He vehemently shakes his head, and he looks defeated. "Not while he's avoiding me. If he doesn't want to talk to me, I don't want to force him. I just want him to know what happened." He raises his gaze from the floor and looks at me. "If you could just—"

"Eric, it's not my place to get between the two of you," I say firmly. What Anthony told me was that he wanted to hit pause on things with Eric, and I promised him I wouldn't meddle or rush him along. Telling Eric anything about Anthony's feelings would undermine his wishes and break my word.

"But—" Eric starts.

"No buts. I'm rooting for you, Eric, but you have to talk to him yourself," I say with finality.

Eric nods forlornly. "I just really like him," he says after a moment's pause. Knocking his knuckles once on the sink, he turns to leave.

"Eric," I call him back. "Give me your phone."

"Why?" Confusion narrows his eyes, but he holds out his phone.

"For when it goes well with Anthony," I tell him while I type my number into his contacts. "I'll want to hear about it *without* you cornering me in the bathroom." I pass the phone back to Eric, whose expression has lifted into a smile.

He gives me a nod and pushes open the door. Briefly, I wonder if anyone notices him exiting the girls' bathroom before I go back into the stall to do what I came here for. I follow Eric out a couple minutes later.

I start to return to our table, but I stop when I see Owen's back on his side of his booth, writing in his journal. I don't know if I wanted him to have moved or not, but it doesn't seem like what a guy would do if he was into whatever was happening between us before.

It hurts a little. I consider dropping into the seat next to him, our shoulders touching like they were minutes ago. Out of an impulse that's part instinct and part something deeper, I want to recapture the way it felt to be pressed against him while he looked at me with guarded anticipation. To—

No. Owen moved for a reason. I should respect that. It felt good to honor what Anthony wanted regarding Eric, and Owen deserves the same consideration. Even if I did like him—which I *probably* don't, not really, not in a way that could last—I wouldn't want to push him into something he obviously doesn't want. Not to mention the fact *he has a girlfriend.*

I slide into the booth opposite him. Feeling bold bordering on reckless, I grab a slice of lukewarm Montague Meat Lovers. Owen doesn't look up from whatever he's writing.

"I'm going to take Will to the club of the college DJs," I nonchalantly announce.

"Wait, why?" Owen's head pops up. Blue ink stains his

throat just beneath the corner of his jaw, and I wonder what he was mulling over while he rubbed his neck. "What happened to Bishop's Peak?" he asks tentatively, either relieved or disappointed.

I'm not going to bother wondering which it is—I just want things back to normal. "You should have it. If you call it quits with the imaginary girlfriend and settle for a humble Stillmont girl, you're going to need a place to get it on."

He says nothing, but he gives his startled smile, and his ears redden.

EIGHTEEN

BENVOLIO: *Alas that love, so gentle in his view,*

Should be so tyrannous and rough in proof!

ROMEO: *Alas that love, whose view is muffled still,*

Should without eyes see pathways to his will!

I.i.174–7

IT'S THE FINAL MOMENTS OF BRIAN ANDERSON and Jason Mitchum's *Rosencrantz and Guildenstern Are Dead* scene. It never fails to surprise me how tranquil everything seems on stage, how measured and quiet. The actors are the only moving pieces on the fixed world of the set, in front of the audience watching in hushed stillness.

Backstage, it's chaos. But I'm not complaining. Despite the nonstop commotion in the wings of the theater, the Senior Showcase is going beautifully, and I love the frenzy of the minutes before a performance.

In the girls' dressing room, I step over piles of midcentury coats and medieval dresses in search of a tie. I spot it sticking out underneath someone's bright purple bra. I pull the tie out and rush for the door. But before I reach it, I glance into the mirror and have to stop.

Jenna Cho, aka my Linda Loman, is smoothing her hair,

seemingly oblivious to the fact she's wearing only one eye-lash.

"Jenna!" I hiss, and she looks at me in the mirror. "Check your eyes. I think you're missing something."

"Ohmygod," she gasps, fumbling for her makeup bag.

I dart from the room and duck into the green room down the hall. It's wall-to-wall insanity. With everyone else's scenes done, the rest of the actors have begun sneaking drinks from the flasks some of the guys smuggled in, still dressed in a wild array of half-costumes and stage makeup. My eyes quickly find Kasey Markowitz in the corner, muttering to herself, re-hearsing her lines.

"Kasey. Here." I hand her the tie. She's dressed in a suit, her hair tucked up under a fedora. She grabs the tie without pausing in her line. "You need help with that?" I ask, the syl-lables stringing together so they sound like one word.

"Nope." Effortlessly, she wraps the tie around her collar and winds it into a perfect knot.

I don't have time to be surprised before a stagehand taps me on the shoulder. "The briefcase prop," he says breathless-ly. It's little Andrew Mehta, a sophomore.

I wait for him to say more. "What about it?" I fire back when he doesn't.

"It's not on the props table."

I sigh. *Of course it isn't.* "Try the guys' dressing room. Tyler keeps forgetting to return it to props." Andrew rushes off, and I find Owen near the door. He's frantically fiddling with his collar, and I have to laugh.

"Need a hand?" I gently tease, coming up beside him and

wrapping my fingers in the tie he's mangled into nothing resembling a proper knot.

He won't meet my eyes. "Uh, thanks." He fidgets with his cuffs like he can hardly stand still while I undo the damage.

"You're going to be great," I reassure him, knowing stage fright when I see it. I begin the knot and find Owen's now looking down at me—I guess I never noticed he's about six feet tall, much taller than I am—a distracted, unconvincing smile on his face.

"*We* will be, the whole cast. You've done an incredible job pulling this together."

I feel warmth spread through me, but I focus on evening out the ends of the tie. "Hey, have you seen Will?"

He looks away again. "He said he might be a little late."

"What?" I pause in mid-knot. Will didn't tell me he'd be late. Once more I hear the vicious voice in my head telling me to be the cool girlfriend, but this isn't just a trip to Verona. "This is the showcase. This is, like, important . . ."

Owen reaches up to his collar and places a hand on mine. Gently, he squeezes my fingers. His wrist is dotted with familiar blue ink, and even though he's in costume I know his notebook and pen aren't far away. The observation relaxes me somehow. When I look up, his eyes have returned to me. "He knows. Don't worry about him," he says delicately. "The show will go perfectly."

His hand is still on mine, and I should pull away, but I'm having a hard time remembering why I like Will and not Owen. I rub the stain on his wrist. "Did no one teach you how to use a pen?"

He blinks once, then his eyes find my finger wiping ineffectually at the blue spot. "I press down on them too hard," he says, his voice a controlled murmur. He doesn't remove his hand. "I can wash it off if you want."

"No, I like it," I say, but I don't stop kneading my thumb across his wrist. Distantly, the applause for the previous scene sounds through the wall. I drop my hand. "That's our cue."

Owen's eyes flicker, like he's just remembered where he is. "Right."

I usher him in the direction of the stage right stairs, then sweep my eyes over the green room for inattentive cast members. Finding no one, I make my own way backstage, noticing faint blue smudges now coloring my fingertips. I smile even as my chest constricts with the mixture of excitement and nerves that begin every performance.

My actors have lined up in the wings, and I watch them file on, Tyler with his briefcase. Peering around the curtain, I look into the audience. But the stage lights are on, and I can only make out the first couple rows. I search the faces of drama underclassmen, proud grandparents, and the occasional teacher.

Nowhere do I find Will.

Fighting disappointment, I turn my attention back to my scene. "Call out the name Willy Loman and see what happens! Big shot!" Tyler proclaims with desperate bravado.

"All right, Pop," Owen replies, placating.

Somebody sneezes in one of the front rows, and I whip my head back to the audience to find a mortified-looking, allergy-stricken freshman sitting next to—*Rose?*

She's by herself, Erin nowhere in sight, and she's put herself together annoyingly perfectly for a woman eight months pregnant. Her hair's done up in a neat bun, and she's wearing the dangly earrings she can't around Erin and a long-sleeve dress that highlights just how little weight she's gained.

Dad's in New York, doing something house-related. I guess Rose would have had to drop Erin off at Aunt Charlotte's, and she came without Dad bringing her. I want to be grateful— she was kind to even look up when the showcase was, let alone make arrangements to come. Yet instead, what I feel is guilty, even a little bitter.

If not for the divorce, it would've been my mom in the front row. She was the one to drag my dad and me to SOTI performances, and she even brought me to the occasional Stillmont High School production when I was younger. She would have loved to be here. Somehow Rose showing up tonight feels like she's encroaching on my mom's and my relationship in a way Rose living under our roof doesn't.

"Don't yell at her, Pop, will ya?" Owen's incensed voice pulls my focus back to the stage. In the moment, because of the way I've blocked the scene and the way Owen's squaring his shoulders, he actually looks bigger than Tyler on the stage. He's bringing an intensity to the final lines that he hadn't in rehearsals, and I'm impressed.

Tyler hunches over and drops his voice to deliver Willy's final line. "Give my best to Bill Oliver—he may remember me." A couple of people in the audience covertly try to wipe their eyes in the heavy pause that follows.

The lights come back on, and the audience applauds as my actors take their bows. Feeling the heady rush of a perfect performance, I begin to step back from the curtain—but then I catch Tyler beckoning me on stage, wearing the ridiculous grin he gets every time he's in front of an adoring audience.

"No way," I mouth while Tyler continues to wave me on.

I watch him—unbelievably—exchange a knowing glance with Owen, who darts to where I'm hiding behind the curtain and, before I know it, hauls me by the elbow onto the stage. He holds me firmly in place under the spotlight.

"Could we give an extra-loud round of applause for Megan Harper," Tyler shouts to the crowd. "Who's probably going to kill me because of this, but not right now. Too many witnesses." The audience laughs, still under Tyler's spell. I can't blame them. Even if he's right and I will kill him after this.

"Not only is Megan an extraordinary director, she put together the entire Senior Showcase," he continues. "She's done amazing work in four years of bringing drama to life on this stage—and giving me more opportunities than I deserve to make a fool of myself in front of you guys." He unleashes his cockiest grin for the span of a second before his features settle into something sincere. "It's been an honor working with her."

Nothing in my history with Tyler prepares me for the way he looks at me then—with genuine respect. A stagehand comes out of the wings bearing a ridiculous bouquet of white orchids, and Owen gives my arm a reassuring squeeze. I turn to look at him, but he's already releasing me and stepping back out of the spotlight. Leaving me alone at the center of everything.

Heat rises in my cheeks. I must have taken the flowers from Andrew Mehta's hands, because distantly I'm aware of the petals pressed against my shoulder while the audience applauds me.

By choosing to be a director, I've tried to avoid moments like these—moments where everyone's eyes are on me, where my classmates' cheers and Rose's loving smile are for me. I thought this would feel like an unwelcome reminder of what I'll inevitably lose when everyone moves on. But it doesn't.

It feels like everything I've missed out on.

I hear someone backstage shout, "Get it!" and I know without a shred of doubt it's Anthony, whose *Pulp Fiction* monologue was, for the record, amazing. Jenna and Kasey laugh behind me, and in the moments that follow, the applause gradually dies down. Everyone begins to shuffle out of the auditorium, everyone except Madeleine. She pushes through the crowd to reach the stage, her smile lit up with pride.

I jump down off the stage next to her. "You on your way to meet Tyler in the boys' dressing room?" I ask, waiting for her to flush.

Which she does. *"No,"* she protests. "I'm waiting for my incredibly talented, gorgeous, director-extraordinaire best friend." She sweeps me up in a crushing hug.

"You're the best for coming," I say into her sweatshirt. "Now seriously, I saw Tyler go backstage."

Madeleine releases me from the hug and glances behind me, hesitating.

"I have to go talk to Rose," I reassure her. "You should congratulate Tyler. I'll find you later." She squeezes me in a final hug, but it's all the encouragement she needs, and she bounces to the stairs up to the stage. I join the crush of people filing into the quad. Hoping to find Will—I figure he has to be here somewhere—I do a quick sweep of the crowd outside. I frown when I don't find him, but then again, it's nearly impossible to tell who all's here.

Rose, however, stands out. She's waiting next to the re-freshments table, and despite how packed the courtyard is, everyone's giving her pregnant stomach a three-foot radius. She looks lost. I understand why—she's never done this kind of thing before.

I walk over to her, not really knowing what I'm going to say. I want to thank her for coming, but we don't often talk one-on-one. It's not like I have a script for this sort of thing. Besides, I still feel like I'm betraying my mom by being happy Rose is here.

Her eyes light up when she spots me coming out of the crowd. Instead of telling her something appreciative, what ends up coming out when I reach her is, "Where's Erin?"

Rose blinks, then her composure returns. "I figured we should wait until she's three before we expose her to *Death of a Salesman*'s suburban nihilism," she replies, and despite myself, I laugh. Encouraged, she smiles gently. "It was won-derful to watch your scene. The whole thing, really. You put on quite an event. I loved your staging—how Willy was in-creasingly isolated from the rest of the actors as his advice grew more delusional."

I reach for words, surprised. It's precisely what I was going for. "You—know the play?"

"I was an English major in college," she says with a smile. Betrayal of Mom or not, I feel guilty I didn't know that about Rose. There's probably a lot I don't know about her, I realize. Where she grew up, her favorite movie, whether she's ever been in a play herself, why she chose to be a paralegal.

"It was really nice of you to come," I finally say, knowing I should've just done so earlier.

"I'm glad I could." She nods to something behind me, her smile turning knowing and playful. "Looks like Biff Loman wants to talk to you, which I think is my cue. I'll see you at home."

"Yeah. See you there."

"You want me to take your flowers?" She points to the bouquet I forgot I was holding.

"Oh." I hold them out to her awkwardly. "Probably a good idea. Thanks," I say, then turn to find Owen a few feet behind me, fidgeting with his tie.

I walk up to him and tug it out of his hands. "You were incredible," I tell him, meaning it. He smiles for only a second before his nervousness returns. He looks just like he did in the green room, wracked with stage anxiety. Except the scene's over. "What's wrong?"

His eyes drop. "Could we, uh, talk somewhere?"

"Definitely, but give me a second. I haven't found Will yet. I should let him know before I disappear on him." I look past Owen to search the quad, where there's still no sign of Will, but Owen takes my hand. My eyes latch on to his.

"That's what I wanted to talk to you about." His voice is lower, urgent now. I feel a tremor tighten my chest.

"Owen, what's going on?"

"We should talk somewhere private."

He gently leads me by the hand back into the auditorium, up the stairs to the vacant backstage, and toward the green room. It's empty except for Brian Anderson, who nods with a smile I'm too wound-up to return. "Kickass job, Megan," he says, stepping over the ears from Courtney's cat costume on his way out.

"Thanks," I say distractedly. "Your Rosencrantz was kickass too, Brian."

"Totally, right?" He shuts the door behind him.

Without a moment's hesitation, I round on Owen. "You've been acting weird today." A horrible explanation drops onto my heart like a lead weight. "Is this about the other day at Verona?"

"No, it's not— Wait, what?" His eyes betray no impression he's bothered by our possibly flirtatious, definitely awkward discussion of Bishop's Peak.

"Never mind," I say, relieved.

Owen goes on, his words coming in a rush. "Will texted before the performance telling me he wasn't going to make it. I should have told you then, but I didn't want you to worry about him instead of watching your scene. You've put so much work into tonight." He looks off into a corner of the room. I watch his jaw clench and the tendons in his neck tense visibly. He's not nervous, he's angry. "I hate Will for doing this. You're my friend, and I don't want to hide stuff from you—"

"Owen," I cut him off, wanting him to just get it over with. "What is it?"

He produces his phone from his pocket, and I catch a glimpse of a photo of the Brooklyn Bridge on the screen—probably a place he took Cosima when they were in New York together for the theater program. Wordlessly, he opens the Messages app and passes me the phone.

The conversation on the screen is with Will. My eyes land on his text reading, **Hey Owen . . . Cover for me, k? I don't think I'm going to make it.** It's time-stamped twenty minutes before we went on stage. Before I fixed Owen's tie and he told me Will would be late.

I scroll down. Owen instantly texted him back. **What the hell?? What could you possibly be doing besides going to your girlfriend's show?**

Will didn't reply until ten minutes ago. **I'm at Alyssa's man! Not leaving anytime soon ;)**

A winky face. It's stunning how hard the semicolon and parenthesis knock the wind out of me.

I return Owen's phone, unable to read the screen a second longer. Will's words repeat in my head like a broken record. Utterly broken. *At Alyssa's. Not leaving anytime soon.* I expected this. I expected this. Didn't I? Even if I'd begun to wonder about . . . someone else, I put away those questions because I cared about Will. Or convinced myself to care. Why was I stupid enough to believe he cared about me?

Owen's watching me with concerned eyes. "I'm sorry, Megan. He's an asshole," he says, and I can tell he means it. I'm not ready to reply. "This is the first I've ever heard of him and Alyssa," he goes on. "I had no idea. Otherwise, I would have said something."

"It's fine," I get out, hearing how hollow my voice sounds. "It's not like I haven't been through this before."

"Don't do that." He frowns. "Don't pretend it's fine, because I know it's not. What Will did was messed up, and you *should* be pissed at him."

The empty ache fills with anger. But not at Will. "I know how to handle a breakup, Owen," I snap, knowing he doesn't deserve my resentment but not bothering to control it. "Don't tell me what I *should be* feeling."

He flinches. "It's not— What I mean is you deserve better."

As quickly as it flared up, my anger collapses. "My boyfriend didn't think so." I feel tears choking my voice, and my eyes start to burn. *Damn it*, I thought I was past being hurt by this kind of thing.

"Will is a moron," Owen says gently. "I'm definitely not giving him any more lyrics for his stupid band." A tearful laugh escapes me, and Owen smiles. "What you deserve is to go out and celebrate this incredible show you put together. Everyone's going to Verona. I'll buy you a real pizza—you know, one we ordered, not someone's leftovers."

I smile weakly. "But what about your costume? Don't you need to change?" I nod to the gray suit and pinstriped tie he's still wearing.

"I'm not worried about it." He shrugs. "Besides, I won't look any more ridiculous than the employees." He holds the door open for me.

"Thanks," I say. He wraps an arm around my shoulder, and I know he understands I don't just mean the door.

Walking into the empty auditorium, I remember every time I've joked with Madeleine, Anthony, and even Owen about my "curse," my "whirlwind romances," my endless stream of breakups. It's less funny now. It's easier to joke when I'm not feeling this, when I'm not feeling replaceable. But the truth is, I have no reason to hope I won't be playing this role forever. To hope one day I'll be the one chosen and not just the girl before.

NINETEEN

FRIAR LAWRENCE: *Confusion's cure lives not*

In these confusions.

IV.v.71–2

I KNOW ABOUT ALYSSA. WE'RE DONE, I text Will the following day. I silence my phone, not wanting to read whatever he replies, and in a final moment of closure, I slide off Will's Ophelia bracelet and throw it behind me.

I'm sitting in my car in front of Luna's Coffee Company, the only coffee shop in town other than Birnam Wood Books and the Starbucks in the mall. It's in the nicer part of Still-mont, up the street from the salon where Madeleine and I had our hair done before junior prom last year. I proposed Randall and I meet here when we coordinated this morning.

It's a testament to the awfulness of my weekend that the prospect of coffee with Randall doesn't sound terrible. I'm here early, but I decide I don't need to spend more time sitting in my car dwelling on Will. I walk in and begin to head for the line, but I stop when I realize Randall's already sitting at a table, giving me a tentative wave. I suppose I shouldn't be surprised he's here early. He sounded especially enthusiastic on the phone this morning.

For whatever reason, he stands up when I reach the table. I try to take a seat, but before I have the chance, he's bending forward for one of those uncomfortable one-armed hugs. "Oh, uh . . ." I stutter, returning his hug.

We sit. It's only then that I notice Randall looks . . . better somehow. He's trimmed his usually overlong curly hair, and it's possible he's lost a couple pounds. He's not wearing one of his customary short-sleeve button-downs and opted for a navy polo instead. His mustache remains, however.

"Thanks for sparing the time to meet me, Megan," he says, grinning bashfully. "I ordered your favorite. Unless your favorite's changed since you visited over the summer." He gestures to the solitary cappuccino on the table.

"Thanks," I say. Despite whatever questions I have about Randall, I can't deny he's thoughtful.

I wait for him to say something. The burden of conversation is on the inviter, right? When a few moments go by and he doesn't, I try the only question coming to mind. "How was the flight?"

He looks startled, like he didn't expect us to talk during this coffee date. "It flew by. I had a full binder of spreadsheets to review," he says as if the one relates in any way to the other.

With no response to that, I wrack my brain for other Randall-related topics while the conversation descends into silence. Finally, one comes. "How's your and Mom's pottery class?" I know I'm fidgeting with the handle on my mug.

"It is terrific," Randall replies unhesitatingly. "Your mother's nearly finished a complete set of bowls for the house."

My mother, finisher of bowls.

"Cool," I say because I have literally no other way to contend with that statement.

"How's *Romeo and Juliet* going?" Randall asks.

I know he's trying. But right now, I'm in no mood to remind myself of playing Juliet on Will's sets, in front of Alyssa whispering behind my back. "It's good," I reply shortly.

He says nothing, and faced with the prospect of having to come up with a third conversation starter, I consider faking a call from my Dad or a forgotten obligation. But I decide to try one final question first. "Why'd your firm send you out to middle-of-nowhere Oregon?"

Randall's demeanor changes visibly. He shifts in his seat, his shoulders rising, and he reaches for a napkin and begins anxiously folding it in his lap. "They, uh, they didn't," he finally says. "It's what I wanted to talk to you about."

If his firm didn't send him to Stillmont, why is he here? "Does Mom know?"

"She doesn't," he replies haltingly, "and I, well, I need you to keep it that way."

"Okay, now you're making me nervous. I don't—"

"I want to propose to your mother," he interrupts.

My hand clenches on the cup of lukewarm cappuccino. "Oh." My mind empties. I'm unable to process what he said. "Um, okay."

Randall's face breaks into a grin. "Okay?"

"Yeah, uh . . . Wait, what?" He's looking at me like I've just done him a huge favor, but I don't know what it is.

"I wanted your permission." His grin falters when he realizes I haven't exactly given it. "You're the most important person in your mother's life, and of course you knew her before I did. I wouldn't feel right trying to build a family with her without your blessing."

The word *family* from Randall flips me upside down and shakes out my thoughts like the pieces of a puzzle. *Family.* Mom and Randall. It's the kind of thought that on most days would have me asking myself all the questions I have for months. If they start a family like Dad and Rose did, where will I fit in? Who will I be except the bump in the road before my parents found the families they wanted?

But today, something's different. My eyes find the place on my wrist where Will's bracelet no longer rests. I know none of my relationships can even begin to compare to what my parents had—years and decades of marriage, of messy effort, of memories stinging and sweet. I've never fallen for someone the way my mom fell for my dad.

Yet I know a piece of her pain. I know what it's like to watch the people you care about replace you and never look back. I've gone through it eight times now. In the hardest moments, when I face my mom and find my reflection, I can't help feeling convinced we'll end up the same in love, forever cast to play the Rosaline in real life. If Randall changes that for her, if he heals even a fraction of the wounds my dad inflicted . . . she should be with him, even if it means starting her own family without me.

I lift my gaze back to Randall. "I think you should definitely propose to my mom. It would make her really happy," I say softly, ignoring how the words ache.

He lets out a breath of relief. "I'm delighted to hear it!" He grins broadly. "I want to do it when the three of us are together. I thought . . . the trip when we're here for your performance in December might be the right time?"

Numb, I force myself to nod. "It sounds perfect."

When I get back to my car, I stupidly check my phone. Force of habit. Six unread messages from Will stare up at me.

> **Wait, what??**

> **I think you might have heard something and gotten the wrong idea . . . Call me, and I'll explain.**

> **You can't just ignore me, Megan. We at least have to talk.**

> **Fine. You're acting really immature, but if this is what you want, then fine.**

I scroll through the first couple, then delete the thread without reading the rest. I delete his number, too, just for good measure.

He and I were supposed to go on our date tonight to the shitty club on Route 46. That won't be happening, which at least spares me from a night amid sweaty, gyrating teenagers and throbbing techno music. With my weekend now pretty much unscheduled, my first thought is to text Madeleine. It's a post-breakup ritual to go to her house, bake homemade Pop-Tarts, and break out the middle-school yearbooks to mock the pictures of the boy in question.

But I hesitate. Madeleine spent the majority of her time with Tyler while I was pursuing Will. I love her, and talking to her would be a comfort, but she's not the one who knows every detail of the relationship. Instead, I find myself remembering the hours spent with Owen discussing even the most insignificant facets of my interactions with Will.

Owen. He's the one who's been there for me through the whole relationship. It's only right he help me with its end.

I drive to his neighborhood on the other end of town. It's nearing nighttime, and the streets are empty. The couple of people out walking are wrapped in coats and scarves, their breath visible under the streetlights. I crank the heat up in my car to compensate for winter settling in.

I park under one of the trees on Owen's street, a couple of houses up from his. Realizing I should probably check if he's busy before arriving on his doorstep, I pull out my phone and send, **hey**, testing the waters.

Hey. You doing okay? he replies a moment later.

my mom's getting married, I watch my thumbs type out and send, not fully knowing why.

It takes Owen longer to respond this time. A couple minutes go by. **Is that good or bad?** he sends.

good i guess. dont want her to be alone. I rub my bracelet-free wrist. It crosses my mind that I drove over here to talk about Will. Yet here I am, talking about my mom after one sentence.

You're not alone either, Megan. Do you want to come over for dinner? It takes him only a few seconds to reply, which is nearly as surprising as what he's said.

i wasnt talking abt me. Once I've sent that, I type out a second text. **but yes i wud thx.**

I'm reasonably certain you were.

I let that one lie, but I'm smiling to myself as I step out of the car. **im outside,** I send, walking up his driveway. He replies a second later.

Outside where?

TWENTY

ROMEO: *Thus with a kiss I die.*

V.iii.120

INSTEAD OF REPLYING, I RING THE DOORBELL. In my billowy floral dress, tights, and a denim jacket, I'm hardly dressed for the weather, and I hug myself while I wait. Running footsteps sound from the other side of the door, followed by Owen's voice.

"Sam, what's the rule about the door?" I hear him yell sternly.

The footsteps stop, and the voice that answers Owen sounds about ten years old. "No opening it without checking who it is first," the voice glumly replies. I step back, smoothing my dress, expecting scrutiny through the small peephole. "It's some girl . . . wearing grandma clothes." I cross my arms, affronted if not a little amused.

"She's pretty," the voice—Sam—continues, redeeming himself. "Prettier than Cosmo."

Ha! I'm going to like Sam.

"It's Cosima," I hear Owen exasperatedly correct him. The door swings open, revealing Owen, his ears their natural shade of red, and a small boy with spiked hair, Owen-y features, and a *Minecraft* T-shirt. *"Very* sorry about my brother," Owen says emphatically, then glances behind me, his lips forming a light smile. "You hang out outside my house often?"

I stride inside, refusing to be embarrassed. "Hey, this is a nice street. Good lighting, great, um—trees."

His grin widens knowingly. "If I'd known how much you liked the *trees*, I would have invited you over more often." He leads me toward the kitchen. "You know you're welcome whenever," he adds after a moment, his voice gentler this time.

In the kitchen, he grabs a striped apron and throws it over his head.

"You're making dinner?" I don't hide my surprise.

He stirs something on a pot on the stove. "Yeah, spaghetti. It's Sam's favorite."

"No, it's not!" Sam bellows from the other room.

Owen chuckles, and I realize they've had this conversation before. "It's his favorite of the things I can make," he explains to me, "which consists of spaghetti and spaghetti." Sam wanders into the kitchen, and Owen points the spoon at me. "Sam, this is my friend Megan. She's going to have dinner with us."

I face Sam, about to give him a wave hello, but he marches right up to me and sticks his hand out. "Nice to meet you," he says formally, shaking my hand in a small but impressive death grip.

"It's nice to meet you, too," I reply. "For your information, no grandmas have ever worn my clothes."

He squints at me. "You sure about that?"

"Sam," Owen warns.

"It's okay." I laugh. "He said I'm prettier than *Cosmo,* so we're cool." I glance at Owen, waiting to see how he'll contend with that, whether he'll defend his girlfriend or put his guest down. I consider it a victory when he wordlessly turns back to the stove and spoons pasta onto the plates.

He carries one into the dining room and places it on the small, scuffed table. Sam clambers into his seat, and I sit down opposite him while Owen returns with the other two plates.

"You're in Owen's play, right?" Sam asks between bites.

My mouth full, Owen replies for me. "Megan's the lead. She's the main character," he clarifies.

Sam's eyes widen, and he looks at me with new respect. "*You're* Juliet?"

"You know *Romeo and Juliet*?" I ask, intrigued. Apparently, a penchant for theater is an Okita family trait.

"Owen told me," Sam answers proudly. "He said it's about this girl who's like the coolest, most beautiful girl everyone's ever seen, and blah blah blah, and she likes some guy, and then everybody dies."

I smile at Owen, not overlooking the adjectives in Sam's summary. "What a deft Shakespearean commentary," I say, still looking at Owen. Then I raise an eyebrow at Sam. "Do *you* think I'll be a good Juliet?"

Sam shrugs. "Owen says you're, like, perfect."

I turn back to Owen, unable to restrain myself from wondering what else he's said about . . . my performance. But before I have the chance to ask, he's leaning over to ruffle his brother's hair. Sam yelps and swats him away, indignant that Owen's messing up his gelled spikes.

"How'd your spelling test go?" Owen asks, withdrawing his hand.

Sam groans, clearly having already forgotten his brother's infraction. "Ninety-eight percent," he mutters resentfully.

"What word did you get wrong?" Owen sounds playfully admonishing.

"Lead, the metal!" Sam pounds an emphatic hand on the table.

Owen laughs. "That one really gives you trouble, huh?"

"Well, Owen," I cut in, "lead's, like, the hardest word ever."

The two Okitas face me, Owen's expression skeptical. "Does that word stump you on your spelling tests, too, Megan?" He's not quite smirking, but the corner of his mouth is upturned.

"Don't be a smartass," I shoot back, then notice Sam's eyes widen. "Sorry," I tell him. "For your information, *Owen*"— I turn back to him—"lead is an inhumanly difficult word. Lead, the metal, is spelled like lead, the verb, which is the present tense of a verb of which the past tense is spelled L-E-D, pronounced led, like the metal, lead," I finish triumphantly.

Owen's smiling now, his mouth half-open in an expression of stunned amusement I don't bother to keep myself from noticing is cute.

"*She* gets it," Sam exclaims, throwing out a hand in my direction.

"I stand reeducated," Owen pronounces, then reaches over

to jostle his brother's shoulder. "Hey, buddy, ninety-eight percent is great. Mom's going to be really proud."

Sam straightens up in his seat, and I realize he's somehow finished all of his spaghetti. "Can I stay up tonight to tell her?"

"*That* depends on if you finish your homework. Quietly, *and* in your room," Owen tells him.

Sam hops off his chair and brings his dish into the kitchen. While he's out of the room, I gesture to where his spotless plate was. "How did he . . . ?" I whisper to Owen.

"He inhales it. I don't know. It's insane," he replies, taking a bite of his own nearly finished dinner.

Sam stomps into the doorway. "You guys aren't going to go *kiss* now, right?" he asks, like the question's a bomb he's been waiting to drop since I got here.

I laugh and dart a glance at Owen, who just points a finger into the hall. "I'm not going to dignify that with a response," he says, doing an impressive job of covering any embarrassment he might be feeling. "Homework. Now." Sam trudges into the hallway wearing a mischievous smirk he definitely didn't learn from Owen.

I spin a forkful of spaghetti. "Sounds like you do this kind of thing often," I say to Owen. "Sweep girls off their feet with the perfect-brother routine, then take them to your room for some *kissing*."

Owen scoffs, obviously playing dumb. "What perfect-brother routine?"

"Oh, please," I say through pasta. "The home-cooked dinner, the helping with his homework. Girls love that."

He feigns surprise. "I had no idea. I've had the perfect chick magnet right here the entire time." He picks up my plate, ever the gentleman, and brings both of our dishes into the kitchen. I walk over to help him. Usually now is when I'd nettle him about Cosima or keep teasing him about Sam's "kissing" remark, but for some indiscernible reason, I don't. Instead, we wash dishes in silence for a couple minutes before he speaks up. "Hey, uh, how are you . . ."

"Since your asshole friend cheated on me?" I supply.

"*Former* asshole friend," he quickly corrects, and I have to smile, knowing I was right when I figured he'd be the one who could lift my spirits.

"I'm okay," I say, and for the first time today I feel it's true. "I sent him a breakup text this afternoon. More than he deserves. Honestly, I'm happier eating spaghetti with you—and Sam, of course—than going to Club Trying-Too-Hard with him." He laughs, and I shrug. "It's for the best. I have a thousand lines to memorize by Monday, and I'm way behind because of the Senior Showcase."

Owen pauses. He takes the towel out of my hand. "You want to stay? I could help," he offers, his voice casual but something searching in his eyes.

I meet them. "It's the Capulet Manor scene. Don't tell Sam, but there's definitely some, uh—kissing involved." *Hm.* I've never known myself to be the kind of girl to stumble over the word *kissing*.

"I'm no Tyler, but I think I'll get the job done." He flashes me a smile, but his phrasing leaves me wordless. *He doesn't mean . . .* No. He's talking about the lines. Definitely the lines.

Like he doesn't know what he's just done to me, he points his thumb over his shoulder. "I have to check on Sam. He plays *Minecraft* if I leave him unsupervised. You want to wait for me in my bedroom?" He looks coy.

And god help me, I blush. "You—your bedroom?"

"Well, where else would we do it?" He walks past me, brushing his shoulder against mine in a move I know is intentional. "Read lines, I mean," he clarifies with a cocked eyebrow.

Wait a second. I follow him into the hall. "I don't believe this," I say to his back. His—*since when?*—well-shouldered, strokeable back.

"Believe what?" he says over his shoulder.

"You're Megan-ing me!"

He throws his head back and laughs. It echoes in the narrow hallway. "Am I?"

I grab his arm and spin him to face me. "You *definitely* are. This is terrible!" How does he expect me to decipher what's for real and what's for fun?

He's grinning, but his voice holds none of the teasing it did before. "Now you know how the rest of us feel. We mere mortals never dare to hope your insinuations are anything but a pastime."

"Wow, you're such a writer sometimes." I don't know what else to say.

He pushes back his hair. "You never told me how fun it is," he says, the humor returning to his voice. He leans a shoulder on the wall pointedly, his eyes inviting—demanding—a reply.

This will not stand. *I* do the Megan-ing around here! I put a hand on my hip and level him a goading stare. "You think *this* is fun? You haven't seen anything yet."

Now his eyes widen, jumping to his door and back. "I have to check on Sam." His voice comes out low and furtive. "I'll only be a second."

I toss my hair over my shoulder and strut past the Yûjirô portrait into Owen's room. "I'll be waiting," I reply.

His room is dark and as orderly as I remember. My hand shakes as I flip on the lights. I force my racing heart to slow down, reminding myself I have no idea what's going to happen when Owen comes in here. I know better than anyone that flirtatious remarks, winks, and nudges don't need to go any further. And how much further do I think they're going to go with *Owen*? He has a girlfriend. *He has a girlfriend.*

I walk around the room, wondering where I should be when he comes in, and my eyes fall on his notebook, half-open on his desk. He's never shown it to me, but he's never told me *not* to read it either. I know I shouldn't. I'd be crossing a line, invading his privacy, and violating his trust. I pause in front of the notebook, willing myself to walk away.

But Owen's writing about Rosaline. About *me*. Part of me—*all* of me—has to know how he sees her.

The sound of Owen's and Sam's muffled voices drifts down the hall, and before I know it, I've picked up the notebook. The open page is covered mostly in illegible and crossed-out half sentences, but I can make out a few lines jammed in between the others.

It's a monologue for Rosaline, and she's . . . a force of nature. She's fierce and honest, her words passionate and heart-breaking. But she isn't tragic, not the way Owen writes her.

"I don't know how far we're taking this but—" I hear his voice from the doorway. I turn, holding the notebook, and his face goes rigid. He crosses the room in a split second. "That's nowhere close to ready." He grabs the notebook from my hands, his voice hard.

"Why? What you've written is good," I protest. It *is* good. It's ringing in my ears, everything he's written about Rosaline.

"It's not good *enough*." He closes the cover and shoves the notebook in a drawer. The subtle shift in his voice weakens my resistance. For the first time, I didn't mean to make him blush.

"When do you think I'll get to read it?" I ask, gentler.

He won't meet my eyes. "I don't know. I haven't exactly made a lot of progress."

"You need more Rosaline insights from the expert?" I want to help him. He's drifting into the shy version of Owen, one I haven't seen in a long time. One it hurts to see.

He smiles slightly. "No. You've been great."

"What then? Is Rosaline just not interesting enough?" I thought he'd written a Rosaline worthy of the page, but I'm beginning to wonder if he disagrees. "You can't say I didn't warn you," I continue, an involuntary edge entering my voice. "There's a reason she never comes on stage."

"No." He shakes his head, intensity in his eyes when they return to mine. "There's *not* a reason except that this play is Romeo and Juliet's. Rosaline could be the central character of her own story. Just because Romeo didn't want her doesn't mean no one else will." He gestures to the drawer. "You read what I wrote. Isn't it obvious how I feel about her?"

There's a pressing current of passion in his voice, passion I don't think was solely pulled from defending his play's premise. I drop my eyes, feeling my neck grow hot. Not wanting to argue with him, to convince him that no, Rosaline is in fact nothing more than the castoff she is in Shakespeare's pages, I mutter, "It sounds like you know exactly what to write."

"Maybe I do." Owen's answer sounds somehow far away, and when I dare to glance up at him, he has that pensive, concentrated look. The look I now recognize as the same one he wore the very first time I admitted he was cute. I hadn't thought anything of it at the time.

"You said you had a thousand lines to memorize," he says suddenly, breaking my reverie, the distance gone from his expression. He bites the corner of his lip in a way that is entirely unfair and holds out a worn copy of *Romeo and Juliet*.

I nod and take the play from him, careful not to brush his hand. Folding the book back against its spine, I find the right scene. For a moment, the words dance in front of me. Not because I don't know these lines, but because I can't get Rosaline out of my head. I need to be Juliet. Just for an hour. *Please can't I be her for just an hour?*

Deep breath in, deep breath out. I let my posture soften, then turn to face my Romeo. He's leaning against his desk, hair falling across his forehead, his hands still ink-stained even after washing the dishes. I offer him my hand, and he stares at it, uncomprehending.

"I believe you are to take my hand, good gentleman," I say in my best Juliet voice. But it still just sounds like me.

Owen's fingers find mine, and all my focus narrows in on the pleasant warmth against my palm. "If I profane with my unworthiest hand—" he begins.

"Wait, what?" I interrupt with a brusqueness Juliet never would.

He drops my hand, eyes uncertain. "What? Did I start at the wrong place? I thought we were doing their meeting."

"No. I mean, yes, we are, but where's your script?"

"Um, you're holding it, Megan." A grin slides across his features.

"You're telling me you know Romeo's lines for this scene?" He nods, and I know he's holding in a laugh. "But you're not Romeo!" I say because it feels like a fact that's been forgotten.

"No. I'm not."

"Then . . . you just happen to have the scene memorized even though it's one without Friar Lawrence?"

"The scene, the play," he says with a wave of his hand as if his words are easily dismissed.

"Oh my god," I groan. "What happened to no time to memorize your lines?"

Owen shrugs. "I ended up reading and rereading it enough times to write my play—and because I love it, honestly. Memorizing everything just kind of . . . happened."

I do my best to look unimpressed. "You're such a showoff."

"Megan, are you maybe procrastinating a little?" Now he isn't bothering to hold in his laugh.

"Ugh, fine." I stick my hand back out, knowing I've completely lost any chance I may have had of being Juliet tonight.

Owen clears his throat theatrically and takes my hand. "If I profane with my unworthiest hand this holy shrine, the gentle sin is this: my lips, two blushing pilgrims, ready stand to smooth that rough touch with a tender kiss." He bends over, his lips hovering close to my hand, and he's about to kiss me—

"I'm sorry, Romeo is *ridiculous*. I mean, comparing his lips to *two blushing pilgrims*?" I blurt for some indefensible reason, and Owen blinks and straightens up. And I want to kick myself. *It's just a kiss on the hand. It doesn't mean anything.* But I can't explain why it makes me nervous like I haven't felt in I don't know how long.

"I think Shakespeare deserves a little credit for poetic language," he says, no hint of nerves in his easy smile.

I consider telling him to run the scene from the top, giving me a second chance at that kiss. But I don't. I'm kicking myself again when I jump right into my line. "Good pilgrim, you do wrong your hand too much, which mannerly devotion . . ." I say the rest of my lines trying to muster the impatient sarcasm that's come easily in every rehearsal. But it's not working, and I know why. It's because I don't really want to turn Owen's advances down, even if they're scripted.

Which is what has me nervous. If this goes further, I *wouldn't* turn him down. But I have to. Because without Will to focus on when I sense my feelings shifting, I'm now forced to confront how much I want to be with Owen.

So much, I know it would destroy me when things collapse between us the way they inevitably would.

Before I'm prepared for it, we've reached the line where Owen's supposed to kiss me. Not on the hand this time. "Then move not while my prayer's effect I take," he says, his voice low. He's not delivering the lines like Tyler, but his speech doesn't sound tight or hesitant like I would have expected. He sounds like Romeo, and I feel myself closer than ever before to the precipice of becoming Juliet. I feel like I could close my eyes and fall in.

But I don't close my eyes. I keep them on Owen. Even though I know in the rational part of my brain he's definitely not going to kiss me just because it's the stage direction, it . . . kind of looks like he's leaning in.

"Romeo might have terrible pick-up lines, but I have to give him credit for going for it," I say abruptly, ending the leaning-in question right there. I walk to the other side of the room, not really having a theatrical explanation for the distance. We recite the lines before their second kiss from opposite ends of the room. When the moment for the kiss comes, I wait for Owen's eyes to find mine, or his voice to waver, or something. But he does nothing.

"You kiss by th' book," I say, and exhale, relieved that's the final line, wanting this pointless, poorly written, totally not-romantic scene to be over.

"Does that mean Romeo's a good kisser or a bad kisser?" Owen wonders aloud, clearly not understanding we *need* to move on to a different scene.

"Bad, definitely bad," I say. He wanders over to the dresser and leans on it, closing some of the distance between us. "Juliet's saying his kisses feel studied and boring," I inform him.

Maybe it's the way he smiles then, or maybe it's how much he loves this play—how he's memorized the entire thing and wants to pull apart its lines and figure out how they work. But I find myself leaning on the dresser too, my nervousness fading.

It'll destroy me to lose Owen after having him. I know that. But it'll destroy me now to never have him at all.

"Okay, then," he says teasingly. "Tell me, kiss expert Megan, what does Juliet think Romeo should do better?"

I pretend to consider, giving in. "It's a fine line. Too stiff or too repetitive and it feels like you're not interested. Too enthusiastic and you're overeager. The key is a lot of passion and a little creativity. You want each brush of lips to feel like the first time, like you don't know where it could lead—"

He kisses me.

Owen Okita kisses *me*, drawing my face in with his hands like it's not enough for only our lips to touch. He hits me with such force that we flatten against the dresser, the script held between us. If I'd ever let myself wonder about kissing Owen, I couldn't have imagined the way his lips draw the breath from mine or the way he guides my head, tilting me to deepen the kiss. It's like nothing I've ever felt. This kiss isn't just one moment—it holds the possibility of innumerable kisses to come. It's extraordinary, and precarious.

It feels real.

He pulls back just an inch, his eyes searching mine. "Is this—"

"Yes," I breathe. I tug his collar to bring us back together. The second kiss—or perhaps it's the second act in one long kiss—is slower, more measured, like he's taking the time to savor every touch. His body becomes flush with mine, and the script falls to the floor.

"By the book or not?" he whispers with a faint smile.

"*Not* by the book. It's like you've never heard of the book. It's like you're illiterate."

Owen's smile widens. "Well, I've thought about doing that for long enough."

I run a hand down his chest in answer. I know a thing or two about kissing, and when I bring my lips to his, I hold none of it back, walking him to the other end of the room and pressing him to the edge of the desk. I know it works, because he withdraws a moment later, his eyes wide. "Whoa," he exhales.

I shush him. "Let's not talk, Owen."

He complies, instead lowering his hands to my waist and spinning us so I'm the one pinned to the desk. The back of my leg hits a drawer with an unexpected bang, causing us both to break apart and laugh at the interruption.

"What about Sam?" I whisper.

"He's fine." Owen pushes a strand of hair behind my ear. "He's probably playing *Minecraft* with the volume up."

He kisses me again, but I pull back a moment later. I don't know how much time we'll have before Sam interrupts us, before everything falls apart and Owen changes his mind. I won't waste a single second. "Should we move to . . . somewhere quieter?" I glance toward the bed.

He swallows, but his eyes say he's not opposed to the idea. I slide out from in front of the desk and take his hand, leading him to the bed. He watches me recline first onto one el-bow, then both on top of the comforter. Without hesitating, he joins me, his body held as if by a thread over mine.

He brings his face to mine, and—he blinks. "What are we doing?" The intensity in his eyes goes distant. He recoils, rolling off me, and onto his knees on the bed. His voice is low with uncertainty.

I sit up. "Hooking up, I thought." I try to say it lightly, but his expression unnerves me. I can feel whatever I have with Owen—whatever I could have—falling apart already.

"You and Will broke up just this afternoon." He runs a hand through his hair.

"So?"

"So . . . what is this, your next fling?"

I jerk back, stunned. Studying his face in the silent sec-onds that follow, I try to work out where this is coming from. How could Owen, who knows me so well, *not* know this—right now—is like nothing I've felt before?

He must notice the way my expression flares with anger, because his face falls. "I didn't mean it like that. It's just, I don't know what to expect because you tend to move from one relationship to the next pretty quickly."

I flush with anger and embarrassment, and like that, I've found my voice. "Hey, *you're* the one who kissed me," I seethe, "while you supposedly still have a girlfriend."

He looks stricken, like he's just remembered her. He hur-riedly climbs off the bed, then fixes me with a narrow stare. "Why do you say 'supposedly'?"

"Because she isn't a real girlfriend, Owen." I slide to sit on the edge of the bed.

"Enough with that, Megan," he snaps. "Now is *not* the time. Cosima's not a joke."

"I'm not joking," I reply coolly. "I know she's real. But your relationship's not. You hardly ever talk to her. I asked you to tell me what she's like, and you told me where she lives. Your entire relationship is based on one summer camp together. You even forgot about her long enough to hook up with me. I think you're only with her because it's easier, or safer or something. You can't get hurt by someone you don't really know, someone you keep at a distance of five thousand miles."

He's clenching his jaw like he did the other times I've seen him really mad, when Tyler insulted me and when Will cheated. "What would you know about my relationship?"

"I watch you, Owen. I watch you delay and hedge and keep your distance with Cosima, and I watch you do the very same with your play." I gesture to his notebook, stuffed in the drawer. "You're scared to finish. You're scared to put yourself out there because the more you do, the worse you might get hurt."

I half expect him to fall silent, but he doesn't even glance at the notebook. "Just because I didn't tell you everything about my girlfriend doesn't mean I don't know her," he shoots back. "She's not just some placeholder."

Of course she's not. I fight to push down tears. *Cosima's not the placeholder. I am. I'm always the placeholder.* I shouldn't have expected anything else, not even with Owen. Owen, who would prefer to be with someone he talks to twice a week than with me.

"Well, if you're in love with her," I say, getting off the bed and crossing my arms, "you shouldn't have kissed me. But whatever. It's not like this meant much to me either."

He flinches. "Then you shouldn't have flirted with me. But I guess that's just what you do. I should have known you never mean it."

"You know me, Owen." My voice is ugly, bitter with resentment. Not only for him, of course. Why did I ever imagine something like this could happen for *me*, the girl who's the punch line of a hundred oh-she's-boy-crazy jokes? I push past Owen to the door, my vision glassy. "I'm going to go."

"Megan—" I hear the regret in his voice, like he knows he went too far. But I don't turn back, knowing there's nothing he could possibly say to fix this—and not wanting him to see the red in my eyes. I slam his front door behind me.

I get into my car and drive up his street. When I know there's no chance of him following me outside, I pull over and do something I haven't in years.

I cry. Really cry, not the couple stray tears and sniffles that follow fights or breakups. I press my forehead to the steering wheel, and my shoulders shake for everything I'm worth.

TWENTY-ONE

BENVOLIO: . . . *one fire burns out another's burning;*

One pain is lessened by another's anguish.

Turn giddy, and be helped by backward turning.

One desperate grief cures with another's languish.

I.ii.47–50

I POINT TO JEREMY HANDLER, BRINGING REHEARSAL to a halt. "Jeremy," I call out from the front row of the auditorium. He pauses on stage, in front of three girls from the cast sitting on a bench. "You're telling those noblewomen that if they don't dance with you, it's because you think they have blisters on their feet. But because you *want* them to dance with you, you shouldn't stand that far from them. You could even try taking one of their hands."

"Okay." Jeremy nervously steps closer to Cate Dawson and gently grabs her hand. "Like this?"

"Perfect." I notice the way Cate's face has lit up, and she's sitting a little straighter. "If Lord Capulet is going to be a creepy old man to his guests, he might as well go the extra mile," I finish.

In the two weeks since my fight with Owen, I've had nothing but a small, stilted Thanksgiving with Dad and Rose—and

Erin, who threw her cranberry sauce on the floor gleefully—and rehearsal to keep me busy. I didn't think it possible, but I hate Juliet more than ever before. It's not getting in the way of my performance. I'm good, to be honest, better than I ever thought I'd be. I never thought I'd say it, but I feel lucky to have Tyler. His loving gazes and passionate delivery smooth over my rougher lines. Which is fortunate, because the Oregon Shakespeare Festival is in a week. We're driving to Ashland two days early and checking into a cheap hotel—Jody wanted time to rehearse in the performance space.

But none of that has me feeling relieved or excited. I just feel empty.

What keeps me going is the thirty minutes a day Jody allows me to direct *Romeo and Juliet*. I guess she noticed my mood lately, or maybe she took pity on my general lack of enthusiasm and wanted to give me something to look forward to.

The only scene I passed up directing was one of Friar Lawrence's. I haven't talked to Owen since I left his house. Nor Will, not that I would have wanted to if he'd tried. But where Will's and my breakup feels distant, like someone else's life, what I lost with Owen—and what I never had—hurts like the day it happened.

It's a sign of my desperation that I spend a lot of time outside of school at Verona. Verona is Will- and Owen-free, and better, I know it's where I'll find Anthony. He and I are both heartbroken, and we spend afternoons and evenings in between his shifts commiserating over old, free pizza. While Madeleine drops by sometimes and tries to join in, it's not like she has a lot of experience with heartbreak. Or any. And Anthony and I have more to do than mope. With his Juilliard audition coming up, I've been helping him narrow down his monologue choices.

I've probably watched him deliver a thousand recitations of a dozen different monologues to the men's bathroom mirror by the time I convince him to choose based on the feedback of a live audience at an open-mic night.

I'm grateful for the distraction. As long as I'm focused on getting Anthony to pick the perfect monologue, I don't have to replay Owen's words in my head or remember the way it felt to be in his arms for one crushing moment. He should be easy to move on from. We were only together for minutes. But those minutes were more than months with Tyler and weeks with Will. I don't know how to move on from something I thought was real.

So I don't. I stay exactly where I am.

I walk into Luna's Coffee Company Thursday evening, and I'm not surprised to find the rest of the drama class already there. Even though he's not as flashy as Tyler, Anthony is looked up to as the undisputed best actor in school. Everyone's tightly packed into the front room, sitting on wooden tables, burgundy leather couches and the rugs on the floor— every inch of space is taken.

"This seat's open," someone says to my left. I spin and find Wyatt Rhodes smirking up at me from one of the built-in benches under the windows. I'm stunned for a moment. I would not have taken Wyatt for an open-mic-night kind of guy. He's not wearing his golf polo—instead, he has on a millennial-pink button-down, the top three buttons undone. It's completely over the top and exactly the kind of outfit that would have had me drooling months ago.

Wyatt nods toward the seat beside him. It's hardly big enough for two, but judging from the look in his eyes, that's probably the point.

"What are you here for?" I ask. He blinks, obviously thrown by the total lack of flirtatiousness in my response.

"Open-mic night. Reading poems has been known to impress the ladies." I notice the Neruda collection on his lap and remember Owen telling me about trying to channel Neruda in his lyric writing.

I flinch, pushing the memory away. This is the point where I say something suggestive, ask Wyatt who he's planning to impress tonight. He's as gorgeous as ever, and he's materialized out of thin air right when I'm in need of someone new.

I say nothing.

"What's up, Megan? I feel like we haven't hung out in a while," he says, a flicker of confusion crossing his face.

"Sorry, Wyatt. I can't," I tell him. I can't flirt with you anymore, because I don't only want flirting. I want everything. I had it for just a moment, and I can't lie to myself any longer. Flirting was never enough. "Good luck with your poems," I say instead, and walk away.

In the middle of the room, I spot Jenna waving me over from a couch. I make my way through the tangle of people seated on every surface possible, and she moves her arm, giving me a place to sit on the armrest right as Anthony steps up to the mic.

"Okay, I know there's often a kind of sharing-is-caring spirit with open mics, but I'm going to hold this shit down for the next half hour." He's dressed in the charcoal suit I know he bought for his audition in New York. "I'm testing monologues. Stomp if you hate it, cheer if you love it. Sound good?"

I cheer with the rest of the drama group, earning eye rolls from the only other open-mic participants I can pick out— two bearded guys with mandolins in the corner.

Anthony extravagantly clears his throat. The rest of us hold our breath, and except for the hiss of the cappuccino machine the room is silent. "About three things I was absolutely positive," Anthony begins. I frown. This isn't one of the monologues we prepped. Chekhov? Ibsen? Beckett?

"First, Edward was a vampire. Second, there was part of him—"

The room erupts into stomping punctuated by a few exuberant cheers. I whoop from the armrest, recognizing Stephenie Meyer's iconic declaration of love from *Twilight*. Anthony collapses onto the mic stand, laughing.

"Okay, for real this time," Anthony promises, straightening his tie. He closes his eyes, taking a beat to find his composure. When he looks back up at us, he's transformed. "Because you can't handle it, son. You can't handle the truth. You can't handle . . ."

He continues the speech, and I watch my classmates' ex

pressions for reactions. He's doing Shakespeare for both the classical monologues Juilliard requires and Chekhov for one of the contemporary, but he needs one more contemporary. I've been trying for weeks to dissuade him from the famous speech from the play version of Aaron Sorkin's *A Few Good Men*. It invites inevitable Jack Nicholson comparisons, and Anthony's talents are better suited to the subtle than the overexpressive. Sure enough, I notice skeptical looks and pursed lips on the faces of the crowd, and while I hear the occasional cheer, the stomping builds slowly until Anthony stops in mid-line.

"Really? You're not feeling Sorkin?" he says, breaking character and rubbing his neck.

The stomping continues, even louder. Anthony shakes his head ruefully.

I call out from my seat. "Scorpius!" I'm expecting the exasperated sigh Anthony heaves when he recognizes my voice. Every time he'd begin the *Few Good Men* speech in the Verona bathroom, I'd cut him off and insist on Scorpius Malfoy's monologue from *Harry Potter and the Cursed Child*. Anthony's been adamantly resisting—he protests that it's too commercial to command respect. But it doesn't matter. He's brilliant at it. He switches seamlessly from righteous anger to wounded vulnerability and captures a world of sorrows in just a few lines.

"Can you even slightly imagine what that's like?" Anthony begins, his voice aching. "Have you even ever tried? No. Because you can't see beyond the end of your nose. Because you can't see beyond the end of your stupid thing with your dad."

Immediately, I'm proven right. The crowd goes quiet, this time watching Anthony with unconcealed interest. Even the baristas stop pouring drinks and listen from the counter. Anthony's eyes dance, and I know he feels the energy in the room. I get up and toss him an I-told-you-so glance. He sees me but doesn't break character. He'll definitely be performing this one in New York. Taking advantage of the lull in the line, I step up to the register, where one of the baristas looks annoyed to be handling my order.

I walk to the other end of the counter to wait for my cappuccino, watching Anthony from behind the coffee machines. When it's been a couple minutes with no cappuccino, I turn to check who's waiting in front of me and—

"Eric?"

He whirls, looking panicked. When he realizes it's me, he relaxes.

"What are you doing here?" I ask.

"I'm, uh—" he stutters like he's searching for an explanation, then stops himself. With a soft smile, he nods toward the stage. "I'm here for Anthony's monologues."

"Thought so." I smile. "Have you two . . . figured things out?" In all the time I've spent at Verona, Anthony's never mentioned Eric, but I haven't wanted to press. It's possible they've talked.

"We haven't," Eric says stiffly, his smile fading. "And we're not going to. I know I'm not the type of guy Anthony wants or deserves to be with. But I wanted to watch the monologues because Anthony told me a lot about the audition before . . ." He looks away. "I heard about tonight and had to come."

I have to give Eric credit. For someone whose wardrobe consists of only lacrosse jerseys, he's pretty emotionally insightful. "But it's clear you still care about him," I say.

"Yeah, I do." Eric's eyes drift to Anthony. "When I'm with him, I feel like there are a million reasons why we should be together. I feel like I'm . . . my entire self, not just . . ."

While he's talking, I notice a familiar head of black hair framed in the doorway. "Playing who you're supposed to be," I finish Eric's sentence as I watch Owen walk into the front and take my seat on the couch.

"But sometimes it doesn't matter," Eric continues. "I'd just mess things up for Anthony—there's too much in the way."

The applause from the other end of the room tells me Anthony's finished his monologue, and I pull my gaze from Owen to find Eric putting on his jacket. "I think I should go," he says.

"Eric. You definitely don't want to talk to him?"

He shakes his head, his eyes pointedly avoiding where Anthony's bowing by the mic. "I don't want to interrupt his night. It's better if he doesn't see me." He nods once before brushing past me to the door.

"Cappuccino," the tattooed barista calls out.

"Thanks," I mutter, taking the ceramic cup and gingerly carrying it back to where Anthony's joined Jenna and everyone on the couches. The room's beginning to clear out, and no one's listening to the folk musicians' gentle Iron & Wine cover. I sit on the edge of the table, putting plenty of distance between myself and Owen.

Jenna drapes her arm around Anthony. "Which one's it

going to be?" she asks, flopping her head on his shoulder.

"*Harry Potter.*" Anthony sighs and gives me a grudging smile. "Definitely *Harry Potter.*"

"It's a really cool pick," Owen speaks up. "You're great at capturing subtler dynamics. Seems like this is definitely your best option."

I scowl. It's enough he's here—he didn't have to go and have the exact same opinion as me.

"You only saw the one!" Jenna straightens up and slaps Owen on the knee. I scowl again. "Where were you? We said we'd meet here an hour ago."

Owen stiffens. "I, uh . . ." His eyes flit to mine for the first time in weeks. It's a glance so quick I nearly miss it, but I know exactly how to read it.

"Talking to Cosima?" I guess loudly.

Now he levels his gaze with mine. "Yeah. I was."

"On a Thursday? Wow," I say with unrestrained bitterness. "What, is she helping you run lines?"

"What's it to you?" Owen's eyes are unreadable.

"Nothing," I say, ignoring the confused expressions on Anthony's and Jenna's faces. "It's nothing to me, Owen." I get up, cappuccino unfinished. "I'm going to get—a muffin," I finish, painfully conscious of how undramatic that sounded.

But turning toward the counter, I freeze in place. Will and Alyssa are stepping up to the line, her hands in his back pockets, and they're kissing for the whole world to see. *Well, perfect.*

"Actually, I'm just going to head out," I tell the group.

I walk past Owen on my way to the door, and out of the

corner of my eye, I see him start to stand. He looks torn, like the part of him that wants to comfort me for what he obviously just saw happen with Will is wrestling with the part of him that remembers we're in a huge fight.

He looks like he wants to follow me, right up until he sits back down.

TWENTY-TWO

PARIS: *Venus smiles not in a house of tears.*

IV.i.8

OWEN AND I DON'T TALK FOR ANOTHER WEEK.

It's December, and Ashland is this weekend. I'm running late for the first full run-through before we leave tomorrow. Not helping matters, it's a dress rehearsal, and right now I'm struggling to stuff a full medieval gown into my bag. I forgot to bring my costume to school—to Jody's open-mouthed horror—because I had a twenty-minute discussion with my dad this morning about dinner plans for when my mom and Randall fly in tonight. Jody had me run home the instant school let out. Apparently, the world will end if the costume designer doesn't have one final opportunity to make alterations before we leave town for the performance.

I rush into the auditorium, nearly colliding with an irate Jody. "Why aren't you *dressed*?" she shouts in the shrill voice she inevitably gets in the final days before a show.

I know how to handle her. "You told me I had to be back in ten minutes. Here I am. Now let me go change," I return over my shoulder, pushing past Tybalt and Benvolio engaged in a duel with their wooden swords.

"Five minutes, Megan!" I hear behind me. "We're doing the Nurse's scene before we take it from the top."

I dash up the stairs to the stage and dart behind the curtain. Everyone's waiting in the wings in full costume, and I have to elbow past lords and ladies and an apothecary on my way to the dressing rooms. Pulling off my scarf and unzipping my jacket, I pass through the green room, where three crewmembers are bent over a mic pack. I open the door to the girls' dressing room, but I'm brought to a halt in the doorway. Cate Dawson's making out sloppily with Jeremy Handler in between racks of clothes, his hand unmistakably up her shirt.

Not a chance I'm going in there.

I hit the stairs to the boys' dressing room two at a time. It's markedly smaller than the girls', but it'll have to do. Ignoring the thick stench of boy clothes, I do a quick sweep of the space, afraid of another uncomfortable walk-in. I drop my bag on the counter, closing the door behind me. Not a minute to waste, I rip the costume out of my bag and fling it onto a hanger, then undo my belt and shimmy out of my jeans.

I peel off my shirt next and throw it over my head. But when I open my eyes—Owen's staring right at me.

Not into my eyes.

My mouth won't work for a couple terrifying seconds. The thought crosses my mind this was a regrettable day to wear my red boy-shorts with "Super Sexy" printed on them.

"What the hell, man?" I yell after what feels like an eternity.

Owen blinks and blushes furiously in his friar's frock. Like he's just remembered his decency, he looks away, then turns a full one hundred and eighty degrees. I guess averting his eyes wasn't enough. "This—this is the guys' dressing room," he stammers.

Remembering he's right, I hastily pull the dress over my head. "Jeremy and Cate were doing something decidedly off-script in the girls'," I mutter by way of explanation. Eager like I've never been for anything to extricate myself from this situation, I yank my dress down and—it gets caught.

I can't figure out on what. I have one arm halfway in a sleeve and the other sticking out what I suspect is the neck hole. The other sleeve is tangled in the straps of my yellow pushup bra. "Fucking shitty costume," I gasp, pirouetting feverishly and trying to fix the problem.

"Is— Um, what's going on?" Owen's voice sounds pinched.

"My fucking costume is stuck." I whack my arm on the counter and swear again.

"Uh, where?" He still doesn't turn.

"If I knew, *Owen*, I'd fix it," I snap. "Just give me a hand."

I hear his voice after a couple more frantic seconds of pulling on the sleeve. "It looks, um, stuck on your bra." He clears his throat, like the effort of keeping his voice level was too much to bear. "I'll go get someone," he offers.

"There's not enough time. Jody's going to kill me if I'm not down in, like, negative-one minutes."

"But, the green room—" he protests.

"The only girl up here is Cate. If you'd really rather interrupt *that* than help me with my bra, then go right ahead."

He looks to the door like he's considering it. But a moment later, I feel his hands on my back, twisting the fabric to unfurl the sleeves.

"Just, pull the collar—" I prompt.

"Move your—"

"Now my arm's stuck."

"How did you—? Have you ever put on a dress before?"

"Have you, Owen?"

"Stay still," he orders me. I feel him struggling with the bra. *This is hopeless.* He circles me to try from the front.

"Just take it off!"

Owen's hands still. "What?"

"Unhook the bra."

He looks up at me, expressionless. "I am *not* taking off your bra right now, Megan."

I let out a short, rattling sigh. "Okay, I will." I reach behind me. But right then, Owen gives the dress a final yank, and mercifully it comes free.

He instantly steps back and turns around again, like he wasn't just nose-deep in my décolletage. Ten hurried seconds later, I've pulled on both sleeves and straightened the bodice over the guilty bra. I'm reaching for the door when I hear, "Wait."

I do, not entirely knowing why. I'm not expecting the fervor of the past few minutes to have prompted him into an apology or a declaration of love, like this is some stupid rom-com.

I feel Owen's hands on my back once more. He sweeps my hair out from under the dress, his fingers brushing the nape of my neck. It's impossible to ignore how I shiver under his touch, try though I might.

"Thanks," I say, a bit breathless.

"No problem." His reply is short and distant. He edges past me to the door.

I follow him, unsteady on my feet, unsure what just happened. Owen's been cold to me for weeks, and he practically told me he's devoted to his girlfriend. But the way he gently touched my neck felt—well, intimate.

Rehearsal keeps my mind from wandering. First full run-throughs never go smoothly, and between remembering my lines and hitting my cues, I have no time to talk to Owen—other than the brief scene in which Friar Lawrence sells Juliet poison, which isn't exactly brimming with sexual tension.

Rehearsal ends twenty minutes behind schedule, and I roll through stop signs on the way home. Dad's waiting impatiently in the driveway. He hustles me into his car with only a "Come on, Megan. We have to go."

It's an hour to the Medford Airport, and I anxiously listen to Dad list off dinner plans and travel arrangements for Ashland while the redwoods fly by in the window. I keep waiting to hear strain in his voice at the prospect of being around his ex-wife again, but it hasn't crept in yet.

We pull up to the terminal, and I'm startled by the little leap my heart does when I catch sight of Mom. Before Dad's even put the car in park, I'm jumping out of my seat and running to give her a hug.

"I wasn't expecting this treatment from my seventeen-year-old daughter," Mom tries to joke, but the lopsided smile on her face betrays how pleased she is. "Shouldn't you be rebellious or something?"

"I missed you," I say into her shoulder. "I'll resume standard operating rebelliousness tomorrow."

Randall's holding the suitcases behind her. He gives me a conspiratorial wink over her shoulder, and my heart sinks a little. In just under a week, my mom's going to be engaged.

I hear the trunk pop, and Dad walks around the car and wraps my mom in a delicate hug. "Catherine, it's great to see you."

Mom gives a small smile in reply, and I notice a faint blush on her cheeks. Dad turns to Randall and reaches for a suitcase, but inevitably Randall insists on carrying it himself. The two of them end up awkwardly walking the suitcase between them the entire way to the trunk.

Mom and I exchange a glance. I follow her into the back of Dad's Rav-4, not ready to give up Mom proximity just yet. "You haven't traded this thing in by now, Henry?" she asks with a laugh while Dad and Randall get in the front. Randall slides his chair back to fit his six-foot-four frame, plowing the back of the seat into my knees.

"No," my dad answers, grinning. "You'd be surprised how long a car can hold out when *someone's* not riding the brakes to every stop."

Mom holds up a hand in defense. "I do not—"

"She does. She really does," Randall confirms, making Dad laugh.

I say nothing, not believing what's happening. I didn't

dare expect this drive would be anything but small talk and long silences, and here we are, laughing already. But this trip's far from over.

Dad and Randall fight over the suitcases the entire walk up to the porch. The house smells like sweet potatoes when I open the front door, and Mom heads straight for Erin, who's shouting *noo-noos* in her playpen.

"Look how big you've gotten," Mom coos, earning a giggle from Erin.

Rose emerges from the kitchen, holding an assortment of silverware, her other hand on her back. I watch my mom for the death glares she gave Rose the last time they were in the same room, and I'm stunned when Mom pulls Rose into a one-armed hug. From the look on Rose's face, she's stunned, too. I can't decipher my mom's unexpected warmth toward her. It could be the years since the divorce, the distance, the fact my mom has a boyfriend, soon-to-be fiancé.

Or it could be an act.

"Megan," Rose says, withdrawing from the hug, "would you finish setting the table?" In mute surprise, I take the silverware from her and walk into the dining room, over-hearing Mom and Rose begin to chat about baby names and nurseries.

We sit down once Dad and Randall have dropped off the suitcases in my bedroom, where Mom and Randall will sleep before everyone drives up to Ashland.

"The whole meal is nut-free, per Randall," Rose proudly announces as the guys file into the room.

"Well, I'll be." Randall grins, sitting down. "So thoughtful of you, Rose. Wow."

As the plates of potatoes and roast chicken are passed around the table, I watch Mom and Dad for signs of strain. They're perfectly normal, Dad serving Mom a spoonful of the potatoes while she chides him for not doing any of the cooking. I chew quietly and listen to Randall recount his victory at the regional bowling tournament. The other three jump in with questions every now and then like they're old friends.

"What time are you guys leaving tomorrow?" Dad asks me when Randall goes into the kitchen to pour everyone refills.

"After rehearsal," I say in between bites.

"And who are you rooming with?" Mom has a knowing smile.

"I don't know, Mom."

"Not Tyler, I hope," she replies teasingly.

I can't keep myself from rolling my eyes. "The rooming is same-sex."

"It's going to stay that way, too," Dad warns, his brows flat.

"Like there's anyone I'd want to invite over." Owen won't talk to me except in the direst of circumstances, and considering the things he said to me in his bedroom, I'm not exactly keen to talk to him either. No matter how good of a kisser he is or how I felt when his fingers brushed my neck. It'll be my first drama trip in years without a hookup.

I catch the look my parents don't even try to hide. "We're not falling for that," Mom says dryly. "This is a class of your drama friends. Even in Texas, where you didn't know a soul, you still had one crush by the end of the summer. One that we know of," she adds a second later.

"Wait, what?" Dad looks up from his plate, startled.

Before I have the chance to defend myself, Randall chimes in. "I caught the neighbor's kid loitering in the backyard one night—"

"Michael was harmless," I interject.

"—the week *after* you left Texas," Randall finishes.

I'd forgotten I ghosted on Michael, honestly. He texted me a couple times after I got home and then promptly found himself a blonde cheerleader. I wonder if they're still together. I bet they are—shit, they're probably engaged. It's Texas.

"Like that kid on the roof," Dad interrupts my train of thought.

I feel the blood rush to my cheeks. "Oh, Jesus."

Mom folds her lips inward, trying not to smile. Rose looks between the two of them, eyebrows arched. "On the *roof*?" she repeats.

I try to nip this in the bud. "We really don't need to relive that. It's . . . It's in the past. There's . . ." I gesture to Erin in her high chair. " . . . a child present."

"Erin's not too young to start learning from her sister's misadventures," Dad says, then nods to Mom. "You tell it, Catherine. You're the one who found him."

I shake my head. But for a moment, it feels like it's four years ago, my parents are together, and Rose and Randall are just a couple we're having over for dinner.

"We were in bed watching some horrible movie . . ." Mom

begins, looking to Dad. "What was it? You really wanted to watch it."

Dad leans back in his chair and crosses his arms. "Hey, *Snakes on a Plane* is a classic of American cinema."

Mom waves off his unsolicited review. "I thought I heard thudding on the roof," she continues. "*Henry* tried to tell me it was just in the movie."

"In my defense, I knew she was looking for every reason to pause the film," Dad cuts in.

"The third time it happened, I went outside to see for myself. Lo and behold, there's somebody standing on the roof over the garage."

"The next thing I know," Dad takes over, "Catherine's running back inside, looking pale, telling me there's some guy trying to break into the house. Not an overreaction *at all*."

Mom laughs into her hand, blushing now, and through my mounting mortification I realize what's happening here. My parents are rediscovering their friendship over what they have in common—embarrassing me.

"I obviously pause *Snakes on a Plane*," Dad goes on, "grab a baseball bat, and go downstairs. We get outside, I take one look at the guy on the roof, turn to Catherine, and say, 'That's a fourteen-year-old boy. Why is there—?' and then I realize he's there to get into Megan's room." He levels me an accusatory look.

"I ask if he's sure." Mom jumps back in. "He just says, 'Believe me, I'm sure.' Then he yells up at the poor kid, and the kid trips and falls on his butt. Henry orders him to get off the roof, but the kid just sits there, looking like he's about to throw up. I take Henry by the arm and tell him I think the kid's stuck."

Rose and Randall shake with laughter. Even I have to admit the situation was kind of funny.

"I get the ladder and climb halfway up. But the kid doesn't move. I hear the upstairs window open, and Megan sticks her head out." Dad looks at me. "Megan, why don't you tell everyone what happened next?"

"Okay, what was I supposed to do?" I protest.

"Not invite the boy on the roof into your room," Dad says.

"You did what?" Rose gasps.

"He was stuck!" I defend myself. "My window was closer than the ladder. I didn't want Charlie to fall!"

"I swear to god, Megan yells down to him, 'Come on up! Just come in here,'" Dad confirms, and I collapse my head into my hands. "Needless to say, that wasn't going to happen."

"Falling wouldn't have even been the worst of Charlie's worries," Mom mutters. "He finally opens his mouth and explains he's *not good with heights*. Let's just say, Henry made it very clear Charlie had to come down *right* then."

"What did you say to the poor kid?" Randall shares a grin with my dad.

"I might have told him . . . I'd throw him off if he didn't," Dad says with a shrug.

"That worked?" Randall returns incredulously.

"Not exactly." Dad bashfully massages the back of his neck. "Catherine coaxed him down eventually." He looks up at Mom. "I'm just glad you were there. I honestly might've killed the kid. You were always the even-tempered one."

It happens so fast, I nearly don't notice. But Mom's eyes flicker, and her smile falters just a touch.

When we finish dinner, I stack dishes to carry into the kitchen while Rose gets dessert ready. Erin begins the frustrated whimper that means we've overtired her, and a tiny spoon clatters to the ground. I hear Dad get up, mumbling about Erin's bedtime.

"Would you mind if I read to her?" my mom asks.

"Please," Dad says. "I could use a night off from reading *Green Eggs and Ham* for the five-thousandth time." Mom lifts Erin out of her high chair and goes upstairs while I load the dishwasher and Rose pulls a pan out of the oven.

In fifteen minutes, Mom still isn't back and Randall's regaling me with the financial intricacies of his current case at work. When Rose comes out of the kitchen, a peach cobbler held in oven mitts, her eyes go to my mom's empty chair, and she frowns. "Megan," she says, interrupting Randall's endless string of details. "Would you go upstairs and tell your mom dessert's ready?"

I shoot her a grateful look and escape into the hallway, passing the photo over the stairs from Dad and Rose's wedding. It's dark in Erin's bedroom, the door ajar. I push it open and find Erin's in her crib, already asleep. "Mom?" I whisper the moment before I see her in the rocking chair, the book closed on her lap.

She hurriedly wipes her eyes. "Hi, honey," she says softly. She forces a smile. "Is everyone having dessert?"

Searching for what to say, I watch her straighten her

blouse and set down the book, clearly intending to just go back downstairs. "You— Are you okay?" I get out.

"Completely," she reassures me. "There are . . . a lot of memories in this house. Nothing to worry about."

I follow her out into the hallway. The picture from Dad and Rose's wedding looks a little too big and a little too beautiful. I feel like I should say something more to Mom, but I decide not to press her further because I know what's upsetting her. There'd be no point in talking about it when there's nothing I can change, and she's obviously struggling enough without me dredging it up one more time.

I knew this trip would be a mistake. The thought burns into my heart like a brand. I knew it would hurt my mom. I knew it would remind her of her old life with my dad and of his new one. It wasn't enough for her to move out when they got divorced—she had to move from Oregon to the Southwest to escape everything that reminded her of the man she's still pining for.

Including me.

It's something she and I have in common. We're always looking backward for the people who've moved on without us.

TWENTY-THREE

FRIAR LAWRENCE: *Affliction is enamored of thy parts,*

And thou art wedded to calamity.

III.iii.2–3

I FLOAT THROUGH THE SCHOOL DAY IN a black cloud.

When afternoon rehearsal ends at 5:30 and the bus for Ashland pulls up outside, I find Anthony in the parking lot. He's drumming his fingers on his leg, and his lips twitch in the way I know means he's dying to run lines. Undoubtedly noticing my expression, he thoughtfully restrains himself and gives me a hug before hunting down Tybalt and Benvolio.

Eager to sit down and close my eyes, I join the line filing onto the bus a couple of people behind Tyler, who's wrapping Madeleine in his arms. Of course she came back to school to send him off. She's not coming to Ashland because she has her alumni interview this weekend for her early action app to Princeton, which obviously she's going to crush.

She and Tyler finally separate, and I glimpse tears in both of their eyes like the prospect of two days apart is nearly unbearable.

I shake my head, and then she turns and I see what she's holding. It's a tiny mountain of brownies on the same flower-shaped plate I remember her bringing to school for me during my parents' divorce. She hasn't brought it out in years— she hasn't needed to.

Her eyes find mine between the heads of our classmates. Without a word, she leaves Tyler and walks down the line to me.

"You didn't have to," I say, taking the plate from her.

"Of course I did," she replies matter-of-factly. "It sucks you're going to Ashland right now, but call me whenever. Seriously."

"I will," I promise. I called her last night about how I found my mom, and before I knew it two hours had gone by. I would've stayed up later talking to her, but sleeping on the couch with adults coming downstairs for trips to the bathroom and drinks of water didn't leave me much privacy.

We've shuffled forward in line, and it's my turn to get on the bus. But on the first step, I hesitate. "Hey," I call, halting her. "I feel like a sleepover's in order when I get home."

She smiles lightly. "Definitely." Giving me a final wave, she walks back toward campus.

I trudge to an empty row near the back and take a seat next to the window. People are beginning to fill the bus, and I catch a couple pairs of eyes checking out the seat beside mine. I place the plate of brownies on the empty cushion, declaring it off-limits. When Owen boards, I watch him in my peripheral vision while pointedly staring out the window.

Finally the bus rumbles to life, and I close my eyes. Just for good measure, I put in my earbuds, the universal sign for *don't talk to me*. For a while I listen to nothing, trying to go over my lines in my head. But I turn on an old playlist when I realize the only words ringing in my ears aren't Juliet's. They're my mom's—*There are a lot of memories in this house. Nothing to worry about.*

I don't open my eyes for forty-five minutes, until we park outside a Burger King for dinner. Between thirty high-school students ordering burgers and freaking out over the premiere, it's not hard for me to hide my nose in my script and avoid the conversation. In an hour, with night falling, we're under way again.

We pass sporting goods stores and strip malls on the way into Ashland, and then the wide street I take to SOTI. I watch coffee shops, bookstores, clothing boutiques go by in the window. We round a corner, and a compound of low buildings in Elizabethan style emerges on the right. And despite my horrible mood, my heart lifts a little when I see it.

The Oregon Shakespeare Festival isn't an event. It's a place, a collection of smaller theaters grouped around a main stage built to resemble Shakespeare's Globe. I don't know why they call it a festival, because they have plays year-round, but I do know the production of *Macbeth* I went to in sophomore year is the best piece of theater I've ever seen.

I've dreamed of having a production on one of those stages. I just never thought I'd be acting in it.

We drive on past a quaint, three-story inn with a picket fence and a gabled roof, and I begin to look forward to falling into bed with a view of the theater. But we keep driving, and two right turns later, we're parked outside a Springview Hotel. Despite the proprietor's meager efforts, including a couple of ceramic plates on the walls, it's charmless and corporate.

I grab my room key from Jody, who's watching me with concern, but she's busy with the thirty other students clamoring for their keys. I slip out to the stairs, not in the mood to bustle into the elevator with my giddy cast-mates.

My room is empty when I open the door. Feeling the irresistible urge to wash off the bus ride, I walk into the bathroom. When I turn on the shower I think I hear the beep and click of my roommate coming into the room, but I'm intent on relaxing in the steam before I'm forced to have a conversation. Under the hot water, half of the tensed muscles in my back unclench.

Once I've put my clothes back on, I open the bathroom door and come face-to-face with Alyssa.

"Unbelievable," I say under my breath at the precise moment she gives me a glare of ice. *Thank you, Jody. A night stuck in a room with Alyssa is exactly what I need right now.*

"Don't worry, I'm not staying," Alyssa says sharply from her seat at the edge of the bed. "I'm waiting for Will to text me, then I'm going to move my stuff to his room. I'll be sleeping there." She tosses her shiny black hair over her shoulder.

"Of course you will," I mutter. I expect the mention of Will to hurt, but it doesn't. I really don't care what he's doing tonight, or who he's doing it with.

But Alyssa's eyes have narrowed. "What's *that* supposed to mean?"

Something in me snaps. The combination of Owen, my parents, this stupid fucking play, and now Alyssa staring at me does *not* have me feeling like playing nice. "I get it now,"

I reply with false lightness. "I wouldn't sleep with him, and you will."

She stands up to her full height of five feet, four inches. "I'm not going to be shamed by a girl who's had ten boyfriends in three years. You go right ahead and tell yourself I'm the bad guy, but I won't feel guilty for *finally* getting with a boy I like."

"It's not that you got with a boy you liked. You got with a boy who had a girlfriend." I push away the memory of kissing Owen, feeling the cold of my wet hair down my back.

"You date everyone, Megan!" Alyssa's voice goes shrill.

"And? Because I've had a lot of boyfriends, my relationships don't matter?"

"No, I don't—" She looks away, and suddenly there's something besides indignation in her tone. Something like pain, or purpose. "I mean, you think you're the only girl who's had a crush on Tyler Dunning? Or Dean Singh? Or Will? Do you even know what it's like to want someone who will never notice you? I watched myself get overlooked for you time after time. Finally, a guy liked *me*, too."

I open my mouth, then close it. Of the ways I've understood my relationships over the years, usurper to Alyssa wasn't one of them. But with everything else pounding through my head right now, I can't deal with hearing her out.

"Whatever," I say with what I hope passes for finality. I walk to the door. "Enjoy your night," I say, the door closing behind me.

🕴

Without knowing where I'm going, I head toward the stairs. I only know I need something to occupy me, to keep me out of Alyssa's way, and to keep my thoughts from Owen and my family. I decide the lobby's the best bet. I'll run some lines until I figure it's safe to return.

Rounding the corner at the other end of the hall, I catch sight of Tyler in front of the vending machine. I pass him with my head down and shoulders squared, hoping to convey I don't want to talk.

"You don't want to go down to the lobby," I hear him say cheerfully before I reach the door to the stairs. "Jody's enlisted everyone in folding programs."

His words bring me to a halt. "Thanks," I mutter, realizing now I have nowhere to go. While I'm considering my dilemma, Tyler swears under his breath, and I turn to find him shaking the vending machine to what sounds like little effect.

"Fucking money-eating piece of . . ."

"Louder. I don't think it heard you," I tell him, unable to resist the urge to heckle Tyler.

He eyes me, and then he clears his throat and repeats himself in his grandest stage voice. "Fucking money-eating piece of vile, execrable filth."

I laugh, surprising myself. "Better. Imagine the vending machine sitting in the back row," I say, adopting my most directorial demeanor.

He's laughing, too, but he halfheartedly kicks the vending machine one final time. "Make fun all you want," he replies, grinning ruefully, "but I'm a man in a crisis right now."

I take two steps toward the vending machine, where I glimpse a bag of Skittles caught in the spindle and hanging half off the shelf. "A Skittles crisis," I elaborate, smiling inwardly at how perfectly Tyler Dunning the situation is.

He nods gravely. "The worst kind." I step up to the glass, scrutinizing the stuck spindle. "I tried shaking it," he explains. "I even reached my arm up through the door—"

I ram my shoulder into the glass, interrupting him. I hit harder than I intended, and the whole machine bounces against the wall with an echoing bang. The Skittles tumble into the bin at the bottom.

Tyler's watching me, mouth half-open. Before he says anything, a door opens across the hallway. Owen's head emerges. "What's going on?" he asks, his eyes round with concern. When they find me, it's like someone's switched off a light in an upstairs room.

"Our Juliet just beat up a vending machine," Tyler says behind me, sounding impressed.

"Oh," Owen replies flatly, his gaze shifting to Tyler. Without a word to me or so much as a glance in my direction, he withdraws and closes the door.

I stare at it after he's gone, feeling the laughter of a couple moments ago ebb away. Tyler nudges me. "Hey, slugger," he says, and I turn, putting Owen and his disinterest firmly behind me. "Do you need some ice? That looked like it hurt."

I rub my shoulder, considering. "It felt kind of good, actually."

Tyler looks at me for a long second before he shrugs, his expression relaxing. He tears open the Skittles and tips the bag in my direction without taking any for himself. "You want some? They never would have happened without you."

I feel myself smiling as I hold out my hand. He shakes the bag, and two purples and a green fall into my palm. We start to wander down the hall, not saying anything while we pass a group of juniors playing cards on the floor. "Final rehearsal tomorrow," Tyler says, slowing down and tipping more Skittles into my hand. "You feel prepared?"

I glance at him out of the corner of my eye. "That depends."

"On?"

"On if you remember to lift your leg before you roll over me in the bedroom scene." I wince, remembering a week of rehearsing the scene in November and the consequent bruises on my thigh.

"It looks good!" Tyler protests. "Jody said it looks good from the audience."

"I don't care! You knee me every time! I'm going to have nerve damage by the end of this play!" He laughs, and I point a finger in his face. "I'm serious. You do it in tomorrow's rehearsal, and I'm eating garlic before the premiere."

He pulls a look of horror. "You wouldn't."

I nod threateningly. "You think playing opposite me is hard *now*? I want to see you 'It was the lark, not the nightingale' me when I smell like ten servings of raw garlic."

"Actresses . . ." Tyler rolls his eyes. Then his voice softens. "But seriously, it's awesome starring with you. You're a great Juliet."

"Really?" I snort, keeping my eyes on the floor. "I feel like

I'm kind of stumbling through it. I still think I'm going to freeze up and forget my lines in front of a real audience." *An audience including members of the SOTI faculty.*

Tyler drifts to a halt in front of a door. "Everyone thinks that's going to happen. But it won't." He smiles reassuringly. "Not if you know it." He nods toward the door, and I realize it must be his room. "We could go over it one more time, if you want?"

Why not? I think to myself. Running lines with Tyler will definitely distract me from my empty room and the look on Owen's face before he closed his door. "That'd be great," I say, following Tyler into his room.

It's empty, but I quickly deduce Jeremy's his roommate from the backpack on one bed with *Jeremy* stitched on it. Walking over to the other bed, I briefly wonder if Cate's managed to sexile her roommate, and if anyone but me will actually sleep in their own room tonight.

I close my eyes, bringing to mind my lines and the staging for my first scene, and feel Tyler sit down on the bed next to me.

"How now—" I begin to recite.

The rest of the line is smothered by Tyler's lips crashing into mine. His hands grab my waist, his nose pressing into my eye. This isn't his Romeo kissing, gentle and thoughtful—this is Tyler, kissing me with the sloppy overenthusiasm I remember from a year ago. *What the fuck is he doing?*

I shove a hand into his chest, pushing him off me. "What the hell?" I gasp, wiping my lips.

"I thought it was obvious." His brow furrows, but his voice sounds impossibly reasonable.

"*What's* obvious?" I jump off the bed.

He gestures at the door, looking at me like I'm the one who's lost my mind. "I invited you into my bedroom to read lines . . ."

I don't believe what I'm hearing. "You think after complimenting my acting and giving me some Skittles, I'll just jump back into bed with you?"

"It doesn't have to be a big deal," he says easily, sending my head spinning all over again.

What doesn't have to be a big deal? I want to ask. Is it that his relationship with Madeleine means so little that he'd throw it away to cheat with me? Or if he really is in love with Madeleine, is hooking up with me so inconsequential he's not even considering what it would do to his relationship? I don't know which one is worse.

"A big deal?" I get out. "I thought you were in love with my best friend."

Tyler shrugs. "Madeleine doesn't have to know. Not if you don't tell her."

I'm stunned speechless for a second. Tyler is somehow a worse guy than I thought he was—than I *knew* he was. Even when he cheated on me and dumped me, I never expected he could be capable of something like this. Hurting Madeleine for no reason just to have something he's had and replaced.

"We did this, Tyler," I hear myself say. "Remember? You're the one who didn't want me anymore."

He tries to place a hand on my arm, but I twist away. "It's just, doing the play with you, being here with you," he begins, "I'm remembering what it was like when we first got together. We had something really great for a while."

"We did." I glare at him. "Until you chose Madeleine."

He holds his hands up in defense. "Okay, okay. Forget it, then." I watch him cross the room to his suitcase and pull out his script. "You want to run the lines?"

I stand there with shock written on my face, not believing anybody could possibly shrug this off. But there he is, already opening the play. "No, I don't want to *run lines*," I spit. Doubting he'll bother to reply, I leave his room and hurl the door closed behind me.

I don't get two steps before my heart sinks. Tomorrow, I'll have to do a lot more than run lines with Tyler. I'll have to run the entire play, in front of everyone. The thought makes me want to drink poison and lock myself in a sepulcher.

TWENTY-FOUR

ROMEO: *Is the day so young?*

BENVOLIO: *But new struck nine.*

ROMEO: *Ay me, sad hours seem long.*

I.i.164–6

I WAKE UP THE NEXT MORNING AT 10:14 a.m., having slept for ten hours. I'm pretty certain it's a personal record. I only woke up briefly before 7:30 room checks when Alyssa snuck back in. The next time I woke up, she was gone.

I reach to the nightstand to grab the schedule Jody passed out on the bus. I've missed breakfast, I discover. Rehearsal's supposed to start in an hour, which means I should get up. I should get ready to endure Owen ignoring me, to withstand Alyssa's scowls and face Tyler, to play the role of a beloved, lovestruck girl who I really, really hate.

I stay in bed instead.

I know I have to tell Madeleine, but I also know doing so will ruin her relationship, a relationship everyone thought was perfect. It's not fair, when I think about it. It'll be my words that hurt her, even though it's Tyler who did something wrong. I'm not up to giving her that call just yet.

If not for me, Madeleine wouldn't have anything to find

out about Tyler. And if not for me, Mom wouldn't have to be reminded of or talk to the person who broke her heart. She would've moved on the way she wanted when she moved out. She might've even been happy if I hadn't been there to reopen wounds she'd tried to forget. None of this is my fault, but it is *because* of me.

The thought hits me then, involuntarily, like it's come from somewhere outside me. Like someone else wrote it down and shoved it into my hand, the world's worst love note.

I'm the reason everyone close to me gets hurt.

Rehearsal time comes and passes. I don't budge, staring up at the ceiling from under the covers. It's six minutes into rehearsal when the texts start. The first three from Bridget Molloy, the stage manager, with increasing urgency culminating in a long string of exclamation points. One from Tyler, just **u coming?** A longer one from Jenna notifying me that Jody's freaking out and is going to send someone to my room in two minutes.

I wait ten minutes, refusing to get out of this bed until I'm dragged by the ankles. Nobody comes.

I'm dozing off when a final text lights up my phone.

WHERE ARE YOU?

Anthony's name on my screen stabs me with a sliver of guilt. I remember what this performance means to him. It'd destroy him if this show was ruined, and especially if his best friend let it happen.

It's not just Anthony, either. There's Jason Mitchum, who really learned to swordfight from YouTube tutorials to play Tybalt. Jenna, whom I overheard murmuring her lines to herself the entire bus ride. And then there's Owen, who loves every word of *Romeo and Juliet* with a deeper appreciation than any actor I've ever worked with.

This play is important to people other than Tyler Dunning. People who are important to me. Showing up and playing Juliet is one small opportunity I have *not* to hurt them. And am I really ready to throw away my chance to go to the college I've dreamt of since I was a kid? I launch myself out of bed, throw on a pair of jeans and a parka, and fly out the door.

I run the three blocks to the theater, the cold biting my lungs, and thread between bicyclists and coffee-carrying pedestrians. I'm out of breath by the time I hit Pioneer Street, which fortunately isn't crowded because it's the Oregon Shakespeare Festival's official off-season. The rounded back of the Elizabethan theater goes by on my left as I rush down the hill to the Angus Bowmer Theatre straight ahead.

Throwing open the door, I burst into the auditorium. Our monastery set is on the stage. No one is seated in the audience, unlike at school, except Bridget with her headset and Jody with her clipboard and a pencil pressed to her lips.

"I long to die if what thou speak'st speak not of remedy," I hear from the stage, and despite my parka and the overactive theater heating, I feel a chill run through me. That's my line . . . but I'm not on stage. I watch motionless as Alyssa walks to my mark while Owen gives Friar Lawrence's reply. She doesn't stumble over a single line, delivering Juliet's desperate dialogue flawlessly. Better than I would've.

"Take thou this vial, being then in bed—" Owen pauses in the middle of his monologue when he sees me. Jody follows his gaze, her eyes narrowing.

Without bothering to call the scene to a halt, she walks up the aisle toward me. Her face is red, her mouth pulled tight in something between irritation and disappointment. "Where have you been?" Her voice rises on the final word and echoes in the empty theater.

"I—I overslept," I mumble.

Her eyes widen. "You *overslept*? In the four years I've known you, Megan, you've never been less than ten minutes *early* to a rehearsal. I know you weren't thrilled to get the Juliet role, but I thought you were mature enough to handle it, or at least that you respected us enough to show up and try."

"I'm here now, aren't I?" I force impudence into my voice to push down the tears.

"You're here an hour late to the most important rehearsal of the entire production. You were off your game in class yesterday, obviously distracted. I'm tired of fighting you on this, Megan." Her expression softens, and she looks unfamiliarly sad. "I don't know what's going on with you, but you win. I'll give you what you've always wanted. You'll play Lady Montague, or nothing."

I don't answer. Alyssa watches me from the stage, and I realize what's happened. They don't need me. They never did. Jody waits for me to decide, but I turn and walk toward the door. Away from what I knew deep down to expect.

If they want to replace me, fine. It's probably better if they do.

I'm halfway to the hotel when I feel my phone vibrate. I pull it out, dreading a gloating text from Alyssa or one from Anthony telling me I'm the worst friend ever.

Instead, it's Owen.

What the hell was that?

Blinking back tears, I send him what I hope will end the conversation.

What should have happened a long time ago, Owen.
Just leave me alone.

It's the first time Owen's voluntarily talked to me in weeks, and under better circumstances I wouldn't pass up the possibility of figuring things out between us. But not today. Not now.

TWENTY-FIVE

CHORUS: *But passion lends them power, time means, to meet,*
Temp'ring extremities with extreme sweet.

II.prologue.13–4

I HAVEN'T LEFT MY ROOM IN SEVEN hours, except for the trip to
the vending machine to pick up what passed for dinner—
which hardly counts. I pretended to sleep when Alyssa returned to the room to be counted for nightly room checks
by a parent chaperone, and while my former understudy
unpacked noisily, probably wanting to wake me up in order
to brag about Juliet, I didn't budge until she left for Will's
again.

I'm flipping channels between two stations of Ashland
nighttime news when there's finally a knock on the door.
Three quick taps, light but deliberate. I've been expecting
Jody to try to talk to me, or maybe lecture me some more, ever
since rehearsal ended. I'm surprised she waited this long.

What if she waited this long because she's sending me home?
Worry constricts my chest. *What if she had to organize my
transportation, or whatever?* Knowing I can't ignore her, I drag
myself to the door.

But I crack it open to find Owen, clutching his notebook.

"What do you want?" I ask, holding the door open only a couple inches.

His expression is guarded but gentle. "I want to show you something."

I start to shut the door. "I'm really not in the mood, Owen."

"I finished it." He holds up his notebook, and in a moment I realize what he means. His play. It surprises me enough that I release my hold on the door, and he brushes by me into the room.

I collect myself, rounding on him. "You ignore me for weeks, and now you barge in here to show me your *play*? That's . . . great. I'm really happy for you," I say sarcastically.

"I wasn't ignoring you." His voice is quiet.

"We haven't talked since . . ." I can't bring myself to complete the sentence. To put a name to whatever happened between us in his room.

"What you said about Cosima and my play stung, and I know I said enough to make you hate me. I was ashamed and frustrated with myself, and I needed distance." He fervently flips the pages of his notebook. "But I couldn't ignore you. Not even if I tried." He looks up at me, a tentative smile curling his lips, and my heart does a familiar Owen-related leap. But it turns back into lead when I remind myself of everything that happened this weekend and everything that stands between us.

"Well, thanks," I say stiffly. "You can go now."

His smile disappears, but he doesn't move. "I won't go until you tell me what's wrong."

"Nothing's wrong."

"I know you better than that, Megan," he says, looking at me intently. "Your text had complete sentences and perfect punctuation. I know something's happened." I say nothing, knowing he'd see through whatever bullshit explanation I give him, and he continues. "What you said to me in my room, you were right."

I look up sharply. *About Cosima?*

"I was afraid to write because I was afraid I'd suck," he goes on, and I deflate a little. "I didn't want to hear it, but I needed to." He places the notebook on the bed. "I wanted to show you the play because it's entirely thanks to you. I thought you might need a reminder of how important you are."

File for future reference: Owen can crush me with a word.

"Owen . . ." I turn away, trying to hide the tears welling in my eyes.

He steps forward and places a hand on my arm. "Does it have something to do with Tyler? I saw you with him last night . . ."

I jerk back. "Did he say something?" On top of everything else today, I couldn't handle it if Tyler was spreading some story about us that didn't happen. Knowing what he's capable of, I wouldn't put it past him.

"No." Owen frowns. "Wait, what would he have said? I just meant that he tries to make you feel bad sometimes."

I sag against the dresser in relief. "No, it wasn't that. He . . . tried to hook up with me. Nothing happened," I rush to say, not wanting Owen to believe I'm the kind of person who could go behind my best friend's back like that. But he's still looking at me with concern, and there isn't a trace of judgment in his dark eyes. "It just changes everything I thought about him and me, and him and Madeleine," I continue.

Confusion traces a crease in his forehead. "Which was what?"

"I guess I could accept being dumped, or even being cheated on, when it meant Madeleine having something perfect." I drop my gaze, unable to meet his, and study his rumpled black sweater and the smudge of ink on his thumb. "But I don't understand why Tyler would break up with me if this is how he's going to treat her."

Owen pauses like he's searching for words. "It's not about you or Madeleine," he says slowly. "It's not about you being inadequate or her being perfect. It's Tyler. The guy's an ass-hole. He was *never* going to be a good boyfriend, to either of you. He's like every guy you date—" He stops, correcting himself. "I mean, they're not assholes, not every one of them. It's just, Will, even Anthony, who was obviously gay—you pick guys who will leave you, who will hurt you, who could never be what you deserve. You're trying to protect yourself from getting your hopes up."

Indignant, I flush. He's one to talk. He hurt me and deserted me just like the rest. "Who do you think you are?" I say, fire in my voice. "You've only known me for a few months. What gives you the right to come in here and tell me that my relationship history is some sort of fucked-up self-fulfilling prophecy—"

"Every prophecy is a self-fulfilling prophecy, Megan," he says seriously. "You taught me that. We *have* only known each other a few months, but you've seen me in a way nobody else ever has, and I think I might know you better than anyone, too." I feel myself softening, until he continues. "You tell yourself you deserve to be dumped, but you don't. You choose it."

"Wow," I say harshly. "Thanks, Owen."

"No, I—" he stutters, backing away from me and beginning to pace across the room. "This isn't coming out right. I mean—I know what you were thinking when you saw Alyssa on stage playing your role. You were thinking what you're always thinking. That you're replaceable."

He *does* know me better than anyone. The realization hits me like a blow, because despite him being here, despite how he's unfailingly loyal and passionately caring, he isn't mine.

"But you're not." He pauses in his pacing to look up at me, and there's an undeniable change in the air. "You're irreplaceable. To your family, to your friends—to me."

The ashes of everything I felt when he was kissing me weeks ago leap into a flame. He's standing in the middle of the room, watching me with his eyes unguarded, and I can read in them everything he wants. It's exactly what I want, too.

I walk forward like I'm being drawn to him, then stop, only inches away. He reaches out and takes my hand, and whatever was between us finally crumbles as I bring my lips to his. He kisses me back softly, still without stepping forward to meet me. Pressing his fingers into my palm, he pulls back.

With his free hand he traces the line of my cheek, and in his touch I feel a hesitation, like he's holding back hope. "How do I know this is for real?" he asks in a whisper.

"Doesn't it feel real?" I'm breathless, hardly able to form the words.

"Yes, but it's felt real to me before, even when you were just flirting for fun. How am I supposed to know you mean it? Especially considering I'm not exactly your type. You know . . . shy, *sweet*." He grimaces on the word.

I tilt my head to find his eyes, forcing him to meet mine. "Here's a hint. With you, it was never just for fun." He nearly smiles. "Besides, my type hasn't exactly worked for me, as you eloquently pointed out. And yes, you're sweet. I like that you're sweet. But you're not only sweet, you're witty, fascinating, charming . . ." I close the distance between us. "And we both know you're not shy." I raise an eyebrow.

He leans in, laughing, and kisses me once more. And this time, there's nothing hesitant about the way he grabs my waist and tugs me tightly against him. Without letting him go, I lead us toward the bed. I remember what I felt the last time we were in this position, how desperate I was to have as much of him as I could, but . . . it's different now. For the first time, I'm not focused on when it will end. I sit down on the sheets and wait for him to climb on top of me.

He doesn't. Instead, he reclines next to me, and with one unexpectedly quick motion he pulls me on top of him. I let out a surprised laugh and lower my face to his. But before our lips meet, I draw back suddenly.

"Wait," I say, leaning up while straddling his waist, my heart plummeting out of my chest and onto the floor. "We did this. You have a—"

Owen cuts me off. "I broke up with Cosima."

"What?" I stutter, reaching for my heart on the floor-boards. *"When?"*

He props himself up and strokes my side. "Pretty much the minute you left my room."

It takes a moment for the words to come together in my head—it's possible his hand on my side isn't helping. But when they do, I'm overwhelmed. Relief, indignation, and adoration fight for space inside me. It's all I can do to kiss him deeply before pulling back and peering at him admon-ishingly. "You really should have told me."

A smile spreads across his face, then slowly fades. "I thought you weren't interested."

I take his face in my hands and stare into his eyes, refusing to let him misunderstand me this time. "Sweet, witty, fasci-nating, charming," I say slowly, "and an idiot." He's laughing when I lean forward to pick up where we left off.

I lift my shirt over my head and take no little pleasure from the way his eyes widen. "Off," I order, pointedly nodding at his sweater. With boyish urgency, he pulls it off, and—

Owen has a six-pack.

Years of pursuing jock-bros like Wyatt Rhodes, and it's *Owen Okita* who's finally going to fulfill my high school goal of hooking up with a six-pack. The universe works in myste-rious ways. They're not the most defined abs I've ever seen—he's not Zac Efron—but they're there. Isn't there some law of nature that the sensitive, writerly guys shouldn't be ripped?

"Owen!" I prod his stomach. "How did this happen? Ex-plain yourself!"

He looks down, uncomprehending. I run a finger down

the line of his muscle, and his face lights up. "I don't know," he says with a lazy smile. "Just enjoy it, Megan."

Laughing, I get off him and walk to the door. But with my hand on the deadbolt, I pause.

I don't want to do what I've done in every one of my relationships before. I don't want to rush. With Owen, though, this doesn't feel like rushing. It feels exactly right, right now. I don't want to be with him in this way because I think I have to now, before he disappears. I'm not doing it under a deadline, under the expectation of everything falling to pieces—it's not rushing because it's not for the wrong reasons. If I know it's real, and Owen knows it's real, it doesn't matter how fast it is. I want to be with him because I *want* to.

I close the deadbolt and turn to face him. "Those too . . ." I point in the general direction of his gray corduroys. I'm expecting the Owen blush, but he only smiles.

"Okay, okay." While he undoes his belt, I step out of my jeans. Thankfully, I'm wearing more respectable underwear today. Nothing written on it.

I climb on top of him, and we kiss in the way people do when there's not a hint of doubt it'll progress to something else. I let my hands explore his chest and—yes, his six-pack. His fingers brush the skin of my back, skimming the lace at the bottom of my bra. I urge him on with my lips.

When I guide one of his hands lower, he pulls back. "I . . ." he starts. "I wasn't expecting anything like this to happen."

I'm thrown, and I tense up. "Do you not want it to?"

"No," he says quickly. "It's not that. It's just . . . I've never . . ." He trails off once more, this time with a vivid blush.

My eyes widen. For the first time I consider the possibility he's not feeling everything I am right now. "I'm sorry, I didn't— If this is too fast, or not special enough—" I move to get off him.

Owen's hand on my hip holds me in place. "It's not that. I just wanted you to know."

"Oh," I say, relieved. "Yeah. I understand. Well, I have," I add, not at all sure how to have this conversation.

"Yeah, Megan. I know. You told me in detail." The corners of his mouth twitch upward. I feel mine do the same.

"Never with Cosima?" I prod his chest. "You guys were at *camp.*"

He grabs my hand. "I hadn't known Cosima for very long." His voice has gone hushed. "I wanted to wait for something meaningful, for someone I cared about so deeply I needed this to express it."

A tiny tremor runs through me. *I* feel everything he's saying, but it wouldn't be unreasonable if—

"I was waiting for this," he says. He pulls me down for a kiss, and for a while we just sink into each other. His hand in my hair, his breath on my cheek, I reach off the bed for my bag.

"I have the . . ." I say, my fingers catching the plastic wrapper.

Straightening up, I notice him watching me questioningly. "Not that I'm not grateful, but who were you planning—?" He stops, reconsidering. "You know what, it *really* doesn't matter." He reaches to kiss me again, but I place a hand on his chest.

"Nobody, for what it's worth." I smile sideways at him. Dropping my gaze, I bring his hand back to my thigh. "Nobody I'd rather . . ." I finish the sentence with a kiss.

We don't rush. Each motion is a step onto uncertain ground, into an unexplored place. My hands find the back of his shoulders, and I clutch him close to me, our hearts pounding together. It's nothing like it was with Tyler. It's how it's supposed to be. From the way Owen's eyes hold mine, I know he feels it, too.

I've spent the day in this bed, in this room, committing to memory every detail of the paint on the walls and the kitschy pattern of the curtains. It's been empty, suffocating, but with Owen it's bursting with light. It doesn't matter the hotel is cheap and plain, the view out the window ordinary—it's perfect. I don't need skinny-dipping under the stars. I only need this.

Owen breathes my name, and I feel like the center of the universe.

We lie in bed for minutes that feel like seconds or hours, my head resting on the hollow of his shoulder.

"Wow," he whispers in the darkness. "No wonder you thought I was insane for having a girlfriend all the way in Italy."

I feel him smile, and I laugh softly. "Yeah, now you know what you've been missing out on."

"I was missing out on a lot before I met you."

I slide my hand up his chest. "To be fair, I didn't know it could be like this either."

"Really?" He tilts his head down.

I look up, meeting his eyes. "Really." I pause, a little nervous to ask the question in my head. "Do you want to stay?"

He hugs me tighter. "Of course I do."

I close my eyes, not bothering to wonder how long he means. Tomorrow, two weeks, it doesn't matter—right now is enough.

TWENTY-SIX

ROMEO: *I have more care to stay than will to go.*

Come death and welcome. Juliet wills it so.

How is 't, my soul? Let's talk. It is not day.

JULIET: *It is, it is. Hie hence, begone, away!*

III.v.23–6

WHEN I WAKE, OWEN'S NEXT TO ME.

I roll onto my side to find him already awake. He's lovingly tracing a finger down my arm, and when our eyes meet, he kisses me lightly on the shoulder.

My stomach growls. Owen looks startled, then amused, and I realize exactly how hungry I am. Madeleine's brownies and the two granola bars I had for dinner aren't holding me after the events of last night. How long *has* it been since I ate? I glance at the clock. "Shit!" I elbow Owen. "It's seven twenty!"

"Ow, Megan." He's rubbing his ribs when I turn back over, and in the morning light I'm given new appreciation of his shirtless chest.

"Sorry," I say, not really meaning it. "Seriously though, you're going to miss morning room checks if you don't leave."

In the back of my mind I notice Alyssa hasn't returned yet either. Whatever she's doing with Will, she's really cutting it close on time.

Owen props himself up on his elbow, blinking. "Oh. Right. Yeah." He tosses off the covers and begins searching for his clothes on the floor. Pulling on his pants, he pauses and faces me, concern in his eyes. "Hey, um," he says hesitantly, "everything's . . . okay, right?"

Touched, and noticing his ears have gone my favorite shade of red, I smile. "Oh my god. You're perfect."

"Um, thanks." A smile flickers on his face. "But you didn't exactly answer the question."

I leap out of bed and fling my arms around his neck. Tilting my head upward so our noses nearly touch, I smile shamelessly. "*Okay* would be putting it mildly." I crush my lips to his, spurred on by his adorableness. Without hesitation his arms encircle my waist, and—I feel him leading us toward the bed.

"Owen!" I say, chastising. Not that I blame him for his enthusiasm. I did just throw myself at him without a stitch of clothing on.

He looks taken aback. "But you just said it was—"

"You have nine minutes," I interrupt, picking up his shirt and halfheartedly offering it to him.

He only grins. "Nine minutes is so much time, Megan."

I laugh and shake the shirt. "No, really. I don't know why Jody didn't drop by yesterday, but she's definitely going to today, to lecture me or something before call time. Besides, do you want *Alyssa* to walk in on us? She'll be back any minute." Owen groans, and I have no choice but to toss the shirt in his face. "Out, Romeo!"

Morning room checks happen with no sign of Jody—or of Alyssa. Brian Anderson's mom, the chaperone, picks up my Juliet costume for quick alterations to fit Alyssa's petite height and measures me for the Lady Montague dress, and I realize Jody's given me the part whether I like it or not. I guess that's her style. I'm beginning to wonder whether she'll *ever* come talk to me or if she's written me off completely.

I've just returned to my room after running downstairs to grab a bowl of oatmeal—I wanted to hit the buffet before everyone else got there—when I hear a knock on the door. I know it's not Jody, who's discussing set placement with the stage crew for their scheduled meeting in the theater. It's probably Owen coming back to get his belt that he left when I kicked him out. I open the door, the belt in hand.

"Dad?"

I hurriedly toss the belt in the trash can behind the door while he strides past me into the room. He looks around without appearing to really take anything in. "We have to talk, Megan," he announces.

"Why are you here?" I ask haltingly.

He raises an incredulous eyebrow. "You disappeared from rehearsal on a school field trip."

"Yeah, but how do you—"

"Jody called me," he says, his voice suddenly lowering.

"She sounded angry, saying something about you no longer playing Juliet. Is that true?"

Now I understand why Jody hasn't come to see me. She brought in the big guns. "Yeah, it's true, but it's fine. I didn't want to be Juliet in the first place." I keep my voice steady despite how I'm still reeling from his intrusion. "I'm Lady Montague now, the part I should have had from the beginning. I have, like, two lines."

Dad perches on the edge of the bed and frowns. "I don't know what you're talking about, the part you should have had from the beginning," he says eventually. "I know you've put a lot of work into this play. It's why your mom flew home to watch you." I hate how innocuously he says *home*, like he doesn't know he forced Mom out of the place where she belongs. "Then we get an irate phone call from a teacher who's always loved you—your mom and I are worried."

"Don't pretend you care how Mom feels," I shoot back, surprising myself, and him. He recoils, confusion written in his eyes.

"What do you mean?" he asks.

I know I probably should take it back, but everything I've watched happen to my family over the past three years is boiling to the surface, and I charge on. "Weren't you paying attention when we had dinner at the house together? Or were you too busy with your new wife to even notice how upset *my* mom was?"

"Your mother's not upset," he says calmly, like I'm the one who has this wrong. "We went out to lunch yesterday, the four of us."

"She was crying, Dad. When she put Erin to bed, I found her in Erin's room crying, alone." I feel a tremor in my own voice. "She's heartbroken. She's always been heartbroken. It's why she shouldn't have even come here in the first place—it only makes her sadder. But what would you care, right?"

"That's not fair." Dad tries to interrupt, but everything I haven't said to him for years is rushing out of me.

"You're the one who divorced her, who stopped loving her. Then you jumped into bed with Rose, not even caring how hurt Mom was." I take a breath. I've run out of words for what I'm feeling.

"I wasn't *in* love with your mom anymore," he says gently, his shoulders sagging, "but I do still love her. I'll always love her. Your mom knows that. She understands why we couldn't be together anymore, but she knows how I feel about her."

"She obviously *doesn't*, Dad," I return. "If she did, I wouldn't have found her crying upstairs in her old home. Remember?"

"Just because your mother understands how I feel about her doesn't mean it won't hurt her sometimes. It hurts me, too." He rubs his face distractedly, his eyes desolate. "It's a hard thing, ending something that permanent. It's a pain that never goes away."

I try to reconcile his words with what I know. It doesn't work. "But you moved on. You moved on so quickly," I say weakly.

Dad straightens up, looking surprised. "I fell in love with Rose, but I haven't moved on," he amends carefully, uncertainly even. "I guess I never considered how it looked to you. How quickly I brought Rose into my life. But finding Rose has nothing to do with what I feel for your mother. Your mom is an invaluable part of my life, and no matter what, she always will be." From the vulnerability in his voice, I feel the truth of what he's saying. He pauses, something searching in his expression. "I hope you know, Megan, if you think Erin and the baby change your place in our family—nothing could ever change that."

I say nothing. I don't know how to tell him he's wrong. They *have* changed my place. It's impossible to admit out loud.

"Hey. Look at me," he says gently. I do, tears I wish I could banish brimming in my eyes. His voice is rough when he continues. "I'm sorry," he says. "I haven't been there for you the way you needed, the way you deserve. I'm trying to figure out how to be a new father *and* raise an intimidatingly smart, self-possessed teenager, and I know I haven't gotten it right every time. But us moving to New York isn't us leaving you behind." He pauses as if for permission, which I give by waiting. He goes on. "You're kind of scarily grown-up now, Megan," he says with a faint grin. "Next year you're going to college. You're going to be pursuing your own future. I want you to have that experience on your own—being the incredibly independent adult you already are."

I smile back, a tear stumbling over my eyelashes.

"That said," he continues, "if you ever need us, or want us, or you're tired of being grown-up for a while, then come home."

Home? I feel my smile fade. "New York's not my home," I say. "It won't be the same. You'll have your own life, and I won't belong."

"Where we are doesn't matter," he says with half a laugh,

as if he's surprised I could imagine otherwise. "Wherever we are, we're family."

His words dissolve the weight on my chest, the weight I hadn't fully realized had lain there for years. He stands up and walks across the room, placing his hands on my shoulders and looking down at me.

"Nothing could ever change how much I love you," he says, and I collapse into a hug against his chest. I'm crying into his shoulder without even realizing it, his hands stroking soothing circles on my back. We remain that way until I'm out of tears.

Finally, I pull back, noticing the ugly snot stain I've left on his shirt. He doesn't seem to mind. "So," I say, casting around for something to defuse the heavy emotion in the room, "how pissed *did* Jody seem on the phone?"

He laughs. "Pissed. Not pissed enough she wouldn't talk to you about the role, though."

"I'm fine with just being Lady Montague. I only need the acting credit for SOTI," I say, stepping away and picking up my new costume. "It doesn't matter what part I play."

"I don't believe that," Dad replies sharply, and I whip to face him, surprised at his sudden conviction. "For months, I've heard nothing but *Romeo and Juliet*. This role is yours. You earned it."

"It doesn't matter," I protest. "They found a new Juliet."

"So what if there's a new Juliet?" he asks, throwing the thought away with a wave of his hand. "I want to know that if you don't go on stage to do what you've worked for, you won't regret it tomorrow."

Still clutching the Lady Montague costume, I picture walking on stage in the Angus Bowmer Theatre just to say two lines. I could do it, but it'd hurt. I've put hours and hours into this play, I've made Juliet my own, and to just walk away . . . Then I picture standing on Juliet's balcony, delivering lines to Tyler Douchebag Dunning—and it doesn't feel impossible.

I thought I wasn't meant to be a main character, on stage or anywhere else. But I also thought Madeleine was perfect and she and Tyler were meant to be, that my dad didn't care about my mom and my place in our family was disappearing, and that Owen could never want someone like me. I thought I couldn't fall for someone absolutely and completely. I've been wrong before.

I look back up at Dad, and I know he sees the resolve in my eyes, because he's smiling. "Jody's in the lobby. I saw her returning when I got here," he says, taking the costume out of my hands. "Go."

In one step I've reached the door. But before I pull it open, I double back and throw my arms around him. "Thanks, Dad."

I enter the lobby, and I'm momentarily overwhelmed by the pre-performance chaos. The noblewomen of Verona have gathered in full costume around the brunch buffet and are chattering excitedly. Nearby, one of the prop masters explains to Anthony for the hundredth time how to use the blood squib for his death scene. The stage crew, Will included, have chosen the center of the room to go over the set changes one final time.

I pick out Jody by the front doors talking to a couple of parent chaperones, none of whom looks happy. Threading in between the costumed girls, I catch snippets of their conversation.

"Heard he was . . ."

"She just called . . ."

". . . Italian girlfriend."

Wait. I stop so abruptly that Jeremy crashes into my back. He mutters an apology and darts around me. I know there's only one person *Italian girlfriend* could refer to, but I have to be certain. I come up beside Courtney, ignoring the indignant looks I get from everyone I just cut in the buffet line.

"Megan! You're here!" Courtney doesn't bother hiding the curiosity in her voice.

"Uh, yeah. I wasn't feeling well," I lie, eager to dodge this conversation. I match their gossipy tone. "Hey, did I hear you talking about Cosima?"

Jenna cranes her head past Courtney. "Yeah, I think she *might* be real." She giggles.

"What—uh—makes you say?"

"Owen's roommate was telling everyone that Owen and Cosima were on the phone this morning," Courtney rushes to say. "They were talking for, like, an hour. Apparently it was . . . *intense.*" She raises her eyebrows suggestively.

"Intense how?" I force myself to ask.

"We heard he was doing a lot of apologizing and reassuring. Whatever Owen did . . . he regrets something." Courtney sounds obviously pleased with herself.

I don't know why I asked. I knew what I would hear. "Still doesn't prove she's real." I fake a laugh as my heart is ripped from my chest. "I'll see you guys later," I say while they're laughing.

Leaving the line, I pause by the stairs to catch my breath, my chest tight. I don't want to be the kind of person who jumps to conclusions based on gossip, but with my romantic history, it's pretty much impossible not to. When Owen left my room this morning, he probably realized he wants to be with Cosima and regrets being with me. He called her to apologize.

I thought I'd done something different when I fell for Owen. He said I'd repeatedly chosen the wrong guys—I thought he was the right one. Instead, I've done exactly what I did every time before. It's like I can't escape putting myself in a position to be discarded and replaced.

Out of the corner of my eye, I catch Jody walking toward the door.

Asking for the Juliet role might just be putting myself in the same position once again. Jody could say no, and I would have to watch Alyssa take everything I've earned. But I have to try. I'm happy I tried with Owen. I know deep down I am. Even if things with him are over without having hardly begun, I don't have time to fall apart right now. The play's too important.

I march up to Jody, sidestepping everyone in my way. Her

hand's on the door. I slide in front of her, stopping her from leaving, and her expression hardens.

"I'm *really* sorry about yesterday," I say in a single breath. "It was unprofessional and disrespectful to you and to everyone involved in the production."

"Yes, it was," she says, unwavering. "I don't have time for this. I'll deal with you after the performance."

"No, we have to talk now," I tell her. I've talked back to Jody before, but this degree of boldness startles even me. It definitely gets her attention—she drops her hand from the door and crosses her arms. "You need to give me the role back," I continue before she can reprimand me.

Surprise joins the sternness in her eyes. "Why's that?"

"I didn't think I could relate to Juliet before. I thought she was an idiot, giving up everything for a guy with mediocre flirting skills." Jody raises an eyebrow but doesn't smile. "But I understand her now." I pause, hoping she's willing to hear more.

"What do you understand, Megan?" she asks, sounding tired.

Encouraged, I go on. "Everyone's an idiot like Juliet sometimes. Or everyone should be. Juliet dares to care about something. It makes her do crazy things—crazy like confronting her director in the middle of a crowded hotel lobby to beg for something she probably doesn't deserve." Jody permits a small grin. "I'm ready to be like that. To care. I want to be Juliet, for you, for everyone in the play who I've worked with—and for me. *I* want this."

I finish my monologue, the most impassioned one I've ever given, and there's a horrible, quiet moment. Not quiet in the lobby, obviously, but between us, there's the silence of the empty stage before the curtain rises.

"Finally," she says at last. "I didn't come talk to you yesterday because I was hoping you'd come to me. You're a wonderful director, Megan. I've seen you break down and explain countless characters, all but delivering the lines yourself. I gave you the role of Juliet because I knew you could do it, but I wanted you to realize you could do it, too."

A grin spreads across my face. "Wait," I say hesitantly, "does this mean I have the role?"

"What do you think?" Jody gives me a wry smile. It's all the answer I need.

Relief races through me, followed by the thrill of this having actually worked. Then—"What about Alyssa?" I wonder aloud.

"That's the other reason I'm glad you came to talk to me." Jody shakes her head, sounding relieved herself. "One of our chaperones caught Alyssa trying to sneak back into her room this morning during room checks. I don't know where she went last night, but the conduct handbook requires I send her home, which would have meant forcing Jenna Cho to memorize the entire play in two hours. Now Jenna won't have to, and one of the stagehands will be reading Lady Montague."

She checks her watch. "Better get in costume, Juliet."

TWENTY-SEVEN

JULIET: *My bounty is as boundless as the sea,*
My love as deep. The more I give to thee,
The more I have, for both are infinite.

II.ii.140–2

I DO A THOUSAND THINGS IN THE next hour. I hurry up to my room, where my dad gives an honest-to-god cheer when I tell him I've got the part. I practically have to push him out the door before I take the world's fastest shower. Throwing on my sweats, I walk with wet hair dangling down my back to the parent chaperones' room, the Lady Montague dress wrapped in a ball under my arm. It takes reciting a portion of my final monologue to convince Jeremy's mom I need the Juliet costume back. I catch her grumbling about having to re-re-alter the dress.

Before I change, I drop by the dining room to grab an apple, which I've eaten by the time I've reached my room. I pull my costume on—no help from Owen this time, unfortunately—and text Anthony, who deserves an explanation, and Eric, who wants directions to the theater. If I survive the play, I'll try to corner him in the back and convince him to at least say hi to Anthony. I don't think that counts as meddling. Eric decided to come on his own, after all.

I do a good job not dwelling on Owen in the fifty-seven minutes it takes me to finish everything. I rush downstairs into the lobby, which I find has emptied out, unsurprisingly. Everyone's already on their way to the theater for an hour of makeup and mic checks before the performance.

I push open the front door, only now remembering I forgot my parka. Even with the sun streaming through the cloudless December sky, the air is eye-wateringly cold. But it's not the end of the world—Juliet's dress involves long sleeves and tights. I step out, hugging my arms to my chest. Only a few pedestrians cut me glances as I walk down Vista Street in full costume. I guess they're used to this sort of thing.

My dress fluttering in the wind, I march into the crosswalk on Fork Street. I'm in the middle of the road when, several steps in front of me, I spot a familiar friar's costume.

"Hey, Owen," I call to his back. How do I talk to someone who was heard having an "intense" conversation with his Italian ex hours after I took his virginity? I'll figure it out.

He turns in the middle of the street, his eyes lighting up when he sees me.

Whatever's going on with Cosima, I'm not going to be weird about it, I decide. I want to keep Owen as a friend, no matter how last night redefined everything for me.

"I heard about your epic speech to Jody," he says when I catch up to him. He's holding the schedule binder Jody handed out to everyone. "I'm really glad you're going to be Juliet."

"Thanks." I scramble to hold together everything his smile unravels in me.

"You look beautiful," he says, not doing me any favors.

The way he's looking at me—I can't help but remember him helping me when I was stuck in the dressing room, his hands brushing my back, his fingers lifting the hem up my body. And yesterday. *Yesterday*. But I play it cool. "You look chaste." I nod to his frock.

Owen steps up onto the sidewalk and twirls in place. "You know, appearances can be deceiving, Megan," he says, stunning me with a wry smile.

I blink. He's 100 percent flirting with me. I know it when I see it. I take a breath, walking beside him. "Hey, so, um, I heard you talked to Cosima this morning." I force myself to sound casual.

His eyes narrow quizzically. "Who told you that?"

"Just . . . some of the girls, you know."

He shoots me a sidewise glance like I've just claimed the Earl of Oxford wrote Shakespeare's plays. "No, I don't know. But, yeah, I did talk to Cosima. She just wanted to clear the air. We left things kind of ugly the last time we talked."

"Oh." I pause, replaying his words in my head and searching for clues. "And . . . ?" I finally ask.

"And . . . then we hung up?" he says like he has no idea what I could be implying. He looks over at me again, and he must notice the desperate curiosity in my expression. "Oh my god. Megan! I was reassuring her the breakup wasn't her fault." His eyes go wide. "Tell me you didn't think I was getting back together with her."

I feel my face redden. "I thought you might feel like last

night was a one-time thing—" I begin defensively. I hear how empty it sounds, how illogical. It's a reflex, born of breakup after breakup.

"I snuck out of my room after room checks," Owen cuts in, talking over me, "I told you you were irreplaceable, I showed you my play, and *then* we—" His face flushes spectacularly, and he gestures emptily in the air. "Which, remember, is something I'd never done before and something I'm desperately hoping is not a *one-time thing*."

We stop in front of the door to the back of the theater. When I look up at Owen, for the first time today I don't hold back what I'm feeling for everything about him, every part of him. Not for the crooked smile he's giving me this very moment. Not for the way he made me laugh while telling me exactly what my heart wanted to hear. Not for his intelligence or his humor. *Nor any other part belonging to a man*, I hear Juliet's voice in my head.

"I'm hoping it's not a one-time thing either," I say softly. "I kind of . . ." I feel a thought forming, and I follow where it leads. "I want to make this official. I don't know. What do you think?" I ask fumblingly.

Owen looks surprised, and then an uncontrolled laugh escapes him. "O, speak again, bright angel," he quotes, and I roll my eyes, recognizing Romeo's line. I move to shove him lightly, but he pins my hand to his chest. "I *really* want to make this official, Megan."

He kisses me, and I feel like call time might as well be in a million years, because I could do nothing but this forever. It's every bit the raging rush it was only hours ago in my hotel bed. His hair—ever too long—brushes my cheeks. My fingers, numb with cold only moments ago, tingle and trace burning lines over his shoulders. My pulse races.

I hear giggles behind me, and I realize what we look like to whoever's walking into the theater. Here I am, Juliet kissing a Romeo she never expected, who's dressed in the costume of a monk. Owen evidently notices them, too, because he holds up the binder to hide us from view, never once breaking our kiss.

I finally pull back and look up at Owen, arms still encircling his waist. "You're in luck, you know," I say. "Every one of my boyfriends finds the perfect girl right after we break up."

Owen kisses the top of my head. "Not every boyfriend," he murmurs into my hair. "I have her right here."

I don't have words for how this feels. I don't know that there are words. Not even in Shakespeare.

Heavy makeup coating my face, I wait in the wings for the curtain to rise. I didn't often force myself to imagine what this moment would feel like, but on the occasions I did, I didn't imagine this. There's no knot in my stomach, but I'm not giddy with excitement either. I feel calm. Centered. Each of my scenes lies before me in a lighted path to the final bows.

The curtain goes up. I peer into the audience, and even though it's dark, I feel my breath catch at the sheer number of people I can see. But I keep looking until I find them. Randall, Mom, Dad, and Rose sitting in the second row. Dad holds Rose's hand, but he leans into Mom's shoulder to whisper in her ear. I watch her smile at whatever he said while Courtney, the narrator, finds her mark.

"Two households, both alike in dignity . . ." I hear her begin.

I go on for my first scene with Romeo and realize it's the first time I've spoken to Tyler since Friday night. We exchange amorous glances across the Capulet Manor set, and I linger downstage before he strides to me and takes my hand. Waiting under the lights, I feel none of the revulsion I do for Tyler himself.

Because I'm not watching Tyler right now. I'm watching Romeo, and I'm Juliet.

He kisses my hand, and I snatch it away, playing the hard-to-get Juliet I've come to love. I exchange hushed dialogue with Nurse Jenna before I exit stage left for the end of Act I. Anthony's by the curtain, his eyes fixed on his mark, his lips moving imperceptibly. I put a hand on his shoulder and whisper, "Juilliard's going to love you." I catch his slight smile in the uneven backstage lighting.

In the wings, I watch a couple of freshmen diligently organizing the prop table. There's the dagger, the apothecary's bottles of poison, Owen's prayer book. The stage crew silently wheels the balcony set into position behind the curtains, and I catch a glimpse of Andrew Mehta and Bridget Molloy standing next to each other watching the narrator on stage, their hands inconspicuously entwined. I smile to myself. I guess *Romeo and Juliet* gets to everyone.

I turn and find Owen, who's helping Jenna with a quick-change from nurse to noblewoman near the wings stage right. And because I'm flushed from the Capulet Manor scene, because he's my *boyfriend*, because I'm ridiculously happy about that, because it's borderline pathetic how much I want to kiss him right now, I can't keep my eyes off him. He looks up, and he returns an unabashedly huge grin. We're *worse* than Romeo and Juliet.

Not taking my eyes off him, I walk backward, knowing I only have a minute to climb the stairs to the top of the balcony set. Mercutio and Benvolio are nearing the final lines of their scene on stage—

There's an enormous crash.

I whirl, restraining myself in the middle of the show from yelling at whoever's fault it was. I find Tyler in a heap on the floor, the wooden trellis in splinters surrounding him. Everyone's frozen, every head turned in our direction. Tyler begins to brush himself off, looking dazed if unhurt, when Bridget rushes over, her face ashen.

"Are—are you okay?" she stutters, clearly fearing the lead has just broken his leg. "What happened?"

"I was practicing the jump, and it just . . . collapsed." Tyler gestures to the trellis. His eyes clear, and a sudden fury fills them. He rounds on the stagehand nearest to him. "What the hell?" he hisses in the loudest whisper he can.

"It wasn't secured properly," Andrew Mehta offers weakly.

"Yeah, no shit." Tyler fixes his glare on Andrew in the dark. "What I want to know is whose fault it was."

"Tyler," I say sharply, stepping in to shield Andrew. "We don't have time for this. Anthony's on the final lines of the scene."

"If we don't have the trellis, we don't have the scene. I have to stop the show until we can fix it," Bridget murmurs in exasperation. She glances over her shoulder. "Where's Will? He's our only carpenter."

Nobody says anything. It's Andrew who finally speaks up. "He, um, left. He said he had to call Alyssa."

Bridget lets out a frustrated groan and begins muttering feverishly into her headset. It's exactly like Will, I realize. I don't know if he's trying to make the production, and by extension me, look bad because he's pissed I got the Juliet role back from Alyssa, or if he just doesn't care about the play anymore. Either way, he's screwed us over.

If we pause the play, it wouldn't be the worst thing ever. It'd just pull the audience out of the story, look unprofessional, reflect poorly on the Stillmont drama program—okay, it'd be the worst thing ever. But without Romeo climbing the trellis and kissing Juliet, I've never been able to pull off the scene. Owen walks up then, and his eyes meet mine.

And just like that, I know.

"However long it takes!" I hear Bridget say. "We need to drop the curtain, and tell the audience we're having technical difficulties—"

"Don't," I cut in. "We'll do the scene without the trellis." I give Tyler a quick look. "Just play it like it's written." He gives a short nod. Anthony comes off stage, and I turn to the stagehands while Bridget hurriedly calls off the curtain. "Roll the balcony on," I tell them as I step onto the set. I climb the staircase, the wooden boards creaking beneath my feet like they have in countless rehearsals.

I'm briefly blinded when the lights come up, and I watch Tyler from where I'm hidden on the set. Once again I'm impressed by how flawlessly he delivers his lines, this time because I know he's tempering his anger from hardly a minute ago.

When it's my cue, I walk onto the balcony and begin Juliet's monologue. Instead of waiting for Romeo to kiss me, I try to coax the love from Juliet's fearful heart. I find myself glancing at my family out of the corner of my eye. I remember Owen's steady heartbeat under my cheek while we drifted off to sleep. The way my dad held me this morning. With every line, I feel Juliet coming to life. I know what it is to love and to be loved.

I wonder breathlessly whether a rose by any other name would smell as sweet, I give Romeo my faithful vow, and when I tell him, "Parting is such sweet sorrow," I feel tears in my eyes.

I die tragically in Act V and come back to life once the curtains have closed. When I walk to the front and take Tyler's hand for my bow, the cheering gets louder, and I can't help it—I'm proud of myself.

I don't know if I'll ever act again. I won't write it off entirely. But I do know I'm glad I did it. Being in the spotlight's not terrible, and it taught me that losing yourself in a character might lead you to find something new in yourself. If I *do* return to acting, maybe I'll play someone without an all-consuming teenage romance.

Then again—where's the fun in that?

We file off the stage. The instant we're out of view, we're no longer noblemen and noblewomen, daughters and cousins, Montagues and Capulets. We're us, smearing stage makeup in a stupidly happy group hug.

I look for Owen and Anthony in the throng. But instead, I find Will waiting behind the crowd, looking uneasy. Out of the corner of my eye, I notice Tyler break off from the group and head directly for him.

"Look who showed up," Tyler says, his voice raised and edged in sarcasm. Everyone falls silent, and I know he's done restraining his anger.

Will doesn't flinch. "What's your problem, man?"

"You, *man*," Tyler returns. "Do you have any idea what could have happened? I could've broken my leg on stage, in front of everyone. You could've ruined the entire show!"

"Whatever. It went fine, didn't it?" Will tries to say. "You got your applause—" but before he finishes the sentence, Tyler steps up in his face.

I'm running toward them in the next moment, knowing their staring match could erupt in the blink of an eye. The excitement and pride and camaraderie of the room are ebbing fast, transforming into something ugly. "Tyler!" I force a hand between them.

"What? You're defending *him*?" Tyler rounds on me.

"It's so not about that," I fire back. "It was shitty"—I glare at Will—"but it doesn't warrant physical violence," I finish, turning back to Tyler.

"I deserve an apology. You do, too. It was your directing he ruined."

"Yeah, I do." For more than Tyler knows. I look back to Will and, surprisingly, from the guilt in his eyes, I know he knows what I mean. With Will in front of me, Tyler at my back, I tell the two guys who've hurt me worst what I know to be true. "If you beg for every apology you're owed, your throat will go dry," I say, noticing Owen watching by the back door. "You can't lose yourself over every problem, hurt, or wrong someone's committed you. Bad things happen. You fix your eyes on the future, and you move on."

I don't wait for Tyler or Will to say something. Without a backward glance, I walk to Owen.

"Ready?" he asks. There's an eager waver in his voice.

I nod, reaching into his heavy sleeve to take his hand. Instead of fighting our way through the crowded theater, we head to the back door behind the dressing rooms. We run into the night, the cold turning our cheeks and noses pink. It's a short sprint to the front foyer where our families and friends are waiting.

I search the room for my parents, and instead my eyes land on Anthony, fake blood staining his tunic. Out of the way of the crowd, Eric's handing him a bouquet of flowers— small, yet they look carefully chosen. Eric's eyes are eager, colored with a little nervousness. Anthony's are understanding, and appreciative. I don't know what's going on between them. But I feel like both of them know they'd be idiots to give up on each other.

Anthony catches my eye, noticing me. And though he gives me only the hint of a grin, he's glowing.

I nod at him and begin to walk away, wanting to give them their moment.

"Megan." I hear Anthony behind me, and I turn around. "You were an amazing Juliet."

"I was, wasn't I?" I say jokingly, but my smile is genuine.

My family's seated when Owen and I get to the restaurant, a white-tablecloth French bistro near the theater. My parents went ahead and got a table while Owen and I changed, scrubbed the stage makeup from our faces, and met Owen's family. His mom, a surprisingly short woman considering Owen's height, looked startled that Owen had a new girlfriend, while Sam tromped around the foyer boasting that his brother was dating Juliet. Owen didn't appear to mind.

When we sit down at the table next to my mom, Rose peers at Owen.

"I know you," she says, her face lighting up. "You're Biff Loman!"

"What?" Dad sits up and sets down his glass. "You've met Megan's new guy already?"

"Dad . . ." I say warningly, not liking the direction this conversation is heading or the way he clarified *"new* guy."

"I'm just really glad I have the chance to meet one of Megan's boyfriends," Mom chimes in while buttering her baguette.

I round on her, my eyes shouting *traitor.* "Mom, you're making it sound like there's one every week! I've only dated one other guy this year."

"School year or calendar year?" Randall asks, raising his eyebrow. Next to me, I hear Owen stifle a laugh. I jab an elbow into his ribs.

"He's handsome, this one," Rose whispers to me like she's finally finished her appraisal of him. "He's got nice eyes."

"Two sets of parents are *way* better than one," I grumble, reddening.

Dad leans in. "You're not afraid of heights, are you?"

"Dad!"

I feel Mom squeeze my hand under the table. "Let's let Owen be," she says reprovingly to my dad. "I'll bet Megan's given him enough trouble." She winks at me, and mercifully the discussion moves on to the new baby and Rose's birthing classes.

Two crepes later without further interrogation of Owen, we're in the middle of ordering dessert when my phone vibrates in my back pocket. I surreptitiously check it under the table, and my heart stops.

The email is from Professor Salsbury at SOTI. I open it with a shaking hand.

Dear Megan,

*I'm terribly sorry I had to run after the play
before we could chat, but I felt I couldn't let a
performance as fine as yours go without prompt
recognition. You played an outstanding Juliet.*

*I've been speaking to your teacher, Ms. Jody
Hewitt, and she couldn't have had higher praise
for your directing achievements. I think you'll be a
wonderful addition to our directing program.*

*I look forward to seeing
you on campus in the fall!*

Michael Salsbury

I glance to the side, wondering if Owen's reading over my shoulder. But he's talking to my dad about *Snakes on a Plane*. I bring my phone up to the table, and I'm about to tell everyone the news until I notice Randall. Wiping sweat from his brow, he raises his knife to his wine glass and taps it once.

"If I could steal the spotlight for just a couple minutes," he begins, everyone's eyes on him. "I would like to say something to Catherine in front of all of you."

I'd almost forgotten. I hold my breath, knowing what's about to happen.

"This has been the greatest year of my life," he continues. "You, Catherine, are the most kind, caring, intelligent, creative, beautiful woman I've ever known."

I glance at Mom. Her eyes glitter with tears.

"You've given me innumerable gifts over the past year," Randall says, "including tonight, here with your family. I didn't have much of my own growing up. Since we met next to the Greek vases in the Blanton Museum—I had no idea what I was looking at, and you showed me everything— there's nothing I've wanted more than to be with you. But the more time I've spent with this family, the more I've realized it would be an equally great joy to be a part of it, too." He shifts his eyes to me. "I know you were joking, Megan, when you said 'two sets of parents,' but the truth is, I feel like we have become a family. And there's nothing I'd like more than to make that permanent."

He takes my mom's hand before he continues. "I never thought I'd be lucky enough to meet someone like you," he tells her, "let alone spend a year with her. If I could just have a little more luck—"

He kneels and pulls out a small black box. Mom gasps.

"Catherine, I love you more than anything. Will you marry me?" Randall asks.

Mom manages a yes through her torrential tears. The restaurant applauds while Randall slides the ring onto her finger and sweeps her into an embrace.

Owen puts his hand on my leg, and I feel him lean into me. He's looking at me questioningly, wondering how I'm handling this.

I watch my mom for my answer. She's staring into Randall's eyes, and I don't know why I ever doubted her feelings, because her gaze holds as much love as I've ever seen when she looked at Dad. I never expected Randall to earn it, but I felt tears in my own eyes when he knelt down with the ring. Randall isn't just an awkward accountant who's in a bowling league—he might be the love of my mom's life. My dad's words from this morning ring in my head. While Mom may never entirely move on from her past marriage, she *has* fallen in love. She's happy.

There's nothing holding my family together, not now, because there's nothing left broken. It doesn't matter where they'll be next year and where I'll be. They're *my* family. Complicated, messy, and mine.

I turn back to Owen. Placing my hand on top of his, I give him my answer in a smile.

I wouldn't change a thing.

TWENTY-EIGHT

ROMEO: *Did my heart love till now?*

I.v.59

THEY NAMED THE BABY JULIET.

I tried to dissuade them, but Rose insisted it's because of Juliet's wit and strong will, not the lovelorn-teenage-lunatic thing. She fell in love with the name after the performance, and I had no choice but to take that as a compliment.

"I don't think the name suits her, honestly," I say to Owen, who's hiking a couple of steps in front of me. I'm not a natural-born hiker, but today's the first day of spring, and I've been planning this since December. "She does nothing but sleep. Erin prepared me for the worst, but Juliet's, like, the most even-tempered baby I've ever heard of. I don't think she's really a Juliet."

"You never know." I hear the smile in Owen's voice. "I've seen Juliet-ish behavior come from the unlikeliest of people."

I roll my eyes even though he can't see me. "Well, I found her chewing on a copy of your play in the living room. Is that Juliet-ish behavior?" He laughs ahead of me. "It was my favorite scene, too. I think I'm going to need you to print me a whole new copy."

"You don't need to read it again, Megan," he says, sounding secretly pleased.

"Of course I do. My boyfriend wrote an amazing play, and I intend to read it every month until forever." We reach the top of the mountain, and I walk to the edge of the campground to take in the view. "Wow, you were right. This *is* nice." The forest opens in every direction below us. It's quiet, and the trees have grown in their new leaves, washing everything in bright green. I remember looking at the photos of this place, Bishop's Peak, on my phone with Owen months ago. It looked beautiful then. It looks nearly unreal now.

I take a quick picture and send it to Madeleine, who graciously lent me her hiking boots this morning. In the months since *Romeo and Juliet*, we've become even better friends. I told her about Tyler when I got home from Ashland, and she promptly broke up with him. She was upset for a couple of days—until she got into Princeton early, continuing her trend of being, well, perfect.

I turn to look for Owen and find him sitting on a log, notebook already out on his lap. I walk over and gently take it out of his hands, setting it down next to him. He glances up at me questioningly. "Owen, I didn't *really* bring you up here to write."

His eyebrows rise. "No?"

I climb into his lap, the bark rough under my knees. "Remember when you told me you hadn't gotten lucky up here, and I told you we should do something about that?"

His hands find the small of my back. "I have a vague memory of that, yes."

"Owen"—I lower my lips to his—"we should do something about that."

In the moment before our mouths meet, he laughs. "You know," he says, pulling back, "I had no idea what to do the first time you said that. I was utterly out of my depth."

"And now . . . ?" I whisper.

"Still utterly out of my depth," he replies, kissing my neck, "but I have an inkling."

This time it's he who moves to meet my lips. His hands tighten on my waist, pulling me closer. "Wait," I breathe, leaning back. "I want to say one thing first."

He nods, waiting with calm curiosity.

"I love you, like, really love you," I begin to ramble. "Like, a lot. Like, so much. So much that if you were to do something stupid like climb my nonexistent balcony in the middle of the night or compare your lips to two blushing pilgrims or something nonsensical like that—I'd still want to kiss your face off." Somehow I stop talking.

Owen brushes a hair from my face, his fingertips tracing the shell of my ear. "I love you, too."

"Wow." My face flares. "This is why you're the writer. Economy of words. I should have gone with that."

"Your way was perfect, Megan. And I would've elaborated, except you, on this mountain, with me, telling me everything you just told me, your hair looking the way it does and your beautiful eyes"—he stares right into them—"have me not at my most eloquent."

"Oh," I say, feeling even less eloquent myself.

His smile softening, Owen presses a long and deep kiss to

my lips, and I realize it was a terrible idea to haul myself to a place with Owen and thin oxygen and expect not to faint.

"Dost thou love me? I know thou wilt say 'Ay,' and I will take thy word," he whispers, catching my chin and tilting me closer.

"Owen," I say, recognizing Juliet's words. "That's my line."

Acknowledgments

THANK YOU, READER, FIRST AND FOREMOST, FOR picking up this book and following Megan's story. Imagining this in your hands is why we do what we do.

We'd be nowhere without the amazing Katie Shea Boutillier, our agent, who believed in this book from the beginning and who's given us incredible guidance in the form of keen editorial comments and an unwavering understanding of exactly what this story should be. We are endlessly grateful.

While we were utterly thrilled for this book to find a home with Puffin and the Penguin Young Readers group, we had no idea how lucky we'd be to work with the wonderful Dana Leydig, editor extraordinaire. For sharpening this story with commentary that consistently rang true, for finding depths where we didn't know to explore them—and for making us laugh in your line edits—thank you from the bottom of our hearts, Dana.

Thank you to Kristie Radwilowicz for capturing the perfect cover design we'd always hoped for and never could have imagined. And thank you to our publicist, Katie Quinn, and the entire Penguin Young Readers marketing and publicity team for getting the book into readers' hands.

To Julie Buxbaum, Huntley Fitzpatrick, Morgan Matson, and Micol Ostow, thank you for the blurbs of our dreams and for your encouragement and wisdom on the publishing journey!

To the Electric Eighteens, you guys rock. Thank you for making our debut year a hundred times better with your enthusiasm and your invaluable insight, and, of course, for giving us so many wonderful books to read!

We owe an enormous debt to our friends for reading our drafts, for following our trials and tribulations with a thoughtful ear and tireless encouragement, and for supporting us every step of the way.

Thank you to Mira Costa High School for introducing us to each other, without which many things would not have happened—this book included—and particularly to the English department for introducing us to Shakespeare.

Finally, we are eternally grateful to our families for, honestly, everything. The Bard said it best, as he often does: "I can no other answer make but thanks, and thanks, and ever thanks."

PREMARITAL COUNSELING

PREMARITAL COUNSELING

H. NORMAN WRIGHT

❧ ❧ ❧
❧ ❧ ❧

MOODY PRESS

CHICAGO

© 1977 by
THE MOODY BIBLE INSTITUTE
OF CHICAGO

Fourth Printing, 1980

Library of Congress Cataloging in Publication Data
Wright, H. Norman.
  Premarital counseling.
  Bibliography: p. 210.
  1. Marriage counseling—United States.   I. Title.
HQ10.W73   362.8'2   77-2355
ISBN 0-8024-6811-X

Printed in the United States of America

Contents

1

The Status of Marriage Today

Literature is saturated with articles describing the plight of the American style of marriage and family. From *Ladies' Home Journal* to the *New Yorker*, *Christianity Today* to *Moody Monthly*, editors, educators, sociologists, anthropologists, politicians, and ministers are voicing their concern. If one is not convinced that difficulties exist, he has not been reading, has not been in touch with people, or is an idealist!

In 1972 the "Report on the American Family" by *Better Homes and Gardens* revealed that 71 percent of more than 340,000 participants felt that "American family life is in trouble."[1] Eighty-nine percent felt that most couples were not well prepared for marriage, and 85 percent felt that religion had lost its influence on family life today. Twenty-five hundred professional family educators and marriage counselors participated in the National Alliance for Family Life Research; a consensus of their opinion was: "There is a definite need for strengthening family life in this nation at the present time."[2] This same group was asked, "Do you feel that, overall, young people are receiving adequate preparation for marriage from their parents?" Ninety-three percent said no.

Are people happy being married today? It is difficult to know, for various reports and specialists differ. Eighty percent of the participants in the *Better Homes and Gardens* study stated that most people they knew were happy in their

---

1. "Report on the American Family." Published by *Better Homes and Gardens* (September 1972), pp. 7, 36, 137.
2. *National Alliance for Family Life Newsletter* (Spring, 1973), p. 1.

marriages. A few years ago, *Life* magazine gave a similar statistic. Yet Dr. J. A. Fritz, in his book *The Essence of Marriage,* has suggested that marriages could be classified into four categories: happy, good, agreeable, and tolerable. He estimates that 5 percent would fall in the happy category, 10 percent in good, and the remaining 85 percent in the last two categories. Dr. James Peterson, professor of sociology at the University of Southern California, made a study of couples who had been married for twenty years or more. He discovered that of every one hundred such couples, only five could be classified as happy.

People today are concerned about marriage. Changes are taking place in family structure and in the permanency of marriage. In 1870 there were twenty-seven divorces for every 1,000 marriages in the United States. In 1972 there were 455 for every 1,000. It has been said that "throwaway marriages" have become part of the fabric of American society. Today, 21 percent of all married couples have divorce somewhere in the background of one or both partners. Among thirty-year-old wives, one of every three has experienced or will experience divorce. If you were married in 1974, your chances of being divorced or separated by 1976 are one in two. In Orange County, California, 13,000 people were married in 1974. During that same year, 13,232 divorces were filed and over 10,000 completed.[3]

The attitude toward marriage today was heard in the office of a marriage counselor when a young woman said, "When I got married I was looking for an ideal but I married an ordeal and now I want a new deal!" A recent cartoon in the *Los Angeles Times* pictured a pastor performing a wedding, and instead of the usual, "till death do you part," he said, "till divorce do you part." This is not entirely unreal. Actual consideration has been given to this very question by Alvin Toffler in *Future Shock.* Toffler said, "As conventional marriage

3. Interview with Brien Burgess, attorney at law, November 1975.

proves itself less and less capable of delivering on its promise of lifelong love, therefore, we can anticipate open public acceptance of temporary marriages."[4]

Margaret Mead suggested "an apprentice period for people contemplating marriage, a five-year terminal point for all marriages with the option of either renewal or cancellation of the contract, and specially trained, government financed substitute parents for the children of dissolved marriages." Another suggestion is a "two level system with the first level of marriage limited to five year period with no children allowed and then either cancellation of the contract or renewal to a permanent nondissolvable relationship and children allowed."[5]

Dr. Carl Rogers, in his book, *Becoming Partners: Marriage and Its Alternatives*, said,

> To me it seems that we are living in an important and uncertain age, and the institution of marriage is most assuredly in an uncertain state. If 50-75 percent of Ford or General Motors cars completely fell apart within the early part of their lifetimes as automobiles, drastic steps would be taken. We have no such well organized way of dealing with our social institutions, so people are groping, more or less blindly, to find alternatives to marriage (which is certainly less than 50 percent successful). Living together without marriage, living in communes, extensive childcare centers, serial monogamy (with one divorce after another), the women's liberation movement to establish the woman as a person in her own right, new divorce laws which do away with the concept of guilt—these are all gropings toward some new form of man-woman relationship for the future. It would take a bolder man than I to predict what will emerge."[6]

The problem is not with the institution of marriage. The

---

4. Alvin Toffler, *Future Shock* (New York: Random House, 1970), p. 251.
5. From *Cherishable: Love and Marriage*, by David W. Augsburger. Copyright © 1971 by Herald Press, Scottdale, Pa. Used by permission.
6. Carl Rogers, *Becoming Partners: Marriage and Its Alternatives* (New York: Delacorte, 1972), p. 11.

problem lies with the individuals within that structure and their attitudes toward it. Richard Lessor wrote, "In the twentieth century it is not a matter of marriage having been tried and found wanting. Marriage is deeply wanted but largely untried."[7] Today, in place of exerting consistent effort and determination to make one's marriage work, the solution is to "bail out." In certain counties of Southern California, the ratio of marriages to divorces is now almost one to one.

Families are being disrupted not only by divorce.

> According to the Federal Bureau of Investigation Statistics, police across the nation receive more calls for family conflicts than for murders, aggravated batteries and all other serious crimes. The category of family conflicts includes not only quarrels between husband and wife but also between parent and child.[8]

> It has ben reported that over fifty percent of all homicides committed are violent physical attacks by one member of a family upon another member of the same family.[9]

Concern over this problem is not limited to families; law enforcement officials are also involved.

> In general, police don't like dealing with family quarrels because they don't know what to expect and frequently the calls prove to be dangerous. FBI statistics show that 22 percent of all police fatalities occur while investigating domestic disturbances.[10]

These events and transitions are bound to have some effect upon people in our society. Nathan Ackerman, a leading family psychiatrist, expressed it in this way:

---

7. Richard Lessor, *Love & Marriage & Trading Stamps* (Niles, IL.: Argus, 1971), p. 7. Reprinted with permission of Argus Communications.
8. Vida Deen, "Family Conflict Calls a Major Police Concern," *Santa Ana Register* (March 28, 1973).
9. William Lederer in *Marriage: For and Against* (New York: Hart, 1972), p. 137.
10. Deen.

At present, anxiety about marriage and family is almost universal. On every hand, one sees nervous concern over teenage marriage, infidelity, divorce, loosening sex standards, women's lib, momism, the decline of parental authority, the anarchy of youth, and so no. One senses deepening disillusion—even despair—surrounding the value of family life.[11]

Statements such as the following do nothing to relieve the high level of anxiety: "In this day of uprooted persons and a world threatened with revolution, the ancient value most endangered seems to be the family."[12] William Wolf, a psychoanalyst as quoted by Toffler, said, "The family is dead except for the first year or two of child rearing."[13]

The ultimate depth of pessimism is seen in the words of Nathan Ackerman concerning the family situation:

> I am a psychiatrist who has devoted a lifetime to studying emotional problems of family living. I have pioneered in the field of family therapy. From where I sit, the picture of marriage and family in present-day society is a gloomy one. Family life seems to be cracking at the seams, and an effective mortar is nowhere available.[14]

There is, however, an effective mortar: the person of Jesus Christ. The presence of Christ, the ministry of the Holy Spirit, and intense effort and work dedicated to the application of Scripture can bring stability, growth, and mutual satisfaction into a marital relationship.

Of all the changes occurring today, four are quite significant in relationship to the future of marriage.

The first change to consider is the movement toward the nuclear family as compared to the traditional extended family, or family of orientation. We have rejected the extended

11. Nathan Ackerman in *Marriage: For and Against* (New York: Hart, 1972), p. 12.
12. Albert McClellan, *New Times* (Nashville: Broadman, 1969), p. 69.
13. William Wolf as quoted in *Future Shock* (New York: Random House, 1970), p. 238.
14. Ackerman, p. 12.

family of the past, the family from which one has come—one's own grandparents and parents. The closeness is no longer there except in rural areas. In America we emphasize separating ourselves from the parents. Little loyalty or obligation is felt toward them. There were many healthy aspects to the way families lived in close proximity to each other in the past. The arrangement gave a person or family someone to depend on. To be sure, the nuclear family unit has its strengths, but it has many problems as well.

A Canadian publication, *Hope for the Family*, said,

> Families have become small isolated, mobile, self-contained units. Very few societies today provide so little support for new parents as our society. As one author put it: "Young parents today are like the pioneers, alone in a wilderness, threatened by uncertainties, no rules but the ones they make themselves." Cut loose from relative and traditions, families have become an easy target for the mass media.[15]

Professor Norman Ashcraft, anthropologist at Adelphi University, suggested:

> Psychiatrists call the "normal" family by a technical term, the "nuclear family," to refer to that supposedly tightly knit unit of father, mother and children. To the family repairmen, the harmonious nuclear family is the only way to live—especially in suburbia. It is right here that I take issue with these so called experts. For I believe that the suburban nuclear household, even in the best of circumstances, does not afford a healthy or happy life. It does not provide stable and emotionally satisfying relationships in the home, nor an environment that children want to live in. In fact, the more we have isolated this domestic unit behind the walls of the suburban home, the more we have alienated children from their parents—and husbands from their wives.[16]

The Bible states in Genesis 2:24: "For this cause a man

15. *Hope for the Family* (Toronto: Wedge, 1971), p. 11.
16. Norman Ashcraft, "The Isolated, Fragile Modern Family," *Los Angeles Times* (May 21, 1973).

shall leave his father and his mother, and shall cleave to his wife; and they shall become one flesh." Notice an emphasis on two verbs: leave and cleave. The word *leave* means to abandon, forsake, to sever one relationship before establishing another. Although the attachment to home and parents should be replaced by the attachment to one's mate, this does not mean disregarding or dishonoring one's parents but rather breaking the tie to one's parents and assuming responsibility for one's spouse.

The fifth commandment states, "Honour thy father and thy mother: that thy days may be long upon the land which the LORD thy God giveth thee" (Exod 20:12). The same command is repeated in Ephesians 6:1-3. To honor is to "regard with high public esteem, to show the spirit of respect and consideration."[17] Honoring parents means to acknowledge them with respect as people to whom one is indebted more than he could ever repay.

Cutting oneself off from relatives, having no regard for the insight and opinions of parents or other family members, not showing concern for the physical well-being of older parents and grandparents—all contradict the teaching of the Word of God. Christians must evaluate what they are doing and why they are doing it in light of the Bible. In the area of relationships with relatives, it appears that families have moved away from biblical teaching. Young people would gain insight into and greater understanding of family relationships if they had a wider experience with other family members. All the experiences of growing up are going to affect one's future marriage.

A second change which developed in our society is that the choice of a mate is left entirely to the individuals involved. Years ago parents were directly involved. It is evident that people strive for independence today. However, we are not

17. William Hendricksen, "Ephesians," *New Testament Commentary* (Grand Rapids: Baker, 1967), p. 259.

arguing the merits of the former system. There is something
to be said for individual choice. But choices seem to be made
on the romantic ideal of love based on feelings. As we shall
see later, this is an unhealthy basis.

Dr. David Mace, a family life sociologist, has pointed out
that marriage has changed from an institution to a companionship arrangement. It is also easier to get out of this arrangement than to get out of a book-of-the-month club. External
pressure will not keep a couple together today. There must
be internal cohesion. The question is, Is romantic love sufficient?

Love is necessary, but many people have an inadequate
concept of what it is. Perhaps a typical definition can be
expressed in this homespun statement: "Love is a feeling you
feel when you feel that you're going to get a feeling that you
never felt before!"

What about common interests, common background, voca-
tional goals, spiritual similarities? What about liking the
other person as a friend and enjoying his or her company?
What about liking to work with the person over an extended
period of time? Being a friend to one another fills many of
the needs that people bring into marriage. There are many
elements that should go into the selection of a mate, but too
many people bypass them.

California has moved to counteract the problem of immature decisions to marry by requiring a court order for permission to marry when one or both persons are under the age of
eighteen. Some countries also require premarital counseling
for these couples. It would be good if in the future the requirement for premarital counseling would be advanced to
all under twenty-one.

Have evangelical churches required and provided mandatory premarital counseling for any who seek marriage? In a
1972 survey of ninety-five churches, only twenty-five required

counseling; fifty admitted to giving very limited counseling or none at all!

A third major change today is that marriage has moved from a relationship of partners with fixed roles to a relationship of partners with fluid roles. Husbands and wives fill many different and unique roles. Two of the most noted writers in the secular field, Wilbur Lederer and Donald Jackson, have stated that one of the elements most destructive to the marital relationship is the failure of spouses to identify, determine, and mutually assign areas of competence and responsibility—who is in charge of what. They feel it is important that the spouses deliberately and mutually develop rules to guide their behavior.[18]

Couples also have moved from a one-vote system to a two-vote system. Within this change it appears that married women have gained more power and assertiveness, and in many cases there is a crippling of male authority at home. Perhaps some women have taken over because of the abdication of men who have turned their energy toward their work. The responsibility for governing American households on a day-to-day basis has fallen largely upon the women.

Nowhere else in the world do women have more real decision-making power than their husbands than in the United States. They have economic power, religious power, and, because of the divorce laws, the power to easily dissolve the marriage.[19] Albert McClellan, in his book *New Times*, stated: "Family life has become mother-centered, with a sharing of responsibility by father and mother, and a decline in the role of the father as the family authority."[20] The parental role is a peripheral role for the American male.

This ambiguity of male authority is a result of the cult of

18. William Lederer and Donald Jackson, *The Mirages of Marriage* (New York: Norton, 1968), pp. 248-49.
19. Lawrence H. Fuchs, *Family Matters* (New York: Random House, 1972), pp. 27-28.
20. McClellan, p. 70.

independence which eventually led to an attack upon the traditional authority of fathers and husbands. It is also partially due to the industrial life of our nation. Lawrence Fuchs states in *Family Matter* that the ambiguity of male authority is perhaps *the most striking and important characteristic of the American family system.* Our American culture places a high premium upon performance in work outside the home; this further undermines male dominance in the home. Some of those outside pressures to perform at work are so great (or the men claim the pressures are so great) that men welcome an escape from the responsibility of being the authority at home.[21] Leonard Benson, in his work *Fatherhood*, goes so far as to say, "The American father is almost invisible, perhaps even at home."[22]

Striving for material success has been part of the reason for the absenteeism of father from the family. In some homes, the mother and children pressure father for more material goods. In others the father himself desires the comforts and gadgets that more money can bring (despite the time payments!).

Our culture has been described in the following manner:

> The success of the religion of consumption is self-evident. North Americans are consumption mad. Many people go around believing that without things they will simply disappear. North Americans are pleasure minded, self-indulgent, materialistic, and selfish.
>
> This vision has captured the hearts of many Christians, young and old. Many Christians try to live according to two visions—to enjoy the best of two worlds—to remain Christians while at the same time pledging to uphold the faith of consumption. Sooner or later, however, one vision, one spiritual force, will gain the upper hand, will become the directing, the determining force in our lives (Luke 12:29-31).[23]

21. Fuchs, p. 26.
22. Leonard Benson, *Fatherhood—A Sociological Perspective* (New York: Random House, 1968), p. 3.
23. *Hope for the Family*, pp. 33-34.

Vance Packard, in the dedication of his book *The Waste Makers*, said: "To my mother and father, who have never confused the possession of goods with the good life."[24] Very few have this philosophy today. To many men, their job is their way of life and their self-image is deeply affected by their ability to provide for their family.

Nathan Ackerman vividly expressed this situation:

> The father strives mightily to show success as a man. He pursues what has been called "the suicidal cult of manliness." To prove his merit, it is not enough to be a man; he must be a superman. In his daily work, he serves some giant industrial organization, or he is a lone wolf in the jungle warfare of modern competitive enterprise. The more he succeeds, the more he dreads failure. He brings his work worries home. Depleted by his exertions, he has little emotional stamina left over to give freely of his love to wife and children.
>
> He wants to be buttressed for the war of tomorrow, but he finds his wife absorbed in her own busy life. He feels deserted and alone and angry that his wife gives him so little understanding. She reproaches him for not taking a more responsible role in the family. She demands more consideration for herself and the children. For the difficulties with the children she feels guilty. But she denies this guilt and projects it to father. Father takes it. He thinks it must really be his fault. Though confused and angry, he appeases mother because of his need for her. He tries to be useful to win her favor.[25]

This is true not just of those in secular work but also of those in Christian service. Many pastors are so involved in their work that their role in the family is nonexistent. There are many who boast that they have not had a day off in

24. Vance Packard, *The Waste Makers* (New York: McKay, 1974), Dedication.
25. Excerpted from pp. 110-15 from *The Psychodynamics of Family Life: Diagnosis and Treatment of Family Relationships,* by Nathan Ackerman, Md.: Basic Books, Inc., Publishers, New York; 1958.

months and that they work seventy to ninety hours each week. That situation is nothing to boast about: it is sick!

A final change is in sexual morality. Much has been written on this subject; it is enough to say that the sexual behavior evident today, both in and out of marriage, threatens family stability, and is also a symptom of other problems.

A recent survey makes this point with graphic finality. The October 1975 issue of *Redbook* magazine presented the results of a survey concerning women's sexuality and sexual behavior. The report was based on surveys completed by 100,000 women. Results indicated that the likelihood that a young woman will have intercourse before marriage has been steadily increasing over the last ten years. For example, 69 percent of the women in this survey who were married prior to 1964 experienced premarital relations. Among those married after 1970, the number was 90 percent. The surveys also revealed that the strongly religious woman was more likely than other women to remain a virgin until marriage, but the influence of religion was less inhibiting than might be expected.[26] For those who have convictions and moral standards, prior sexual involvement can affect the marriage unless the total forgiveness of Jesus Christ is experienced.

In the midst of all these changes, the church can have an impact. Imagine what would happen if every couple who married in the next ten years experienced six to eight hours of premarital counseling in their local church and also spent twenty-five hours of outside preparation through books and tapes. This idea is the message of this book.

---

26. Robert and Amy Levin, "Sexual Pleasure: The Surprising Preferences of 100,000 Women," *Redbook* (October 1975), pp. 51-58.

2

Taking the Risk out of Mate Selection

A young man came in one morning and said, "It's not worth it! I see so many of my friends' marriages breaking up, I'm never getting married. Marriage appears to be such a gamble—and it's the only game in town where both players can lose! There's too much risk involved in getting married! I don't want to end up a statistic." Perhaps he was running scared and being a bit overcautious. Yet his concern is echoed by many young people. In some cases this attitude lends itself to the move toward simply living together.

There is a risk involved in the marriage process, but the essential element is not so much finding the right person as it is becoming the right person. Both individuals can lose in the game of marriage, but it is just as possible for both to win!

What is involved in the process of selecting a mate? What factors, conscious and unconscious (some have said that all couples in love are unconscious), move people toward one another? What does the evangelical church have to say to young people about their choice of a life partner? Do we say that God has one person that He has selected to be your mate, or is there an unlimited stockpile that you could select from and still be within God's will? Often the church says only that a believer must marry a believer. This is scripturally true, but there are more factors involved in the selection of a mate than spiritual oneness.

REASONS FOR MARRIAGE

There are numerous reasons for marriage apart from being

19

in love. *Pregnancy* is still a reason for marriage. In fact, about one-fourth of all marriages occur when the bride is pregnant. Probably many of these marriages would not have occurred had the woman not been pregnant. Research on these marriages shows a relationship between a premarital pregnancy and unhappiness in marriage.[1] In God's grace, these marriages do not have to end in a higher divorce rate or have a greater rate of unhappiness than others; the forgiveness of Jesus Christ can affect this situation as well as any other.

Rebound is a reason for marriage when a person attempts to find a marriage partner immediately after a relationship terminates. In a sense it is a frantic attempt to establish desirability in the eyes of the person who terminated the relationship. Marriage on the rebound is questionable because the marriage occurs in reference to the previous man or woman and not in reference to the new person.

Rebellion is a motivation for marriage and occurs in both secular and Christian homes. This is a situation in which the parents say "no" and the young person says "yes." This is a demonstration of one's control over one's own life, and possibly an attempt to demonstrate independence. Unfortunately, a person uses the marriage partner to get back at parents.

Escape from an unhappy home environment is another reason for marriage. Some of the reasons given are fighting, drinking, and molestation. This type of marriage is risky, as the knot-tying is often accomplished before genuine feelings of mutual trust, respect, and mature love have had any opportunity to develop.

Loneliness is a reason that stands by itself. Some cannot bear the thought of remaining alone for the rest of their days; they do not realize that a person can be married and still feel terribly lonely. Instantaneous intimacy does not occur at the

---

1. David Knox, *Marriage: Who? When? Why?* © 1975. Reprinted by permission of Prentice-Hall, Inc., Englewood Cliffs, N. J.

altar, but must be developed over months and years of sharing and involvement. The flight from loneliness may place a strain upon the relationship. One person may be saying, "I'm so lonely. Be with me all the time and make me happy." The problems stemming from this attitude are apparent.

Physical appearance is a factor that probably influences everyone to some degree or another. Our society is highly influenced by the cult of youth and beauty. Often our standards for a partner's physical appearance are set not so much to satisfy our own needs, but simply to gain the approval and admiration of others. Some build their self-concept upon their partner's physical attributes.

Social pressure may be direct or indirect and can come from many sources. Friends, parents, churches, schools convey the message, "It is normal to be married; to fit the norm you should get with it." On some college campuses a malady known as "senior panic" occurs. Engagement and marriage may be a means of gaining status; fears of being left behind are reinforced by others. In some churches when a young unmarried pastor arrives, matchmaking becomes the order of the day. Some churches will not hire a minister unless he is married; thus a young minister must either marry before he is ready to or desires to or spend months looking for a church.

Guilt and pity are still involved in some marriages. Marrying a person because one feels sorry for him or her because of physical defects, illness, or having a poor lot in life does not make a stable marital relationship.[2]

What about *romance*? Aren't love and romance a factor? Yes, but it is important to distinguish between genuine love and romantic love. Romantic love has been labeled cardiac-respiratory love. This is love with an emphasis upon excitement, thrills, and palpitations of the heart! Some people react as though there were a lack of oxygen in the area. Ecstasy, daydreaming, a deep physical yearning, and an apparent

2. Ibid., pp. 136-42, adapted.

fever are all indications of this malady. Not only is this type of love blind, it is also destructive. Past or future is not taken into consideration in evaluating the potential of the relationship. Dr. James Peterson has aptly described the dangers of marriage for this reason:

> First, romance results in such distortions of personality that after marriage the two people can never fulfill the roles that they expect of each other. Second, romance so idealizes marriage and even sex that when the day-to-day experiences of marriage are encountered there must be disillusionment involved. Third, the romantic complex is so short-sighted that the premarital relationship is conducted almost entirely on the emotional level and consequently such problems as temperamental or value differences, religious or cultural differences, financial, occupational, or health problems are never considered. Fourth, romance develops such a false ecstasy that there is implied in courtship a promise of a kind of happiness which could never be maintained during the realities of married life. Fifth, romance is such an escape from the negative aspects of personality to the extent that their repression obscures the real person. Later in marriage these negative factors to marital adjustment are bound to appear, and they do so in far greater detail and far more importantly simply because they were not evident earlier. Sixth, people engrossed in romance seem to be prohibited from wise planning for the basic needs of the future even to the point of failing to discuss the significant problems of early marriage.
>
> It is difficult to know how pervasive the romantic fallacy really is. I suspect that it creates the greatest havoc with high school seniors or that half of the population who are married before they are twenty years old. Nevertheless, even in a college or young adult population one constantly finds as a final criterion for marriage the question of being in love. This is due to the distortion of the meaning of a true companionship in marriage by the press, by the magazines, and by cultural impact upon the last two or three generations.

The result is that more serious and sober aspects of marital choice and marital expectations are not only neglected but sometimes ridiculed.[3]

MATE SELECTION

Ask college students the question, "Why do most people get married?" and one usually still receives the answer, because of romantic love, or people are destined to marry each other, or they just have this attraction for one another and marriage is the logical outcome. One fact that is often overlooked is that marriage partners need to fulfill certain qualifications to be suited to each other. In reality, however, more couples are thrown together by factors other than romance or the logic of intelligence!

There are many limits on mate selection. Physical location is the most significant limitation, a fact which seems highly unromantic.[4] The farther two people live apart, the more intervening opportunities there are to choose someone else. There is a limit to how much time and money a man will spend traveling to see a woman when there are other women closer by. Occasionally romantic love breaks all barriers, but these cases are the exception.

Research studies regarding marriage indicate that persons marry with greater than chance frequency within their own social class.[5] Any overall tendency for people to marry either "up" or "down" in social class is negligible.

When a person marries, does he choose a person just the opposite of himself? For years the statement "opposites attract" has been used to explain part of the attraction process. And yet the results of hundreds of studies of married couples indicate that, almost without exception, in physical, social, and psychological characteristics the mates were more alike

3. Lyle B. Gangsei, ed., *Manual for Group Premarital Counseling* (New York: Association, 1971), pp. 56-57.
4. J. Richard Udry, *The Social Context of Marriage,* 3d ed. (New York: Lippincott, 1974), p. 157, adapted.
5. Ibid., p. 157, adapted.

than different. The exceptions, or those that appear to be exceptions, do not alter this overall tendency.

Within the framework of like marrying like, however, some characteristics appear to be quite opposite in each spouse. Since the fulfillment of needs is at the heart of much of mate selection, one will find that some needs in couples are complementary while some are contradictory.

It is in the area of complementary characteristics and needs that the concept "opposites attract" is seen to be somewhat accurate. The most important complementary needs involve dominance and submissiveness. If a person has a need to dominate he will tend to marry and be gratified by a person who needs to be submissive. If a man marries a woman who has the need to be dominant and he is submissive, there will be some conflict because the social expectations of our society call for the male to be dominant and the female to be submissive. In spite of social pressures, many couples choose to go against the expectation. If one has a need to nurture others, such as giving sympathy, love, protection, and indulgence, he would be happy with a partner who has the need to be nurtured. (Most people, fortunately, are capable of both, and this is healthier.) A person who needs to admire and praise others would enjoy being married to a person who needs to receive respect and admiration. If the needs of one spouse change years later, the relationship could be disrupted. Complementary needs help determine how two people treat each other.

It is important to keep in mind the distinction between complement and contradiction. Unfortunately, some couples label any difference between themselves as complementary. Complementary needs fit so well together that no compromise is required, whereas contradictory needs require a compromise on some middle ground, but not usually on a happy medium. For example, if one is extremely thrifty and the other is a big spender, the needs will clash head on. If one enjoys social contacts and the other is a recluse, conflict is almost inevitable.[6]

In our American culture people choose a partner whom they expect to be gratifying to them. It is interesting to note that both engaged and married couples see things in each other that cannot be found through testing. What an individual sees in another person is what pleases him. "What would ever attract him to that girl?" we ask, because we cannot see in her the things he sees. A couple's choice of each other is based upon a set of relationships pleasing to themselves which they attribute to one another.

As people date and are attracted to one another, basic needs are met. Much of a couple's relationship is based upon the meeting of those needs. This means that there are literally thousands of people of the opposite sex who could fulfill those needs if the person has appropriate status qualities. Being held in esteem in someone else's eye confirms our worth in our own eyes. The need to fall in love and to have someone else fall in love with us does not require a particular person. The first step is having those basic needs met. Then the details of "personality meshing" can be filled in imaginatively. This personality meshing probably determines the future of the relationship established by a couple.

Further complicating the matter of mate selection is the factor of the cultural "ideal mate" image, depending upon what marriage means in a particular society. If, for example, marriage is primarily a division of labor and childrearing, the the ideal wife would be one who is physically strong with broad shoulders and broad hips. Descriptions of masculine and feminine characteristics provided by a culture influence the ideal mate images. In one society the ideal woman is sweet and delicate, in another she is extroverted and sexually provocative. Culture defines it; we fit into the pattern.

6. Robert Blood, Jr., *Marriage* (New York: Free Press, 1969), pp. 38-43, adapted.

Cultural definitions of the ideal mate can influence mate selection in two ways. Because this definition identifies what is desirable in a mate, it almost labels the desirability of each person. The closer a person gets to this cultural ideal, the more attractive he or she becomes to a greater number of people. And if the person realizes that he is approaching the ideal, he can be more selective in his own choice of a mate and hold out for the one closest to the ideal.

The second way in which this cultural definition of the ideal mate can influence mate selection is called "idealization of the mate." It means that, even if your choice does not meet the cultural standard of idealization, you attribute those characteristics to the person with whom you have fallen in love.

The choice of the partner is complicated by this human penchant for wishful thinking. Unfortunately, the more insecure a person is, the greater is his need for idealizing his partner.

Most people do not think about mate selection in a logical, analytical manner, but we are unconsciously influenced by these factors and in subtle ways we probably do adhere to them. Yet many people would vehemently deny these ideas, protesting that "it is our love that brought us together."

If cultural images influence one's selection of a mate, what about the images that parents have of their offspring's future mate? Parents exert considerable indirect control over the associations of their children; this in turn limits the field of possibilities for mate selection. College students feel this pressure less than those who remain at home. Parents help determine an acceptable grouping of eligibles from which their child may choose a mate.[7] Interestingly enough, when a woman's parents disapproved of her relationship with a young man (according to a study by Burgess and Wallin), more than twice as many relationships ended in broken engagements or early divorce as when both parents approved.

7. Udry, p. 187, adapted.

The approval of the man's parents does not seem to be nearly as important.[8]

After all is said and done, however, most people still come back to "we married because we loved one another." So what constitutes love? Many of the elements involved in mate selection discussed earlier are behind what we call love. But the emotional element of love lingers with us. Earlier the description of one romanticist was given: "Love is a feeling you feel when you feel that you're going to get a feeling that you never felt before." This is about the only way some people know how to describe their relationship.

What does all this have to do with the pastor and premarital counseling? It has everything to do with the potential success of the marriage relationship. If the pastor is the one conducting the premarital counseling, all the previously mentioned information should be etched upon his mind as he evaluates the motivation for a marriage. One should look for apparent and not-so-apparent reasons for marriage. Through skillful questioning, some of these before-mentioned factors may emerge. It is important to remember that the courtship and engagement period can be a deceptive time when fogged by romance.

Just where does the will of God enter into all this? How does one determine God's will for a mate?

Many people seem to rely upon inner impressions or feelings. Others say that the Lord revealed to them what they should do, and yet they are a bit fuzzy as to the means of this revelation. Many have the leading or impression that they should marry a certain person. What principles could a person follow? Dr. James Dobson has suggested four basic principles that a person may follow in knowing God's will for any area of his or her life. These principles should be applied to any impressions that a person might have regarding marriage.

Is the impression scriptural? Guidance from God is always

8. Ibid.

in accordance with His Word. If a Christian is considering marrying a non-Christian, there is no use in praying for God's will; the Scripture is clear concerning this situation. In searching the Scripture, verses should be taken within context, not in a random sampling.

Is the impression right? The expression of God's will should conform to God's universal principles of morality and decency. If human worth is depreciated or the integrity of the family is undermined by some "special leading," then it is probably not a leading from God.

Is it providential? Every impression ought to be considered in the light of providential circumstances. Are necessary doors opening or closing? Is God speaking through events?

Is the impression reasonable? Does the impression make sense? Is it consistent with the character of God to require it?[9]

If a person has numerous mixed feelings about marrying the other individual, if there is no peace over the upcoming event, and if the majority of friends and relatives are opposed to the wedding, the decision ought to be reconsidered.

MARRIAGEABILITY TRAITS

Since most people eventually get married, it is important to be aware of the traits that make an individual a better partner and give him or her more potential to make a marriage work. There are eight basic factors which have been called marriageability traits: adaptability and flexibility, empathy, ability to work through problems, ability to give and receive love, emotional stability, similar family backgrounds, similarities between the couple themselves, and communication. If these elements are present, there is a greater likelihood of marital satisfaction and stability. As the counseling proceeds, one should be evaluating the couple in light of these factors.

    9. James Dobson, *Dr. James Dobson Talks About God's Will* (Glendale, CA: Regal, 1974), pp. 13-21, adapted.

Perhaps all these factors could be considered as some of the elements of compatibility. Many couples ask, "Are we compatible?" Compatibility can mean how well the intrinsic characteristics of two people *fit*. Compatibility between individuals can also determine how easily a relationship can be established. However, this provides only the potential for a good marriage; it is necessary, but not sufficient. The more compatible the better, but the potential must be activated and used. Compatibility is a matter of becoming and developing as well as being. No two people are ever entirely compatible.

Adaptability and *flexibility* are necessary ingredients. This means the person must be able to adjust to change with a minimum of rigidity. He must be able to accept the differences in his partner, adapt, and work toward a different lifestyle if necessary.

Charles Shedd, in his book, *Letters to Phillip*, tells the story of two rivers flowing smoothly and quietly along until they came together and joined. When this happened, they clashed and hurled themselves at one another. But as the newly formed river flowed downstream, it gradually quieted down and flowed smoothly again. Now it was broader and more majestic and had much more power. Dr. Shedd suggested that a good marriage is often like that. When two independent streams of existence come together, there will probably be some dashing of life against life at the junction. Personalities rush against one another, preferences clash, ideas contend for power, and habits vie for position. Sometimes, like the waves, they throw up a spray that leaves you breathless and makes you wonder where the loveliness has gone. But that's all right. Like the two rivers, what comes out of this struggle may be something deeper, more powerful than each river was on its own. This is what occurs in the adaptability process. Ephesians 4:2 says, "Because we love one another, we are willing to make allowances for one another" (Amplified). It is vital that one learn to look at the interests of the other person, to consider the other's needs and ideas, and, because of love, to be willing to allow the other to think and do things differently. It means that a person evaluates his or her spouse's differences as being only differences—not marks of inferiority.

Empathy is a positive characteristic necessary for all interpersonal relationships, and especially for those who are married. It is the ability to be sensitive to the needs, hurts, and desires of others, feeling with them and experiencing their world from their perspective. If they hurt, we hurt. If they are excited, we can be excited with them and understand and perceive their feeling response. Romans 12:15 tells us that we are to rejoice with those that rejoice and to weep with those that weep. This passage from the Word of God seems to reflect the idea of empathy.

Dr. Judson Landis, one of the foremost family sociologists, has said that the most marriageable people are those whose ability to empathize is high. They are able to use their empathetic ability in a very positive manner. They can control their words and actions so they do not say the wrong things that hurt the other individual.

A third marriageability trait is the *ability to work through problems.* Problems, conflicts, and differences are part and parcel of marriage. Some couples run from and ignore problems, or give each other the silent treatment. Couples who accept and properly dispel and control their emotional reactions and clarify and define their problems and work together toward solutions, will in all likelihood remain married.

The *ability to give and receive love* is a trait that needs both elements for success. The giving of love involves more than just verbalizing it. It must also be evident in tangible ways which are identifiable and recognizable to both parties. Behavior, actions, and attitudes convey this in a meaningful manner. But just as important is the ability to accept love from another. Some people have such a need to be needed that they feel fulfilled by giving. To receive and accept love threatens them and lowers their sense of self-worth. If this nonacceptance response is continued, usually the other partner will give up or find someone else who will accept his love.

Emotional stability—accepting one's emotions and controlling them—lends balance to a relationship. We depend upon a person who has a consistent, dependable emotional response. Extreme flare-ups and decisions based upon emotional responses do not lend themselves to stable relationships.

The *more similar the family backgrounds,* the more contributions each can make to the marriage relationship. The greater the differences—economic, cultural, religious, being an only child compared to having several siblings, permanent living quarters compared to a high mobility rate—the more adjustments must be made. These adjustments can add even more pressures to learning to live together. Naturally, the more mature the couple, the more easily these adjustments can be made.

Another trait, closely tied to similarity in family background, is *similarities between the couple themselves.* Earlier it was mentioned that like tends to marry like more than the opposite. If a couple has similar interests, likes and dislikes, friends, educational level, and religion, the marriage relationship is greatly enhanced.

The final trait which is necessary for a love relationship to develop is *communication.* There are differences in ability, styles, and beliefs about communication. Free interchange of ideas is essential. Communication is the ability to share in such a way that the other person can understand and accept what is being said. But listening is also involved. True listening means not thinking about what you are going to say when the other person stops talking. It means not making value judgments as to how the other person expressed himself and the words he used. It means that if you are really listening you can reflect back both the meaning and feeling of what was expressed. The tendency in our culture is for men not to communicate on a feeling response level, to verbalize less, and to be more solution-oriented instead of talking about the problem. This puts a great strain upon the marriage relationship.

Numerous studies made over the past two decades provide additional indicators of marital success which cannot be discounted. It appears to be a trait of human nature for those who differ radically from the norm in these characteristics to believe that they will be the exceptions and will make their marriage work in spite of gross differences. For a few it may work.

Various studies point out the importance of significant relationships with other people. If a person has experienced warm and satisfying relationships with both his father and mother, his marriage will be influenced positively. If the parents were affectionate, firm, consistent, and fairly well adjusted in their own marriage, this contributes to the new marriage relationship. Another interesting factor centers on friends of both sexes: if each person has friends, and these become and remain mutual friends after marriage, the marriage relationship will be enhanced.

Environmental conditions in the person's background, both social and physical, can influence the marriage somewhat. A happy childhood, lack of poverty, and completion of extensive formal education can contribute to success in marriage.

The socioeconomic level of a man's parents seems to affect the economic status of his own marriage. Research has indicated that stability and adjustment of the marriage are directly related to the income of the husband. The lower the husband's income, the greater the possibility that the marriage will be more unstable and maladjusted.

Another factor affecting marital success centers on particular events in the person's past and the timing of those events. Marriage at an early age is not favorable to a healthy adjustment nor to marital longevity. A brief whirlwind romance or a premarital pregnancy is an additional adverse condition. A good work record, definite and reasonable occupational plans, and a low residence-mobility factor contribute positively.

The most difficult factors to measure are the psychological attributes of the individuals. Yet they are important. A strong interest in family life, just as strong a commitment to make it succeed, and a willingness to work together are the positive points. Even if one person within a relationship will exert effort there is more chance of that marriage succeeding than if both just coast along.[10]

In past research there was some indication that for marital satisfaction to occur the wife must be able to understand and adapt to her husband. It seemed less important for the husband to understand his wife. But with the current emphasis upon greater equality within marriage, these findings should change.[11]

Couples who have reported happy marriages appear to concentrate their energy on their relationship. Those who seem less happy concentrate on situational aspects of marriage such as home, children, and social life as sources of their marital happiness. Feelings of happiness in marriage have a direct correlation to the way the partners are relating to one another.

Other studies reveal that in the area of communication happily married couples differ from unhappily married couples in the following ways: They (1) talk more to each other; (2) convey the feeling that they understand what is being said to them; (3) have a wider range of subjects available to them to discuss; (4) preserve their communication channels and work on keeping them open; (5) show more sensitivity to each other's feelings; (6) personalize their language sym-

10. Udry, p. 236, adapted.
11. Leonard Benson, *The Family Bond—Marriage, Love and Sex in America* (New York: Random House, 1971), pp. 144-45, adapted.

bols; and (7) make more use of additional nonverbal techniques of communication.[12]

One final element that must be present for any possibility of success is commitment. Robert Blood has summarized it best:

> Commitment is dangerous. It can be exploited. If my wife takes my commitment for granted, she may rest too easily on her laurels. Perhaps commitment should be not simply to each other as we are but to the highest potentialities we can achieve together. Commitment then would be to marriage not simply as a status but as a dynamic process. Let me commit myself to a lifelong adventure, the adventure of living with this woman. The route of this adventure has been only dimly charted by those who have gone before. Because I am unique and my partner is unique, our marriage will also be unique. We commit ourselves to undertaking this adventure together, and to following wherever it may lead. Part of the excitement of marriage is not knowing in advance what either the joys or the sorrows will be. We can be sure, however, that we will be confronted with countless challenges. Commitment provides the momentum for going forward in the face of those challenges.[13]

All these facts, then, should be part of the pastor's filtering system as he works with the couple. The counseling session will give him an opportunity to determine the potential qualities of the future relationship as well as family and individual differences.

---

12. Carlfred B. Broderick, ed., *A Decade of Family Research and Action* (Minneapolis: National Council on Family Relations, 1972), p. 66, adapted.
13. Blood, pp. 10-11.

3

Premarital Counseling—Purpose, Results, and Various Styles

At this point it should be apparent that there is an urgent need for premarital preparation. The local church or those who have some type of Christian ministry are in the best position to provide such a service. It is interesting and sad to note how lax the local church has been in having an ongoing, intensive, and mandatory program of premarital counseling.

Several states have taken steps to stem the number of divorces that occur in youthful marriages. California and other states have passed legislation requiring persons under eighteen to obtain not only parental consent but also a court order giving permission to obtain the marriage license.

The Superior Court of Los Angeles County, along with courts in many other counties, mandated premarital counseling as a prerequisite for obtaining a marriage license by minors. Many churches and public health agencies offer their services to young couples seeking permission to marry. In 1972, of the 4,000 couples who applied for marriage licenses and needed court orders, 2,745 turned to ministers for their counseling. Many of the other couples used community health services. Even though the law and the program are just a few years old, initial findings have indicated the following conclusions concerning those couples involved in premarital counseling provided by public health services: couples used the information given to them as well as the resources of the public health program and many returned for counseling after marriage. The findings reinforced the conviction that premarital counseling is a valuable means of offering primary prevention about common problems, responsibilities, and satisfactions of marriage.[1]

What is the purpose of premarital counseling? What does the pastor or other counselor hope to accomplish by spending several hours with a couple? There are several goals for Christian premarital counseling. In the following discussion, these goals are not listed in order of importance.

One of the goals of the counseling is to make arrangements for the procedural details of the wedding ceremony itself. The couple can express their desires and the pastor can make suggestions and provide guidelines. Tremendous variation is found in wedding invitations and ceremonies today. A pastor should be flexible in his approach to the ceremony. Christian couples are becoming more vocal and personal in sharing their faith in Jesus Christ through their invitations and ceremony, thus allowing both to serve as vehicles for testimony as well as commitment and celebration.

Premarital counseling is a choice opportunity for the pastor or other counselor to build an in-depth relationship with the couple which could lead to a continuing ministry in the future. The rapport established now will make it easier to be involved in the excitement of the couple's marriage in years ahead.

A vital goal is providing correction. Correction of faulty information concerning marriage relationships, the communication process, finances, in-laws, sex, and so on, will be a regular part of the counseling for most couples. In fact, the pastor may be one of the few individuals involved in the life of the couple who can provide this corrective. Unfortunately, some pastors believe that, at this point, couples are not open

1. Helen Shonick, "Pre-Marital Counseling, Three Years' Experience of a Unique Service," *The Family Coordinator* (July 1975), p. 321.

to assistance and their minds are made up or romantically blinded. To the contrary, if counseling is presented in the proper manner and the pastor is well prepared, couples will look forward to each session as a unique learning experience and value it highly. Many couples have suggested that the content of premarital counseling should be given to college students prior to mate selection and then again at premarital counseling.

Providing information is another goal and is congruous with the process of correction. Probably more teaching occurs in this type of counseling than in any other. Part of this teaching involves helping the couple to understand themselves and what each one brings to marriage, to discover their strengths and weaknesses, and to be realistic about the adjustments they must make to have a successful relationship.

The counselor must have expertise in many areas, because the couple is looking to him or her as the conveyer of helpful information. This is an opportunity to provide an atmosphere in which the couple can relieve themselves of fears and anxieties concerning marriage and settle questions or doubts that they have. This may also be a time in which strained and severed relationships with parents and in-laws will be restored.

Counseling also provides an opportunity for Christian growth. Anyone giving premarital counseling should use it to assist the individuals to develop spiritually and thus build a firmer basis for the marriage relationship. Couples should be given instruction in personal and family devotions before marriage. As they develop a pattern and grow in their marriages, these couples could eventually minister to other couples in the congregation.

The final purpose for counseling may seem foreign to some and yet could be one of the most important goals. This is a time to assist the couple in making their final decision, Should we marry? They may not come with that in mind, but engagement is not finality. Research indicates that between 35 and 45 percent of all engagements in this country are terminated. Many people do change their mind. Perhaps the process of premarital counseling, some couples will decide to postpone their wedding or completely terminate their relationship. On the other side, there will be some cases in which the pastor will decide that he cannot, in good conscience, perform the wedding because of the apparent mismatch or immaturity of the couple. Some couples will listen to his advice; others will simply go elsewhere and find someone who does not require so much and will perform the ceremony.

Couples will change their mind. During the spring of one year I worked with nine different couples in premarital counseling, spending six sessions with each couple. Six of the couples proceeded with their weddings and three chose not to proceed. One of the latter decided two weeks before the ceremony. Two couples had such a poor relationship that I planned to tell them their marriages would be too much of a risk; before I did, they told me they decided to break off their relationships.

What are the results of this program of counseling and are they significant? Very little has been done in terms of extensive research and statistical studies with a long-range approach. Two research reports will be cited, as well as individual responses. A Baptist pastor in Oregon made his own follow-up study of couples who had completed his five sessions of premarital counseling. In 1973 he stated that he had performed between 170 and 180 weddings since 1958. He followed up on these couples and learned that six had divorced. He also had refused to marry a number of couples because he felt their marriages would be too risky. (Remaining married is not always an indication of success; many tolerate unhappy and unfulfilling marriages for years.)

Lt. Col. John Williams, a faculty member of the United States Air Force Academy in Colorado Springs, reported in his doctoral thesis that divorce among U.S. military officers is significantly lower than among the population as a whole. Among military officers, air force officers were found to have the lowest divorce rate, with the lowest of all found among officers graduating from the Air Force Academy. Between the years of 1959, when the first class graduated, and 1970, only 21 of the 4,500 Air Force Academy graduates (.004 percent) were divorced.

These statistics may be explained in part by the high value placed on stable marriage. A premarital counseling program conducted by the chaplaincy is an indication of the importance of successful marriage to the air force. Cadets and their fiancées are given intensive preparation for marriage which takes place after graduation from the academy. Protestant, Catholic, and Jewish chaplains conduct their own programs.

Catholic chaplains spend eight to fourteen hours counseling each couple, covering basic areas of communication, finances, love, responsible child planning, and in-laws. The final preparation is accomplished at a weekend retreat where marriage counselors, gynecologists, and lawyers share their views and experiences with the couples.

The Protestant program includes seminars on Sunday afternoons in January, February, and March. The subjects discussed include the success rate of air force marriages, methods of communication, and the physical and spiritual aspects of marriage. A marriage retreat is conducted in April.[2]

In the winter of 1976 a research study was conducted concerning the types, extent, and results of premarital counseling done in churches. Over one thousand churches were contacted, and four hundred and seven returned usable surveys. Over twenty-five different denominations were represented, with churches ranging in size from thirty people to over six thousand people. Some important results are: The average

2. *Religious News Service* (May 15, 1974), p. 2.

number of sessions required for premarital counseling was three. Forty-five pastors required only one session and forty-four required at least six sessions. Two hundred and seventy-four stated that they performed weddings for non-believers and sixty-nine reported they did not. Three hundred and sixty-nine indicated that premarital counseling was required and thirty-eight stated that it was not. Three of the most significant questions asked the participants were:

1. What are the four most significant questions that you ask the couples during the counseling? The results of this question were very helpful but space does not allow a complete presentation of this information. (A complete report of this study is available, including these questions, from Christian Marriage Enrichment, 8000 E. Girard, Denver, Co. 80231.)

2. If counseling is mandatory, how do couples react? How does the church respond to this? Over 90 percent of the responses to this question were positive. People were in favor of the policy, felt that it helped, and encouraged their friends to come for counseling. Some couples were hesitant or went elsewhere.

3. What are the results of premarital counseling in your experience and how do you know?

A representative sampling of responses is as follows:

• Very good: based upon the couples' feedback and the strength of their marriages.

• Several have postponed or canceled weddings.

• It has opened up couples to marital counseling they otherwise would not have had.

• About 20 percent do not marry. They cancel their arrangements.

• Some couples decide that they are not ready for marriage. Some have come to know Christ as Saviour.

• Many have expressed gratitude. Only two have been divorced (about 70 marriages in 22 years).

- Most couples have appreciated the sessions.
- The best type of counseling I believe.
- Twenty-five percent of couples from one church decided not to get married. Almost another 25 percent have postponed their wedding date. Many couples have been very outspoken in their appreciation and in encouraging friends to take the course.
- One pastor counseled fifty-seven couples and conducted weddings for twenty-three. Out of the first eleven he married before he learned how to conduct premarital counseling, one couple divorced and five couples are still having real struggles. After training, he counseled forty-five couples. They now have proper ground rules for their marriages and even for disagreeing and are developing successful marriages.

The basic structure of the premarital counseling suggested in this book is six one-hour sessions before the wedding plus one session three to six months after the wedding. Your initial reaction might be, "How do we fill all of that time?" The problem is actually just the opposite—sometimes the time allotted is not sufficient to cover all the material.

Other readers might react by saying, "I marry twenty to thirty couples a year. What you're suggesting could amount to 200 hours. Where do I get that time, with everything else that I have to do?" It is true that counseling takes time. However, it might be well for each minister to regularly analyze what he is doing with his time. Are his gifts and abilities being used to their best advantage? It is all too easy in the ministry to become overwhelmed with tasks that have little to do with a real ministry to people. Often it comes down to a matter of priority; we do what we feel is important. Premarital counseling is one of the most important opportunities for ministry.

There are several ways to approach this problem of time. One is to restructure one's use of time so that counseling takes a higher priority and other activities are delegated. When we keep adding ministries to our already busy schedule and fail to relinquish or delegate some, a number of difficulties arise. (See Exod 18 and Num 11; note the difficulty Moses experienced because he had not delegated responsibilities to others.)

If the church has a multiple staff, several or all of the ministers could conduct the premarital counseling. A number of churches have trained lay couples to do portions of the counseling, thus using the gifts of many as well as helping the pastoral staff.

Another approach is to conduct some or all of the premarital counseling in group sessions. Examples of this will be given later in the chapter.

It is important to educate the congregation concerning the pastor's policy of premarital counseling—a task that could take a full year. Through the pulpit, classes, the church newsletter, and the bulletin, the pastoral staff has the opportunity to educate the congregation concerning the importance of marriage and the family and to describe in detail what is covered in premarital counseling. People in many congregations have expressed the wish that premarital counseling had been available to them years before.

On the other hand, some will resent a mandatory program and will threaten to go elsewhere for their wedding and perhaps even find another church home. That is their choice! If they so decide, the pastor should not allow himself to be manipulated and pressured into lowering his standards. Too often it has been too easy to be married within the local church. A couple must be willing to take time to adequately prepare for marriage. Through a consistent program such as this, the community and the people in the congregation will come to a deeper level of respect for the ministry of the church.

It is also true that a pastor may have fewer weddings under his new policy. But those he does have will be significant.

The Reverend Robert Dulin, Jr., expressed this standard in his excellent address at the Congress on the Family in 1975 when he said, "Pastors should refuse to sell the birthright of their ministry to nurture marriages, for the pottage of conducting a wedding. The church's ministry is not to conduct weddings. Its ministry is to nurture marriages, before marriage and during marriage. If couples cannot make a commitment to nurture their marriage prior to the event, then the church should say we cannot have your marriage solemnized here."

There may be board members or relatives of members of the church who will ask for a special dispensation in the case of their own young person. A son who is home on leave from the army for a week wants to get married; a couple where there is a pregnancy wants a quick and quiet wedding. Many other unique circumstances will arise. Couples involved in these situations are usually in even greater need of counseling and preparation than the ordinary couple, and they too should complete the total program of premarital counseling.

Part of the process of educating the congregation will be to give periodic reminders about the steps involved in scheduling a wedding at the church. Couples should consider starting their counseling at the time of engagement, or in some cases, prior to engagement. It is best to conduct the counseling no later than four to six months before the wedding. There are two reasons for this. One is that the counseling lasts six to eight weeks, since the sessions are a week or ten days apart.

The second reason for starting counseling early is that the wedding date is not put on the church calendar when the couple first calls the church. The pastor waits until he feels that he favors the marriage and that he can conduct the wedding; at that point the couple can go ahead and set the date on the church calendar. This may occur after two sessions, or, for some, after five. A couple may ask to have a date on the calendar held for them, with the clear understanding that this does not constitute setting the date officially.

Undertaking the counseling does not automatically insure the couple that the wedding will be performed. The pastor will have several criteria to use in making this determination. (These will be discussed later.) With this approach, couples will soon learn to make their plans well in advance. This has advantages for the entire church.

If several churches in a community would adopt this approach, couples would soon begin to see how deeply the church values the marriage relationship and how important the preparation is. At a large church in southern California, a couple asked to see one of the pastors on the staff. When this pastor said that he would require five to six sessions of counseling, the couple said they did not want to have that much counseling and would ask one of the other staff members to perform the ceremony. When they arrived for their appointment with the next minister, they were surprised to hear he had the same requirement. They tried a third minister on the staff, and when they heard the same approach, they returned to the first one and said, "If so many of you on this staff believe so much in premarital counseling and its value, we've decided that we ought to have it. We'd like you to put us through the counseling."

Another way of providing the premarital counseling is through a group preparation program. A Catholic priest in Dodge City, Kansas, reports a program of premarital counseling in which lay couples had been trained to conduct the sessions. Forty couples were spread throughout the area and took two or three engaged couples at a time into their homes and provided several sessions of premarital counseling.

Grace Community Church in Panorama City, California, has a large number of couples married each year. To adequately provide for premarital counseling, a class session is conducted on Sunday mornings. Each couple must attend at least five sessions in order to be married at the church. Some of the couples receive individual sessions as well, based upon the results of their personality tests. Between twenty and thirty couples take this course. Listed here is the outline.

Session	Topics	
1	Purpose of Course	
	Purpose of Engagement	
	Outline of Course	
2	T-JTA (Taylor-Johnson Temperament Analysis) Test Results Returned	
3	Communication	
4	Health	Family Background
	Education	Employment
	Housing	Leisure Time
5	In-laws	Children
	Finances	Sexual Adjustment

Weekly homework assignments assist the individuals, as persons and as a couple, to think through and evaluate their beliefs, values, and goals. The assignments also enable those counseling to better evaluate the strengths and potential weaknesses of the couples in order to be of greater assistance to them. The contact couple assigned (explained below) are the only individuals other than the teaching staff who ever see the work turned in. Homework is handed in on a weekly basis because the assignments are coordinated with the subjects discussed at the next session.

Contact couples are carefully selected married couples who are asked to work on a one-to-one basis with an engaged couple in the course. Each engaged couple is afforded the opportunity to receive personal counsel, interaction, and exposure to a Christian married couple within the latter's own home setting. Homework assignments or any other topic may be discussed. The time spent is left to the discretion of the contact couple.

Optional discussion and fellowship studies are held on selected Friday evenings during the course. The studies are designed to provide additional input, interaction, and fellowship. Topics of practical importance for a mature marriage relationship are covered. Selected couples from Grace Church are invited to lead the discussions.

A resource library of excellent books and tapes is provided for those involved in the course. A packet of four tapes from *Marriage Divine Style,* a series of messages by the Reverend John MacArthur, pastor of Grace Church, is given to every couple at the beginning of the course to help provide a sound understanding of the marriage relationship as God designed it.

A question that most pastors ask is, "What standard do we use in evaluating whom we marry and whom we don't? Do we marry just Christians or do we become involved with non-Christians? What about those who have been divorced? What should be done here?"

A pastor will have two Christians coming to be married, two non-Christians, and one Christian and one non-Christian. One cannot assume that just because two believers are involved the marriage should occur automatically. A Christian profession alone is not sufficient. And that is what the premarital counseling is all about—making this determination.

A basic standard that could be used with any couple is that if they are immature, have unrealistic expectations about marriage, have low motivation to complete the assignments during counseling, and cannot adapt or change, they should postpone the marriage. Some might be urged not to marry at all.

The material given in this book will help a counselor establish criteria for marrying or not marrying. Some of the questions to consider during evaluation are:

Are any legal requirements being violated, such as license,

consent of parents for minors, health test, waiting period? Are any of your own church requirements being ignored?

Do these persons give frivolous reasons for wanting to get married?

Is one or are both entering marriage under duress?

Are they so immature mentally and emotionally that they do not understand the meaning of the vows or give reasonable promise of fulfilling them?

Are their indications that they do not intend to fulfill their marriage vows?

Are there any serious mental, emotional, physical, or other handicaps that might endanger their marriage? Have these been adequately understood, accepted, and dealt with insofar as possible?

Is there such marked personality incompatibility that the need for psychological testing is indicated?

Are there differences in age, background, values, and so forth, which will enrich or threaten their relationship?

If this is a second marriage, has sufficient time elapsed since the death or divorce for the widowed or divorced person to have overcome the hurt and made adequate preparation for the new marriage?

Some pastors favor a preliminary brief session with the couple to discuss their spiritual life. Whether this is done prior to the onset of the actual premarital counseling or during the first session is up to the individual counselor. The details for this session are presented in the next chapter.

When it comes to a believer and an unbeliever seeking marriage, the Scriptures clearly forbid the uniting of such a couple (see 2 Cor 6:14); this would be the standard for refusing to perform the ceremony. As a couple comes for the interview where this information is shared, the pastor's response in love and concern and his high regard for the scriptural teaching could make an impression upon the unbeliever so that the door for discussion remains open. This is an opportunity for evangelism. Yet if one does make a response at this time it is important to spend time with the person to eliminate the possibility that it was a pseudoprofession designed to get the pastor to conduct the wedding.

It is very difficult to judge motives. The pastor dealing with a premarital conversion should engage the person in a thorough discussion of the meaning of a commitment to Christ. He should watch for external evidence that indicates a change of life.

If a person does respond to the claim of the Gospel, he or she should be guided into a group which will assist him or her in the Christian life. In many such cases the wedding date, if it is relatively close at hand, might be postponed in order to let the new convert grow in the faith. This growth is especially important for men because of the biblical concept of the leadership role of the Christian husband. If both partners are at a similar level in their Christian walk it is easier for them to grow together and study together. In some instances the new convert may pass the other person in Christian development and become a source of spiritual encouragement.

A number of pastors in evangelical churches have stated that they do perform weddings joining believer and unbeliever. Their reasons include pressure from parents who are members, board-member pressure, fear of offending long-standing friends, and doubt that the non-Christian would respond to any proclamation at this time. A pastor may weigh in his mind what his congregation will think about what he does. His feeling of the approval or disapproval of the church figures in his decision. A common, final reason is that if the couple is allowed to marry, the unbeliever may eventually respond to the church and its message through this contact. Too often, though, the opposite occurs: because of the influence of the one, both individuals are lost to the church and the faith of the believer begins to wane. In most of these cases it is the woman who is the Christian and the man who is not. As difficult as it may seem to some, the biblical standard must remain the guide for the church.

Wayne Oates has graphically summarized the church's position:

> Marriage under the auspices of the church is an institution ordained of God, blessed by Christ's presence, and subject to the instruction of the Holy Spirit. This is what is meant when a church says it will not "join any person together other than as God's Word doth allow." If there is any other standard, the church is consciously yoking two people together unequally. The Christian experience of regeneration is a necessary prerequisite for a congregation's participating in a Christian wedding through the ministry of its pastor. God has not promised that even a Christian marriage will be free of tribulation. However, when a church joins couples together apart from the Christian faith, it shares the responsibility for any future failure of the marriage for the very reason it did not communicate the redemptive transforming love of Christ at the time of the wedding.
>
> One very real objection can legitimately be raised here. Some people say that a pastor and a congregation can marry a couple, even if one or both may not be Christians, with the hope that by being kind at this point, by doing things they may want it to do, it will have an opportunity later to win them to Christ. However, being kind to people does not necessarily consist of doing what they want done. It may even be the deepest sort of unkindness. Furthermore, there is always suspicion of the wisdom of the man or woman who marries with an eye to "reforming" the mate. If this is true of the couple's individual relationship to each other, it certainly is true of the relationship of the pastor and the church to them. When a church offers the services of its pastor with a view to the couple's being changed at some later date, it forthwith misrepresents reality to the couple.[3]

---

3. Wayne Oates and Wade Rowatt, *Before You Marry Them* (Nashville: Broadman, 1975), p. 34. Used by permission.

Pastors are divided over the question of what to do for couples when both claim to be unbelievers. Such a couple seeks a church wedding not to reflect their commitment to Christ, but because of sentiment, status, or because the church represents the place to be married. Some pastors agree to perform this service for a couple, acting more as an agent of the state than as a minister of the Gospel. The ceremony is usually held in the pastor's study and does not involve a regular church wedding. The content of this ceremony includes only what is necessary to fulfill the law. Yet it seems that this function could be performed by a justice of the peace. The pastor's time should be committed to bringing people to Christ and building strong, enriched marriages; time available for weddings should be reserved for believers.

A Christian wedding involves vows taken before God, scriptural teaching and references which pertain to Christians, a blessing and benediction from God upon the husband and wife, a time of testimony to their faith in Christ, a commitment to build their marriage upon biblical teachings, and a time of celebration and praise. This should also be a time when those who attend the celebration are asked to uphold the couple in prayer and encouragement. Is it possible that nonbelievers could honestly go through this ceremony? Could a pastor honestly lead them through it?

When unbelieving couples ask for a wedding, these reasons can be clearly and lovingly explained. The pastor could also suggest that they continue meeting to explore together the meaning of the Christian faith. Some will respond, but some will never return; they will seek a place where their request will be honored. If a couple remains and professes faith in Christ, then the process of Christian growth begins, and a wedding is a possibility in the future.

It would be difficult to leave this section of the book without facing what some have called a dilemma. What are the guidelines to follow when faced with a couple of whom one or both have been married and divorced? One concern should be with the person's relationship to Christ and his or her Christian walk. Another concern should be with the previous relationship. The discussion should determine whether all past matters have been settled biblically.

There are many views today concerning divorce and remarriage. Some take the position that there is no biblical basis for divorce or for remarriage. However, it does appear from certain passages that divorce is permissible in some cases, and if so, remarriage would also seem to be accepted. (For a thorough discussion of divorce and remarriage, see *Divorce* by John Murray, Presbyterian & Reformed Publishing Co., and *Divorce and Remarriage* by Guy Duty, Bethany Fellowship.)

It is difficult to obtain all the facts concerning the previous marriage situation, but the pastor ought to try to determine whether the divorce occurred according to biblical grounds: if there were attempts at reconciliation, if the divorced person is bitter or forgiving, and so on. If a person states that the spouse was the one at fault, the one who did the cheating, it is still important to ask, "Can you think of any way in which you might have had some responsibility in the demise of the first marriage?" or, "In what way do you feel that you contributed to the problems?" It is rare that only one person is at fault.

Another question to ask is, What would you like to be different in this second marriage than it was in the first, and how will you make this difference? What did you learn from the first experience that will benefit you in this new relationship?

If one or both have children, spend time exploring their understanding of the process of child rearing from a biblical perspective. Philosophies of discipline usually conflict; the counselor can provide suggestions for handling the situation. (Materials for this purpose are suggested in a later chapter.)

As a pastor interviews a person or a couple considering marriage after divorce, the following questions should be considered:

What is the level of spiritual maturity of each individual? What is the evidence of the presence of Christ in their relationship?

Were these people Christians at the time of the divorce (one or both), or have they become Christians since the divorce? What effect has divorce had upon them in terms of their relationship to Christ?

What did the person(s) learn from the first experience? In what way are they the same or different since the divorce?

Has this person undergone some type of counseling or therapy during the first marriage or since that time? Are there any psychological or medical problems which need treatment before this person enters into this marriage? (This is where the testing portion of the premarital counseling program may help to uncover some problem areas.)

Is this couple capable of making a marriage work financially? The man's financial commitments to the first marriage may jeopardize the second. Finances undermine many marriages.

What do they see as the church's response to their marriage and what are they seeking in terms of their future life in the local church?

Again Wayne Oates summarizes the church's position:

> If a couple have become faithful Christians and have demonstrated their change of heart and life since they have been divorced, a church will be hard put to refuse to marry them without placing its teaching concerning divorce above its doctrine of regeneration. Especially is this true if these people are deprived of a Christian wedding and at the same time awarded the privileges of church membership and of holding positions of leadership in the church. The wisdom of an earlier Episcopal ruling is still valid: a couple is re-

quired to wait at least one whole year after the date of the legal decree of divorce before remarriage. This ruling prevents a couple from "by-passing" the grief process of the previous marital break-up and from hastening into a premature relationship that may have been one precipitating cause of the previous marital collapse.[4]

4. Ibid., pp. 38-39. Used by permission.

4

Resources to Use in Premarital Counseling

Earlier I suggested that a couple be required to have at least six sessions of premarital counseling. Here is how these sessions are organized. During the first session the pastor meets with both partners. Next he sees each one individually, each for one hour. It makes no difference whether the man or the woman is seen first. These sessions may occur during the same week or could be a week apart. The individual sessions are considered the second session. The third through the sixth sessions are held with the couple together. Sometimes additional individual sessions may be called for because of emotional difficulties discovered through testing.

The setting where the counseling takes place is very important. The pastor's office or a study at home could be used if they have sufficient privacy and a homey, informal atmosphere. Freedom from interruptions is crucial; the pastor should make arrangements to prevent people from walking into the room, knocking on the door, and calling on the phone. When the pastor and the couple sit near each other in easy chairs, an informal setting is created that helps alleviate the couple's anxieties.

Part of the structure of this counseling and one of the requirements for the couple is that they must agree to complete the assignments given during the time of training. Several books, tapes, and tests are used in the assignments.

Many books are available that could be used. Each pastor

will probably have certain volumes which appeal to him. However, it is of value to be widely read in the area of marriage and family, as some books are more applicable for one couple than for another. Each person is asked to read one book that applies only to himself or herself. The woman is asked to read *Woman: Aware and Choosing* by Betty Coble, Broadman Press. Of the multitude of books written today for women, this work seems to have a balanced approach to the role of the wife without emphasizing a number of subtle manipulation techniques. The man is asked to read *Do Yourself a Favor—Love Your Wife* by Sherman Williams, Logos publishers. This author has taken a directive approach that penetrates some of the typical defenses of men. Reading this book prior to marriage should help a man avoid some common problems that occur.

Each partner is asked to read *Intended for Pleasure* by Dr. Ed and Gail Wheat, Revell. Reading this book and listening to the tape series mentioned later should give any couple a thorough understanding of the physical process. These resources save hours of counseling time, as the pastor needs only to deal with any questions or reactions that arise from the input of these materials.

Communication—Key to Your Marriage is my own book, published by Regal. I ask couples to read a chapter, write their answers to the discussion questions, then discuss their responses. There will be times when the couple could spend hours in discussion—and this is the very purpose of the premarital counseling program.

When the couple comes for the first session it is vital that they be told that they will probably spend twenty to twenty-five hours of work outside the sessions. They should look over their schedules and arrange time for study and discussion. This is another reason the actual counseling should take place well ahead of the wedding, for wedding preparations could take precedence over the counseling and its homework, which are more important.

One other book which could be used by the couple, or at least some of the information could be imparted by the pastor, is *Love Is Something You Do* by John Bisagno, Harper & Row. One of the financial and money management resources mentioned later in this book should also be assigned during the later sessions.

Many tape resources available today can be used to cover the roles of husband and wife. It would be advantageous if a pastor listened to the various sets mentioned here and had them available to use with couples. The selection will depend upon what a couple has already listened to and upon the emphasis the pastor feels the couple needs. Two available sets are *God's Order for Wives* and *God's Order for Husbands* by Larry Christensen, available from Bethany Fellowship. *The Role of the Husband and the Role of the Wife* is a series recorded by Dr. Howard Hendricks from Dallas Theological Seminary and produced by the One Way Library. Each pastor may know of other tapes available for this same purpose or may have made his own to use in this manner.

One of the finest sets of tapes available on sex was made by Dr. Ed Wheat, a Christian physician and surgeon, founder of The Bible Believer Cassette Ministry in Springdale, Arkansas. The series, titled *Sex Problems and Sex Techniques in Marriage,* has been of tremendous assistance to thousands of couples who have been married for many years as well as to those preparing for marriage. The couple is asked to listen to this series together a month or so before the wedding. Topics covered in this series include "The Command to Have Sexual Union," "Anatomy of the Male and Female Reproductive System," "Phases of Sexual Response," "Sexual Problems," "Explanation of the Menstrual Cycle," "Birth Control," "Sex After 60-70-80," "Frequently Asked Questions and Answers About Sex," "The Greatest Enjoyment in the Sexual Union," and "The Purpose of the Sexual Union." For some reason, listening to a qualified doctor discuss this material frankly and openly has greater impact than reading the same words in print. One of the tapes concludes with a clear Gospel presentation. This series is available from Christian Marriage Enrichment, 8000 E. Girard, Denver, Colorado 80231.

Tests and evaluation forms for premarital counseling provide valuable information and save time. One such test is the *Sex Knowledge Inventory*, from Family Life Publications, which has been used in this type of counseling to help a couple and their pastor determine the couple's level of knowledge and understanding of the basic physiology of the sexual response. However, the use of the book and the tapes by the Wheats should cover this subject adequately, and a pastor may not need the inventory.

From time to time, one encounters an individual, usually a man, who feels that the book and tapes would be a waste of time as he considers himself quite knowledgeable in this field. Having him take the *Sex Knowledge Inventory* quickly dispels that belief and makes him more receptive to the instruction. Form Y of this test deals with such technical subjects as anatomy, physiology, and contraception. Form X may be more helpful in the counseling process as the questions are broader in scope and can also reflect some of the individual's attitudes. Several sample questions from form X are listed here.

What is the relation[ship] between being sexually attracted to a man or woman and being in love with that person?

A. Sex attraction is physical desire; love is an attitude.
B. Sex attraction and being in love are the same thing.
C. If there is no sex attraction, there can be no love.
D. Sex attraction may mean that love also is present.
E. If there is no love there will be no sex attraction.

Sex relations are:

A. For physical pleasure.
B. A way to relieve tension.
C. A way to express love.
D. A biological urge.
E. All of the above.

Of the following, which one supplies the best evidence for predicting that a prospective husband or wife will be a good sex partner?

A. The "sex appeal" of the man or woman.
B. His or her interest in or conversation about sex.
C. His or her physical demonstrations of affection.
D. All of his or her behavior during courtship.
E. His or her response to physical closeness.

What is the probable reason[s] when muscles of a wife's vaginal entrance go into spasm, which may prevent intercourse altogether or cause her pain in intercourse?

A. Insufficient or inadequate sex play before intercourse.
B. No sex desire or inability to enjoy sex relations.
C. A learned involuntary reaction to sex relations as painful, dangerous.
D. Normal expectation that sex relations are threatening or painful.
E. An intentional act from fear of pregnancy or of intercourse.

How often is unsatisfactory intercourse caused by a difference in size of the male and female sex organs?

A. Almost always.
B. Very often.
C. Often.
D. At times.
E. Rarely.

What kind of intercourse is necessary for a woman to become pregnant?

A. She must reach orgasm before the man.
B. The man and woman must reach orgasm at the same time.
C. She must reach orgasm after the man.
D. Pregnancy is possible whenever sperm cells enter the vagina.
E. The man must reach orgasm for the pregnancy to be possible.

At what time in her cycle of menstruation is a woman most likely to become pregnant?

A. About two weeks before menstruation begins.
B. During the three days before menstruation begins.
C. During menstruation.
D. In the first day after menstruation begins.
E. During the first week after menstruation ends.*

Another helpful form is the "Marriage Prediction Schedule" from Family Life Publications. This particular tool will give the pastor background information on each individual. This information reveals potential areas of conflict and adjustment as well as attitudes concerning the family. A scoring key on this form is supposed to indicate the probability of success for the marriage, but its validity is questionable. The main value of the test is being able to note differences between the couple in such things as attitudes toward family members. Listed here are some of the actual questions from this form so you may see how it can be used.

Indicate your attitudes toward your parents on the following scales:

1. Your attitude toward your father when you were a child: very strong attachment; considerable attachment; mild

*Used by permission.

attachment; mild hostility; considerable hostility; very strong hostility

2. Your present attitude toward your father: very strong attachment; considerable attachment; mild attachment; mild hostility; considerable hostility; very strong hostility; no attitude as he is dead

3. Your attitude toward your mother when you were a child: very strong attachment; considerable attachment; mild attachment; mild hostility; considerable hostility; very strong hostility

4. Your present attitude toward your mother: very strong attachment; considerable attachment; mild attachment; mild hostility; considerable hostility; very strong hostility; no attitude as she is dead

---

1. What is the attitude of your closest friend or friends to your fiancé(e); approve highly; approve with qualification; are resigned; disapprove mildly; disapprove seriously

2. How many of your present men and women friends are also friends of your fiancé(e)? all; most of them; a few; none

3. How would you rate the physical appearance of your fiancé(e)? very good looking; good looking; fairly good looking; plain looking; very plain looking

4. Do you think your fiancé(e) is spending a disproportionate amount of present income on any of the following (check only one)? clothes (or personal ornamentation); recreation; hobbies; food; rent; education; do not think so†

An illustration will help demonstrate how the form would be of value. Perhaps we have a couple who have completed this form. The young man's present attitude toward his father is that of mild hostility; he has also indicated that he has considerable hostility toward his mother. The young woman had a very strong attachment to her father when she

†Used by permission.

was a child and still has that strong attachment. How will the differences in these feelings affect the marriage relationship? Will the young man project feelings of hostility toward the woman's father as well? What is the cause for his feeling this way? What attempts have been made to resolve this problem? Will he be suspicious of his wife's parents? Could he develop hostility toward her if she desires a close contact with her father? Are his parents aware of his feelings? Has there been a time of confession, forgiveness, and reconciliation? Other significant questions are found in the "Marriage Prediction Schedule." Without this tool it might be difficult to discover some of the potential areas of marital disturbance.

The major test used in premarital counseling is the "Taylor-Johnson Temperament Analysis," (T-JTA). In the January, 1973, issue of the *Family Coordinator,* Dr. Clinton Phillips published an article, "Some Useful Tests for Marriage Counselors." The Taylor-Johnson test was mentioned as one of the five tests. The American Institute of Family Relations in Hollywood has given this test to more than seventy thousand couples over the years, and thousands of other counselors and ministers have used it extensively. It is used for individual, premarital, marital, and family counseling, business and industry placement, placement of Sunday school teachers, evaluation of counselors for Christian camps, and assessment of college and seminary students. This test has been used as the basis for Bible studies in groups, as the traits lend themselves well to biblical teaching.

The test takes between thirty and forty-five minutes to complete. The profile derived from the test is very readable; lay people can understand it readily. Norms for this test are available for high school, college, and adult ages. It is important to remember that a minister must take a training course in order to qualify to administer and work with this test. Many seminaries give this training. Numerous one-day seminars are conducted throughout the United States which qualify ministers and counselors to use this test. For information regarding a seminar in your area write to Christian Marriage Enrichment, 8000 E. Girard, Suite 602, Denver, Colorado 80231, or to the publisher of the test.

Before the couple comes for their first counseling session, they are asked to take the test. They may pick up the forms at the church office, or these may be mailed to them. The counselor goes over the instructions with them before they take the test. Each one takes it twice. The woman takes it as she sees herself, and then as she sees her fiancé. He takes the test as he sees himself and then as he sees her. This is called a criss-cross. The information derived from each person's perception of himself or herself and of the partner is invaluable and saves several hours of counseling.

Since many emotional problems such as uncontrolled anger, depression, worry, lack of empathy, or a low self-image are at the heart of numerous marital problems, it is crucial to take an intense look at this area for each person. Following are four profiles of a married couple, showing the scores for themselves and then the criss-cross. Look at the profiles, noting the nine traits and their definitions and the four shaded areas (from "excellent" to "improvement urgent"). Study the differences in the scores of this couple to see if you can determine areas in which they both have strengths and weaknesses as well as problem areas between them.

By having the test returned to you before the couple's first session, you will have time to score the forms before you meet with them. Even though you do not go over the results until the individual sessions, you may want to probe into certain areas of their life or relationship because of what the tests have revealed.

Several other alternate resources could be used to help couples thoroughly evaluate their relationship and provide helpful information. A booklet called *Grounds for Marriage,* by James R. Hines and published by Interstate Publishers

HUSBAND

TAYLOR-JOHNSON TEMPERAMENT ANALYSIS PROFILE
Profile Revision of 1967

These Answers Describe **BROWN, RICHARD**   Age **46**   Sex **M**   Date **8-1-66**

School **U. OF CALIF.**   Grade_____ Degree **PHD.** Major **CHEM. ENG.** Occupation **CHEM. ENGINEER**   Counselor **W.E.**

Single____ Years Married **20** Years Divorced____ Years Widowed____ Children: M **1** Ages **18**   F **1** Ages **16**

Answers made by: SELF $\frac{and}{or}$ husband, wife, father, mother, son, daughter, brother, sister, or_____of the person described.

Norm(s): **67-68** GEN. POP.	A	B	C	D	E	F	G	H	I	Attitude (Sten) Score: **6**
Mids		1	2	1		1			1	Total Mids: **6**
Raw score	4	7	20	17	34	1	20	8	37	Raw score
Percentile	20	50	19	11	65	5	26	39	96	Percentile
TRAIT	Nervous	Depressive	Active-Social	Expressive-Responsive	Sympathetic	Subjective	Dominant	Hostile	Self-disciplined	TRAIT

| TRAIT OPPOSITE | Composed | Light-hearted | Quiet | Inhibited | Indifferent | Objective | Submissive | Tolerant | Impulsive | TRAIT OPPOSITE |

Excellent   Acceptable   Improvement desirable   Improvement urgent

DEFINITIONS

TRAITS
Nervous — Tense, high-strung, apprehensive.
Depressive — Pessimistic, discouraged, dejected.
Active-Social — Energetic, enthusiastic, socially involved.
Expressive-Responsive — Spontaneous, affectionate, demonstrative.
Sympathetic — Kind, understanding, compassionate.
Subjective — Emotional, illogical, self-absorbed.
Dominant — Confident, assertive, competitive.
Hostile — Critical, argumentative, punitive.
Self-disciplined — Controlled, methodical, persevering.

OPPOSITES
Composed — Calm, relaxed, tranquil.
Light-hearted — Happy, cheerful, optimistic.
Quiet — Socially inactive, lethargic, withdrawn.
Inhibited — Restrained, unresponsive, repressed.
Indifferent — Unsympathetic, insensitive, unfeeling.
Objective — Fair-minded, reasonable, logical.
Submissive — Passive, compliant, dependent.
Tolerant — Accepting, patient, humane.
Impulsive — Uncontrolled, disorganized, changeable.

Note: Important decisions should not be made on the basis of this profile without confirmation of these results by other means.

1. *Taylor-Johnson Temperament Analysis* (T-JTA), Taylor, Robert M., and Morrison, Lucile Philips, by Psychological Publications, Inc., 5300 Hollywood Blvd., Los Angeles, CA 90027, 1966-74.

Printed by permission of Robert M. Taylor & Psychological Publications, Inc.

WIFE

TAYLOR-JOHNSON TEMPERAMENT ANALYSIS PROFILE
Profile Revision of 1967

These Answers Describe **BROWN, HELEN** ___ Age **40** ___ Sex **F** ___ Date **8-1-66**

School **COMPLETED** ___ Grade **11** ___ Degree ___ Major ___ Occupation **HOUSEWIFE** ___ Counselor **W.E.**

Single ___ Years Married **20** Years Divorced ___ Years Widowed ___ Children: M **1** Ages **18** ___ F **1** Ages **16**

Answers made by: SELF $\frac{and}{or}$ husband, wife, father, mother, son, daughter, brother, sister, or ___ of the person described.

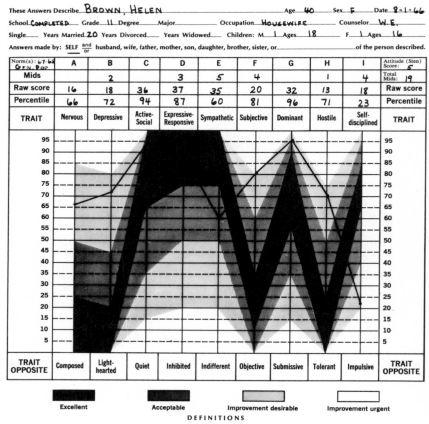

Norm(s): 67-68 GEN. POP.	A	B	C	D	E	F	G	H	I	Attitude (Sten) Score: 5
Mids		2		3	5	4		1	4	Total Mids: 19
Raw score	16	18	36	37	35	20	32	13	18	Raw score
Percentile	66	72	94	87	60	81	96	71	23	Percentile
TRAIT	Nervous	Depressive	Active-Social	Expressive-Responsive	Sympathetic	Subjective	Dominant	Hostile	Self-disciplined	TRAIT

| TRAIT OPPOSITE | Composed | Light-hearted | Quiet | Inhibited | Indifferent | Objective | Submissive | Tolerant | Impulsive | TRAIT OPPOSITE |

Excellent   Acceptable   Improvement desirable   Improvement urgent

DEFINITIONS

TRAITS

Nervous — Tense, high-strung, apprehensive.
Depressive — Pessimistic, discouraged, dejected.
Active-Social — Energetic, enthusiastic, socially involved.
Expressive-Responsive — Spontaneous, affectionate, demonstrative.
Sympathetic — Kind, understanding, compassionate.
Subjective — Emotional, illogical, self-absorbed.
Dominant — Confident, assertive, competitive.
Hostile — Critical, argumentative, punitive.
Self-disciplined — Controlled, methodical, persevering.

OPPOSITES

Composed — Calm, relaxed, tranquil.
Light-hearted — Happy, cheerful, optimistic.
Quiet — Socially inactive, lethargic, withdrawn.
Inhibited — Restrained, unresponsive, repressed.
Indifferent — Unsympathetic, insensitive, unfeeling.
Objective — Fair-minded, reasonable, logical.
Submissive — Passive, compliant, dependent.
Tolerant — Accepting, patient, humane.
Impulsive — Uncontrolled, disorganized, changeable.

Note: Important decisions should not be made on the basis of this profile without confirmation of these results by other means.

Printed by permission of Robert M. Taylor & Psychological Publications, Inc.

HUSBAND BY WIFE
CRISS - CROSS

TAYLOR-JOHNSON TEMPERAMENT ANALYSIS PROFILE
Profile Revision of 1967

These Answers Describe **BROWN, RICHARD** Age **46** Sex **M** Date **8-1-66**

School **U. OF CALIF.** Grade _____ Degree **Ph.D.** Major **CHEM. ENG.** Occupation **CHEM - ENGINEER** Counselor **W.E.**

Single _____ Years Married **20** Years Divorced _____ Years Widowed _____ Children: M **1** Ages **18** F **1** Ages **16**

Answers made by: SELF **and or** husband, wife, father, mother, son, daughter, brother, sister, or _____ of the person described.

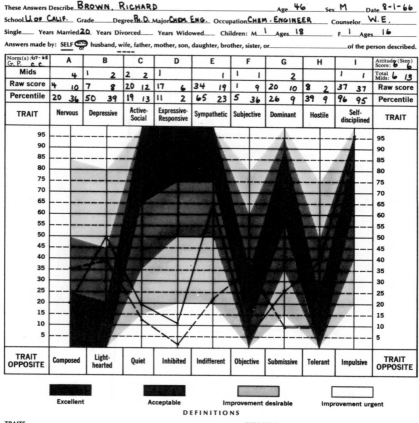

Norm(s) :67-68 Gr. P. c.c.	A		B		C		D		E		F		G		H		I		Attitude (Sten) Score: **6** **6**
Mids		**4**	**1**		**2**	**2**	**2**		**1**	**1**	**1**	**1**		**2**			**1**	**1**	Total **6** **13** Mids
Raw score	**4**	**10**	**7**	**8**	**20**	**12**	**17**	**6**	**34**	**19**	**1**	**9**	**20**	**10**	**8**	**2**	**37**	**37**	Raw score
Percentile	**20**	**36**	**50**	**39**	**19**	**13**	**11**	**2**	**65**	**23**	**5**	**36**	**26**	**9**	**39**	**9**	**96**	**95**	Percentile
TRAIT	Nervous		Depressive		Active-Social		Expressive-Responsive		Sympathetic		Subjective		Dominant		Hostile		Self-disciplined		TRAIT

TRAIT OPPOSITE	Composed	Light-hearted	Quiet	Inhibited	Indifferent	Objective	Submissive	Tolerant	Impulsive	TRAIT OPPOSITE

Excellent **Acceptable** **Improvement desirable** **Improvement urgent**

DEFINITIONS

TRAITS

Nervous — Tense, high-strung, apprehensive.
Depressive — Pessimistic, discouraged, dejected.
Active-Social — Energetic, enthusiastic, socially involved.
Expressive-Responsive — Spontaneous, affectionate, demonstrative.
Sympathetic — Kind, understanding, compassionate.
Subjective — Emotional, illogical, self-absorbed.
Dominant — Confident, assertive, competitive.
Hostile — Critical, argumentative, punitive.
Self-disciplined — Controlled, methodical, persevering.

OPPOSITES

Composed — Calm, relaxed, tranquil.
Light-hearted — Happy, cheerful, optimistic.
Quiet — Socially inactive, lethargic, withdrawn.
Inhibited — Restrained, unresponsive, repressed.
Indifferent — Unsympathetic, insensitive, unfeeling.
Objective — Fair-minded, reasonable, logical.
Submissive — Passive, compliant, dependent.
Tolerant — Accepting, patient, humane.
Impulsive — Uncontrolled, disorganized, changeable.

Note: Important decisions should not be made on the basis of this profile without confirmation of these results by other means.

Printed by permission of Robert M. Taylor & Psychological Publications, Inc.

WIFE BY HUSBAND

CRISS - CROSS

TAYLOR-JOHNSON TEMPERAMENT ANALYSIS PROFILE
Profile Revision of 1967

These Answers Describe **BROWN, HELEN**   Age **40**   Sex **F**   Date **8-1-66**

School **COMPLETED** Grade **11** Degree____ Major____ Occupation **HOUSEWIFE** Counselor **W.E.**

Single____ Years Married **20** Years Divorced____ Years Widowed____ Children: M **1** Ages **18** F **1** Ages **16**

Answers made by: SELF **and/or** husband, wife, father, mother, son, daughter, brother, sister, or____ of the person described.

Norm(s): 67-68 G.P. C.C.	A		B		C		D		E		F		G		H		I		Attitude (Sten) Score: **5 4**
Mids		2	1		1	3	1	5	1	4	2		1	1	1	4	1		Total Mids: **19 9**
Raw score	16	28	18	21	36	37	37	33	35	19	20	24	32	33	13	25	18	29	Raw score
Percentile	66	90	72	74	94	94	87	72	60	23	81	84	96	89	71	80	23	68	Percentile
TRAIT	Nervous		Depressive		Active-Social		Expressive-Responsive		Sympathetic		Subjective		Dominant		Hostile		Self-disciplined		TRAIT

| TRAIT OPPOSITE | Composed | Light-hearted | Quiet | Inhibited | Indifferent | Objective | Submissive | Tolerant | Impulsive | TRAIT OPPOSITE |

Excellent   Acceptable   Improvement desirable   Improvement urgent

DEFINITIONS

TRAITS

Nervous — Tense, high-strung, apprehensive.
Depressive — Pessimistic, discouraged, dejected.
Active-Social — Energetic, enthusiastic, socially involved.
Expressive-Responsive — Spontaneous, affectionate, demonstrative.
Sympathetic — Kind, understanding, compassionate.
Subjective — Emotional, illogical, self-absorbed.
Dominant — Confident, assertive, competitive.
Hostile — Critical, argumentative, punitive.
Self-disciplined — Controlled, methodical, persevering.

OPPOSITES

Composed — Calm, relaxed, tranquil.
Light-hearted — Happy, cheerful, optimistic.
Quiet — Socially inactive, lethargic, withdrawn.
Inhibited — Restrained, unresponsive, repressed.
Indifferent — Unsympathetic, insensitive, unfeeling.
Objective — Fair-minded, reasonable, logical.
Submissive — Passive, compliant, dependent.
Tolerant — Accepting, patient, humane.
Impulsive — Uncontrolled, disorganized, changeable.

Note: Important decisions should not be made on the basis of this profile without confirmation of these results by other means.

Printed by permission of Robert M. Taylor & Psychological Publications, Inc.

(19 Jackson St., Danville, IL. 61832), has a number of topic areas that could be adapted to a program of premarital counseling. Titles of the topic areas are "What You Bring to Your Marriage," "Adventure into Mutuality," "Personality Traits Compared," "The Marriage Union," "Financing the Home and the Future," and "Religious Homes are Happy Homes."

Family Life Publications has produced another form titled the *Marriage Expectation Inventory for Engaged Couples.* A sampling of some of the questions is listed here.

1. Loving my future partner means for me . . .

2. Recall four instances of how your future partner demonstrated love toward you during the last month:

3. List four situations in which you, intentionally or unintentionally, were hurtful to your future partner in the last month:

4. List two ways you and your future spouse differ:

5. List two ways you and your future spouse are alike:

6. List four things your future partner has "bugged" you about recently which you could have corrected, but did not:

7. Explain why.

8. What is the best strength you will bring to your marriage?

9. What is your future partner's best strength?

The "Premarital Counseling Inventory" has been developed by Research Press. The instructions on this form give the best explanation of its use:

This inventory asks several series of questions aimed at describing who you are, what you like about your present relationship, and how you would like to see it evolve. Based upon your thoughtful answers to these questions, the counselor can help you to determine your level of satisfaction with things as they are now. You can also be helped to redefine, together, some aspects of your relationship which could be improved. Based upon this information, you may be able to make a more confident decision about whether to marry or you may be able to strengthen the decision which you have already made.

Topic areas covered in this inventory are family background, past marital history, history of your present relationship, attitudes concerning roles, time, and money, and development of marital contract. Here is a sample section from this inventory, titled "History of Your Present Relationship."

III. History of your present relationship
    A. When did you first meet?
    B. For how many years and months have you known each other?
    C. What five strong points attract you to the other person?
    D. Have you decided to marry? Yes_____ No_____. If no, please go on to question E. If yes, please answer the following questions.
        1. How confident are you about the wisdom of your decision?
        Very much so_____ Pretty confident_____
        Have some doubt_____ Very unsure_____
        2. What reaction have your parents had to your decision?
        Very positive_____ Positive_____ Neutral_____
        Negative_____
        3. What reaction have your friends had to your decision?
        Very positive_____ Positive_____ Neutral_____
        Negative_____
    E. Have you ever called off your plans to marry?
    Yes_____ No_____. If no, please go on to question F. If yes, please answer the following questions.
        1. When did this happen?
        2. What would you say was the cause?
        3. How did you resolve the situation?

.   .   .   .

G. Please list three ways in which you think a positive and specific change in the behavior of the other person would help you to enjoy your relationship more. For example, please write "Ask me how I spent my day" (positive and specific), rather than "Don't ignore me" (negative and vague).

	Is this:			
	Very important		Unimportant	
1. _____	1	2	3	4
1. _____	1	2	3	4
1. _____	1	2	3	4

H. What are your three most important personal interests?

I. What are the three things which you and your friend most enjoy doing together?

A final resource that is helpful in the area of communication is the "Premarital Communication Inventory" developed by Dr. Millard J. Bienvenu, Sr. This form must be ordered directly from the author at Northwestern State University of Louisiana, Natchitoches, Louisiana 71457. A few of the questions will give you an idea of the contents of this discussion tool designed for the couple to use by themselves or with the pastor.

	Yes Usually	Sel- dom	Some- times
Do you have a tendency to keep your feelings to yourself?	_____	_____	_____
Does your fiancé tell you when he/she is angry with you?	_____	_____	_____
Does your fiancé fail to ask your opinion in making plans involving the two of you?	_____	_____	_____
Do you communicate successfully with each other's families?	_____	_____	_____

Does it bother you *unduly* for   _____   _____   _____
your fiancé to express his/her own
beliefs if they differ from yours?
Does your fiancé nag you?   _____   _____   _____
Does your fiancé wait until you   _____   _____   _____
are through talking before saying
what he/she has to say?
Do the two of you discuss what   _____   _____   _____
you expect of one another in terms
of a future mother and father?

One final area must be noted: the cost of counseling. Is there any charge when it is done at the church? What would it cost if the couple went to a professional marriage counselor? In answer to the second question, it would cost a couple between $60.00 and $120.00 for this preparation. Most churches do not charge for counseling. However, the wedding service fee usually pays for church use, utilities, janitorial service, and other expenses. A number of churches have begun to include an additional twenty-five or thirty-dollar fee to cover the cost of counseling. This money pays for the books which the pastor gives to the couple. It is important for the couple to own the books. Many have stated that after they were married they reread the books, which took on a new meaning for them. The fee also pays for the testing materials used by the couple and several series of tapes used in the counseling ministry.

One final word of instruction is necessary. Before proceeding with this ministry of counseling, the pastor or lay person must be totally familiar with the tapes, books, tests, and other materials to be used. It may take several weeks of study, but this in turn enhances the ministry of marital preparation. In addition to reading the books already mentioned, a pastor or counselor will benefit greatly and add depth to his counseling ministry by reading the following books. Remember that these authors hold various views, and the reader will not agree with everything they say. That will be beneficial since it will cause the reader to think and to examine his beliefs.

Bisagno, John. *Love Is Something You Do.* New York: Harper & Row, 1975.

Hollis, Harry Jr. *Thank God for Sex.* Nashville: Broadman, 1975.

Jackson, Don; and Lederer, William. *The Mirages of Marriage.* New York: Norton, 1968.

Small, Dwight. *After You've Said I Do.* Old Tappan, N.J.: Revell, 1968.

———. *Design for Christian Marriage.* Old Tappan, N. J.: Revell, 1959.

5

The First and Second Sessions

The first session is about to begin. The couple is arriving at the church for their first premarital interview. Prior to this session they have completed the "Taylor-Johnson Temperament Analysis." They have also answered, individually, several questions that will be covered in this particular session. The questions were given or mailed to them along with the Taylor-Johnson test. The following questions should be answered before the session:

1. What is your definition of marriage?
2. How were feelings of love, warmth, and tenderness shown in your home as you were growing up? How would you like feelings of love, warmth, and tenderness shown to you in public and in your home?
3. How have your attitudes toward marriage been influenced, and who influenced them?
4. What fears do you have about marriage?

Other questions are posed during the counseling session.

After the couple arrives, it is important to spend time getting acquainted. Some of the couples will be people a pastor has known for years, others will be strangers. It is helpful for the pastor to share information about himself such as background, family, hobbies, schools, and some of his interesting experiences in marriage.

One of the basic ground rules of the premarital counseling is stated in the beginning: there is nothing that cannot be discussed in these sessions. The couple should not hesitate to ask the pastor any questions they have, and he will take the same privilege of asking them anything he feels is necessary.

It is important to remind the couple of the agreement that they complete their outside assignments if the counseling is to continue.

The session is then under way with the question, "Why are you coming to the church to be married, instead of going to a justice of the peace?" Why is a church important? Such a question helps the couple clarify their motivation for being married in the church and causes them to think of the testimonial aspect of the wedding ceremony. Perhaps they have to verbalize their reasons for the first time. This may be a new revelation to each of them. For some individuals the church has little or no meaning. Others are very committed to having Jesus Christ at the center of their marriage relationship.

Next they are asked to share their definition of marriage. This they do individually. At this point the pastor can share several definitions of marriage with them, his own and others which have been formulated. There are three definitions that I like to explain at this point; sometimes these are incorporated into the wedding itself. One was written by David Augsburger:

> Is marriage a private action of two persons in love, or a public act of two pledging a contract? Neither, it is something other. Very much other! Basically, the Christian view of marriage is not that it is primarily or essentially a binding legal and social contract. The Christian understands marriage as a covenant made under God and in the presence of fellow members of the Christian Family. Such a pledge endures, not because of the force of law or the fear of its sanctions, but because an unconditional covenant has been made. A covenant more solemn, more binding, more permanent than any legal contract.[1]

1. David Augsburger, *Cherishable: Love and Marriage* (Scottsdale, Pa.: Herald Press, 1971), p. 16.

Another interesting definition was shared in a message by Dr. David Hubbard:

> Marriage does not demand perfection. But it must be given priority. It is an institution for sinners. No one else need apply. But it finds its finest glory when sinners see it as God's way of leading us through His ultimate curriculum of love and righteousness.[2]

The definition that I have been formulating for several years is the one that I concentrate on with the couple. It is given here, followed by an amplification that I share in counseling and in classes with married couples. This will give you an example of the personal aspect of this counseling.

> A Christian marriage is a total commitment of two people to the person of Jesus Christ and to one another. It is a commitment in which there is no holding back of anything. Marriage is a pledge of mutual fidelity; it is a partnership of mutual subordination. A Christian marriage is similar to a solvent, a freeing up of the man and woman to be themselves and become all that God intends for them to become. Marriage is the refining process that God will use to have us develop into the man or woman He wants us to become.
>
> There is one phrase there that I would like to focus on; this phrase is "the refining process." Have you ever thought of your marriage as a refining process? That God is going to allow certain events to happen in your life that will cause you to grow and develop into the man or woman He wants you to become? What would happen if you were to have that attitude toward the events that occur within your marriage—that those events are something that God can use to cause you to grow deeper together and to cause each to grow more as an individual?
>
> Each of you has had different experiences. In every marriage it will be different. We've had a unique situation in our relationship. We have two children, a daughter in junior

2. David Hubbard, president of Fuller Theological Seminary, in an address.

high, and a son who will be eight years of age. He's about eighteen months old mentally and will probably never be more than three or four years old mentally. He is a brain-damaged, mentally retarded child. When Matthew was first born we didn't know this. At about eight months of age, he began having seizures. We took him to the UCLA medical clinic where the diagnosis was made.

The name "Matthew" means "God's gift," or "gift from God." Matthew is God's gift to us. We have experienced times of pain, disappointment, and heartache, but we've experienced other times of joy and delight. I can remember when we prayed for Matthew to walk. All of us in our family prayed for about three and a half years. And one day when we were together, he stood up and took about five steps. I said something like, "Isn't that wonderful?" Joyce said something like, "Isn't that great?" Then our nine-year-old daughter said, "Let's stop right now and thank God for answering our prayer." It is interesting how our children will teach us and will cause us to give thanks to the proper person.

You consider some of the events that may occur in your life and you wonder, "How in the world am I going to handle them when I don't even know what's going to happen?" But God gives us the resources to handle whatever happens; He does this in His wonderful and marvelous way, even when we're not aware of it. God can be preparing us for some of those situations that are going to hit us.

Before Matthew was born and I was in seminary, I had to write a thesis. I didn't know what to write about. When I went in, the professor said to me, "Nobody's written a thesis on the Christian education of the mentally retarded child. You write it." So I did. I read books, studied, went to schools, and observed Sunday school classes for these children. I learned a lot about them. Then I wrote the thesis.

My wife typed the thesis the first time, a second time, and finally a third time, and she learned about retarded children as well. After it was finally turned in and accepted, I went to work at my church while I was working on a psychology degree. I had to do an internship in the public school district for the school psychologist credential. I was assigned to test and re-test mentally retarded children. At my church I was given the responsibility of training teachers to teach mentally retarded children within the church, and so I had to develop a program.

One night two years before Matthew was born, Joyce and I were talking; we said, "Isn't it interesting all the experience we've had with retarded children? Could it be that God is preparing us for something that is going to occur later in our life?" That is all we said. Two years later Matthew came into our lives. We saw how God prepared us.

When an event occurs in your life that some would call a tragedy, can you look back and see how God has been preparing you for that, or how He's going to give you the extra strength, wisdom, and patience right at the right time for you to handle it?

Marriage is a refining process. An adequate concept of what marriage is about is the first foundation of marriage preparation.

The next topic area which we explore is the couple's individual family background. For example, the woman could be asked to share something about her home and family, such as where she lived, in what type of home, what her parents did, whether they are still together, whether she has brothers and sisters and what type of relationships they have, the financial status of the home, whether the family moved around or lived in one place. She also answers the following question: How did your parents' physical and mental health relate to you in growing up? How did your parents handle disagreements? Which parent did you admire the most? Then the man can give the same information about his background.

Two questions are asked which the couple were requested to give written answers for before the session. How were feelings of love, warmth, and tenderness shown in your home as you were growing up? How would you like feelings of love, warmth, and tenderness shown to you in public and in your home?

Part of the problem you are looking for here is the fact that when people come out of their own home they might carry with them some of the behavior that was detrimental in that home. They also might have certain expectations. For example, a person might come into marriage with the expectation that his or her mate will be like a parent whom he or she admired. Or, one partner may have the expectation that the mate will *not* be like a parent with whom this individual had a number of differences. One may believe that the lifestyle in the new home will be the same as in the parental home; another may wish it to be radically different.

There is also the problem that a person might have a personal conviction that his or her description of a mate and a parent is the only acceptable description. He or she will not allow latitude for the other person's ideas and perceptions; this inflexibility can create difficulties later in the marriage relationship. An example may illustrate this.

The young man's name was Bob. His mother died in childbirth. He had no brothers or sisters. He was reared solely by his father and had no contact with women in his home as he was growing up. His father was lower middle class. They moved every year or two. Bob went to many different schools, lived in different cities all over the nation, and had no settled roots.

Bob did not date very much. When he was in high school he dated a girl only once or twice. Later he went to college by himself. He worked very hard; he spent a lot of time studying, and a lot of time working at a job. When he was twenty-three years of age, he met a young woman named Janet; they fell in love and decided to be married.

Janet came from an upper middle-class home. The family had lived in the same location for the past fifteen years. Janet had two brothers and three sisters. The family was very stable. They did many things together; they were a very close-knit group. The grandparents lived nearby, and there were aunts and uncles in the same town. Janet never had to want for much. She had money when she needed it, and the parents took a great deal of interest in all their children.

Here was a couple with great differences in their backgrounds. Premarital counseling was vital for them. There were some major differences which needed to be explored, for the marriage could have suffered greatly because of these differences. The young man had had very little contact with females. He did not know what it is like to live in a home with women around. He did not have a mother or any sisters, and he did not date much, so after marriage he could have been in for a very real cultural shock. He had not had much experience in sharing a home with other individuals. What happens when he is married? In the morning he walks into the bathroom and runs into nylons, drying on the towel rack. He realizes that he is living with a person who is very different than himself.

If he is very frugal and she is accustomed to spending money freely, what conflicts will come about? An unfortunate factor in this situation is that, at least from what we know, this young man did not have a good model of what a family should be like.

These are just a few of the areas of adjustment. The couple must be made aware of differences and must be asked to develop a plan and approach to solve these potential problems.

Another topic is the dating background of this couple: How long have they been going together, and what kind of dates have they had? For example, here are two different couples. One couple has been dating for the past two and one-half years. They live in the same town. Their dates occur mostly on Friday and Saturday nights, and sometimes on Sunday evenings. During the week they have very little contact with one another. Quite often when they go out on Friday or

Saturday night they go to a movie or some type of entertainment. Now and then they go to a party, but they really do not have that much time to communicate with one another.

On the other hand, a couple may have a completely different history. They have been dating and thinking seriously about marriage. They have been dating for eight months, but during that period they have spent quite a few hours together each day. During the summer they worked together washing dishes in the kitchen of a Christian camp, and they saw each other at times when they were happy, when they felt sad, and when they were in bad moods. All of this contributed to a good relationship.

Now as you look at the two couples, you might think, "Well, here's a couple who has gone together for over two years. They might have a better relationship." That is not necessarily true. The couple who spent more varied and realistic time together, even though the time was shorter, could have a better adjustment.

The couple to be counseled should be asked what they have done on their dates, where they have gone, whether they have included other friends, or if they have just gone places alone. It is also important that each individual has become acquainted with the other's parents. In fact, young couples who are seriously dating should be encouraged to spend time in the evenings in each other's parents' homes. On some occasions I have met couples whose families have gotten together on vacations and all spent a week together in the mountains. This has contributed to a healthy relationship.

Recently a couple who came for premarital counseling had a unique experience to share along this line. He was twenty-nine and she was twenty-six. He was a lawyer in Los Angeles, and she held a job with a Christian organization in Seattle, Washington. Several months before the wedding he drove to Seattle to spend time with her, and they decided to take a week together and tour Vancouver, British Columbia. This would mean that they would spend several days together in close contact under varied conditions. Prior to their trip, they discussed it in depth and planned where they would go and what they would do. They also determined that on this trip they would not so much as hold hands, as they did not want to allow for any possibility of difficulty occurring in their physical relationship. At night they obtained separate motel rooms.

They made this commitment, prayed together, and enjoyed their trip. This couple had a deep commitment to the Lord and to one another. It was a delight to work with a couple such as this in counseling. Not every couple could or should have this type of experience. But realistic dating is essential.

The fifth area that is discussed can be delicate. We should be concerned about the extent of their sexual involvement and the attitude the couple has toward this important aspect of their relationship. This topic may be introduced by asking each of them about the sexual information that has been given to them over the years: Who prepared you in terms of your understanding about sex? Who talked with you? What books have you read?

One of the questions I ask, which quite often brings on a silence, is this: "Most couples desire to express their affection in some physical manner. To what extent have you expressed your affection to one another?" If I do not get any response from the couple at that particular time, then I might go a little more into detail by explaining that when a couple is in love they have certain feelings toward each other and they like to express these feelings sexually. Now I may get continued silence from a couple. Or I might get a response that says, "Well, I do not think I understand what you mean." Most of the time a couple does understand what is meant.

These questions are not a attempt to pry and probe into a very personal area of their life. I am really not trying to be voyeuristic in any way, but I am concerned about the extent of the physical relationship for a very sound reason. If the couple has built their relationship upon a physical basis only, they are asking for difficulties later on in the marriage. And if they have gone too far, or further than their standards permit, they might have feelings of guilt, fear, resentment, or even hostility.

In counseling it is important to have the atmosphere and opportunity in which to explore the physical relationship. From time to time a couple sits there, and then one of them might venture to say, "Well, I think we've gone a little further than we really wanted." And then I can say, "Well, could you be more specific for me? Are you saying that you were involved in light petting or heavy petting, or have you been sleeping with one another?" The attitude depends upon the couple. Some couples feel bothered, upset, and guilty if they have been involved in petting. Other couples are bothered only when they have been going to bed together.

I explore further by asking, "Can you tell me some of the feelings that you've had about the extent of your physical relationship? Are you satisfied with it? Have there been problems? What attitudes do you have?" If they have been sleeping together—and I do run into Christian couples, born-again people who have been involved in sexual relations—I simply share with them part of my beliefs. I tell them that I believe it is very important at this particular time for them to stop having complete sexual relations for two basic reasons. One reason is to find out if their relationship is built on something other than just the physical; refraining from sleeping together will really help them to make this decision.

The second major reason for asking them to stop having sexual relations is based on the Scripture. The New Testament teaches that we are not to engage in premarital relations. The Scripture calls this fornication. This should be discussed thoroughly with the couple. (See the Appendix for an overview of this teaching.)

So far I have not encountered a couple who has refused to follow this guideline, though from time to time you might find one. The pastor of a large church in southern California follows this particular principle. On many occasions, directly from the pulpit, he has stated this principle which he holds for premarital counseling. He also states that if a couple is not willing to refrain from premarital intercourse, he will not agree to continue the counseling nor to perform the ceremony. This is basically my feeling, too. If a couple will not follow this guideline, then the counseling ought to stop.

It is very important for a couple to go into marriage with the proper attitudes and proper behavior. If they have been involved in premarital intercourse there should be a discussion of their feelings. There should be confession of sin with one another and a time of forgiveness and prayer.

One area that must be considered as one talks about sex is whether or not the young woman is pregnant. If she is pregnant, then various alternatives must be considered. Marriage might not be the best one.

If pregnancy is the main motivation for marriage, it is not sufficient. If the couple is mature, deeply committed to one another, and willing to wait to complete the counseling, and if they realize the adjustments that will be necessary, then marriage could occur. Many couples, however, feel pressured to marry by parents, friends, their own guilt, and even the church.

Other alternatives would be not marrying and either giving up the child for adoption, or, in some cases, keeping the child. The number of abortions each year is increasing steadily; there are many different views regarding this procedure. Pastors differ greatly in their attitudes. My own personal stance is that abortion is not an alternative; if the subject arises, I advise against it. One of the best preventives against abortion in churches and even in secular schools would be the presentation of the outstanding film, *First Days of Life* produced by For Life, Inc., 1917 Xerxes Avenue, North, Minne-apolis, Minnesota 55411. This film depicts the development of the child from conception to birth. With the use of X-ray film it shows the fetus in various stages of development.

The sixth area considered in this first session is the extent of their preparation for marriage. You may ask, What prep-aration have you had for marriage? Have you been reading any books? If so, what books have you read? Have you taken any classes in church or in college, and did you have the classes separately or together? It is necessary to find out what preparation they have had, because some might have been good and some might have been poor.

Another major area to explore is: How have your attitudes toward marriage been influenced, and who influenced them? Quite often parents and brothers and sisters will have had a part in this. The young couple may also have friends who have been married for some time and who provide a model of a good marriage relationship. The "Marriage Prediction Schedule" is helpful in exploring this particular area.

You will find some couples that have come out of very poor backgrounds with tremendous hostilities, fighting, and multi-ple divorces within a home; either the man or the woman might have suffered sexual abuse as a young child, and as a result has some problems with his feelings and attitudes in the area of sex. You need to explore and talk with the couple about their background.

One question to ask the couple is: What fears do you have about marriage? Reassure them that most people looking forward to marriage have certain fears, questions, and doubts; you want them to have the opportunity to talk about some of these. You might not get a response; the couple might say, "Well, we really have no fears. We've talked this over and we really think we know all about it." You may want to drop the question at that point. But later on, you will probably discover that they do have some fears. Do not pressure them when they are not ready to discuss their fears; drop the questions for now. You will probably get another chance to help them later.

Another area to discuss is the couple's Christian beliefs. (Some pastors choose to have an extra preliminary interview for this purpose.) I do not ask the question, "Are you a Christian?" It is too easy to respond with a "Yes" which terminates the conversation. You will learn more by phrasing the question differently. For example, you might ask one of them, "Just tell me a little bit about your own personal spiritual growth and what you believe about the person of Jesus Christ and God." Then sit back and let the person talk.

The majority of the couples that you and I see are born-again believers. But there can be differences between born-again believers. One might be a very strong, growing, maturing Christian. The other may have been a Christian for ten years, but has never really developed any depth in Bible study and prayer, nor become particularly involved in the church. If these differences are sensed now, you can begin to work with the couple and help them develop some spiritual growth. This is especially important if the young woman is the one who is very strong as a believer and the man, who is supposed to be the spiritual leader within the marriage relationship, is weak at this time.

Every now and then you will deal with a couple where one is a Christian and the other flatly declares, "No, I'm not a Christian, I do not believe." What do you say at that particular time? If I am counseling such a couple and one partner has shared with me the fact that he or she is not a Christian, I thank him or her for that honesty. Then I take the opportunity to present the Gospel and talk about how important spiritual harmony is to a marriage relationship. The unbeliever may then say, "Well, I am really not interested," and that will close the conversation, at least for that particular time. Later on you may have another opportunity to speak of spiritual things.

Do you continue with the premarital counseling when one person remains an unbeliever, or do you stop it? I think it is best to go ahead with the counseling and explain again that you reserve the right to decide whether you will perform the wedding ceremony until later on in the sessions. You can also take the opportunity to explain the teaching of Scripture regarding the marriage of a believer to an unbeliever. The believer may be aware of it and could already have some conflicts over this. Or perhaps he or she is not aware of it. You can point out that the Scripture teaches that a couple is not to be unequally yoked together. You might experience some different reactions at this point: the Christian could be angry or hostile, or he or she might be very agreeable to continuing the premarital counseling.

Pastors who have followed this procedure say they have had varied experiences. A number of the couples have agreed to continue the premarital counseling, realizing that without it the pastor would not agree to perform the ceremony.

What happens in this particular kind of a counseling problem when the non-Christian professes to be a Christian? Would this solve the difficulty? Would you feel like going ahead with the ceremony on the date the couple had planned? It might be best to talk to the couple about postponing the wedding date so the new Christian will have an opportunity to grow in his or her new Christian life. This is important, especially when the new Christian is the young man. A marriage relationship in which the woman is spiritually stronger and more knowledgeable of the Scriptures can have problems unless she is very sensitive about her role. You will have many different experiences here.

When a person has accepted the Lord, you could put him or her in contact with other Christians who are involved in Bible study and help them assist the new Christian person in his or her growth. If the new Christian is not concerned about developing his or her spiritual life, that should raise questions as to the genuineness of the decision.

Finally, I like to hear the couple's definition of love. If time has vanished by this point in the discussion, this question may be carried over to the two individual sessions. Each is asked to give his or her definition of love and to answer the question, Why do you believe that you're in love with this particular person? After I have heard what they have to say, I can take the opportunity to share some different ideas and concepts.

There are two definitions that I like to share with a couple. One is this: "A person is in love with another individual when meeting the emotional needs of that person becomes an emotional need of his or her own life." We discuss and explore this statement to discover what it means in practical daily life.

Another definition is this: "Real love means an unconditional commitment to an imperfect person." This is the love that one needs to have for the person one marries. It is also an illustration of the kind of love that God has toward humanity. His is an unconditional commitment, and all of us are imperfect. If each person realizes that the future mate is imperfect and accepts him or her that way, there is hope!

One young couple I was counseling had an interesting experience. The young woman was delighted about it. She was so happy and jubilant when I saw her that I had to ask, "What are you so happy about?" And she said that about three days before, they were out one evening and her fiancé was just miserable. She said he was stubborn, obstinate, and out-of-sorts. He was really a rat, and yet, in spite of all that, she had the firm conviction that she really loved him. She said, "That was so affirming to me to realize that even at the times when he might be very disagreeable and I might not really like everything he was doing, I'd still have this conviction of love."

An important biblical passage to share is 1 Corinthians 13. I go over it and talk about the ideas it contains, using the Amplified version.

Another thing that I discuss with a couple is that in order to really love another person you must love yourself first—you must have a good feeling about yourself. This concept may come up again in connection with the couple's T-JTA scores.

Several other definitions of love may be shared at this point. One is, "Love is a learned emotional reaction." "One does not fall in or out of love; one grows in love."[3] Another is, "Love is not a commodity that can be bartered for, or bought or sold; nor can it be forced upon or from someone. It can only voluntarily be given away."[4] Eric Fromm gave an extensive definition: "Love means to commit oneself without guarantee, to give oneself completely in the hope that our love will produce love in the loved person. Love is an act of faith, and whoever is of little faith is also of little love. The perfect love would be one that gives all and expects nothing. It would, of course, be willing and delighted to take anything it was offered, the more the better. But it would ask for nothing. For if one expects nothing and asks nothing, he can never be deceived or disappointed. It is only when love demands that it brings on pain."[5] This statement sounds very basic and very simple, but it is difficult in practice.

At this point the first homework assignment is given to the couple. This assignment, like the others that follow, is to be completed individually and not discussed between them. The first assignment should be completed before the third session, which is the next session in which they will be together as a couple. The second session consists of the separate meetings with the counselor.

3. Leo Buscoaglia, *Love* (Thorofare, N.J.: Shack, 1972), pp. 61-62.
4. Ibid., p. 63.
5. Ibid., p. 66.

In presenting the first homework assignment, give each person a copy of the chart representing Maslow's levels of needs (fig. A). Explain the chart, using the following information.

MASLOW'S LEVELS OF NEEDS

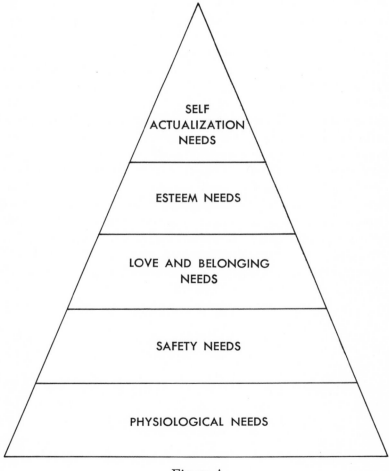

Figure A

Years ago a psychologist named Maslow suggested that each person has certain basic needs in his or her life. These needs are listed in order of their importance: (1) physiological needs, (2) safety needs, (3) love and belonging needs, (4) esteem needs, and (5) self-actualization needs.

Physiological needs are those necessary to maintain human life, such as food, water, oxygen, and rest. Safety needs include a life-style that gives protection and avoidance of danger; structure, rather than disorder. The need for love includes a desire for affectionate relationships with people. Esteem suggests receiving recognition as a worthwhile person. Self-actualization is the need to become the person one has the potential to become.

It is fairly obvious that most spouses fulfill one another's needs in the areas of physiological and safety needs. There may be occasions, however, when one does not put forth the effort to meet the other's needs for love, esteem, and self-actualization. He or she may not provide opportunities for the spouse to become all he or she could become. As you look at these three areas of needs, it is important to try to determine how one could fill these needs within his spouse.

Each individual is to write his or her answers to the following questions concerning the hierarchy of needs:

1. The ways in which my needs in the last three areas of the hierarchy can best be met by my spouse-to-be are:

2. These are the ways in which I will attempt to meet the needs of my spouse in the areas of love and belongingness, esteem and self-actualization:

At the end of the session I explain any other tests that I will ask the couple to take. I tell them the books they are to read and help them develop a time schedule for the books. Then I give them the written work to complete before the third session. In addition to the material on Maslow's hierarchy, I ask them to answer these questions:

1. Write twelve to fifteen reasons why you want to marry this person.

2. Describe the goals you have for your marriage. (Often a couple might not know what is meant by a goal. It is the direction or purpose of the marriage, or what a person wants the marriage relationship to accomplish. Some couples understand it better when expressed this way: "What dreams do you have for your marriage relationship?")

3. Write a paragraph on what you are bringing to this marriage that will make it work. (This deals with what each one has to contribute to the marriage.)

4. Write down your role and the responsibilities that you will have within the marriage; then write down what you believe the role and responsibilities of your spouse will be. (Each person is to do this individually, and they are to be very specific and detailed.)

5. What will you get out of marriage that you would not have gotten if you had remained single?

If both sets of parents are in favor of the marriage, I give one final assignment, not to the couple but to their parents. I have each person ask his or her parents to write a letter to me telling why they want this young man or woman to become their son- or daughter-in-law. They are not to share this with their son or daughter, but to mail it to me. During the last counseling session I read these letters to the couple. This is an affirming time and greatly enhances total family relationships.

You may find that you will need longer than a hour for the first session. You may choose to extend it to an hour and one-half. Or you might want to insert different questions and delete some of those suggested. The material given here is what I have used for several years; many pastors have also worked with this material successfully.

It is often helpful to conclude each session with a significant idea or illustration. The following has given insight to many couples:

> You must work at your marriage both to give it life and to keep it vigorous. Divorce is not the only thing that will kill a marriage.
>
> Indifference will kill a marriage. Neglect will kill a marriage. Drifting apart and separating in interests and associations will kill a marriage. I once came across the story of a childless couple whose marriage had been in a state of living death for many years. Nevertheless, for reasons convincing to themselves, they wished to avoid a legal separation. Instead, for years they went their separate ways, maintaining separate bedrooms, eating breakfast and lunch separately and engaging in separate activities during the day. If they met at the dinner table or for social engagements, it was generally in the presence of friends. They avoided being alone with each other.
>
> One day, the husband, who was a very prominent citizen, learned from some friends that his wife had written a book which was becoming a literary success. He read it and discovered it was autobiographical. Its contents contained a suspicion of scandal. It told of the author's heartbreak in the loss of a man whom she had lived with many years ago and who now was gone forever. The date of her deep interest in this man with whom she had lived as revealed in the book was after they had been married. The husband angrily confronted his wife and charged her with adultery. He demanded to know the name of her secret lover. For a long time she refused to tell him. At length, she cried: "You were that man. You were once the wonderful, idealistic young man whom I loved and adored. But that man died long ago. Now all I have left is the man he became—one whom I know to be selfish, mean and a cheat, one whom I can no longer love or respect."[6]

For the second session you will see each person separately,

6. Louis Binstock, *The Power of Maturity* (New York: Hawthorn, 1969), pp. 104-5.

so you really have two meetings. This is the time when I
show each person the results of the "Taylor-Johnson Temperament Analysis." As mentioned, they were asked to complete these tests at home without discussing them with one
another and to send them back before the first session. The
tests are ready when they come in for individual sessions.

I explore with the person the results of the test that he
answered regarding himself, and the results of his answers
regarding his fiancé. I do not show the results of the other
person's answers regarding himself or the fiancé. These I hold
until the session when they come together. For now they can
see their own score and the score reflecting the way they saw
the other person. We might spend ten or twenty minutes on
this, or we might spend the entire session. I have found that
some people need several private counseling sessions because
of information discovered through the T-JTA.

The test is very helpful in uncovering problem areas or
potential problem areas that could erupt within the marriage.
As you look at a person's profile, you may discover that he has
a very high score in nervousness, or depressiveness, or one
may be too submissive. Another may be too subjective, or too
hostile, or very, very impulsive. All these could contribute to
difficulties within the marriage relationship. We look not only
at the profile reflecting the person's view of himself, but also
at the profile reflecting his view of his fiancé.

After going over the T-JTA scores, I ask some of the same
questions that I have asked when two of them were together
in the first session. You may wonder, "Why do you do this?"
One reason is that I often get different answers the second
time around. If a person is hesitant about revealing some of
his or her fears, anxieties, or guilt over sexual behavior, this
provides an opportunity to share these without the presence
of the other person. And so I do ask some of the same questions, especially if I have been somewhat suspicious or con-

cerned about the answers received during the initial interview.

One couple who had been engaged in heavy petting both told me in the first session, "It really doesn't bother us." But when we started the individual session the young lady said, "I wanted to bring up something we discussed in the first interview. I really have felt very badly about the sexual behavior, and I didn't know how to discuss this with my fiancé. I didn't want to hurt his feelings, and I didn't want to get into an argument, because I feel he is much more dominant than I am. What can I do about this?" So we discussed her feelings. Actually I felt that she wanted *me* to tell her fiancé that she did not like the sexual behavior. My response was that if I did this I would be assuming a responsibility that was not mine. So I spent time helping her to formulate how she would share this with her fiancé. And she was able to do so.

Sometimes a couple will choose to discuss their feelings further on the outside when I am not present. On other occasions they wait until I am there so that all three of us can be involved in the discussion.

After going over some of these repeat questions, we spend time on any problems that the person anticipates in the marriage. Topics vary from individual differences to in-laws, where they're going to live, schooling, and finances. Again I make it clear that there is nothing that the person cannot ask me or bring up.

Finally, we discuss the question that I asked the person to answer in preparation for the session: What do you think that you are going to get out of marriage that you would not get if you were to remain single? That question has provoked quite a bit of discussion and response, not only when it is asked of an individual, but in groups of married couples.

Each session with an individual will be different. With one person you might concentrate on topics that do not even come up with another person. Usually this session takes a good hour, sometimes even more; and again, as mentioned earlier, if there are some difficulties revealed by the Taylor-Johnson test, you might have to arrange for additional individual sessions ministering to that person.

Getting Acquainted

1. Pastor shares information about himself such as background, family, hobbies, schools, and some of his interesting experiences in marriage.
2. Lay ground rules: (a) There is nothing that cannot be discussed in these sessions; (b) the couple must complete their outside assignments if the counseling is to continue.

Marriage Defined

1. Ask couple why they are coming to the church to be married instead of going to a justice of the peace. Why is the church important?
2. Ask couple to share their definition of marriage.
3. Pastor shares definitions given in this chapter.

Family Backgrounds

1. Have the couple share something about their homes and families, such as where they lived, in what type of home, what their parents did, are they still together, whether they have brothers and sisters, and what type of relationships they have, the financial status of the home, whether the family moved around or lived in one place.
2. Ask how did their parents' physical and mental health relate to them in growing up? How did their parents handle disagreements? Which parents did each admire the most?
3. How were feelings of love, warmth, and tenderness shown in their homes as they were growing up?
4. How would they like to have feelings of love, warmth, and tenderness shown to them in public and in their home?

5. What differences do they see between themselves? Are these differences sources of potential problems? What can they do to solve the problems?

Dating Background

1. How long have they been going together? What kind of dates have they had? What have they done on their dates and where have they gone? Have they included other friends or have they just dated together?
2. Have they had opportunities to become acquainted with each other's parents?

Sexual Understanding

1. Who prepared them in terms of their understanding about sex? Who talked with them? What books have they read?
2. Most couples desire to express their affection in some physical manner. To what extent have they expressed their affection to one another?
3. Can they tell you some of the feelings that they've had about the extent of their physical relationship? Are they satisfied with it? Have there been problems? What attitudes do they have?
4. (If applicable) Is the woman pregnant?

Preparation for Marriage

1. What preparation have they had for marriage? Have they been reading any books? If so, what books have they read? Have they taken any classes in church or in college, and did they have the classes separately or together?

Attitudes Toward Marriage

1. Who has influenced their attitudes toward marriage, and how have the attitudes been influenced?
2. What fears do they have concerning marriage?

Spiritual Maturity

1. Ask them about their spiritual growth and what they believe about the person of Jesus Christ and God.

Love Defined

1. Ask each one why he believes he's in love with this particular person.
2. Discuss and explore the statement: "A person is in love with another individual when meeting the emotional needs of that person becomes an emotional need of his or her own life."
3. Talk about 1 Corinthians 13, using the Amplified version.
4. Discuss the fact that one must love himself before he can love others.

Homework Assignment

1. Assign questions to be answered before the third counseling session.
2. Give the couple a copy of Maslow's chart and explain it to them.
3. Explain any other tests you want them to take.
4. Conclude with quote, page 91.

SUGGESTED OUTLINE FOR SESSION TWO

Taylor-Johnson test

1. Explore the results of the test.
2. Answer questions.

Anticipation of Marriage

1. Ask what problems they anticipate in their marriage.
2. Ask what do they think they will get out of marriage that they would not get if they remained single.

6

The Third and Fourth Sessions

The content of the third and fourth sessions in premarital counseling is listed together as it is difficult to know how much will be covered in the third session. In some cases much of this material will be covered; in others, most of the time will be spent talking about the "Taylor-Johnson Temperament Analysis." As you work with different couples you will find that with some you will need three sessions to cover all this material; with others you will be able to cover it very comfortably in two sessions.

When the couple arrives for the third session they are usually very interested in looking at the Taylor-Johnson test. They have seen their own profile and how they perceive the other person, but they have not seen the other's profile nor how their fiancé perceives them. The discusion centers upon the test. You might start by showing the man's profile to the woman and discussing potential problems, then show the woman's to the man. Finally, show them how they see one another. Usually they will have a number of questions.

A typical situation may be that of a young man who scores himself very high on sympathy; when he sees that his fiancée scored him very low, he wants to know, "Why do you see me like that? I am a very loving and caring individual." Perhaps he is, but he might not be sharing this with her or verbalizing it so that she perceives it.

It is important to focus on the personality differences, the areas of possible adjustment. I like to focus on how the two

people are alike and how they are different. You are not looking for a couple to have identical profiles. There are very, very
few who are identical in their T-JTA profile. In fact, some
who are too much alike may have difficulties. Maybe the man
and the woman both score ninety-five on the dominant scale.
Look at one of the Taylor-Johnson profiles now and you will
see what the potential problem might be with the couple.
Two individuals who are very dominant may be headed for
trouble if they do not learn to ease off, to give, and to adjust to
the other person.

At this time it is helpful to ask, In what way are your
parents like you? How are you like them? Which of the
traits or qualities of your parents are you looking for in your
spouse? We discuss how the personalities of the parents may
have influenced the young people. It is helpful to discuss how
this might carry over into the marriage relationship.

It is difficult to know how long it will take to cover the
T-JTA. If there are problem areas evident, I give specific
assignments which must be completed during the time of the
premarital counseling. See the Appendix for books and tapes
which can be used with the T-JTA. After the discussion of the
T-JTA, we might spend time discussing the "Marriage Prediction Schedule," particularly if it has uncovered some extremes
and noticeable differences.

Next we discuss the assignments and questions given as
homework. These were: (1) give twelve reasons why you
want to marry the other person; (2) write the goals you have
for your marriage; (3) write a paragraph on what you are
bringing to this marriage that will make the marriage work;
(4) write out your own role and responsibility and the role
and responsibility of your spouse; and (5) answer the ques-
tian, What will you get out of marriage that you wouldn't get
if you remained single?

The following is one woman's list of reasons for wanting to
marry her fiancé. She entitled this, "Why I Want to Marry

Jack," and then gave ten reasons: "I love him. He knows and loves Christ as Savior. He is excited about life and wants to accomplish much for God. I want to share and be a part of Jack's life. I want to help Jack become all that God intended him to be. I enjoy being with Jack. We have a good time together. I am physically attracted to him. I can relax and be myself with Jack. I want to care for him, to take care of his home, the meals. He is the kind of man I would want for the father of my children." A person could be quite encouraged by these, for they show a healthy, realistic balance.

Look for a balance as the individuals read their reasons for wanting to marry the other. Occasionally somebody will give reasons like these: I want to marry him because he fulfills all my needs, he takes care of me, he does this for me, he does that for me. The reasons focus on "what the other person can do for me," without the balance of "what I can do for the other person." When a situation like that is encountered, the person should be confronted with what he or she has said.

I remember an occasion when a young lady was listening to her fiancé's reasons for marrying her. The more he read the angrier she became, and before he completed the reasons, she broke in and said, "The reason you want to marry me is for me to do everything for you! What are you going to do for me? Don't you really love me?" The rest of the session was spent talking about the reasons and motivations for their marriage. We were able to settle some of the differences right then and there.

We should be just as concerned, however, when we see an individual giving reasons that indicate that he is going to do everything for the other person. Can this individual accept love? Can he accept the other person's doing something for him? There has to be a balance.

Here is a young man's list of reasons, exactly as he wrote them and shared them in the session:

The Whys and Goals of Our Marriage

The twelve reasons why I'm marrying Betty:

1. The Lord is first in her life. It happened last January, tired of calling her own shots. Consistently has followed that up with a desire to learn, prayer, fellowship, and witnessing.

2. Little girl nature—modest dress, looks young, spontaneity, loves cows, and cute things.

3. Reaches out to other people—senses needs and puts love into action, not just on a one-time basis, but consistent followup. Example—neighbors, friends and work.

4. Responsibility and common sense—Boss said that seldom has he seen a more dedicated person, and one with so much skill in speech therapy. I trust her with maps and directions, to sometimes handle arrangements where I'm not able. Sets goals and meets them, a budget.

5. She laughs with joy in her heart—she loves pure things, clean and crisp. She wakes up with a smile on her face. She doesn't complain a lot, is willing to roll with the punches. She loves life and wants to reach out and grab it.

6. She cries—she has a depth of feeling for many different situations, work, person who is lost. She uses it to accent her womanhood.

7. She's devoted to our relationship—she's uplifting, encouraging. She speaks the truth in love. She cares what I feel, and respects my desires and interests. She desires to work hard at making it work. She's affectionate and warm.

8. She's intelligent—similar educational background.

9. She sees our relationship as a team ministry. We're walking in the same direction with a common goal, to spread the teaching and life of our Lord Jesus.

10. She's cute (size, shape, face, hair) and clean (neat in appearance, takes care of herself).

11. She's a quick learner. When new things come her way she desires to incorporate them into her life and moves on to the next step.

12. She loves fires, daisies and poems, i.e., very romantic,

loves beauty, and purity. Enjoys relaxing with the simple things.

13. I love her. I feel good when I'm around her.

The next question to consider is the goals that they have for their marriage relationship. Here are some goals that were brought in by a young woman. These are just as she expressed them:

First of all, to encourage the spiritual growth of each person. To encourage the physical, mental, and emotional growth of the other person. To produce an environment and relationship that reflects God's love to others. To raise children who know and love God and are equipped to live in society. To produce a relationship and home that is full of joy and excitement. To have a relationship where the basic needs of each person can be met in the other.

One of the questions to explore at this time is, "What are you going to do to meet these goals or to reach them?" You can determine how detailed a plan the individual or the couple has worked out to achieve their mutual goals. If they need help, you can assist them in the process.

A third area to cover is the question about roles and responsibilities. Here is a paragraph that one young woman wrote in response to this particular question; the title is her own.

My Role

As his wife, I should be a companion and a friend. I must support and encourage him in spiritual growth and his daily work. I should be someone he can share with and find acceptance, security and love no matter what mistakes he has made. I have the responsibility and joy of meeting his physical needs. My role as wife is submissive in the sense that God has given him primary responsibility in our relationship. The final decisions do not rest with me. My job is to create an environment where he and our children can become all that God intended them to be.

I find that most couples do not go into sufficient detail in the area of roles, and for that reason it helps to give them what I call, "Your Role Concepts Comparison Sheet." A copy is presented in the Appendix; duplicate copies to use in your counseling. Each individual is given a copy of this and asked to take a few minutes answering. Each question may be answered in one of five ways: agree, strongly agree, mildly agree, or strongly disagree. The partners answer without looking at one another's copy.

Note that the second question states, "The wife should not be employed outside of the home." You might find one person who is not sure and one who strongly agrees or disagrees. It is important to stop at this time and talk about this area to see why they have differences of opinion and how this is going to affect their marriage relationship.

Looking down the sheet, you find other questions that might bring up discussion. For example, "The husband should babysit one night a week so the wife can get away and do what she wants," or, "A couple should spend their recreational and leisure time together," or, "It is all right for the wife to initiate love-making with her husband." If you find differences of opinion here, then you need to discuss these.

One of the areas of concern that will arise is the question of "Should the wife work?" A couple of questions on the sheet relate to that area, and you need to explore some of the particular problems that might arise if she works. However, you must also allow the freedom for the couple to make the final decision.

You may have a man who is very adamant against his wife working, yet his fiancée is a college graduate and has a profession. She has spent years training for her position and feels that it is very important for her to be able to continue in it. This is where you have to explore some of the reasons behind each person's attitude as well as work toward some type of reconciliation of the two conflicting opinions. One personal conviction that I try to get across is that it's very important when children are in the preschool years for the mother to be the one who is responsible for training, guiding them, and nurturing them. I think it can be difficult if the children at that age are given out to someone else. After the children are old enough to go to school, then perhaps the wife might find it beneficial to be employed part-time. Her salary, though, should not be used just for her own needs, but for the entire family. However, there will be exceptions. You may want to share some practical principles to follow if a wife is going to work. Some helpful material is found in the Appendix of this book titled "Husband-Wife Roles in the Twentieth Century."

The final "homework" question that is discussed is, "What are you bringing to this marriage that will make it work?" One woman wrote:

> I am bringing a love for Jack and a desire to meet his needs. I am aware of his strengths and his weaknesses. I realize the importance of unselfish giving and feel, for the most part, I am capable of that. I have common sense, intelligence, and leadership abilities that are important in caring for a home and a family. I am not governed by emotions and I usually am willing to express and talk about problems. I have a forgiving spirit and a sense of humor.

Here is one written by a young man as he came in to the premarital counseling session.

> I believe that I am bringing much to marriage that will help it to be successful. My faith in Christ is the greatest single element that will make our marriage successful. I believe beyond all doubt that God designed for us to be joined in marriage. I have abilities in leadership that will allow me to carry out my role as head of my house. I have confidence that I can carry the responsibility of marriage. I am willing to sacrifice things that I want for the attainment of the highest good. I have an understanding of what God intended a marriage to be. I have tremendous determination to make

my marriage successful above all else. I see marriage as a
top priority. I have an ability to sense the needs of others,
and I have strengths in being able to listen to people.

Here you have two examples of what people feel they are
bringing to a marriage relationship that will make it work.
Of course, people's comments are not always of this quality.
Some are lacking; their reasons for marriage might be very
immature. I can remember one person who wrote, "He makes
me feel good all the time. He causes me to laugh. I feel fun
with him." It was very superficial. When people's comments
are of this nature, we need to discuss their ideas and the
realities of marriage in depth. If one's reasons for marriage
are superficial—looks, youth—those reasons might disappear;
then what is left of the marriage relationship?

There are several more questions that I like to ask at this
time to direct the couple's thinking deeper. The first is:
"Name the personal characteristics that you possess that will
build up a marriage. Name the personal characteristics your
partner possesses that might tend to tear down the marriage."
I have the couple write down their answers; then we share
them. By this time the couple is quite perceptive, with a real
freedom to discuss and share.

The next question elicits some surprise: "How are you
going to change your mate?" Sometimes they look back as
though to say, "What do you mean, 'change my mate'? He's
perfect the way he is." You might have to reemphasize this
by saying, "Well, most people do find some behavior or attitudes in their fiancé or their spouse that irritate or bother
them, and they might want to change them. Now how are
you going to go about changing this person?" Or, better yet,
"What have you already done to change the person?" The
person might share, "I don't want to change her. She's exactly
as I like her." This might be very true and very honest for
now. On the other hand, some people who appear to have

this attitude are actually thinking, "After I get married, I'm going to start modifying him."

It is unfortunate when one attempts to turn the other person into a revised edition of himself. In marriage counseling, I sometimes encounter a spouse who will say, "You know, the thing that attracted me to this individual when we were dating and when we were engaged is the very thing that I'm trying so desperately to change right now. I liked it to begin with, but now I am trying to change it." I may ask, "Are you being successful?" More often than not the response is, "Why, no, that's why I'm here. It isn't working."

As we look at this matter of attempting to change one's mate, we start exploring some of the attitudes and ideas that the two people might have toward each other. Basically what I want to get across to them is a statement presented by Cecil Osborne in *The Art of Understanding Your Mate*. He suggests a way in which you can change your spouse. To summarize it, if you really want to change the person that you're married to, you change yourself. The other person will change in response to the changes that he or she sees in your life. But if your goal is trying to modify or change the other person, it is not going to work. We have to begin with ourselves.

A friend told me that for years and years he kept praying that God would change his wife and change his children. And for some reason God did not seem to answer him in the way he wanted, and his wife and children did not change. Then one day he started praying in a very different way. He said, "Lord, change my life. Change me, mold me into the kind of man and husband and father I need to be." Then the man said, "You know, the strangest thing happened. My wife and my children changed." They changed because he changed.

If young married people would work on needed changes in their own lives, then the partner's defects and problems would not seem as large. Naturally, most couples do find areas that concern them. It is unrealistic to think that a person will be totally accepting. Some faults or behavior ought to be altered. A couple needs the freedom to express their concerns and irritations to one another, but they cannot force one another to change. All they can do is to bring problems to the other's awareness, then leave it up to the other to respond as he or she sees fit.

At this point you may want to spend some time getting the couple's reactions to the reading material. By now they should have completed their individual books and the book by Ed and Gail Wheat, *Intended for Pleasure.*

Sometimes when you ask, "What do you think of the material you're reading?" One person may say, "I really didn't like it. It didn't help me at all. I don't see why you asked me to read it." This is a time when you need to be careful and refrain from being defensive. Simply ask the person to elaborate: "Well, can you tell me more about that? What are some of the things you didn't like?" This leads into a discussion, and perhaps you will see that the reading was hitting too close to home. The person may have seen himself in some of the cases mentioned. Or he found some problems brought out in his life for the first time and did not know how to handle them.

It is helpful to get feedback concerning the books; it also serves as a reminder to the couple that they need to keep up on their reading. I require a couple to complete all the reading before we have finished premarital counseling.

Now we spend some time talking about sex, the honeymoon, and children. Attitudes expressed earlier may indicate that it is essential to spend some time talking in this area. It is helpful to talk with the couple about the way in which the Scriptures present the subject of sex. God created sex, and it is to be used for several specific purposes. Procreation is not the only purpose of sex; sex is also meant for pleasure; it is a means of relating to one another and being close to one another; it is a time of giving to each other.

We also need to talk about specific details, because sometimes couples make mistakes as they go into the sexual relationship. Quite often the woman has heard quite a bit of discussion about the question, "Do women really have orgasms?" They might have misconceptions. The series of tapes by Dr. Wheat helps reduce the time spent in counseling in this area. They answer many questions ahead of time. The book by the Wheats should also help.

Encourage the couple to be able to talk together freely about sex. One of the factors that contributes to a healthy sexual relationship is the ability to talk about what they are doing when they are doing it. If something is not pleasing to one, he or she should say so. If one is not comfortable, he or she should express it. I also point out that if one person is having difficulty adjusting sexually, it might not be just his or her own fault or responsibility, but a matter of both partners working together. There is a kind of tuning process that has to occur as each individual comes to know what the other person's body is like and how they relate together.

Additional books may be helpful. One is *The Key to Feminine Response in Marriage* by Ronald Deutsch, which gives specific guidelines concerning what an orgasm is actually like and how the husband can assist his wife in coming to a complete climax. Another recent and thought-provoking book is *The Joy of Being a Woman* written by Ingrid Trobisch, Harper & Row.

I tell the couple that there is no set time or set place in the house where the sexual relationship must occur. They need flexibility and freedom about time and place. They also need to be made aware of the importance of cleanliness; taking a shower or a bath is very important because the nose is so sensitive to odors. Odor can either excite an individual or actually inhibit excitement.

It is necessary to talk frankly and directly to the man, because men sometimes have a tendency to be insensitive to

some of the little things that are important to a woman, especially the idea of showing her affection at all times during the
day. A man should give his wife frequent hugs and kisses
without each one having to lead to the bedroom. Some women
have complained that the only time their husbands expressed
affection to them was when they wanted intercourse. Affection and attention should occur every day whether intercourse
is intended or not. Often couples rush around all day at a
frantic pace, and then all of a sudden they arrive in the bedroom. They're exhausted, but they feel, "Well, now's the time
that we have to express our love toward one another sexually,"
and they do not achieve the satisfaction they ought to be
achieving. Timing and sensitivity are basic.

It is also basic procedure that both individuals should have
thorough physical exams by their medical doctor before the
wedding. In most states certain blood tests have to be performed before a couple can obtain a marriage license. If
neither party has a doctor or knows of one in the area, I give
them a list of several names. The tape series by Dr. Wheat
discusses methods of contraception; encourage the couple to
continue this discussion with their doctor.

When it comes to the honeymoon, there are several suggestions to make concerning sexual behavior. Some couples seem
to be convinced that intercourse is mandatory on the wedding
night. But this could be the worst time if the couple has had
a busy day, an eight o'clock wedding, a reception at the
church, another reception at the parents' home afterwards,
the get-away at one o'clock in the morning, a drive of a hundred miles, and the arrival at a strange motel at two or three
in the morning. The couple is exhausted physically and emotionally, but then they feel, "We must have relations." Often
it is a disappointment for both. If they are going to be very
busy and going to have a late wedding, I suggest that they
just get some sleep, and when they awake in the morning,

they will have plenty of time, they will be relaxed and have their strength back, and they can have an experience that will be very beautiful. We must also caution them against expecting too much from the sexual relationship, especially if it is the first time. Most couples learn to respond to one another; the satisfaction and enjoyment they derive from the sexual relationship ten years later is generally much better than the initial encounter.

Tell them a sense of humor helps, because both of them could make some mistakes. They may feel uncomfortable, awkward, slightly embarrassed, and not know exactly what to do. We have heard of situations where the bed has collapsed or somebody has fallen out of bed, or there's a short in the wiring in the building and suddenly the lights come on. These are shocking events, but a sense of humor will help the couple work toward a healthy adjustment.

Now is a good time to discuss how many children the couple would like to have, and when they plan to have children. Even though they do not have children at this point (at least, most of the couples we see do not have children), this is an opportunity to talk with them about the importance of being united in their principles for disciplining and rearing their children. Two or three books could be suggested to them at this time. One book I have found very helpful is *Help, I'm a Parent* by Dr. Bruce Narramore. A workbook accompanies this volume. I suggest that they read and discuss the book and work through the workbook before they have children.

I also suggest that when it comes time for them to consider having a family, one of the best educational experiences they could have to prepare themselves for children would be to volunteer to work in either the nursery department or the toddler department of their church. They should work as a team, teaching and helping the children for six to ten months.

They will become better acquainted with what children are like, and have a better idea of what to expect when their own children come along.

From time to time a pastor finds himself counseling people who present an unusual set of circumstances. One such couple that I counseled arrived for the session together. The woman was twenty-eight years of age and had been married before. Her previous husband had been on drugs, had been involved with several other women, and had deserted the family. There was one child, who was about eight or nine. The woman was on welfare because of the lack of support from her previous husband. She was a born-again Christian.

The man was forty and had never been married. He had not had any real dating experience before meeting this woman, but they had been dating now for about a year and one-half, and seemed to be very much in love. She was about four or five inches taller than he and other differences were apparent in terms of their personality makeup. What would be your response to this couple? What areas of adjustment would you focus on? And what are some of the questions you might ask them?

I explored several areas with these two individuals. The woman had been living on her own for some time and had assumed the role and responsibility of both mother and father. She had been required to take responsibility for all areas of the home. Would she be willing to give up appropriate areas to her new husband? They had already discussed this and worked out a solution.

Another potential problem was that he had not dated much and had waited until he was almost forty before deciding to get married. What was the reason for this? He just had not found the woman God wanted him to marry.

Another area of concern was the difference in their stature. We discussed it; both of them felt very comfortable about it.

Was this man going to be able to adjust to the woman's

eight-year-old daughter? One of the positive elements in the relationship was related to his employment: he had been an elementary school physical education teacher for eighteen years. He knew what elementary-age children were like and had worked with them; in fact, he had already assumed some of the role of helping to discipline within the home. This had already been worked out, and the woman's daughter felt very positively about this man. There were differences and yet they were aware of them and were working on them.

Another factor had to be considered: Would he be aware of what it was going to cost to care for a family? We discussed in detail some of the new expenses he would be having in this family life. In a case like this it would be helpful for the man to shop with the woman in a department store and discover the cost of women's and children's clothing.

All in all, this couple was a delight to counsel. They were both genuine Christians; the person of Christ seemed to be at the center of their relationship. They had already made a positive adjustment.

In-laws are a topic for discussion. Unfortunately, over the years in-laws have been the brunt of so many jokes that we assume that a couple will experience difficulty with them. It is important to explore a couple's feelings about and relationships with both sets of parents. Many questions can be asked here. What is each one's attitude toward their parents and their fiancé's parents? Much of this may have been discussed already. We ask, "How close are you going to live to them?" Do you feel that it would be possible for you to live a thousand miles away from your own parents?" If a couple or individual is incapable of living far away from their own parents, they might not be ready for marriage. Genesis 2:24 states, A person shall "leave" his parents and "cleave" to his wife. The word *leave* in the Hebrew actually means "to abandon, to forsake, to cut off, to sever a relationship before you start a new one." Those words are used in a positive sense and do not mean alienation of family members. But it is important to realize that some people may leave home physically but not emotionally. Perhaps the idea of living that far away can assist us in determining whether the person can really make that separation from the parents.

There are several other questions to be asked. They include, How do you anticipate dealing with your parents after marriage? How do you anticipate dealing with your in-laws? How much time do you feel you will want to spend with your parents and in-laws in the first year of your marriage? How near do you plan to live to your parents or in-laws? If you visit one set of parents one week, do you feel that you need to visit the other set of parents that week? These are basic questions, but they are subject areas that have not been dealt with by most couples.

In-laws can be an excellent resource in terms of emotional support and advice. Young couples need to look at them as they would at other friends. Looking at them with a positive attitude builds the relationship. If you are counseling a couple where one individual is having difficulty with the other's parents, you could ask, "What might you have been doing to bring on this problem? What might they have been doing?" "What have you done to try to bring about a reconciliation?"

One time a young man in counseling said he felt that his fiancée's parents did not really like or even respect him. My initial response was, "How much time have you taken to sit down with them and allow them the privilege of getting to know you? Have you really shared with them some of the things of your life? Have you ever taken them out to dinner—and paid the bill?" He had done none of these things, so we developed a plan: during the next week he would spend time with them, talking about things that would be of interest to them, talking with his fiancée's father about his job, and getting to know them more. On Sunday the young couple took the parents to church and then to dinner. The results were very positive. The young man came back the next week and said, "You know, I never realized how much they cared for me." The main reason for the problem was that he was not reaching out. In order to have others respond to us, we cannot wait for them to take the initiative but must reach out ourselves.

There are certain guidelines about in-laws which can be shared with the couple. Some of these are just commonsense principles. A person should treat his in-laws with the same consideration and respect that he gives to friends who are not in-laws. When in-laws take an interest in your life and give advice, do what you would do if a friend gave advice. If it is good, follow it; if it is not good, accept it graciously and then ignore it. Remember that many times when in-laws appear too concerned with your affairs, they are not trying to interfere in your life but are sincerely interested in your welfare. Look for the good points in your in-laws. When you visit them, make the visits short. When visiting the in-laws, be as thoughtful, courteous, and helpful as you are when you are at other friends'. Accept the in-laws as they are. Remember that they would probably like to make changes in you, too. Mothers-in-law have been close to their children before marriage; give them time to find new interests in life. Go into marriage with a positive attitude toward your in-laws. You believe it is a good family to marry into, and you intend to enjoy your new family. Give advice to your in-laws only if they ask for it. Express the faults of your spouse only to your spouse, not to your family. Do not quote your family or hold them up as models to your spouse. Remember it takes at least two people to create an in-law problem; no one person is ever solely to blame. (See the Appendix for additional information concerning in-laws.)

You may want to have the preceding principles duplicated and available to give to the couple so they can take them home and restudy them. As you read this material to them, it is interesting to observe their reactions as the various points are covered. Now and then one might jab the other or look at the other with raised eyebrows, as they may have encountered problems already.

Communication is a critical topic for any couple. A question to ask is, How do you communicate now, and what would you like to change about your communication style? If a couple is having difficulty with their communication (and this is usually detected on the "Taylor-Johnson Temperament Analysis") I might ask them to take the "Premarital Communications Inventory," as it can indicate specific areas that we need to strengthen.

Sometimes I ask a couple to discuss a subject that they have not talked about much, or a controversial subject. It is healthy for the couple to disagree in your presence; it allows you to see some of the communication principles they might be employing to handle their disagreements. If they have such a discussion, ask them to sit face-to-face, to move their chairs so they are looking at one another. Many times married couples learn to communicate "from the hip," as we call it. They run past each other on the way to the other room, or the wife is in one room fixing the dinner, and the husband is in the other room reading the paper. They talk to one another but rarely have eye contact. I want the couple to experience looking into each other's face and to note some of the nonverbal communication. Once they are settled face-to-face, I sit back and let them talk for two or three minutes, or even for ten minutes.

Another method that will aid communication is to record the conversation (asking their permission to do so, and keeping the tape recorder out of their view). Then play back some of the discussion so that all of you can analyze communication. This can be a very enjoyable experience. People are surprised to hear how they express themselves to others.

As counselors we look at a couple to determine if they have

the ability to share on a deep emotional and feeling level. We want them to be able to share their convictions, their ideas, their philosophies, and not only that, but how they feel about some of their ideas and beliefs. Many people communicate only on what we call the "cliché level." They talk about the weather; they talk about how they feel physically; they talk about some mundane subject, but they do not get down to serious problems and topics. They do not talk about their relationship. In premarital counseling, in a sense, we are forcing people to talk about items that they have not wanted to talk about but really need to discuss.

Counseling gives us an opportunity to share some basic principles of communication with the couple. A basis for communication is an atmosphere where people can share their ideas and their beliefs, no matter what they are. We also emphasize that they cannot really avoid controversy, so they might as well learn to face some of the difficulties. Using the silent treatment against another person is very unfair and does not solve the problem. If you have a couple who already has this tendency, you could work with the more verbal individual and ask, When your partner retreats and becomes silent and won't communicate with you, how are you going to get him or her to communicate?

Often people who are verbal fall into the trap of putting pressure on that nonverbal person. They will say, "Why don't you talk to me? I want to listen to you. Tell me what you're thinking." And the more pressure they put on, the more the other individual withdraws. And the more the other individual withdraws, the more irritated and agitated the verbal one becomes and the more pressure he or she exerts.

One of the best ways to solve this problem is for the verbal person to say, "I do want to hear what you have to say, and I do want to listen. I'm also willing to wait until you find it comfortable to express yourself." Then back off and do not mention it again. It might take ten minutes; it might take an hour for the person to share. And when he does talk, it is imperative for the verbal one not to make value judgments such as, "Well, where did you ever get a ridiculous idea like that? That's really stupid!" If this happens the quiet one realizes that it is not worthwhile to share what he believes, because he will be criticized!

By now the couple may be reading the book on communication. If not, ask them to begin. After they have completed the first five chapters, have them bring in a list of the ten most important principles which will assist them in their life together.

By now you have covered much of the content of the third and fourth sessions. These are occasions in which you will not cover it all in two sessions and may have to continue it into the fifth session.

Between the third and fourth sessions the couple is given several assignments which are due by the fifth session. First, they are asked to have Bible study and prayer together. Many couples have already started, but some have not. In fact, some have said, "What do we do? We've never done it before." This is an opportunity to share some basic principles with them. *Two Become One* by J. Allen Peterson is an excellent biblical study workbook covering some of the main areas of marriage. The couple can work on this together, and it gives them a structure that many are lacking.

They are also asked to list Scripture verses they feel they would like to build their marriage relationship upon. They are to do this by themselves without discussing it and to bring this to the fifth session. I ask them not to list passages such as Proverbs 31, Ephesians 5, or 1 Peter 3. These passages are very important to the marriage relationship, but I ask the couple not to use them and to do some creative thinking about the rest of Scripture.

They are asked to choose one of the series of tapes on roles and responsibilities, to listen to it together, and to discuss and react to what they have heard.

The final assignment is to write out in as much detail as possible the budget that they feel they are going to be able to live with when they are married.

I like to close the third or fourth session with a quote for them to consider, one which causes them to think and discuss. This is from Dr. Dwight Small's *Christian: Celebrate Your Sexuality.*

> When a man and a woman unite in marriage, humanity experiences a restoration to wholeness. The glory of the man is the acknowledgement that woman was created for him; the glory of the woman is the acknowledgement that man is incomplete without her. The humility of the woman is the acknowledgement that she was made for him; the humility of the man is the acknowledgement that he is incomplete without her. Both share an equal dignity, honor and worth. Yes, and each shares a humility before the other also. Each is necessarily the completion of the other, each is necessarily dependent upon the other.[1]

SUGGESTED OUTLINE FOR SESSIONS THREE AND FOUR

Test Results

1. Examine the T-JTA profiles and note the differences and the similarities between the individuals.
2. Ask them in what way their parents are like them. How is the couple like their parents? Which of the traits and qualities of their parents are the man and the woman looking for in each other?
3. Discuss results of the "Marriage Prediction Schedule."

Discussion of Homework Assignment

1. Ask why they want to marry each other.

1. Dwight Small, *Christian: Celebrate Your Sexuality* (Old Tappan, N.J.: Revell, 1974), p. 144.

2. Ask what goals they have for their marriage.
3. Ask what each is bringing to this marriage that will make it work.
4. Have them detail what each one's role and responsibility will be.
5. Ask what they would get out of marriage that they won't get if they remained single.
6. Discuss "Your Role Concepts Comparison Sheet" (found in the Appendix of this book).
7. Have each name the personal characteristics that he possesses that will build up a marriage. Have each name the personal characteristics his partner possesses that might tend to tear down the marriage.
8. Ask how each intends to change his mate.
9. Ask what they think of the material they're reading. (Remember to complete reading materials before the conclusion of the counseling sessions.)

Sex, the Honeymoon, and Children

1. Discuss the sexual relationship.
2. Discuss the need for a limited physical relationship before marriage.
3. Talk about the honeymoon and offer suggestions as given in this chapter.
4. Explore the couple's attitude toward children—how many they want to have and when.

In-laws and Parents

1. Ask what their attitudes are toward both sets of parents.
2. How close will the couple live to them? Does each feel that it would be possible for him to live a thousand miles away from his own parents?
3. How does each one anticipate dealing with parents after marriage?

4. How does each one anticipate dealing with in-laws?
5. How much time do they feel they will want to spend with parents and in-laws in the first year of marriage?
6. How near do they plan to live to parents or in-laws?
7. If they visit one set of parents one week, do they feel they need to visit the other set of parents that week?
8. Discuss the positive influence of in-laws.

Communication

1. How do they communicate now, and what would they like to change about communication style?

Assign Homework

1. Bible study and prayer.
2. List Scripture upon which to build a marriage.
3. Listen to one of the tapes on roles and responsibilities.
4. Prepare in detail a comfortable budget.

Close with quote by Small.

7

The Fifth Session

By now you may have discovered that there is so much material to cover that you question whether it can be done in the suggested number of sessions. But the fifth session gives you a chance to catch up on anything you have not covered so far. It is best to talk in detail about each topic so the couple reaches a solid understanding. In addition, they need to ask questions so they can apply this material to their lives.

Many questions have already been suggested for you to ask, but there are several more that you could cover with the couple. These deal with various subjects, and you can work them in where you see fit.

The first is, Do you like sympathy and attention when you are ill? That might sound like a strange question, but people come from different backgrounds. They have had different experiences; where one individual might like a lot of attention, the other might prefer to be left alone. If this is not discussed ahead of time, conflicts can arise. A wife, trying to care for her husband who has the flu, might give a tremendous amount of attention. But this irritates him. He does not appreciate it. She wants to know, "Why is he like this? I'm just trying to show him my love and compassion and concern." He does not see it in that way; or, for some reason, because of background experiences, he reacts negatively to it.

A second question is, As a general rule, do you enjoy the companionship of the opposite sex as much as that of your own sex? In this particular question we are trying to see how the people relate to both sexes. Here is a young woman who enjoys spending more time with men, perhaps because she is employed in a situation with more men than women. How is her husband going to react? Is this a trusting relationship? Is there any jealousy?

You can also ask, "After you're married, do you think that either of you will look at members of the opposite sex? Do you feel that in any way you might be attracted to members of the opposite sex?" Many different answers have come. Some say, "No, oh no, we're just completely suited for one another. We'll have no interest in another individual and that's it." Others have been quite honest and stated, "Even during our engagement we've found that there are people who come into our lives that we might admire; and in some cases we might even be attracted to them." I have talked to a number of couples who have been surprised, shocked, disappointed, and even upset because, even on their honeymoon, they've discovered they notice members of the opposite sex, and are attracted to them. Honesty and realism are needed in this area.

Going into the marriage relationship with the idea that "we are never going to notice a person of the opposite sex" is unrealistic. Every man and woman will have to battle sexual temptation, particularly with the emphasis upon sex in our society, including the way people dress. We do try to clarify with the couple the fact that they will notice others and sometimes be attracted to them.

Many couples who have been married for some time have developed healthy relationships and can actually talk about others whom they admire or find very attractive. Some couples will talk about this quite openly. Often a husband will share with his wife that he is having trouble in his thought life at work because of the behavior and dress of the women. They talk about this very openly and his wife is not threatened in any way. They discuss it, they pray about it, and they work on it together. They do not hide these things from one another.

I like to suggest that if their relationship is what it should be, and their sexual relationship and love for one another are on a high plane, the couple is going to have less difficulty with temptation. This does not mean they will not notice and admire others. That is just part of being human, and physical beauty is part of God's creation. We can, however, caution them about what they do with their thought life. It is one thing to look at a person of the opposite sex and notice that he or she is attractive. But when one indulges in sexual fantasies concerning that individual, he is guilty of lust, which is sin. It is healthy for the counselor to share honestly. You could talk about this area and tell some of the ways you have learned to deal with it.

In concluding this area of discussion you may want to share with the couple this prayer from the book *Thank God for Sex* by Harry Hollis, Jr. The profound insights of this prayer have a lasting effect upon the couple.

> Lord, it's hard to know what sex really is—
> Is it some demon put here to torment me?
> Or some delicious seducer from reality?
> It is neither of these, Lord.
>
> I know what sex is—
>   It is body and spirit,
>   It is passion and tenderness,
>   It is strong embrace and gentle hand-holding,
>   It is open nakedness and hidden mystery,
>   It is joyful tears on honeymoon faces, and
>   It is tears on wrinkled faces at a golden
>   wedding anniversary.
>
> Sex is a quiet look across the room,
>   a love note on a pillow,
>   a rose laid on a breakfast plate,
>   laughter in the night.

Sex is life—not all of life—
but wrapped up in the meaning of life.

Sex is your good gift, O God,
To enrich life,
To continue the race,
To communicate,
To show me who I am,
To reveal my mate,
To cleanse through "one flesh."

Lord, some people say
sex and religion don't mix;
But your Word says sex is good.
Help me to keep it good in my life.
Help me to be open about sex
And still protect its mystery.
Help me to see that sex
Is neither demon nor deity.
Help me not to climb into a fantasy world
Of imaginary sexual partners;
Keep me in the real world
To love the people you have created.

Teach me that my soul does not have to frown at sex
for me to be a Christian.
It's hard for many people to say, "Thank God for sex!"
Because for them sex is more a problem than a gift.
They need to know that sex and gospel
Can be linked together again.
They need to hear the good news about sex.
Show me how I can help them.

Thank you, Lord, for making me a sexual being.
Thank you for showing me how to treat others
with trust and love.
Thank you for letting me talk to you about sex.
Thank you that I feel free to say:
"Thank God for sex!"[1]

1. Harry Hollis, Jr., *Thank God for Sex* (Nashville: Broadman, 1975), pp. 11-12. Used by permission.

A third question is, How much praise do you feel you need? Some individuals say they can exist with very little praise. However, they might need more than they realize, and it is crucial to determine how important praise is to each one.

We also talk about the area of friendship. You can ask, Do you like the friends of the person you're going to marry? Do you have many friends? How close are you to them? After you marry, how will you choose friends? Are you going to do this as a couple, or are you going to have your individual friends and go your separate ways? Often this contributes to conflict, because a young woman might not care for the friends of her future husband or the man dislikes friends of his future wife. Inwardly she would like him to give them up, but has not, as yet, verbalized this. Here it is brought out, talked about, and determined what can be worked out.

Another question is, What activities will you want to continue to do separately once you are married? One couple says, "We're going to do everything together; nothing is going to be separate." My response to them may be, "Is this realistic? Have you really discussed this? Have you looked into it?" I ask both of them to tell me about their hobbies and the things they enjoy. Then I ask, "Do you see yourself doing this with your wife? Do you see yourself doing this with your husband?" They may come to realize that they have balance in their relationship already. Of course there are many things a couple should enjoy doing together, but there may be activities that one enjoys by himself.

Initially when a couple marries they may feel they need to spend all their time together. This is why, when you talk to them about the honeymoon, you could bring out some principles to assist them, such as, When you go on your honeymoon, make sure there are a number of activities. If you go to a place and just sit there in a motel room for the next week or two, there is bound to be some boredom; then some feelings may come out that are not the healthiest for the marriage relationship. It is important that a couple have activities together but also learn to do some things separately.

I also like to pick up any questions or topics that we have not covered previously, then talk about their proposed budget. How realistic are they in terms of what it takes to live today? That is what to look for. Often a couple has thoroughly worked this through; other times there is a tremendous amount of unrealism. I remember one couple who had gone into detail on the budget. Both of them were working, and they went through every item and had $350 to put into the bank each month. Together we worked on that budget to determine the level of realism. Yet they still came out with $250 they could put away. This couple had planned to use both paychecks, but the future needed to be explored. I asked, "What will happen if the wife becomes pregnant and you have to rely upon one paycheck? Are you going to be able to do this?" If both are working, it may be well to recommend that they try to live on one paycheck so they become accustomed to this life-style.

Most couples I have worked with over the past few years have not thought very much about what it takes to live. They might come in and tell me that they have put aside $100 for their rent. I may respond with "Fine. Where are you going to find a place for $100? Have you looked?" They usually say, "No, we haven't really looked, but we think we'll be able to find one." The next assignment is to send them out and ask them to look in the area where they want to live and see what they can find for $100. Perhaps they can find something, but they might not want to live in it.

We do the same with some of the other budget items. One couple, just recently, said that they could live on fifteen dollars a week for food. Neither had ever done any shopping. They both lived at home, and the parents were buying the food. It was a delightful experience to have them go to a market and see what they could buy for fifteen dollars. They quickly revised their budget. It is standard practice now to ask couples to shop at a market together and purchase a week's supply of food for their family. It might also be helpful if the man would accompany the woman as she shops in a department store to become aware of costs.

We go into great detail with the budget since so much marital disruption is caused by financial strain. Sometimes a couple leaves out insurance costs or clothing. One young woman said that she had set aside $10 a month for clothing. That is not realistic. Medical expense is another thing to keep in mind. Hospitalization insurance is an important factor. The tithe to the church is important; if a couple has not made any provisions for this, it should be discussed. This item ought to be on the top of the list.

A sample form, "Your First-Year Budget," is found in the Appendix of this book. This could be used in helping a couple determine their budget.

There are several resources which can be used to assist the couple with developing their financial skills. During this session, I use a form called the "Finances Questionnaire." (This is found in the Appendix and may be duplicated for use in premarital counseling.) Each person is given a copy and asked to answer each question quickly. After completing it, they are asked to exchange papers and note how their partner answered the questions. This may cause one or both some surprise, yet it helps them understand each other's priorities. They could be encouraged to continue their discussion of this inventory after the counseling session.

Several excellent money management and budget outlines and resources are available. Several of the best are suggested here, one of which should be mandatory reading. You may want to obtain all of them and then determine which would best suit your ministry. These resources could easily be used in a financial seminar for the congregation. *Christian Family Money Management and Financial Planning* is a twenty-four-page booklet which assists a couple in determining their assets as well as assisting them in planning a budget. This booklet and other helpful pamphlets are available from Louis Neebaver Co., Old York Road & Township Line, Benson East, Jenkintown, Pennsylvania 19046. *Handbook for Financial Faithfulness, a Scriptural Approach to Financial Planning*, by Floyd Sharp and Al MacDonald, is published by Zondervan.

Household Finance Corporation has developed an economical "Money Management Library" consisting of several forty- to fifty-page pamphlets on various helpful topics. This material may be included in the mandatory reading by the couple. The titles are *Your Health and Recreation Dollar, Your Shopping Dollar, Your Equipment Dollar, Your Home Furnishings Dollar, Your Housing Dollar, Your Clothing Dollar, Your Food Dollar, Children's Spending, It's Your Credit— Manage It Wisely*, and *Reaching Your Financial Goals*.

Other areas that need to be considered include the ways the two people have handled money in the past. Have they had a sufficient amount of money to handle? Have they had a savings account? Have they ever had a checking account?

Another question to consider is, When they are married, who is going to be responsible for handling the finances? Who will pay the bills and handle the checks? And how have they arrived at this particular decision? There seems to be discussion and controversy today over the idea that this must be the husband's responsibility. Now and then you find a man who says, "Well, I don't have a head for figures. I really haven't had any experience here." Whether it is the man or the woman who has not had financial experience, both ought to develop financial proficiency. No matter who is paying the bills, both need to be fully aware of the amount of money coming in and where it is going. If a wife is responsible for purchasing groceries each week and the husband expresses concern over the amount of money she is spending, he should go shopping with her. That way he will know what it is like to go out and pay for food; he can see for himself what food costs.

Three basic principles to develop financial unity are: (1) All money brought in should be regarded as "family" money with each person informed of its sources and destination; (2) money should be used after mutual discussion and agreement; and (3) each person should receive a small amount for their own use without having to account for it.

A prior assignment was listening to the tapes on roles and responsibilities. Time is spent talking about their feelings about and reactions to the tapes, and whether they agreed or disagreed with them. Now and then someone will say, "I really can't believe everything that that man said on the tape." That's all right. Talk about it and see in what way he or she disagreed with it. Quite often they just say, "It was tremendous. I wish I'd heard teaching like that years ago." Different reactions are given, but the discussion helps clarify points on the tape.

Another prior assignment to discuss is the couple's time of Bible study and prayer together. How did they feel as they went through it? What did they experience? Some couples say, "Oh, it was very awkward at first. I'd never prayed in the presence of my fiancé before. But, you know, even though it was awkward, I really did enjoy it and it was a good experience. And when it came to Bible study, we just followed the outline that was given in that book *Two Become One*, and we filled in the questions and answers and then we talked about them and how they will apply to our marriage."

It is a valuable experience during the premarital counseling (and perhaps even earlier than I suggested) that a couple learn to pray together, to develop a time of sharing in the Word together, to discuss and talk about spiritual things. Often couples do feel awkward if they have not done it before. If they wait until after the marriage, they might not get into it. It's interesting to talk to some couples who say, "You know, it took us four years to pray together, because both of us were sitting back and waiting for the other one to suggest it. We didn't want to bring it up ourselves, so we just assumed the other person would." You, as the pastor-counselor, can be very helpful at this time; it would be well to share some of your own experiences while at the same time allowing the couple to develop the type of relationship that would suit them.

For the rest of the session, consider the verses that the couple has selected to build their marriage relationship upon. They were asked to do this individually. We may start out with the young woman and ask her to share the verses and tell why she thinks these are important. This is the first time that her fiancé has heard these. After the woman has shared, the same process is repeated with the man.

Over the years I have gained a great deal from the insight, perception, and honesty of young couples as they have pointed out concepts that have been new to me or that I had never thought of before. We need to have a receptive attitude as we practice premarital counseling.

Next I spend ten to thirty minutes sharing the verses I want them to consider. The verses I use are printed in the Appendix under the title, "The Family Communications Guideline." I have these printed on good paper, and I give a copy to the couple. They have one in front of them and I have one in front of me. Some of these are a review and reinforcement of verses from their assigned reading. Many of the verses that I feel are important in building a marriage relationship have to do with communication.

After talking about communication, I read the letters their parents wrote. Most couples are very eager to hear these and to have a copy. Here are examples of two recent letters:

> We have prayed since Chuck was a young boy that the Lord would direct him in selecting his life partner. We are

very pleased and excited that the Lord has led Chuck to
Pattie. They met at Biola and have had the privileges of
getting to know each other these past two years. We are
pleased that Pattie first of all loves the Lord and wants to
serve Him and secondly loves Chuck and wants to be his
mate and serve him.

Pattie has many fine qualities such as a very pleasing personality and is very loving and kind to others. She is concerned with others and above all wants to serve the Lord.

We feel that Pattie will fit into our family as if she always
belonged. Chuck's two brothers love her as do his sister
and grandparents. We consider her as another daughter.
We are looking forward to many happy times together in
the Lord and as a family. Our prayers will be continually
with them.

Why We Appreciate Charles Becoming
Our Son-in-Law

There are many reasons why we appreciate Chuck, to become our son-in-law in less than two months. Here are just
a few:

He is a fine Christian, raised in a wonderful, godly family—
his parents, two brothers and sister have also shown their
warmth and love—a great Church—Church of the Open
Door, L.A.—and in training at Biola College.

His goals, aspirations and plans for Christian service are
solid, as he plans to go on for further studies in Seminary. . . .

He has so many of the character qualities described in
Advanced Basic Youth Conflicts' Seminar and so comple-
ments Pattie well. He has helped to give her stability, purpose and new avenues of services, as he has drawn her out,
with his outgoing personality.

He appears to be a man of prayer and devotion to God,
with a desire to serve Him, as both Chuck and Pattie have
set goals for His glory, for themselves—meaningful goals in
Christian life and service for their future. This pleases us
very much.

Chuck is very honest, direct, disciplined, organized (as seen in his school life and whole pattern of living), humble (seen in his sports, especially) and virtuous. He has high moral standards.

We have witnessed, over the past two years, especially in the last eleven months, sufficiently, to be convinced that he will take good care of Pattie, will provide for her and endeavor to make her life as much as God intends for it to be to the best of his ability. We believe he will strive for the highest and best for both of them, for God's glory.

His warmhearted generosity, sympathetic nature, keen interest in others and handsomeness are other additional features not to be overlooked.

We are thus very happy to have Chuck becoming the husband of Pattie. We pray daily for them both, asking God's will for them and their lives.

We could wish no greater joy than that they be full of Christ, His Holy Spirit and the Word, as they serve Him.

You will spend a lot of time discussing the details of the wedding ceremony with a couple. A pastor needs to be flexible because marriage ceremonies are changing today. Couples desire to write their own ceremonies, and they want to plan in greater detail than before. Many of them might choose to be married in a place other than the church sanctuary. They might prefer a home, a hillside, or a park. I think we need to allow for the changes that are coming about. Some of the wedding ceremonies young people have designed have been very creative and enriching, and they glorify the Lord. Many couples want more of a Christian emphasis, and a time of dedication and testimony in the service.

One of the resources you might want to give to the couple is *Your Wedding Workbook* (Interstate Printers, Danville, IL). This resource gives suggestions such as the time schedule, financial obligations, planning the dress, flowers, color schemes, wedding music suggestions, and the music plan for the ceremony. It also gives a suggested order of service for a wedding with guidelines for the reception, the receiving line, a checklist for newspaper information sheets and many different little items that some couples do not know or think about. If you have what is generally called a wedding counselor or a person in charge of the weddings at your church, he or she might find this extremely helpful as well.

When you are coming to the end of the counseling with the couple, you might make some suggestions for their honeymoon. The honeymoon can be a time of spiritual growth and development. I suggest that they read through the book of Proverbs, finding every passage that would help to build their marriage relationship, specifically those passages dealing with one's emotional life and with communication. I also recommend that they get a copy of Paul Tournier's book, *To Understand Each Other*, and read this aloud to one another as a devotional guide. One other resource that I like to ask them to read out loud is the Song of Solomon (Living Bible version), because it's a very beautiful portrayal of love in the physical relationship.

One book which I enjoy giving to couples as their wedding present is *The Living Marriage*, published by Revell, a compilation of Scriptures from the Living Bible along with helpful quotes from other sources. The couples have been very delighted with it; it has helped them and they have expressed their appreciation for it.

Before concluding premarital counseling, I remind the couple of their postmarital visit. There are important reasons for this visit: basically, it is to provide them with an opportunity to share how their relationship has been developing, and what they have learned and discovered. It also gives them an opportunity to bring up questions or problems. Some couples need two or three postmarital sessions to work out problems that have arisen. I tell them that it is their responsibility to call me. However, if I don't hear from them, then I will call and ask them to come in.

A last point to stress is that if they ever experience serious difficulties in their marriage relationship, they should never hesitate to seek help. Often pride, particularly on the part of the man, keeps them from seeking assistance. If they have tried to work out the problem and have not come to any solution, or if one is so frustrated that they just cannot see daylight, they ought to go to their pastor or to a professional counselor. One of the worst problems that can develop is a couple waiting too long to go for professional help. In fact, many marriage counselors say that it takes approximately seven years from the onset of a problem before a couple seeks assistance. Such delay makes it very difficult for a counselor or pastor to be of much help.

If a married person is having difficulties, it is important that he or she communicate with the spouse first and be careful about talking over problems with friends. It is important that we have close friends, but we need to go to our spouse first. If we do seek out a friend, are we seeking him out for assistance, or for sympathy and to take our side? If a woman wants to talk over a problem with a friend, she ought to talk to another woman; a man ought to talk to another man. If one goes to an individual of the opposite sex, entanglements can develop.

For the last premarital visit, or the postmarital visit, some pastors have the couple over for dinner to spend time with the entire family. After a time of fellowship, the pastor and the couple can talk privately.

A time of prayer together usually concludes the premarital counseling sessions.

Now we need to discuss situations in which it would be difficult to perform the wedding ceremony. Even though this was discussed earlier, it is important to reinforce some of the principles. I believe that age is one of the factors that may lead a pastor to decide against the wedding. Several states now have laws prohibiting the marriage of individuals under a certain age. The state of California prohibits persons under the age of eighteen from being married unless they have parental consent and a court order giving permission. Some courts require premarital counseling before issuing an order.

You might encounter a couple who are both eighteen; even though they meet the legal requirements, you need to consider other factors. It is difficult, yet essential, to confront them with the facts about couples who marry at this age: they are more prone to divorce, they are losing out on friendships, perhaps they have not dated much, and many difficulties can arise. But, after counseling, you still might marry some of these couples because they are mature enough to make it work.

Tender age is not the only consideration. What happens if a man of thirty-five wants to marry a woman who is twenty-two? There is an age difference but they might be very close in maturity level, in emotional stability, and in their Christian walk. How would you feel about a couple if the woman is thirty-five and the man is twenty-two? An attitude in our society implies that it is all right for the man to be much older than the woman, but not the reverse. Our culture feels that such a marriage is not proper and that there are too many problems. Now and then you may run into such a couple, and you must examine your own attitudes. Such a couple might have a very good relationship.

What about some of the other problems that we encounter? When a couple refuses or fails to complete the assignments, it is an indication that their motivation level is so low that they will probably not work on problems that will arise in their marriage. In order for them to stay in the premarital counseling, they must complete the assignments. If they fail to complete their assignments, then I talk to them. I point out that this is an indication to me that their motivation level is too low for a marriage relationship. They must be willing to work on their marriage; they have to be willing to grow and move ahead in their life together. I might ask them to postpone the wedding until they see the importance of making an effort. If too many differences show up on the "Taylor-Johnson Temperament Analysis" test and the "Marriage Prediction Schedule," if they have a low ability to adjust, and if they are not concerned about changing, then I would not feel comfortable marrying them.

When you tell a couple you cannot marry them, you will find different reactions. It is helpful to formulate beforehand the words you will say and how you will say them, giving reasons and showing what you feel would be the probable consequences of their marriage at this time. Some couples might become hostile. They might say, "We can go down the street and find another church, and the pastor there will perform the ceremony. We don't have to be married here." Or somebody might say, "My father is a deacon in this church and he's going to be very unhappy with you, pastor." These are possibilities. You are going to have other couples who sit in stunned silence and say, "We really never thought of it that way before." Perhaps six months later this couple will come back and will be ready for marriage.

Some couples will be relieved upon hearing your decision. They have been waiting and hoping for someone to confront them and let them know that their marriage will not work out. It takes boldness and sensitivity on the counselor's part. We need to pray about this decision and think it through carefully, for we are influencing not just one life, but two—not only separately, but together in a marriage relationship.

SUGGESTED OUTLINE FOR SESSION FIVE

MARITAL ADJUSTMENT

1. Do they both like sympathy and attention when they are ill?

2. As a general rule, do both enjoy the companionship of the opposite sex as much as that of their own sex?
3. After they're married, do they think that either of them will look at members of the opposite sex? Do they feel they might be attracted to members of the opposite sex?
4. Share prayer from *Thank God for Sex* by Harry Hollis, Jr.
5. How much praise does each feel he needs?

FRIENDSHIP

1. Do they like their fiancé's friends? Do either have many friends? How close is each one to their friends? After they marry, how will they choose friends? Will they do this as a couple, or will they have individual friends and go separate ways?
2. What activities will they want to continue to do separately once they are married?
3. What hobbies and activities does each enjoy? Will they do any together?
4. Discuss the need for activities, especially on the honeymoon.

BUDGET

1. Discuss "Your First Year Budget," found in the Appendix of this book.
2. How have they handled money in the past? Has each had a sufficient amount of money to handle? Has each had a savings account?
3. Has either of them ever had a checking account?
4. When they are married, who will be responsible for handling the finances? Who will pay the bills and handle the checks? How have they arrived at this particular decision?
5. Share principles from this chapter on developing financial unity.

DISCUSSION OF HOMEWORK ASSIGNMENT

1. Discuss reactions to the tape on roles and responsibilities.
2. Discuss couple's time of Bible study and prayer together. How did they feel as they went through it? What did they experience?
3. Discuss prayer together.
4. Have the couple share the verses they found upon which they can build their marriage. Have them explain why they think these are important.
5. Pastor shares verses. See "The Family Communications Guideline" in the Appendix.
6. Share letters from the couple's parents.

WEDDING PLANS

1. Discuss ceremony details.
2. Make suggestions for honeymoon.

POSTMARITAL COUNSELING

1. Remind the couple of their postmarital visit.
2. Encourage them to seek help if needed.

CLOSE in prayer.

8

Special Problems in Premarital Counseling

You will see couples who have unique situations. As much as possible, you need to plan your procedure and develop a standard to help you decide when a couple is ready for marriage. Your standard will be tested as you apply it to varying situations.

What happens if you have a widow or a widower in your church who wants to marry? Perhaps both partners have been married before, or perhaps one has been married and one has never been married. At this stage in life do they really need to go through premarital counseling? And yet, why not? If a man was married for thirty years, was widowed, lived alone for five years, and now plans to marry a woman who has never been married before, counseling is very necessary. Every newly married couple faces adjustments, and especially a couple such as this.

For example, you may encounter a couple where he is sixty-five and she's sixty-eight. She was married for forty years and he was married for thirty-five years. Now they have fallen in love and want to be married. Working with such a couple can be one of the most delightful experiences of your life, because they have so much to offer and share. But you as a pastor have a lot to offer to them, too. They might be living in the past, holding on to the memories of those wonderful years, or maybe those not-so-wonderful years, with the other person; maybe they are going to bring these memories into the new marriage relationship. You have to look at their areas of expectations and adjustments and also their ability to adapt and adjust at this time.

No matter what their age or circumstances are, questions must be considered if children are a part of this newly formed family: Can the person who may never have been married before accept the experiences of the other's love life with someone else in years gone by? If there are children still in the home, can the new partner accept and love them? Will the children accept someone else in mother's or father's place? If one has never married before, can he or she suddenly take on a ready-made family and adjust to them? Often, the new parent fails to understand the psychological problem of the stepchild and may retaliate by rejecting the child, or by showing favoritism if his children are involved. When older children are involved they could oppose the marriage and even from the beginning of courtship manifest hostility toward the new partner.

If one has never been married, he or she must be able to accept the fact that the spouse has loved another, perhaps had children by the other, and that a big part of his or her life was inseparably involved with someone else and always will be. He or she must see that love objectively and accept it as a part of the new partner. To expect one never to talk about the first mate, never to look at the picture, is hardly reasonable. It is healthy to encourage the mate to talk about the first spouse, not to compare with the present one, but to help him to accept the present one in the other's place. It is very damaging for either to bring up the first relationship with such remarks as "John never treated me as you do," or "Mary never would have said that."

Another potential problem that arises now and then is, "What do you do with interracial marriages? What does the Bible have to say about this?" It does not appear that the Scripture has anything to say about interracial marriages. You are probably going to have more and more couples from different races wanting to be united in marriage. What will you say to a Christian couple who are of different nationalities and different backgrounds?

If I were counseling an interracial couple, I would want to know their motivations for marriage, as with any other couple. Are they mature individuals? Are they really in love, or is this marriage a reaction against parents or society? Are they trying to prove something? Have they really looked at some of the particular problems that will occur because of a marriage like this? It would be helpful to them to take the time to speak with other interracial couples who have been married for a number of years, couples who have had a successful experience, so that they go into marriage very realistically.

There are several main adjustment factors that a couple in a mixed marriage will face in varying degrees. The first is that of housing. In spite of legal action with civil rights boards, many mixed couples find resistance to their settling in various sections of cities and in many churches.

A second problem faced by the interracial couple is that of companionship with other families. Judson T. and Mary G. Landis said, "Young people who make mixed marriages while in a university community, where attitudes are likely to be more inclined toward acceptance of such marriages than in other communities, may encounter new problems if they leave the university community and settle elsewhere."[1] The couple may have to find more of their companionship with each other than the normal couple does. This, too, can add strains to a relationship which it may not be able to handle.

An interracial marriage will probably face in-law problems. Many families, including some who reared their children to be very liberal in racial attitudes, cannot accept the idea that their child is going to marry someone of a different race.

The greatest problem faced by this couple is the difficulty

1. Cleveland McDonald, *Creating a Successful Christian Marriage* (Grand Rapids: Baker, 1975), pp. 288-94, adapted.

of rearing children who are marginal to two different cultures. The adjustments faced by the couple in an interracial marriage can be insignificant in comparison to those faced by children of such a marriage.

Dwight Small said:

> Not infrequently there is a very dark child and a very light one in the same family. The colored child loves the colored parent and dislikes the other. Or the parent takes to the child of the same color but rejects the other. This is aggravated when other children make fun of the fact that two children in the same family are different in color. Our cruel and competitive culture still brands such children as "half-breeds." So the crucial question is whether parents have the right to impose upon unborn generations a radical decision of their own.[2]

Albert Gordon stated,

> Persons anticipating cross-marriages, however much in love they may be, have an important obligation to unborn children. It is not enough to say that such children will have to solve their own problems "when the time comes." Intermarriage frequently produces major psychological problems that are not readily solvable for the children of the intermarried. Living as we do in a world that emphasizes the importance of family and religious affiliations, it is not likely that the child will come through the maze of road blocks without doing some damage to himself.[3]

Children may be the recipients of cruel remarks and other unpleasantness. People can be hostile and cruel, and these factors must be considered.

Evidence indicates that couples contemplating an interracial marriage face many obstacles to adjustment and happiness. When a couple disregards the need for similarity of

2. Dwight Small, *Design for Christian Marriage* (Old Tappan, N.J.: (Revell, 1959), p. 149.
3. Albert I. Gordon, *Intermarriage* (Boston: Beacon, 1964), p. 354.

racial background, they could encounter adjustments that could be overwhelming.

There are many other individual cases that you will have. No matter what couple comes to us, we need to develop a standard, based as much as possible upon the Word of God, and we must hold to that standard. We have to educate the congregation concerning this policy. In time, our congregations will realize the importance of marriage and will appreciate our stand.

Here are two different cases. Consider some of the problems that they present, and decide how you would handle each one. What would you suggest and what would you do?

The first case has to do with a young man, Richard, who is telling the story of his background. Think about what you would say to him if he were there in your study sharing this with you:

> My father divorced my mother when I was only two and a half. I guess I was her only real happiness after that. She never remarried, and I was the only child she ever had. Sometimes when I was little I wasn't sure if I really did make her happy. She cried a lot and it was very hard for me to distinguish whether she was crying because my father was gone or whether she was crying because she was happy I was there. She was always very sensitive. Things other people said hurt her, and even when I was just growing up she'd come to me for comfort. It seemed to make her feel better to tell me her problems even though she knew that I, as a child, couldn't do anything about them.
>
> She tried to do everything she could for me. She went without new clothes herself so that I could have everything I needed. She worked long hours, and part of the time she had a second job doing work at home. I used to feel terribly guilty about it, but she would always say, "There, there, you're my little boy to take care of now, but someday you will be my big man to take care of me." We were very close.
>
> I started sleeping in her bed soon after my father left. I

still do. I don't tell anybody that because they would think it was kind of queer for a grown man to be sleeping with his mother, but there's nothing sexual about it. I guess it's habit. I don't like to sleep alone any more than she does.

When I got to high school, I didn't have many dates. I was sort of shy and not very athletic. I didn't have much chance to play with the other boys. I'd been too busy with my studies because that's what Mother encouraged me to do. The girls didn't pay much attention to me either. I turned out to be kind of sensitive, too. My feelings were easily hurt. They still are.

My senior year in high school Mother started getting sick. I had talked some about going away to the state university, but when I found out the anxiety connected with my leaving made her even sicker, I decided not to do that and I went to college right here in town. She continued to have some types of illnesses and the doctors have never decided exactly what it is, but everything that upsets her now puts her to bed for a few days. While I was in college I went out with a few girls. I might have gone out more often but I couldn't stand to think of Mother sitting home alone.

When I got to graduate school, I met Ruth and for the first time I think I experienced some real feelings of love. It upset Mother terribly for me to talk about it. Mother didn't like her. She pointed out to me a lot of things that I probably should have seen myself about Ruth. She was from a different background and she was very selfish. Anyway, I broke up with her after about a year. That was eight years ago. My mother is much older now and I guess I'm her only source of support because economically, emotionally, she literally lives for me.

Recently I met a girl named Janice and I've been going with her about six months. Now Mother is starting to talk about her the same way she talked about Ruth, but worse. Janice says that I have to choose between her and my mother. I just can't do that. What am I going to do?

In many ways Richard is an emotional infant. He is very,

very dependent upon his mother and he does have to come to the place where he makes a choice, but the choice is not all or nothing. He can learn to become more independent from his mother. She might try to manipulate him and she might threaten suicide. Her illness could become worse. Yet one of the healthiest events that could occur is for Richard to proceed to become more of a man and to develop his own life. She is trying to control him. Before he marries Janice, Richard will need counseling so that he can develop into the type of man that he should be. A pastor might even find occasion to talk to Richard and his mother or Richard and Janice or perhaps all three of them together.

Here is a different problem. Mary was a very attractive woman, a twenty-eight-year-old fashion designer. But she was extremely critical. She seemed to find something wrong with every man she went out with. She said,

> I like to have a good time, but after I go out with a fellow for several weeks I just begin to see how many faults he has and just about that time he starts to get serious and wants to paw me. I've got a well-paying job and a beautiful car. My life is very convenient and well planned. Many times I've said to myself, "Why should I marry someone just for the sake of being married?"
>
> The other girls try to make me feel as if I am missing something but I thought I knew better. I'm still sure I know more about love and more about men than most of them will ever learn. My mother was married twice, and both times it was to an irresponsible man who failed to provide for us. My father was the first one; he was an alcoholic. He had an overwhelming need for affection and response. He tried all the time to beg, demand or buy my love. Even as a tiny child I had to live with complex emotional problems. I had to learn to see through and sometimes give deceptive satisfactions to his impossible demands. I knew all about the weaknesses of men long before I started going out.
>
> Unfortunately my father didn't stop when my mother

divorced him. In fact, I think it got worse. He needed me more than ever. He used to call me long distance when I was in school. I didn't know what to say to him. I didn't know what to say to him then, and I don't know now. I just try to do the best I can, but that's never good enough.

After my father left, my mother married someone else just like him. It would almost be funny if it weren't so tragic. She used to swear that if she ever got out of the situation she was in, she'd never look at another man as long as she lived. But she wasn't unmarried a year before she found another man to abuse her. In many ways he was worse.

Now I'm twenty-eight. It hit me all of a sudden that in another ten years I'm going to be too old to have children, and I don't have much to live for right now. Last week for the first time in a long while a man was really serious about wanting to marry me. John's a nice guy; he's not very exciting though. But he's nice. I don't really love him, but I am fond of him, and I do know if I go ahead and marry him I'll start looking for his faults right from the wedding day. I just can't seem to help myself, and I know that I'll try to manipulate him, and I'm sure I can do it because I've had lots of practice. In some ways I guess I could be good for him because I think he really needs me. I know how to cheer him up and make him feel successful. My problem is, what should I do at this point? I don't know.

What are some of the basic problems that Mary has that are going to hinder a marriage relationship?

A person like this needs individual help before she will be ready for marriage. It could be that this young woman is very critical of herself. That could easily lead to the criticism of men. It is also a factor that her poor experiences with men and her ability to manipulate them have caused her to develop a bad attitude toward males in general. Before she considers marriage she should look into her own life and deal with some of her basic attitudes. She should probably not go through with this particular marriage. Fondness is one thing, but deep love is something else. A marriage relationship requires an ability to adjust and to accept oneself and another individual.

One other area that must be considered is a situation that occurs more and more today. Couples come in and say, "Why bother to be married? We're Christians, we've submitted ourselves to one another and we're living together. Isn't that marriage in the sight of God?"

One could take time debating whether a person is really married or "not" married. The piece of paper and the ceremony do not necessarily make it more of a marriage, but we need to consider that one of the marks of a Christian is that his or her life should not be the cause of anyone's stumbling. The Christian's life is a witness to others, and it reflects the love of Jesus Christ. A relationship should avoid the very appearance of evil, according to the Scripture. In our society we have certain laws that we are expected to follow. A Christian couple that decides, "We don't need that piece of paper in order to be married," may cause others to stumble.

Dr. David Freeman, professor of philosophy at the University of Rhode Island, wrote an article titled, "Why Get Married?" It is published in the *Theology News and Notes* of Fuller Seminary. He was speaking to the question, Who needs a piece of paper in order to be married? and he said,

> To the Christian couple, the answer is simple: you do, not because it will insure that your love will mature more quickly, not because the license or the ceremony will insure the permanence of your love, but because the Christian is under obligation to obey laws that insure the wellbeing of their neighbor, laws including fairness and the fulfillment of contractual obligations. Our society is complex. We are related to others by many crisscrossing, interlocking relationships. The relationship between two people in real love, while personal and intimate, is not solely private. It is a public affair. Two people shipwrecked on a desert island would hardly

need a license or a minister to marry them. Their relationship would undoubtedly be private, with God alone as a witness. But the rest of us live in a community, belong to a family, are citizens of a state, and are dependent upon numerous individuals and organizations for our very survival. Marriage is a relationship between man and woman intended by God to be a monogamous relationship, intended to be a permanent bond in which many needs are satisfied—the need to love and be loved, the need for deep friendship, for sharing, for companionship, for sexual satisfaction, for children, the need to escape loneliness. Marriage ought to be a bond of love, reflecting the love Christ has for His people, a bond of sacrificial love where husband and wife have become one, one flesh, a unity.[4]

4. Daniel Freeman, "Why Get Married?" *Theology News and Notes of Fuller Theological Seminary* (Dec. 1973, 19:4), p. 17.

9

Group Premarital Counseling and Preparation

This series on marriage preparation is designed to be used with a minimum of four couples and a maximum of fifteen. Premarital counseling usually involves one couple meeting for several sessions with the pastor or another staff member. This is the ideal. However, it is possible to combine individual premarital counseling of couples with group counseling. The couples can learn from one another during the group sessions. If several couples are planning to be married within a brief span of time, the group sessions can also save the pastor time.

In order to prepare yourself for this type of teaching situation, you may want to read *Ways to Help Them Learn— Adults* by H. Norman Wright, published by Regal. This book outlines, in detail, learning principles and teaching methods that will be used in this series.

Please be sure that you begin your own preparations in advance and carefully follow the advance preparation suggestions for materials to read, order, select, and reproduce.

Cost: Include $25-30 with the wedding service or church fee. This fee will cover the purchase of materials, tests, tapes, film rental, duplicating materials, and any other costs incurred. (The purchase of tapes is a one-time expense; they can be used again.) Part of the money should be used to purchase a set of the recommended books for each couple so they can keep these to read again. Some couples may ask if they can obtain copies of the tapes used in the series. The church could have an extra supply available or let the couples order them directly from the publishers.

Leaders for this series: The pastoral staff can be involved in conducting this series. It is also possible to train selected married couples to conduct the series. The training consists of having several married couples actually go through this course and having them listen to any tapes suggested.

Time: These sessions should be started at least three months before the weddings. The meetings could be conducted on any evening for two and three-quarters hours—from 7:00 to 9:45—including a fifteen-minute coffee break. Schedule the meetings one week apart.

ADVANCE PREPARATION SECTION
Prior to the sessions

I. For your own preparation:
    A. Be sure you have completed the first portion of this book.
    B. Be sure you read over this entire series before you set up the program.

II. Materials you will need for the series (order all materials at least one month in advance):
    A. Books: a copy of each of the following for each couple
        1. Coble, Betty. *Woman: Aware and Choosing.* Nashville: Broadman, 1975.
        2. Williams, H. Page. *Do Yourself a Favor—Love Your Wife.* Plainfield, N.J.: Logos, 1973.
        3. Wheat, Ed; and Wheat, Gail. *Intended for Pleasure.* Old Tappan, N.J.: Revell, 1977.
        4. Wright, H. Norman. *Communication—Key to Your Marriage.* Glendale, CA.: Regal, 1974.
        5. ———. *The Living Marriage.* Old Tappan, N.J.: Revell, 1975.
    B. Tapes
        1. Wheat, Ed. "Sex Technique and Sex Problems in

Marriage." Denver: Christian Marriage Enrichment.

2. Wright, H. Norman. "Communication—Key to Your Marriage." Denver: Christian Marriage Enrichment.

C. Tests

1. "Marriage Expectation Inventory for Engaged Couples." Soluda, N.C.: Family Life Publications.

2. "Sex Knowledge Inventory." Soluda, N.C.: Family Life Publications.

3. "Taylor-Johnson Temperament Analysis." Los Angeles: Psychological Publications.

D. Reserve the films *We Do! We Do!* and *Johnny Lingo* for the appropriate meetings. Order from a Christian film distributor or Augsburg Films, 3224 Beverly Blvd., Los Angeles, Calif. 90057.

E. Select speaker for the finances presentation and select three couples for the final meeting.

F. Prepare transparencies in advance and have an overhead projector and screen at each meeting.

G. Have paper and pencils available at all sessions.

STEP-BY-STEP PROCEDURE FOR EACH SESSION

Carefully read the instructions for each session. Prepare in advance any materials needed for the session. Check the instructions below and compare them with the session instructions so you will know that you have made all the necessary preparations.

SESSION	WHAT TO ORDER OR PREPARE PRIOR TO EACH SESSION
1.	1. Prepare transparencies.
	2. Be certain films are ordered. *We Do! We Do!* is used for session 1.
	3. Listen to the tape and select the section on the definition of marriage from the tape "Founda-

tions of a Christian Marriage." (This tape is part of the series, "Communication—Key to Your Marriage.") Have the tape set at this point so you can play the proper section at the right time.

4. Have the "Marriage Expectation Inventory for Engaged Couples" and the "Sex Knowledge Inventory" available.

5. Have available the book *Communication—Key to Your Marriage.*

6. Have a 16-mm projector and a cassette tape recorder available.

7. Duplicate copies of "Love Dies," found in the Appendix.

---

2.   1. Have the T-JTA test booklets and answer sheets available.

2. Have available copies of *Intended for Pleasure* by the Wheats.

3. Prepare copies of "Your Role Concepts Comparison" and the "Case Studies on Conflicts in Marriage," found in the Appendix of this book.

4. Have the "Sex Knowledge Inventory" available.

---

3.   1. Have a set of Dr. Wheat's tapes available for each couple.

2. Have 3 x 5 cards available.

3. Prepare transparencies.

4. Have the film *Johnny Lingo* and a 16-mm projector available.

5. Obtain and read *Christian: Celebrate Your Sexuality* by Dwight Small (Revell).

---

4.   1. Prepare the "What Is Your Opinion" agree-disagree sheet.

2. Have the tape, "Communication Is the Key" available.
3. Have the T-JTA profiles available.
4. Prepare transparencies.
5. Have books and tape resources available for those who wish to use them in light of their test scores.
6. Prepare copies of "Your First Year Budget," found in the Appendix of this book.
7. Order a copy of "The Pre-Marital Communication Inventory" by Millard J. Bienvenu, Sr., Northwestern State University of Louisiana, Natchitoches, Louisiana 71457. Upon receiving a copy, decide if you want to use these for the session.

---

5. 1. Prepare copies of the "Finances Questionnaire," found in the Appendix of this book.
2. Prepare transparencies.
3. Duplicate material on in-laws, found in the Appendix.
4. Remind the speaker for this session.

---

6. 1. Have three couples available to share at this meeting.
2. Prepare tape or transparency of the wedding vows.
3. Have copies of *The Living Marriage* available.

THE INTERVIEW PRECEDING GROUP COUNSELING

Meet with each couple three to four weeks before the first session. Use this as a time to get better acquainted and to lay a foundation for the series. You may use some of the questions and ideas from session one or from the portion of this book that deals with the initial interview in the individual counseling. In addition, listed here are some simple background questions that you can use with each couple. This get-acquainted meeting is a time to explore each individual's commitment to Jesus Christ and to ascertain their spiritual level and growth.

What do you think marriage is? (Let one answer; then ask the other partner whether he or she can add to the first answer.)

How long have you been going together?

Since you've been going together, what has it been like?

What types of families do you come from?

Are your families basically alike?

How do you get along with each other's parents?

Will the wife work after you get married?

How would you like your marriage relationship to be different from your parents'?

Are you running into any roadblocks as you plan for your marriage ceremony? (Ask both partners.)

DESCRIPTION OF THE ACTIVITY
SESSION 1

5 minutes

1. *All together.*

Introduction by the session leader: Share background information about yourself; then share the purpose of premarital counseling:

a. to help a couple evaluate their own relationship,
b. to form realistic expectations for marriage,
c. to correct inaccurate attitudes and beliefs about marriage,
d. to develop proper habits of thinking and skills of communicating which will enrich the marriage,

   e. to gain information about sex, marriage roles, in-laws,
      finances, and the spiritual relationship so this informa-
      can be translated into practice.

   Structure and Content: Explain the details of this program
to the participants. There will be six sessions, two and three-
quarters hours in length, with a fifteen-minute break in the
middle of each session. There will be homework between
sessions averaging three to five hours a week, depending upon
the individual.
   Let couples know that there will be adequate time for
questions, and that there is nothing which cannot be discussed or asked during the series. If any individuals or
couples would like to meet individually with the leader, they
may ask for an appointment.

15 minutes

2. *Small groups.*

   The purpose of this activity is to get acquainted. Ask class
members to form groups of three or four, depending upon
how many there are, so the groups are the same size.
   Ask members to number off in their group. Then start with
the highest number in each group. Each person has two minutes in which to tell about him or herself. Each explains:
This is what you need to know about me in order to understand me. At the end of two minutes, the rest of the group
can ask questions. Then another member shares and the entire process is repeated until every person has been through
the experience.
   As the leader, watch the time for everyone. When the activity ends, ask how people felt as they were going through
the process. Ask for several to share insights they learned
about one another during this procedure.

45 minutes

3. *All together.*

Attitudes toward marriage: Ask the members to complete the following sentences (1-6, and to state "agree" or "disagree" to number 7. They should write their answers on a piece of paper.

- a. Marriage is . . .
- b. Men are . . .
- c. Sex is . . .
- d. My attitudes toward marriage have been shaped by . . .
- e. In marriage a man is . . .
- f. In marriage a woman is . . .
- g. Agree or disagree with this statement: Marriage is a contract.

Show the film *We Do! We Do!* After the film, have students form small groups of three or four persons for a ten-minute discussion; then have the total group discuss the film. Use these questions both times: What attitudes toward marriage did you see in the film? What could be done to correct these attitudes? You may also want to use some of the questions that come with the discussion guide for the film. Put the questions on the chalkboard or on a transparency.

Ask members to look at some of their own attitudes as expressed by the sentence completion and agree-disagree they worked on before the film. Discuss with the whole group the question, Where have you received your attitudes toward marriage?

25 minutes

4. *Small groups.*

Discuss the following questions in small groups of four to six. Put the questions on the chalkboard or make a transparency.

1. What do you hope to get out of your marriage that you would not get if you remain single?
2. Formulate your own definition of marriage.
3. What is the difference between love and infatuation? How can you be sure?
4. What kind of love is it necessary to have before you marry that other individual?

25 minutes

5. *All together—teaching session.*

Take five minutes for brief summaries of what the groups decided. Then take twenty minutes for your teaching, using the following material and suggestions:

a. Share a few of your own ideas of what a person should receive from marriage.
b. Using an overhead projector, show the transparency on the differences between mature love and immature love (or infatuation). You will find this material in the Appendix. Read to them "The Romantic Fallacy."
c. Share the two definitions of love on a transparency ("Real love is" and "Love is a feeling". These are on one sheet in the Appendix.) You may want to amplify these definitions. They are discussed on the tape which will be used next.
d. Use the tape "Foundations of a Christian Marriage" from the series "Communication—Key to Your Marriage." Find the section near the beginning of the tape where the speaker discusses the definition of marriage. Use this definition on the overhead as the speaker reads it. Take down the transparency during the portion of the message when the speaker is sharing his testimony about his retarded son. This way the class can give their full attention to the testimony being given. Reproduce the definition so class members can take it with them. It is in the Appendix.

15-20 minutes

6. *Meet as couples, face to face.*

Have the couples discuss the following questions. Ask them to be sure they discuss all of these questions. Put these on the chalkboard or a transparency.

  a. Of how many models of a good marriage are you aware?
  b. What makes these marriages good?
  c. What will you do to make your marriage different from poor marriages? (Some examples might be: building one another's self-esteem, setting goals, actively pursuing activities that would build the marriage such as reading books, attending seminars, keeping lines of communication open, continuing to grow as an individual and encouraging your partner to grow.)
  d. When is a person ready for marriage?

10-15 minutes

7. *All together—summary lecture.*

During this time share the marriageability traits. These are discussed in detail in the earlier portion of this book in chapter two.

5 minutes

8. *All together—summary and closing.*

Assign homework:

  a. Ask each person to list ten goals that he or she has for marriage. They should do this without discussion and bring these to the next session.
  b. Distribute the "Marriage Expectation Inventory for Engaged Couples" and the "Sex Knowledge Inventory," form Y. Ask them to complete these individually.
  c. Distribute the book *Communication—Key to Your Marriage* and ask them to read and complete the first chapter

for this week. The remainder of the book should be
completed by the end of the course.

d. Distribute a copy of "Love Dies" by David Knox to each
couple. Ask them to read this together during the week.
It is in the Appendix.

SESSION 2

10 minutes

1. *All together.*

Provide the "Sex Knowledge Inventory" answer sheets and
have them take these with them when the session is over so
they can grade their own test. Ask each couple to share the
goals that they wrote for their marriage. Allow three minutes
for this. Then ask the group to share what they believe are
the most important goals that they devised.

20-25 minutes

2. *Couples together.*

Ask each couple to combine their lists of individual goals
into one list.

a. Have them choose the four most important goals.
b. Have them develop the plan and steps necessary to
achieve these goals. If possible have them set some
target dates for accomplishing the goals. Emphasize the
fact that goal setting is the first step, but it is most important to develop a plan to follow in order to attain the
goal.

25 minutes

3. *Individuals, then couples face to face.*

"Your Role Concepts Comparison:" Distribute a copy of
this questionnaire to each person.

a. Have each person answer the questions according to his
or her own belief.

    b. Ask them to indicate next to each question the source for their own belief. Who or what influenced them? For example, parents, friends, pastor, the Bible, or they thought it up.

    c. Then ask them to answer in the way they think their fiancé would answer.

    d. Ask the couples to sit face to face and discuss their answers. Ask the men to start by picking one statement and saying, "This is how I answered, and this is how I think you answered the statement." Then they should proceed to discuss their answers. When a couple has finished the discussion of one statement, the woman should select the next one, using the same procedure.

20 minutes

4. *All together.*

Ask for reactions and questions concerning the statements of the role comparison sheet. There will be many varied opinions and questions from the group. Be sure you have read over these statements carefully and have thought through your own response. Some members may ask about the woman working or having a career. If not, you may want to bring up the question and share the information from the Appendix. This is titled, "Husband-Wife Roles in the 20th Century" and "How Does a Couple Try to Resolve Role Confusion?"

5. *Small groups.*

"Conflicts in Marriage Case Studies": Have the couples meet in groups of two or three couples. Distribute a copy of the case study sheet to each one. Ask them to spend a few moments on two or three of the cases that are most interesting to each of them. Ask them to decide how they would solve these case problems. During the last five minutes, ask for suggestions. The case studies are in the Appendix.

15 minutes

6. *Face to face: then all together.*

Have couples sit face to face and work out the principles and procedures they will follow in handling conflict in their upcoming marriage. During the last five minutes, have the group share insights.

25 minutes

7. *Individuals, then groups of four without partners.*

Ask each person to write answers to these questions:

a. Why are you getting married now?
b. Why are you marrying this person? Give at least eight reasons.

As they meet in the groups, each person should take three minutes to share his or her answers; then the others can ask questions for two minutes. Encourage members to share their answers with their fiancé after the session.

5-10 minutes

8. *All together—summary and closing.*

Assignment: Distribute the "Taylor-Johnson Temperament Analysis." Give each person one test booklet and two answer sheets. Ask members to answer the test questions as they see themselves and as they see their fiancé. See chapter four of this book for information on the T-JTA.

Distribute the Wheats' *Intended for Pleasure: Sexual Happiness in Marriage* and ask members to read this book for the next week. Suggest that couples spend some time sharing their answers from the "Marriage Expectation Inventory for Engaged Couples." Have them think about questions or fears they have about their forthcoming marriage.

Close in prayer.

SESSION 3

5 minutes

1. *All together.*

Have everyone turn in their T-JTA on themselves and their fiancé. Ask if there are any questions related to the "Marriage Expectation Inventory for Engaged Couples."

25 minutes

2. *All together.*

Show the film *Johnny Lingo.* You can order it from many Christian or secular film distributors or from Augsburg Films, 3224 Beverly Blvd., Los Angeles, Calif. 90057. This is an outstanding film on building self-esteem.

20 minutes

3. *Large or small groups.*

If you have a large group for this series, have six or seven sit in the center of the room and discuss the questions while the others listen. If this is a smaller group have them discuss it together or in groups of three.

Discussion questions: Put these questions on the chalkboard or make a transparency.

  a. What can a person do to build self-esteem in his or her mate?
  b. What are the most common ways to destroy self-esteem?
  c. What has helped you the most to feel worthwhile?
  d. How is a person likely to act or respond when he or she does not like himself or herself?

During the last five minutes, have each individual write down what he or she can do to build self-esteem in his or her partner. Ask them not to share this but to put it into practice.

30 minutes

4. *All together.*

Give a 3 x 5 card to every person. Ask them to write down any questions or fears that they have about marriage. They may ask about anything; you may want to mention or suggest some topic areas. For example: sex, contraception, unwanted pregnancy, pain during intercourse, premature ejaculation, difference in the intensity of the sex drive, losing interest in each other, the morality of oral sex, deviant sex behavior, scriptural teaching on sex, children, or divorce. Do not have members put their names on the cards. Collect the cards.

Start off the discussion by raising the questions, To what extent should a Christian couple be involved sexually prior to marriage? How can a person deal with guilt if going too far prior to marriage? See the Appendix for "God's Word: Wait Until Marriage." You may want to make this into a transparency to use at this point.

Now read some of the questions that the members wrote. Allow the group to discuss the questions and you can add or correct information as needed.

For your own preparation you could listen to the tape series that will be distributed at the close of this session; you may also want to listen to the series entitled "Sex and the Bible" by H. Norman Wright, from Christian Marriage Enrichment, 8000 E. Girard, Denver, Colorado 80231. Read Dwight Small's book *Christian: Celebrate Your Sexuality,* published by Revell, or *Thank God for Sex* by Harry Hollis, Jr., Broadman.

If this portion of the session takes longer than thirty minutes, do not cut it short. These are important questions. Adjust your schedule by reducing the times for 5 and 6; or have 6 later, or as a homework assignment.

15 minutes

5. *Small groups.*

Have the couples discuss the following questions:

a. How were feelings of love, warmth, and tenderness shown in your home as you were growing up?
b. How would you like to have feelings of love, warmth, and tenderness shown to you in public and in your home?

15 minutes

6. *Face to face.*

List the following questions on a transparency and have members write their answers. Then ask couples to sit face to face, share their answers, and work out any differences they might have.

a. Do you like sympathy and attention when you are ill?
b. Generally, do you enjoy the companionship of the opposite sex as much, or more, than your own? After you are married, do you think you will look at members of the opposite sex?
c. How much praise do you feel you need?
d. Do you like your future spouse's friends?
e. Do you have many friends?
f. How will you select friends after you are married?
g. What activities do you desire to do together and apart after marriage?

40 minutes

7. *Small groups.*

Ask groups of four to six to work out ten Scriptures that they feel a married couple should base their marriage upon. See *The Living Marriage* for suggestions. Ask them not to select the traditional passages such as Ephesians 5, 1 Peter 3, 1 Corinthians 13, or Proverbs 31. These passages are important, and we take it for granted that they would be a part of a couple's life. The idea here is to come up with some Scriptures not always associated with marriage.

During the last fifteen minutes, show Ephesians 4:2, Amplified version, on a transparency. Ask members to individually visualize or describe what they would do to put that passage into practice in their married life. Ask them to write down their suggestions and then have several share these with the group.

5 minutes

8. *All together.*

Closing: Ask everyone to continue reading the book, *Communication—Key to Your Marriage*. Read chapters 2 through 5 before next time. Give each couple a set of the tapes "Sex Problems and Sex Technique in Marriage" by Dr. Ed Wheat. (These are to be returned to you later.) Ask them to set aside time during the week to listen to the tapes together. Explain that this is a very frank, detailed presentation from a Christian medical doctor. When you preview these tapes yourself, decide whether you will suggest that couples listen just to the first one, or to both.

Close with prayer.

SESSION 4

1 hour and 20 minutes

1. *All together.*

Distribute the session 4 "What Is Your Opinion" agree-disagree sheet from the Appendix to each class member. Provide pencils. After the sheets have been distributed, give the following instructions:

Each of you has been given an agree-disagree sheet. On the sheet you will find several statements concerning the specifics of the marriage relationship. I would like each of you (without talking with any one else) to read each statement and decide whether you agree or disagree with it as it is presented there. If you agree place a check mark in the blank under "agree." If you disagree place a check in the blank marked "disagree." You will be given sufficient time to answer the statements. Please work individually and as quickly as possible.

Give the class enough time to complete their work. When everyone has finished, thank them for completing the sheet. Then ask all those who agreed with statement number one to raise their hands. Then ask how many of them disagreed with statement number one. Proceed to statement number two and ask how many agreed and how many disagreed. Do this for each of the agree-disagree statements without stopping to discuss any of the statements.

Give members seven minutes to discuss their response in small groups of three.

You will need one hour for the tape presentation. Listen to the tape entitled "Communication Is the Key" from the series "Communication—Key to Your Marriage." Make an overhead transparency or a chart of the main points and Scriptures. You may want to make a fill-in outline so the participants could copy down the main points. A number of these points will be reinforced by their continued reading in the communication book.

Following the tape show this statement on the overhead: "What do you think about this? Most problems in communication occur because each person communicates on a different level than the other. The longer a couple is married the more they learn what *not* to talk about."

Ask, "In light of the five levels of communication in your reading during the past week, what level do you communicate on? (Refer to pages 67 and 68 of *Communication—Key to Your Marriage*.) Is there a difference in your level as compared with your fiancé's? Are there things now that you hesitate to talk about?" (You may want to read these five levels to them.) Take your break at this time and have them consider these questions. They may want to bring these up again later.

Note: You may want to use the "Premarital Communication Inventory." See the Advance Preparation Section.

30 minutes

2. *All together.*

Explain the background and scope of the "Taylor-Johnson Temperament Analysis" test. Define the traits. You may want to have a large blow-up of the T-JTA profile. This is available from the publishers of the test; one is now available with an acetate so you can draw upon it. (See address in the Advance Preparation Section.)

Ask each person to predict his or her own profile. Be sure to explain the mid-scores and the attitude score. After each one has predicted his or her own score, return the completed profiles so they can see the result of their test.

Allow time for questions. Discuss the potential inter-relationships of trait scores on a couple's profile and how these might affect the marriage.

Note: You will probably have some profiles which will indicate that the person needs further counseling on an individual basis. Be sure that you indicate that this is available. You may ask individuals in for counseling if you see too many scores in the white area of the test or if you see great differences in the couples' scores and their perception of one another.

Be sure you have available many of the books and tape resources suggested for improving any of the scores. Note the materials recommended under the listing of T-JTA resources and Scriptures. Refer to the Appendix for this listing.

25 minutes

3. *Small groups.*

This is a time for a discussion of some of the trait scores, such as:

    a. How can a person become less nervous?

    b. How should a person handle hostility constructively?

    c. In what ways could impulsiveness become detrimental?

    d. How could self-discipline stabilize a marriage?

    e. Is the submission talked about on this test the same kind of submission discussed in the Scriptures?

    f. What effect would a high score in subjectivity have upon the marriage?

Have the members discuss how they feel about their own scores and the way they saw their fiancé. Have them share what they would like to change and have the members in the group suggest ways to change or improve.

15 minutes

4. *All together.*

Take questions and reactions at this point from the entire group. Suggest reading and tape material for each trait's improvement.

Spend some time taking prayer requests; close this meeting with a time of concentrated prayer. Let members know again that you or other pastoral staff are available for individual discussions of the test.

Homework assignment: Have each couple work out a budget. Distribute a copy of "Your First Year Budget." See Appendix.

Ask the members to find out the cost of items normally taken care of by the other partner; for example, the women could find out how much it would cost to buy a set of tires and have a car lubricated. Ask men to find out the cost of women's clothing, food, baby items, or furniture. If anyone still lives at home, have him or her volunteer to do the grocery shopping for the next week. This will be valuable experience.

SESSION 5

20 minutes

1. *All together.*

This time should be spent in an open discussion using some of the following questions:

   a. Were you aware of what things cost today? Were you surprised?
   b. Have you ever used a budget before? How can you control spending of money that is not budgeted?
   c. Should marriage partners have an allowance that they do not have to account for? Why or why not?
   d. Who should take the responsibility of working out the budget and paying the bills? Why? Where does the concept of spiritual gifts come into play here?

20 minutes

2. *Individuals, then couples, face to face.*

Distribute a copy of the "Finances Questionnaire." Have each person complete it; then ask the couples to sit face to face and discuss the various items.

45 minutes

3. *All together.*

This portion of the meeting is given to a special speaker that you have invited. This should be a Christian businessman or accountant who can give specific and practical guidelines on making and living within a budget. Be very selective when you choose this person; ask him or her to give as many helpful hints as possible during the forty-five minutes. If this person represents a company or organization, let him or her know that this is a teaching situation, not a promotional time.

25 minutes

4. *Groups of three couples.*

Place the following questions on an overhead transparency. Ask the couples to discuss as many as possible in the time allotted.

a. When should you spend more to get quality, and when can you skimp on quality in order to save? Discuss the following: car (new or used; "transportation" or "sports"); housing (rent or buy); furniture (mattress, stove, refrigerator, sofa, stereo, etc.); food (steak, casseroles, leftovers); wearing apparel (clothes, shoes, cosmetics); dishes and silverware; gifts (to your mate, to others).

b. What type of vacation do you want? (Camping or a Caribbean cruise?) How much will it cost? How will you save for it? How often will you take a vacation?

c. What kind of honeymoon will you take? How much will it cost? How will you pay for it?

d. How was money handled in each of your families? What attitudes regarding money do you bring to your marriage? What were considered luxuries, what necessities?

e. What types of charge accounts will you have (gasoline, department store, bank card)? What amount of money would each partner feel comfortable owing on charge accounts? Will charge accounts be used regularly or only for emergencies?

f. What do you think about borrowing money from relatives?

g. What are your financial goals?

h. How soon will you attempt to buy furniture? What type (expensive, fix-it-yourself, or in-between)? How much will you spend? What major appliances will you buy? How soon? How much will you spend?

i. What things do you consider necessities or luxuries?

5-10 minutes

5. *All together.*

The group leader should give information about the following:

a. It is important to establish good credit (for major expenditures as a house, car, having a baby, or emergencies).

b. What you pay in gasoline tax is deductible on your income tax, and charging gas is a good way to keep track of it. Or you can keep a record of mileage driven during the year and use government gas tax tables to estimate taxes paid.

c. Do you know that utility companies usually require a deposit in order to begin service? (Sometimes $25 to $50 each!)

d. Do you know where to borrow money? There is a great difference in what finance charge you will have to pay. Usually a credit union is best, a bank is next, and a "mouse house" (finance company) worst.

e. Your application for a marriage license is public record. Many firms use the list of marriage license applicants as a list of new prospects. Expect to be barraged by mail, telephone, and door-to-door solicitation. Can you say, "NO!"?

f. Beware the door-to-door salesman. Your unborn child does not *need* a complete encyclopedia set!

g. Any sale made at your home in California may be canceled if written notice is mailed to the company within three days of the sale. Other states may have this law, too.

30 minutes

6. *Individuals, then all together.*

The remaining time should be spent looking at attitudes toward in-laws and sharing principles to follow in dealing with in-laws. Make a transparency of the following questions for a brief agree-disagree sheet.

Agree Disagree   Statement

‾‾‾‾ ‾‾‾‾ 1. If you have any difficulties in your own marriage, it might be helpful to get advice from your parents.

‾‾‾‾ ‾‾‾‾ 2. Most in-law problems come from the mother-in-law, not the father-in-law.

‾‾‾‾ ‾‾‾‾ 3. You should visit or call one set of parents just as much as the other.

‾‾‾‾ ‾‾‾‾ 4. It might be best at the start of the marriage to let parents and in-laws know that you would like to learn on your own and would appreciate not receiving any advice.

‾‾‾‾ ‾‾‾‾ 5. If a wife has a disagreement with his mother, the husband should stay out of the discussion and let them work it out.

Follow the usual procedure for an agree-disagree sheet, but this time have a five- to ten-minute discussion. Then complete this session by sharing the principles of "Dealing with In-laws" from Landis and Landis and Lobenz and Blackburn. Make a transparency of these items and use this for a lecture base for your presentation. Duplicate a copy of the material and give to each couple. This material is found in the Appendix. Also read over the adapted material from David Mace as that will help your presentation. This material has been adapted from his book *We Can Have Better*

Marriages if We Really Want Them. You may want to read this material in the original.

3 minutes

7. *Close.*

Suggest that each couple think of one positive act they could perform during this coming week for each set of parents. Ask them to continue reading *Communication—Key to Your Marriage* and other books or resources they might be using in conjunction with their T-JTA. Ask them to plan at least one session together this week for Bible study and prayer. Suggest J. Allan Pederson's excellent workbook *Two Become One* published by Tyndale and available in Christian bookstores. This would give them the format and structure that they might be looking for.

Close in prayer.

Session 6

5 minutes

1. *All together.*

Ask the couples to share their reactions and feelings about their Bible study and praying together. Be willing to share some of your own feelings and insights with them.

15 minutes

2. *Groups of two or three couples.*

Discussion question: What provision are you making for continuing your own spiritual growth? Ask the couples to discuss this together. Ask them to also discuss these questions:

  a. Should a couple pray and study the Scriptures together every day?
  b. Who decides what church they attend and how often?

30 minutes

3. *Two groups and then all together.*

Ask the women to meet in a group and the men to meet in a group. Each group is to discuss, How will I contribute to my partner's spiritual growth? After fifteen minutes, ask each group to share their ideas with the total group.

As group leader you may want to make some of the following suggestions:

a. Individual study of the same passage, then share findings together.

b. Use a Bible study guide or commentary, such as *Barclay's Daily Study Bible* or the *Aldersgate Adult Bible Study material.* (This Free Methodist material is inductive in approach.)

c. Use a concordance for a topical study.

d. Listen to tapes or use Bible studies on family topics.

e. Play the "Ungame" or use the game's Christian and Bible study cards as discussion topics. (For information on the game and the Bible study cards, write to Christian Marriage Enrichment, 8000 E. Girard, Suite 602, Denver, CO 80231).

f. Each morning you might ask each other what you could pray for during that day; then have a time of sharing together, and close by reading 1 Samuel 12:23.

45 minutes to one hour

4. *All together.*

Now three married couples you have selected will share insights they have learned over the years. Select one couple that has been married a few years, another married ten to twenty years, and one who has been married more than twenty years. Select couples who have something to offer and can be open, honest, and responsive.

Let the couples know that they will be asked all kinds of questions. Ask each couple to share specifically what Jesus Christ has meant in their marriage and how they have grown spiritually and helped each other to grow during their marriage. Let the class members know that they can ask any questions that they would like to have answered at this time.

10 minutes

5. *Groups of three individuals.*

It is important to introduce the topic of child rearing and discipline so the couples will plan to equip themselves well before having children. Ask them to discuss the following questions:

    a. How did your parents discipline you?
    b. How do you feel about it now?
    c. Would you do things the same or differently?
    d. If differently, how do you know that you will be able to do it differently?

5 minutes

6. *All together.*

Just as it requires study and learning to become skilled craftsmen, it requires study and learning to become a good parent. Many people want to rear their own children differently than they were reared. However, most people revert to the same procedures their parents used unless the couple puts forth an effort to learn new procedure and principles.

Suggest to the members that before they have children they could do the following:

    a. Spend time with small children so they can receive some firsthand experience.
    b. Consider working in the church's nursery or two-year-old department for three months; this could be an education in itself!

c. Listen to the series of tapes by the Reverend Charles R. Swindoll on parent-child relationships. Order from the First Evangelical Free Church, 642 W. Malvern, Fullerton, California 92632. Also listen to *The Family in Today's Society,* available from your Christian bookstore or from Herald Press, Scottsdale, Pennsylvania 15683.

d. Read the following books (available from Christian bookstores):

1) *Help! I'm a Parent,* by Bruce Narramore
2) *Your Child's Self-Esteem,* by Dorothy Briggs
3) *Hide or Seek,* by James Dobson
4) *The Concordia Sex Education Series.*

20 minutes

7. *Men in groups and women in groups.*

Make a transparency or tape recording of the sample vows in the Appendix. Show or play this for the group. With the help of the group, each person should write, in everyday language, what he or she wants to promise to his or her partner. Each person's vows may be different from others in the group, but each may benefit from sharing ideas.

10 minutes

8. *Couples face to face.*

The couples should read their vows to each other and discuss any part that is not clear. They may share their feelings about the promises they have received and given. Are the promises realistic?

Close session with couples praying together in small groups.

As your wedding gift to them, give each couple a copy of *The Living Marriage,* published by Revell. Encourage them not to read this together until their honeymoon, so they could use it as the first devotional study of their married life.

Appendix

THE DIFFERENCE BETWEEN IMMATURE LOVE AND MATURE LOVE[1]

Immature Love	*Mature Love*
1. Love is born at first sight and will conquer all.	1. Love is a developing relationship and deepens with realistically shared experiences.
2. Love demands exclusive attention and devotion, and is jealous of outsiders.	2. Love is built upon self-acceptance and is shared unselfishly with others.
3. Love is characterized by exploitation and direct need gratification.	3. Love seeks to aid and strengthen the loved one without striving for recompense.
4. Love is built upon physical attraction and sexual gratification. Sex often dominates the relationship.	4. Love includes sexual satisfaction, but not to the exclusion of sharing in other areas of life.
5. Love is static and egocentric. Change is sought in the partner in order to satisfy one's own needs and desires.	5. Love is growing and developing reality. Love expands to include the growth and creativity of the loved one.

1. Robert K. Kelley, *Courtship, Marriage and the Family* (New York: Harcourt, Brace & World, 1969), pp. 212-13. Used by permission.

176

6. Love is romanticized. The couple does not face reality or is frightened by it.

6. Love enhances reality and makes the partners more complete and adequate persons.

7. Love is irresponsible and fails to consider the future consequences of today's action.

7. Love is responsible and gladly accepts the consequences of mutual involvement.

THE ROMANTIC FALLACY[2]

First, romance results in such distortions of personality that after marriage the two people can never fulfill the roles that they expect of each other. Second, romance so idealizes marriage and even sex that when the day-to-day experiences of marriage are encountered there must be disillusionment involved. Third, the romantic complex is so short-sighted that the pre-marital relationship is conducted almost entirely on the emotional level and consequently such problems as temperamental or value differences, religious or cultural, or health problems are never considered. Fourth, romance develops such a false ecstasy that there is implied in courtship a promise of a kind of happiness which could never be maintained during the realities of married life. Fifth, romance is such an escape from the negative aspects of personality to the extent that their repression obscures the real person. Later in marriage these negative factors in marital adjustment are bound to appear, and they do so in far greater detail and far more importantly simply because they were not evident earlier. Sixth, people engrossed in romance seem to be prohibited from wise planning for the basic needs of the future even to the extent of failing to discuss the significant problems of early marriage.

It is difficult to know how pervasive the romantic fallacy really is. I suspect that it creates the greatest havoc with

2. Lyle B. Gangsei, *Manual for Group Pre-Marital Counseling* (New York: Association Press, 1971), pp. 56-57. Used by permission.

REAL LOVE MEANS AN

UNCONDITIONAL COMMITMENT

TO AN IMPERFECT PERSON

LOVE IS A FEELING YOU

FEEL WHEN YOU FEEL THAT

YOU'RE GOING TO GET A FEELING

THAT YOU NEVER FELT BEFORE

high school seniors or that half of the population who are married before they are twenty years old. Nevertheless, even in a college or young adult population, one constantly finds as a final criterion for marriage the question of being in love. This is due to the distortion of the meaning of a true companionship in marriage by the press, by the magazines, and by cultural impact upon the last two or three generations. The result is that more serious and sober aspects of marital choice and marital expectations are not only neglected but sometimes ridiculed.

A DEFINITION OF MARRIAGE

A Christian marriage is a total commitment of two people to the Person of Jesus Christ and to one another. It is a commitment in which there is no holding back of anything. A Christian marriage is similar to a solvent, a freeing up of the man and woman to be themselves and become all that God intends for them to become. Marriage is the refining process that God will use to have us develop into the man or woman he wants us to be.

LOVE DIES[3]

Love feelings are not "built in" but come from learned social responses, for example, a smile, a touch, a laugh. Most of the things that make us feel good are incorporated into our cultural system of dating and courtship; we treat the other person very courteously, smile a lot, try to be pleasant, avoid saying offensive things, dress to look attractive, use best manners, and perhaps dine on food and enjoy entertainment that takes us beyond our budget. More importantly, all of these pleasurable features appear against a background of escalating physical stimulation or sexual excitement. Indeed, we have a social interaction in which one's dating partner is paired with the widest possible range of pleasurable sensa-

---

3. David Knox, *Marriage—Who? When? Why?* (Englewood Cliffs, N.J.: Prentice-Hall, 1975), pp. 101-2. Used by permission.

tions and activities. (Bartz and Rasor, 1972, used by permission.)

Consider this explanation of love in your dating relationship. Think about someone you just met. It is not possible for this person to elicit love feelings in you unless you have already shared a number of pleasurable experiences (e.g., eating together, seeing movies together, talking together). The "love at first sight" experience is the result of seeing someone whose features (eyes, face, body type) have already been paired with love feelings. For example, it would be difficult for you to fall romantically in love with someone three times your age. This love possibility with an elderly person is reduced because you have not experienced love (romantic) feelings with someone that age nor have you been taught to expect love feelings. The experience of love requires a cultural readiness.

The behaviors which cause love feelings must be reinforced to be maintained. This implies that during a developing relationship, couples have a high frequency of reinforcing each other for appropriate behavior. This results in the partner continuing the desired behavior which results in the continuation of love feelings. If you want your partner to continue to engage in behavior which you define as desirable, you must reinforce or reward that behavior.

Love dies when partners spend little time together and stop sharing activities that are mutually enjoyable.... As a test..., identify an unhappy couple you know and specify how much time they spend together engaging in enjoyable behavior. Contrast this with a couple you define as being in love and observe the amount of time they spend in mutually enjoyable activities. Love can be created or destroyed by pairing or failing to pair the partner with pleasurable activities over time.

The death of love also results from failure on the part of both partners to reinforce appropriate behavior in each other.

For example, smiling, caressing, complimenting, spending time together, and helping with the baby are behaviors in marriage that may not be reinforced. When these behaviors are no longer reinforced, they will stop. If your partner stops doing things that you like, your love feelings will disappear. It is important that you reinforce your partner for positive behavior (so that the behavior will continue) to insure that there is a continued basis for your love feelings.

In summary, love is a function of sharing pleasurable activities with each other over time, reinforcing your partner, and being reinforced by your partner for appropriate behavior. When partners stop spending time with each other in pleasurable mutual activities and stop reinforcing each other for appropriate behavior, love dies.

How Does a Couple Try to Resolve Role Confusion?

In recent studies, husband and wife role differences are the result of "balance of power" in the marriage. The "sources of power are in the comparative resources which the husband and wife bring to the marriage." "A resource may be designated as anything that one partner may make available to the other, helping the other satisfy his needs or attain his goals. The balance of power will be on the side of that partner who contributes the greater resources to the marriage." In the past, this power was allocated to the one with the greater physical strength.

THERE ARE SEVEN BASES OF FAMILY POWER:

1. Personalities of spouses: It might be assumed that the more dominant personality would wield the greater power in marriage. However, studies show that this is more valid with the dominant male than the female.

2. The relative age of spouses: When there is a large dif-

YOUR ROLE CONCEPTS COMPARISON[4]

What do you believe about your role in marriage?

Answer Key:
1. Strongly agree
2. Mildly agree
3. Not sure
4. Mildly disagree
5. Strongly disagree

	Wife						Husband				
The husband is the head of the home.	1	2	3	4	5		1	2	3	4	5
The wife should not be employed outside of the home.	1	2	3	4	5		1	2	3	4	5
The husband should help regularly with the dishes.	1	2	3	4	5		1	2	3	4	5
The wife has the greater responsibility for the children.	1	2	3	4	5		1	2	3	4	5
Money that the wife earns is her money.	1	2	3	4	5		1	2	3	4	5
The husband should have at least one night a week out with his friends.	1	2	3	4	5		1	2	3	4	5
The wife should always be the one to cook.	1	2	3	4	5		1	2	3	4	5
The husband's responsibility is to his job and the wife's responsibility is to the home and children.	1	2	3	4	5		1	2	3	4	5
Money can best be handled through a joint checking account.	1	2	3	4	5		1	2	3	4	5
Marriage is a 50-50 proposition.	1	2	3	4	5		1	2	3	4	5
Major decisions should be made by the husband in case of an impasse.	1	2	3	4	5		1	2	3	4	5
The husband should babysit one night a week so the wife can get away and do what she wants.	1	2	3	4	5		1	2	3	4	5
A couple should spend their recreation leisure activities with one another.	1	2	3	4	5		1	2	3	4	5
It is all right for the wife to initiate love-making with her husband.	1	2	3	4	5		1	2	3	4	5

1 2 3 4 5		1 2 3 4 5
1 2 3 4 5	The husband and wife should plan the budget and manage money matters together.	1 2 3 4 5
1 2 3 4 5	Neither the husband nor the wife should purchase an item costing over fifteen dollars without consulting the other.	1 2 3 4 5
1 2 3 4 5	The father is the one responsible for disciplining the children.	1 2 3 4 5
1 2 3 4 5	A wife who has special talent should have a career.	1 2 3 4 5
1 2 3 4 5	It is the wife's responsibility to have the house neat and clean.	1 2 3 4 5
1 2 3 4 5	The husband should take his wife out somewhere twice a month.	1 2 3 4 5
1 2 3 4 5	The wife is just as responsible for the children's discipline as the husband.	1 2 3 4 5
1 2 3 4 5	It is the husband's job to do the yard work.	1 2 3 4 5
1 2 3 4 5	The mother should be the teacher of values to the children.	1 2 3 4 5
1 2 3 4 5	Women are more emotional than men.	1 2 3 4 5
1 2 3 4 5	Children should be allowed to help plan family activities.	1 2 3 4 5
1 2 3 4 5	Children develop better in a home with parents who are strict disciplinarians.	1 2 3 4 5
1 2 3 4 5	The wife should always obey what her husband asks her to do.	1 2 3 4 5
1 2 3 4 5	The husband should decide which areas each should be responsible for.	1 2 3 4 5
1 2 3 4 5	Neither husband nor wife should bring their parents into the home to live.	1 2 3 4 5

4. James R. Hine, *Your Marriage Analysis and Renewal* (Danville, IL.: Interstate Publishers and Printers, 1966), pp. 19-20, adapted.

ference in age, the scale is tipped in favor of the older spouse, usually the husband.

3. The relative education of spouses: Generally the spouse with the higher educational level has more influence in the marriage than he or she would otherwise have. Influence seems particularly noticeable when one mate is college educated.

4. The employment status of the wife: Power wielded by additional income is probably the decision factor. The full-time working wife has the most influence in family decisions. Other studies show the housewife exerts more influence. More study is needed in this area.

5. The occupational status of husband: This has a great deal to do with his status in the home. Most wives will recognize they owe their status to the good position of their husbands. Therefore, they will be more dependent, even though they may be well-educated women. In lower class situations where the wife's income is essential to family welfare, the husband's bargaining power is not as great.

6. The presence and number of children in the family: It has been demonstrated that childless couples tend to be more equalitarian than couples with children. The more children in the family, the more influence the husband has.

7. The stage in the family cycle: In early years of marriage there is a more equalitarian pattern. With the coming of children, the husband seems to dominate. Once children leave and there is the empty nest, very few wives are dominated by their husbands. This shows that the balance of power shifts throughout a marriage.

HUSBAND-WIFE ROLES IN THE TWENTIETH CENTURY

One of the greatest areas of adjustments, change, and concern in today's marriages centers around the roles of the husband and wife.

In our American culture an assumption has existed concerning sex-role distinctions and definitions. For example, traditionally expressive behavior has been designated to women and instrumental behavior to men. But is this actually true? The patterns of interaction within marriage are not always that clear cut nor are the roles that segregated. We have certain expectations and stereotypes for behavior, such as the behavior of a father toward his children. But within this expectation there is tremendous variation because of personality, work, and pressures. Our roles are actually more like stereotypes.

Perhaps as man and woman begin to interact there is some segregation of the roles. But after the relationship develops, the roles begin to drop off and more realistic methods of functioning together are developed.

In most American marriages the husband is still the main income provider, and the wife cares for the children. Both are instrumental roles. And there is little evidence to prove that the woman is the only one involved in emotional expressive behavior. In families with children at home, it is too difficult to have a simple division of roles along instrumental-expressive lines because of the complexity of living together. Each person, whether husband or wife, needs to be instrumental and expressive in his behavior. Actually, husbands who are not emotionally supportive to their wives and affectionate to their children could be disruptive to family life. And wives who do not effectively direct the affairs of the household could also be a disruptive influence to the family.[5]

One of the greatest changes evidenced in today's marriages is that of the working wife or career wife.

The traditional view of the American wife is domestic: she marries early and spends the remainder of her life caring for her children and husband. But that picture has changed. Today half of all girls are married by age twenty-one and by

5. Richard Udry, *The Social Content of Marriage*, 3rd ed. (New York: J. B. Lippincott, 1974, p. 265.

thirty-two the average American woman has her youngest child in school. By forty-five, her children have left home and her life expectancy is seventy-seven.

In February 1974, there were 35 million women in the United States labor force, comprising 45 percent of all women age sixteen and over—up nine percentage points since 1955. Mothers, with children under age three and husbands present, had a labor force participation rate of 29 percent in 1973, about a 100 percent increase since 1960. Wives who worked full time year round in 1972 accounted for a median of nearly 40 percent of family income. There has also been a sharp expansion in the proportion of women heading families and households. In 1973, 6.6 million U.S. families were headed by women. It is projected that by 1980 one in four households will be headed by a woman.[6]

The traditional role of the woman keeping house is unfulfilling to many women and understandably so. In years past the woman not only kept house but was involved in part of the productive labor of an economic enterprise (see Prov 31). Much of the wife's work and production responsibility was withdrawn from the household, and this exaggerated the division of labor between husband and wife. The trend today toward women's employment outside the home is a logical consequence of moving all of the production out of the home, including the husband's work. In the past the woman's functions could be fulfilled in one location and outside employment was unnecessary.

There are several reasons why wives are drawn into employment outside of the home. Ginzberg and Yohalem in *Educated American Women: Self Portraits* suggest four basic categories of women and their reasons for seeking employment outside the home. The first group are the "planners." These women have had definite goals from a young age and

6. Data Track Research Services Institute of Life Insurance, New York. No. 1 Women, Summer 1974, p. 3.

have pursued those goals without allowing anything to deter them. The second group are the "recasters," women who shift their interests, plans, and goals when something else is more desirable. They may have had original ideas about what they wanted to do with their lives but because of some obstacles they settled for another choice. Some of these women simply decided that what they chose in the beginning was not what they wanted so they sought something better.

A third group is the "adapters," highly flexible women. They realize early in adulthood there will be many adjustments and changes. No matter what happens at the various stages of marriage, they are ready to make the adjustment.

The last group is given the title "unsettled." These women may have been at one time in any of the other three categories. But because their plans have not been realized, they now fumble and search for a new style and are still somewhat frustrated.[7]

In addition to the above, other practical reasons for employment enter in. As living costs keep rising, many couples find that both partners must work to make ends meet. The desire to add items to the home, to maintain too high a standard of living, or a belief that the husband cannot provide adequately motivates some wives to work. A common goal of saving money for a child's education sends some wives looking for a job.

The wife's personality is another factor. For many women measuring the soap for the dishwasher, choosing the right cycle on the dryer, or cleaning the living room for the sixth time in a week is not very fulfilling. What happens when all of the children are in school and the wife is well organized? It takes more than soap operas and magazines to provide fulfillment. Outside employment is just one means of fulfillment, however.

7. Letha Scanzoni and Nancy Hardesty, *All We're Meant to Be* (Waco, Texas: Word Books, 1974), p. 197. Adapted.

In the past wives were not expected to work. Today society not only accepts working women but in some ways may even expect it. Now the pressure has been reversed. The work ethic must go on and if wives cannot find enough to do within the home then the ethic pushes them to work outside of the home.

The move toward employment is not without emotional upheaval, however. Wives who are committed to work for achievement goals and who aspire to a career often have anxieties, doubts, occasional feelings of role conflict and guilt. Questions arise such as Is it really all right to work? Is this best for my family? How am I doing in my profession? Some women actually begin worrying about their own normality when the freedom of choice replaces rigid cultural norms, and they must make their own standards and decisions. Uncertainty about their femininity arises when a career atypical for a woman is chosen.[8]

It will take years for attitudes to change and new roles to be accepted. A recent poll showed that 31 percent of American wives feel that "a woman's ultimate fulfillment in life is the realization of her own personal goals," but 67 percent felt that "a woman's ultimate fulfillment in life is marriage and motherhood." And the majority of the wives rejected the idea of complete equality with their husbands: 60 percent of the wives who did want more from life than a husband and children did *not* want complete equality with their spouses.[9]

What is the effect of the working wife upon the marriage relationship? The conclusions of research are not that clear cut. In white families, the wife decreases her housekeeping activities while the husband increases his by performing masculine tasks more unilaterally and helping with more feminine tasks. But in many families conflict arises because of the revised division of labor. It has also been found that the

8. Ibid., p. 198. Adapted.
9. Udry, p. 305. Adapted.

power structure shifts in the direction of the wife who now has a greater voice in major economic decisions and a lesser voice in routine household decisions. Some studies have shown that when both the husband and wife were career oriented, pursuing such goals as law, college teaching, or medicine, husbands did not appear threatened or dominated. But this study also indicated that none of the wives wanted to be more successful than her husband.[10]

A common assumption about working wives is that the couple's amount of interaction will lessen. But again this has not been found to be the case. Some time-consuming leisure activities may be curtailed but there is still ample interaction and involvement together.

In terms of marital happiness, some findings indicate that there is no difference in the marital adjustment of working and nonworking wives. But what really matters is the husband's attitude toward the wife's employment. Nearly all recent studies show a relationship between a wife's full-time employment and conflict in the marriage, but unfortunately this relationship is not that clear and not that accurately defined. It is apparent that both partners experience more tensions and less companionship in their marriage when the wife works by necessity than by choice. When the wife works only because she wants to, tensions are lower and companionship higher than if the wife chose to stay at home. When the wife works part-time as compared to full-time, the marriages tend to be happier.

One interesting study found that the wife's working is evidently a source of marital conflict. But the added income puts the family on a higher socioeconomic level and this has a positive effect upon the family. These two items balance each other so that the final effect of the wife's employment is really negligible.[11]

10. Ibid., p. 304. Adapted.
11. Ibid., pp. 305-7. Adapted.

Perhaps all of these findings seem confusing and contradictory but what they do indicate is that more extensive studies are needed. It may be too soon to know all of the results, but each couple ought to be aware of some possible effects of the wife's employment. If employment is the couple's choice then they must work together to resolve and eliminate detrimental effects upon their relationship.

Because so many wives with small children work, Robert Kelley has suggested ten ideal conditions for this situation.

1. Any career for a woman should offer sufficient financial compensation. The salary should be commensurate with her education and should allow her enough money to pay for child care, housekeeping, and other expenses incurred because of working. If there is insufficient money left over to meet family needs, the position might not be worthwhile.

2. Personal satisfaction should be derived from the career. A combination of fulfillment with challenge and stimulation is necessary as compared with jobs that are simply an energy drain.

3. An adequate mother-substitute must be obtained to take care of the children while the mother is at work. This may be the most difficult condition to fulfill. A reevaluation of the nursery school or individual taking care of the child must be done consistently by both the husband and wife.

4. The employed wife needs the understanding and encouragement of her husband. If this does not occur, not only the marriage but the wife's effectiveness on the job can suffer.

5. A mother who is career oriented should be just as interested in the social, moral, and intellectual development of the children. As a child is entrusted to others during the formative years and especially during the three-to-five-year-old age, the quality of the care and education must be high.

6. An employed wife must balance her life so she has time and energy to give to her husband and children. This may

require adjustments at home but also the career might have to be selected with this in mind.

7. In a two-career family, the quality of living should remain high, otherwise working is detrimental. For a home to be dirty, meals poorly planned, with little leisure or family time, the mother's job does not help; it hurts. Good planning and a willingness to work together should keep living at a quality level.

8. A long-range benefit of a wife's career should be the improvement of the marital relationship. This is difficult to achieve and difficult to measure. Perhaps a career can assist a woman in developing her resources and interests. She may make more effort regarding personal attractiveness than one who is much more restricted.

9. It is possible for the woman to gain increased appreciation for her husband and children as they work to make the home surroundings a place of refuge and comfort. This condition is important for any working wife or husband.

10. Community expectations must be considered since certain areas of the country and certain cities are more open to the newer life-styles than are others. In selecting a community in which to live this ought to be taken into consideration. Positive reinforcement from community and acquaintances can lessen the adjustment difficulties.[12]

Is there any effect upon the children when both mother and father are employed outside of the home? Some alarmist articles imply a picture of increased divorces, messy homes and messy children, and delinquency or emotional disturbances in the children because of the mother working. However, these conditions can also occur when the mother is at home.

In all actuality, the studies appear to be contradictory and somewhat uncertain as to the effect a mother's working has

12. Robert Kelley, *Courtship, Marriage and the Family*, 2d ed. (New York: Harcourt, Brace, Jovanovich, 1974), pp. 367-68. Adapted.

upon the children. If mothers feel guilty about working or dislike their jobs there could be some negative effects upon the children. Other mothers could be so stimulated and thus grow so much personally that they become even better mothers during the time they spend with their children.

There are mixed attitudes toward mothers of preschool children working. It appears that more middle-class mothers who have children of this age would not work as compared with those that must out of economic necessity.

There does appear to be some evidence indicating that the mother's employment affects boys differently than girls. The employment may have a positive effect for the girls and a negative effect for the boys. A few studies indicate that there may be a higher rate of delinquency in middle-class homes where both parents work. Another study indicates that boys are affected negatively when the motives for the mother's working reflects failure on the part of the father as the head of the household. Some studies indicate that boys of working mothers may be more dependent and withdrawn. Girls, on the other hand, may admire their mothers more and develop a more clearly formed self-concept.[13]

There are indications that mothers who are employed have a better adjustment to their children than those who are not employed. They seem to share positive feelings more, use milder methods of discipline, and desire more pleasure from their children. However, employed mothers report more frequent doubts and feelings of inadequacy as parents than non-working mothers.[14]

Case Studies on Conflicts in Marriage[15]

1. We've been married eleven weeks, and Frank has just told me that with fall coming on, he is planning four or five nights a month out with the boys, bowling or just doing some

13. Udry, pp. 307-8. Adapted.
14. Ibid.
15. Adapted from *Marriage: Discoveries and Encounters,* The Cana Conference of Chicago, pp. 11-12.

talking. He says we both need private lives and our own circle of friends and that I should make similar arrangements.

Now, I can understand occasional nights out, but this planning to be apart bothers me. I married him to be with him and to do things together. Besides, my girl friends just do not go out much without their husbands.

What do you suggest?

2. Our wedding is only one week away, so please reply promptly. We finally got around to talking about children seriously the other night, and Jim said straight out that he does not want children for at least three or four years. He maintains we deserve this kind of freedom "before we are tied down with kids."

I frankly don't see children as a burden. These days, with a little planning, you can fit them right into your social life, travel, and almost anything. Money is no problem and I am afraid of the attitude that says you have to have everything nailed down and secure before you have a baby. We've both been around a good deal, and I for one am more than ready to start a family. What do you think?

3. About the only thing that bugs me about my fiancé is that he makes no plans.

When he calls, the second sentence out of his mouth is always, "What do you want to do?" Then I say, "I do not know," and we waste time floundering around and end up irritated and doing nothing. It just seems stupid!

I think it's the man's responsibility to think up things and make definite suggestions and plans. He says there just are not that many things he likes to do, and that I like to move around too much.

I'm afraid his attitude could make for a lot of boredom in marriage. What should I do?

4. My wife is Mrs. Clean. She's forever dusting, mopping, and straightening. . . . Any spill, rip, tear, or wrinkle is a crisis.

Now, I've always thought of myself as a neat person. But, if I skip a shoeshine or a shave on a weekend, wear the same shorts or socks two days running, leave a match on the floor, miss using enough deodorant, or drop a jacket on a chair instead of hanging it up—it's war! I'm all for comfort. There are a lot more things in life than cleanliness. Whoever said, "Cleanliness is next to Godliness," was a heretic! How can I straighten her out?

5. If my mother-in-law makes one more comment on my cooking or housekeeping, I think I will scream. She has nothing to do at all so she drops in two or three times a week and tells me what's wrong with my recipes, why I should change furniture polish, how the plant won't grow in that corner, and why I shouldn't spend money on having laundry done. There is never a word that comes out of her mouth that isn't some direct or implied criticism.

I keep telling John to shape her up on this matter. He says he knows his mother can sometimes be a pain but that I am too sensitive too. Besides, he adds, I'm a big girl and can fight my own battles. What do you suggest?

GOD'S WORD: WAIT UNTIL MARRIAGE[16]

A. Both adultery (sexual intercourse between a married man and a woman not his wife, or between a married woman and a man not her husband) and fornication (sexual intercourse between any two people not married to each other) are condemned in Scripture.

1. Adultery is prohibited expressly in the Ten Commandments (Exod 20:14) and is condemned in many other passages in the Old Testament. (See Gen 20:3; Prov 6:32-33; Jer 5:7-8.)

2. Jesus repeated the commandment prohibiting adultery (Mark 10:19) and even added that looking upon a woman to lust after her amounts to the commission of

16. Adapted from *Lutheran Youth Alive Newsletter.*

adultery with her in one's heart (Matt 5:27-28). He condemned both adultery and fornication in Mark 7: 20-23. (See also Mark 10:11-12.)

3. One of the few "essentials" that the apostles felt necessary to touch upon in their letter to the Antioch Christians was that they abstain from fornication (Acts 15: 28-29).

4. Paul speaks out strongly against sex outside of marriage in many of his letters. For example:

    a. 1 Corinthians 6:9-20. Paul warns us that those who continue to practice fornication or adultery "shall not inherit the kingdom of God" (vv. 9-10). He adds that "our bodies are not for sexual immorality, but for the Lord" (v. 13). Indeed, our bodies are "members of Christ" (v. 15) and "temples of the Holy Spirit" who is in us (v. 19). Accordingly, we are to glorify God in our bodies (v. 20) by fleeing sexual immorality (v. 18).

    b. Galatians 5:19-21. Sexual immorality, impurity, sensuality, and carousings are all included in Paul's list of the "deeds of the flesh," the doers of which "shall not inherit the kingdom of God." We are to display the fruit of the Holy Spirit, which includes love, patience, faithfulness, and self-control (vv. 22-23).

    c. Ephesians 5:3-12. Paul urges the Ephesian Christians not to let sexual immorality or impurity "even be named" among them (v. 3). Moreover, they are not to participate in the "unfruitful deeds of darkness," and they are to expose and reprove them (v. 11).

    d. See also Romans 13:9; 1 Corinthians 5:9-11; 10:8; 2 Corinthians 12:21; Colossians 3:5-7; 1 Thessalonians 4:1-8; 2 Timothy 2:22.

5. Other New Testament authors were equally emphatic in their condemnation of sex outside of marriage. He-

brews 13:4; James 2:11; 2 Peter 2:9-16; Jude 7; Revelation 2:20-22; 9:21.

B. A biblical figure who "fled" from sexual immorality is Joseph (see Gen 39:7-12). His master's wife asked him repeatedly, day after day, to lie with her, but Joseph refused each time: "How then could I do this great evil, and sin against God?" (v. 9). One day when he was doing his work around the house, she caught him by his garment and asked him again. Understanding the seriousness of this temptation, Joseph "left his garment in her hand and fled, and went outside" (v. 12).

BENEFITS OF WAITING UNTIL MARRIAGE

A. No guilt. God tells us to wait until marriage. Not waiting will create guilt that will hamper your relationships with Him, with your sexual partner, and with everyone else. By waiting you can know, because God says so, that Jesus Christ smiles on your marriage bed.

B. No fear. Waiting insures that you will never have to be afraid, not even to the extent of one fleeting thought, of having to build a marriage on an unexpected pregnancy.

C. No comparison. Waiting insures that you will never fall into the devastating trap of comparing your spouse's sexual performance with that of a previous sexual partner.

D. Spiritual growth. On the positive side, waiting will help you subject your physical drives to the lordship of Christ, and thereby develop your self-control, an important aspect of the fruit of the Holy Spirit. Also, if you get married and are later separated temporarily (e.g., for a business trip), then this discipline early in your relationship will give both of you confidence and trust in each other during that time of separation.

E. Greater joy. Waiting insures that there will be something saved for your marriage relationship, for that first night and for the many nights thereafter. The anticipation of the fulfillment of your relationship in sexual union is exciting. Don't spoil it by jumping the gun.

HOW FAR SHALL WE GO BEFORE MARRIAGE?

Given our conviction to refrain from sexual intercourse until marriage, the question remains: How far shall we go, short of sexual intercourse, before marriage?

A. The answer to this question depends upon how far along you are in your relationship together (first date or engaged) and upon your abilities to withstand the very strong temptation to have sexual intercourse.

B. However, a general principle which we feel applies to everyone is the following: That which has its natural end in sexual intercourse should be held to your wedding night.

1. This means, at the very least, that heavy petting, direct stimulation of each other's sexual organs, and mutual masturbation should be out. Don't build up your sexual drives and desires to the point of no return, lest your physical relationship becomes a source of frustration rather than of joy for you.

2. This also means that you should not engage in any physical activity which will build up the other person's sexual drives to the point of no return. In the context of a different problem, that of eating certain types of food, Paul puts forth the general exhortation that we not do anything which causes our brother (or sister) to stumble (see Rom 12:13, 21). Thus, both persons must be sensitive to each other and must place the other's spiritual health ahead of their own desire for physical fulfillment now. When in doubt, don't! For "whatever is not from faith is sin" (Rom 14:23). Pray, alone and together, about your physical relationship. If you can't visualize Jesus Christ smiling at the two of you, the Holy Spirit may be urging you to pull back the reins a

little, for the sake of your love for the Lord and for each other.

C. This does not mean that the two of you are not going to relate physically before marriage, nor does it mean that your sexual drives will not increase as you do relate physically. And it certainly does not mean that you will not want to go to bed with each other. But it does mean that the two of you will make Jesus Christ the Lord of your sexual life and that you are going to wait for the green light from Him.

Your First Year Budget[17]

(Try to figure out your expenses for the first twelve months of marriage.)

Flexible Expenses
    Clothing $ _____
    Furniture and Equipment, including repairs   _____
    Medical and Dental Care   _____
    Contributions to Charity   _____
    Gifts, Entertainment, Recreation, Hobbies   _____
    Day-to-Day Living Costs   _____
        Food and Household Supplies   _____
        Laundry and Cleaning   _____
        Drug Store Sundries   _____
        Books, Papers, Magazines   _____
        Car Upkeep   _____
        Personal Allowances   _____
        Total Flexible Expenses $ _____

    Add all flexible expenses and divide by 12. This is the amount you need set aside each month to take care of flexible expenses.

Fixed Expenses

Paycheck deductions for Taxes $ _____
            Social Security   _____
            Other   _____

17. H. Norman Wright, *The Christian Faces . . . Emotions, Marriage, and Family Relationships* (Denver, Colo.: Christian Marriage Enrichment, 1975), pp. 80-81.

Housing—Rent   _____
        Mortgage Payments   _____
        Taxes, Special Assessments   _____
Utilities— Gas   _____
        Electric   _____
        Phone   _____
        Water   _____
Church Support—Sunday Collections   _____
                Special Collections   _____
Union or Professional Association Dues   _____
Membership Fees in Organizations   _____
Insurance Premiums   _____
Vehicle Licenses   _____
Regular Payments—Loans   _____
              Installment Purchases   _____
              Christmas Savings Club   _____
              Other   _____
Regular Savings   _____
Add *Total Fixed Expenses* $_____

Then divide by 12—this is the amount you will need to set aside each month to take care of fixed expenses.

(1) Figure out your total income for your first year of marriage.
(Total Annual Income) $_____

(2) Add your yearly flexible expenses and fixed expenses.
(Total Annual Expenses) $_____

Deduct (2) from (1) to find out if you are in the black or red. $_____

What Is Your Opinion?[18]

Agree   Disagree

_____   _____   1. It is all right to modify the truth to avoid unpleasantness in the home.

18. H. Norman Wright, *Communication—Key to Your Marriage,* Leader's Manual (Glendale, Calif.: Gospel Light, 1974), p. 31.

———— ———— 2. An argument is a destructive force in married life.

———— ———— 3. Quarreling is always wrong for a Christian couple even though insights are gained thereby.

———— ———— 4. Every couple should have friends with whom they can talk over their marital problems and adjustments.

———— ———— 5. The wisest course to take when an argument seems to be developing is to remain silent or leave the room.

———— ———— 6. When a Christian couple are at an impasse in their discussion or communication, the best solution is to pray together about their differences.

———— ———— 7. It is sometimes necessary to nag another person in order to get him to respond.

———— ———— 8. There are certain matters about marriage that are best not discussed by a couple.

———— ———— 9. The Bible teaches that we should avoid people who get angry much of the time.

———— ———— 10. Only positive feelings should be expressed in the marriage relationship.

———— ———— 11. If we are married and something our mate does bothers us, we should go ahead and tell him or her and try to change him or her.

———— ———— 12. It is a sign of spiritual and emotional immaturity for a person to be angry at another individual.

FINANCES QUESTIONNAIRE

Circle the answer describing how you feel about the following:

> E—Extra
> D—Desirable
> U—Useful
> N—Necessary

Life Insurance	E	D	U	N
A Color TV	E	D	U	N
New Furniture	E	D	U	N
A Stereo Set	E	D	U	N
A Wig	E	D	U	N
Having a Car *(new car)*	E	D	U	N
Having Two Cars	E	D	U	N
Owning a Boat	E	D	U	N
Planning a Family Budget	E	D	U	N
Owning Your Own Home within Five Years	E	D	U	N
Giving 10% to the Church	E	D	U	N
A Dishwasher	E	D	U	N
A Blender	E	D	U	N
Laundry Service	E	D	U	N
A Camper	E	D	U	N
Pets	E	D	U	N
A Complete Set of China	E	D	U	N
Donations to Charity	E	D	U	N
A Working Wife	E	D	U	N
Vacation Once a Year	E	D	U	N
Air Conditioner	E	D	U	N
Continued Formal Education After Marriage	E	D	U	N
Long Term Savings Plan	E	D	U	N
Medical Insurance	E	D	U	N
Credit Cards	E	D	U	N
Installment Buying	E	D	U	N
A Motorcycle	E	D	U	N
Beauty Shop Once a Week	E	D	U	N

Dealing with In-laws[19]

The following suggestions by Landis and Landis could provide guidelines for couples in relation to their in-laws:

1. Treat your in-laws with the same consideration and respect that you give to friends who are not in-laws.
2. When in-laws take an interest in your life and give advice, do just as you would if any friend gave advice: if it is good, follow it; if it is not good, accept it graciously and then ignore it.
3. Remember that many times when the in-laws appear to be too concerned with your affairs, they are not trying to interfere in your life but are sincerely interested in your welfare.
4. Look for the good points in your in-laws.
5. When you visit your in-laws, make the visits reasonably short.
6. When visiting in-laws, be as thoughtful, courteous, and helpful as you are when you are visiting other friends.
7. Accept your in-laws as they are; remember that they would probably like to make changes in you, too.
8. Mothers-in-law have been close to their children before marriage; give them time to find new interests in life.
9. Go into marriage with a positive attitude toward your in-laws—you believe it is a good family to marry into and you intend to enjoy your new family.
10. Give advice to your in-laws only if they ask for it; even then, use self-restraint.
11. Discuss the faults of your spouse only with him, not with your family.
12. Do not quote your family or hold them up as models to your spouse.

19. Judson T. and Mary G. Landis, *Personal Adjustment, Marriage and Family Living* (Englewood Cliffs, N.J.: Prentice-Hall, 1966), pp. 238-39.

13. Remember that it takes at least two people to create an in-law problem. No one person is ever entirely to blame.

For a married couple to handle relationships with parents and in-laws on a positive basis, they need to:[20]

1. Be mindful of the fact that family ties are normal, necessary, and important and that a brusque rejection of them can only bring unhappiness to all;
2. Make the process of separating themselves gradual rather than abrupt;
3. Accept the spouse's concern for his parental family;
4. Accept the fact that parents cannot automatically stop being interested in, and concerned about, their children just because the latter get married, and that parental help can sometimes be a wonderful thing to have;
5. Present a united front to any attempt by parents or in-laws to interfere; firmness is more effective than hostility.

THOUGHTS AND PRINCIPLES ABOUT IN-LAWS[21]

The main facts about in-law tensions are as follows:

1. The person who causes most of these conflicts is unfortunately the mother-in-law. One study found that she initiated as much trouble as all the other in-laws put together.
2. Victims of in-law interference are nearly always the daughters-in-law. Often the mother-in-law is jealous of her daughter-in-law for dividing the affection of her son and tries to win back the central position in his life by alienating him from his wife.

20. Norman Lobenz and Clark Blackburn, *How to Stay Married* (New York: Cowles, 1968), pp. 55-56.
21. J. Richard Udry, *The Social Context of Marriage*, 3rd ed. (New York: Lippincott, 1974), pp. 288-93, adapted.

3. Competition and conflict between these two women reaches its most violent form when they have to live together in the same house.

4. Rearing of the children is frequently another area in which the mother-in-law interferes.

5. A mother-in-law who acts in these ways can be very troublesome. But she deserves your pity more than your hostility. What this person really needs is the love of those around her, but since she seems unable to get it she tries instead to gain her ends by manipulation and intrigue. Unfortunately she usually does not realize that she is completely defeating her own purpose.

Principles to follow with in-laws:

1. No in-law interference can damage a sound marriage. In-laws cannot drive a wedge between husband and wife who stand firm together.

2. The policy to adopt is to make it clear that you want to be friendly and you want to work for harmony between the generations, but you will not tolerate unwarranted interference in your marriage. This must be made clear with no compromise.

3. A confrontation or discussion should be followed up by sincere and genuine attempts to be friendly and conciliatory. You can behave lovingly towards them even if you don't feel loving, and the action tends to promote the feeling. It will help and encourage your spouse if you make a real effort in this direction. Experience shows that this policy can, in time, achieve a surprising degree of success.

4. If you and your in-laws really have very little in common, short visits from time to time are best.

5. Remember family ties cannot be broken, and they last throughout a lifetime. Even if your relationships with your in-laws are as they should be right now, a time

may come when you may need their help or they may need yours.

SAMPLE WEDDING VOWS[22]

I, Ronald, take you Carolyn, to be my lawfully wedded wife. I promise to love and honor you, using as my example the love which Christ has for the Church in that He loved her and gave Himself for her. I promise to take you into my home and to provide for your material needs; to bring you affection and cheer, understanding and companionship; to be to you a source of strength; and to render to you all that is rightfully due a wife from her husband. I promise to do these things with all my energies, whether for better or worse, in sickness or in health, in riches or in poverty, according to God's holy ordinance, and forsaking all others, to give myself only and always to you, until death itself parts us.

I, Carolyn, take you Ronald, to be my lawfully wedded husband. I promise to love and honor you and be subject to you as unto the Lord, to be a help meet to you, to provide those things in our home which are necessary for your happiness and comfort; to bring you affection and encouragement, understanding and companionship, and to render to you all that is rightfully due a husband from his wife. I promise to do these things with all my energies whether for better or for worse, in sickness or in health, in riches or in poverty, according to God's holy ordinance, and forsaking all others, to give myself only and always to you until death itself parts us. "Entreat me not to leave you, nor to return from following you. For where you go, I will go, and where you lodge I will lodge. Your people shall be my people, and your god, my God."

The exchange of rings:

With this ring, I take you to be my wife and endow you

---

22. Written by Ron and Carolyn Klaus, now of Philadelphia, for their wedding in June 1968.

with all my earthly goods. I give it as a token of our mutual vows and of my love for you. The ring is circular, having neither beginning nor end. My love for you did have a beginning, but by God's grace, it will never have an end. In the Name of the Father, and of the Son, and of the Holy Spirit, Amen.

With this ring, I take you to be my husband. I give it as a token of our mutual vows and of my love for you. The ring is gold, long the most precious of metals, and I give it as a symbol of the pricelessness in God's sight of the oneness He has created between us. In the Name of the Father, and of the Son, and of the Holy Spirit, Amen.

You Paid How Much for That?[23]

Secret thoughts of a husband: "I just can't understand why my wife is always short of money. Now if I took over, things would be more efficient and there would be money to spare."

A wife broods: "I don't know why my husband says he can't take me out more often. His expenses aren't that high."

Do you confess to thinking like that occasionally? Here is your chance to show how much you know about the day-to-day money problems your spouse faces. This quiz for married couples is divided into two sections, one for each partner. Each of you is asked the approximate cost of twenty-five items or services that the other usually pays for. Here are the rules:

Wives ask their husbands the questions headed "For Men." Husbands ask their wives the questions headed "For Women." In some cases a price range rather than the approximate cost may be allowed.

Score four points for each correct answer. Don't be too strict. Give your spouse credit for a correct answer if he or she comes within, say, 10 percent of the right amount.

___

23. Reprinted by permission from *Changing Times,* The Kiplinger Magazine (June 1972). Copyright 1972 by The Kiplinger Washington Editors, Inc., 1729 H Street, N.W. Washington, D.C. 20006.

If you want to compare scores, go ahead. But that's not the point of the quiz. The idea is simply to show you how well you understand your mate's side of the spending. And maybe the quiz will teach you a lesson: Don't beef about somebody's spending habits until you know what you are talking about.

For Men

How much would you have to pay for these?

1. A ten-pound turkey _____
2. A five-pound bag of potatoes _____
3. A chocolate cake mix _____
4. A chuck roast for six _____
5. A week's supply of milk _____
6. A broom _____
7. A large box of detergent _____
8. A two-quart ceramic casserole with lid _____
9. A set of eight water glasses _____
10. A set of six steak knives _____
11. A fake fur coat _____
12. A pair of pantyhose _____
13. A three-piece polyester pants suit _____
14. A woman's swim suit _____
15. A girl's blouse _____
16. A pair of kid's jeans _____
17. A pair of children's shoes _____
18. A nylon lace half slip _____
19. A king-size no-iron sheet _____
20. A machine-washable, drip-dry tablecloth _____
21. 3½ yards of double-knit fabric _____
22. A pair of steel sewing shears _____
23. A pair of sheer Dacron window curtains _____
24. A permanent wave _____
25. A tube of lipstick _____

For Women

How much would you pay for these?

1. A quart of motor oil   _____
2. A chassis lubrication   _____
3. A set of shock absorbers   _____
4. A pair of first-line tires   _____
5. A 20-inch power mower   _____
6. Fertilizer to cover the lawn   _____
7. A 6-foot aluminum stepladder   _____
8. A set of four screwdrivers   _____
9. An adjustable wrench   _____
10. A gallon of latex paint   _____
11. A fiber glass fishing rod   _____
12. A boy's baseball mitt   _____
13. A haircut, including tip   _____
14. The home heating bill for a year   _____
15. The yearly federal income tax   _____
16. Your husband's annual life insurance
    premiums   _____
17. An 'off-the-rack' worsted suit   _____
18. A man's raincoat   _____
19. A medium-priced pair of shoes   _____
20. A pair of knit slacks   _____
21. A wash-and-wear shirt
22. Ten shares of American Tel & Tel   _____
23. Dinner for four at a good restaurant,
    including tip   _____
24. A businessman's lunch for two   _____
25. Two tickets to a football or baseball game   _____

FAMILY COMMUNICATIONS GUIDELINES

Job 19:2; Proverbs 18:21; 25:11; James 3:8-10; 1 Peter 3:10

1. Be a ready listener and do not answer until the other person has finished talking (Prov 18:13; James 1:19).

2. Be slow to speak. Think first. Don't be hasty in your words. Speak in such a way that the other person can understand and accept what you say (Prov 15:23, 28; 21:23; 29:20; James 1:19).

3. Speak the truth always, but do it in love. Do not exaggerate (Eph 4:15, 25; Col 3:9).

4. Do not use silence to frustrate the other person. Explain why you are hesitant to talk at this time.

5. Do not become involved in quarrels. It is possible to disagree without quarreling (Prov 17:14; 20:3; Rom 13:13; Eph 4:31).

6. Do not respond in anger. Use a soft and kind response (Prov 14:29; 15:1; 25:15; 29:11; Eph 4:26, 31).

7. When you are in the wrong, admit it and ask for forgiveness (James 5:16). When someone confesses to you, tell him you forgive him. Be sure it is *forgotten* and not brought up to the person (Prov 17:9; Eph 4:32; Col 3:13; 1 Pet 4:8).

8. Avoid nagging (Prov 10:19; 17:9).

9. Do not blame or criticize the other but restore him, encourage him, and edify him (Rom 14:13; Gal 6:1; 1 Thess 5:11). If someone verbally attacks, criticizes, or blames you, do not respond in the same manner (Rom 12:17, 21; 1 Pet 2:23; 3:9).

10. Try to understand the other person's opinion. Make allowances for differences. Be concerned about their interests (Phil 2:1-4; Eph 4:2).

T-JTA Resources and Scriptures

A. NERVOUS

1. Gockel, Herman. *Answer to Anxiety.* St. Louis, MO.: Concordia, 1965.
2. Hauck, Paul H. *Overcoming Worry and Fear.* Philadelphia: Westminster, 1975.
3. Jones, D. Martyn L. *Spiritual Depression: Its Causes and Cures.* (Chapters 8, 10, 11.) Grand Rapids: Eerdmans, 1965.
4. Lee, Earl G. *Recycled for Living.* Glendale, CA.: Regal, 1973.
5. Seamands, David. "How Jesus Handled His Emotions." Pasadena: Tape Ministries.°
6. ———. "God's Prescription for Life's Greatest Fears." Pasadena: Tape Ministries.
7. ———. "Damaged Emotions." Pasadena: Tape Ministries.
8. Wright, H. Norman. *An Answer to Worry and Anxiety.* Irvine, CA.: Harvest, 1976.
9. ———. "Handling Worry and Anxiety." Denver: Christian Marriage Enrichment.†
10. Psalm 131:2   John 16:33   Hebrews 13:6
    Isaiah 26:3   Romans 5:1; 15:13   1 Peter 5:7
    Matthew 6:34; 11:28 Philippians 4:6-7   1 John 4:18

B. DEPRESSIVE

1. Cammer, Leonard. *Up from Depression.* New York: Pocket Books, 1971.
2. Flach, Frederic. *The Secret Strength of Depression.* New York: Lippincott, 1971.
3. Hauck, Paul H. *Overcoming Depression.* Philadelphia: Westminster, 1973.

°Order tapes by David Seamands from Tape Ministries, P.O. Box 3389, Pasadena, CA 91103.
†Order tapes by H. Norman Wright from Christian Marriage Enrichment, 8000 E. Girard, Suite 206, Denver, CO 80231.

4. Jones, D. Martyn L. *Spiritual Depression: Its Causes and Cures.* New York: Pocket Books, 1965.
5. Kraines, Samuel, and Thetford, Eloise. *Help for the Depressed.* Springfield, IL.: C. C. Thomas, 1972.
6. Seamands, David. "How Jesus Handled His Emotions." Pasadena: Tape Ministries.
7. ———. "God's Prescription for Life's Greatest Fears." Pasadena: Tape Ministries.
8. ———. "Damaged Emotions." Pasadena: Tape Ministries.
9. ———. "The Spirit of a Person." Pasadena: Tape Ministries.
10. ———. "The Hidden Tormentors." Pasadena: Tape Ministries.
11. Wright, H. Norman. *An Answer to Depression.* Irvine, CA.: Harvest, 1976.
12. ———. "Can Anything Good Come Out of Anger or Depression?" Denver: Christian Marriage Enrichment.
13. ———. *The Christian Use of Emotional Power.* Old Tappan, N.J.: Revell, 1974.
14. Job 4:6
    Psalm 3:5-6; 40:1-2; 42:5, 11; 43:5; 147:3
    Proverbs 14:30
    Matthew 12:20
    Luke 4:18

C. ACTIVE SOCIAL AND
D. EXPRESSIVE RESPONSIVE

1. Augsburger, David. *Caring Enough to Confront.* Glendale, CA.: Regal, 1975.
2. Nirenberg, Jesse S. *Getting Through to People.* Englewood Cliffs, N.J.: Prentice-Hall, 1968.
3. Powell, John. *Why Am I Afraid to Love?* Niles, IL.: Argus, 1967.
4. ———. *"Why Am I Afraid to Tell You Who I Am?* Niles, IL.: Argus, 1969.
5. Seamands, David. "Wishing, Wanting and Willing." Pasadena: Tape Ministries.
6. ———. "Is Everyday Halloween for You?" Pasadena: Tape Ministries.

7. Wright, H. Norman. *Communication—Key to Your Marriage.* Glendale, CA.: Regal, 1974.
8. ———. "Communication—Key to Your Marriage." Denver: Christian Marriage Enrichment.
9. Zunin, Leonard. *Contact—The First Four Minutes.* New York: Ballantine, 1974.
10. 2 Timothy 1:7   James 5:16

E. SYMPATHETIC

1. Becker, Wilhard. *Love in Action.* Grand Rapids: Zondervan, 1969.
2. Bisagno, John. *Love Is Something You Do.* New York: Harper & Row, 1975.
3. Buscaglia, Leo. *Love.* Thorofare, N.J.: Slack, 1973.
4. Powell, John. *The Secret of Staying in Love.* Niles, IL.: Argus, 1974.
5. ———. *Why Am I Afraid to Love?* Niles, IL.: Argus, 1967.
6. 1 Samuel 12:23; 23:21   Ephesians 4:31-32
   Romans 12:10, 15; 14:19; 15:1   Hebrews 2:18; 4:15-16
   1 Corinthians 13   1 John 4:7
   Galatians 6:2

F. SUBJECTIVE

1. Collins, Vincent P. *Me, Myself and You.* St. Meinrads, IN.: Abbey, 1974.
2. Keyes, Kenneth S. *Taming Your Mind.* (Orig. title, *How to Develop Your Thinking Ability.*) Berkeley: Living Love, 1975.
3. Lembo, John. *Help Yourself.* Niles, IL.: Argus, 1974.
4. Missildine, W. Hugh. *Your Inner Child of the Past.* New York: Simon & Schuster, 1963.
5. Seamands, David. "Is Your God Fit to Love?" Pasadena: Tape Ministries.
6. ———. "The Hidden Child in Us All." Pasadena: Tape Ministries.
7. ———. "The Healing of Memories." Pasadena: Tape Ministries.

8. ———. "My Grace Is Sufficient for You." Pasadena: Tape Ministries.
9. Wright, H. Norman. *The Christian Use of Emotional Power.* Old Tappan, N.J.: Revell, 1974.
10. Psalm 119:66   Philippians 1:27; 2:5; 4:8-9
    1 Corinthians 9:27   Colossians 1:10
    2 Corinthians 13:5   1 Peter 1:14

G. DOMINANT OR SUBMISSIVE

1. Ahlem, Lloyd H. *Do I Have to Be Me?* Glendale, CA.: Regal, 1973.
2. Augsburger, David. *Caring Enough to Confront.* Glendale, CA.: Regal, 1973.
3. Hoekema, Anthony A. *The Christian Looks at Himself.* Grand Rapids: Eerdmans, 1975.
4. Jabay, Earl. *The God Players.* Grand Rapids: Zondervan, 1970.
5. Lembo, John. *Help Yourself.* Niles, IL.: Argus, 1974.
6. Maltz, Maxwell. *Magic Power of Self-Image Psychology: The New Way to a Bright Full Life.* Englewood Cliffs, N.J.: Prentice-Hall, 1964.
7. Narramore, Bruce, and Counts, Bill. *Guilt and Freedom.* Irvine, CA.: Harvest House, 1974.
8. Narramore, Bruce. "Guilt and Self-Image." Forest Falls, CA.: First Ev. Free Church, 1975.
9. Smith, Manuel. *When I Say No, I Feel Guilty.* New York: Bantam, 1975.
10. Swindoll, Charles. "Lessons Learned from Failure." Fullerton, CA.: First Evangelical Free Church.‡
11. Wright, H. Norman. "The Christian Faces Emotions, Marriage, and Family Relationships." Denver: Christian Marriage Enrichment, 1975.

H. HOSTILE

1. Hauck, Paul H. *Overcoming Frustration and Anger.* Philadelphia: Westminster, 1973.

‡Order tapes by Charles Swindoll from the First Evangelical Free Church, 643 Malvern, Fullerton CA. 92732.

2. Phillips, J. B. *New Testament in Modern English.* New York: Macmillan, 1958.
3. Wright, H. Norman. *An Answer to Frustration and Anger.* Irvine, CA.: Harvest House, 1977.
4. ———. "Can Anything Good Come Out of Anger or Depression?" Denver: Christian Marriage Enrichment.
5. ———. *The Christian Use of Emotional Power.* Old Tappan, N.J.: Revell, 1974.
6. Psalm 4:4
   Proverbs 14:29; 15:1, 18; 16:32; 29:11
   Ecclesiastes 7:7-9
   Matthew 5:22
   Romans 12:19; 14:13
   Ephesians 4:26, 31-32
   Colossians 3:8, 10
   James 1:19

I. SELF-DISCIPLINED

1. Carlson, Dwight. *Run and Not Be Weary.* Old Tappan, N.J.: Revell, 1974.
2. Lembo, John. *Help Yourself.* Niles, IL.: Argus, 1974.
3. Missildine, W. Hugh. *Your Inner Child of the Past.* Chapters 13 and 14. New York: Simon & Schuster, 1963.
4. Oates, Wayne. *Confessions of a Workaholic.* Nashville: Abingdon, 1972.
5. Swindoll, Charles. "Lessons Learned from Failure." Fullerton, CA.: First Evangelical Free Church.
6. Proverbs 14:17   Titus 2:2
   Romans 11:12   Hebrews 10:36
   1 Corinthians 9:27; 14:40; 15:58   James 1:4; 5:7
   Galatians 5:22-24   1 Peter 1:13-15
   Philippians 3:14; 4:13

J. GUILT

1. Jabay, Earl. *The God Players.* Grand Rapids: Zondervan, 1970.

2. Narramore, Bruce, and Counts, Bill. *Guilt and Freedom.* Irvine, CA.: Harvest House, 1962.
3. Seamands, David. "Damaged Emotions." Pasadena: Tape Ministries.
4. ———. "The Spirit of a Person." Pasadena: Tape Ministries.
5. ———. "The Hidden Tormentors." Pasadena: Tape Ministries.
6. ———. "Is Your God Fit to Love?" Pasadena: Tape Ministries.
7. ———. "The Hidden Child in Us All." Pasadena: Tape Ministries.
8. ———. "The Healing of the Memories." Pasadena: Tape Ministries.
9. ———. "My Grace Is Sufficient for You." Pasadena: Tape Ministries.
10. ———. "Wishing, Wanting and Willing." Pasadena: Tape Ministries.
11. ———. "Is Everyday Halloween for You?" Pasadena: Tape Ministries.
12. Tournier, Paul. *Guilt and Grace.* New York: Harper & Row, 1962.

K. FORGIVENESS

1. Augsburger, David. *The Freedom of Forgiveness.* Chicago: Moody, 1973.
2. Linn, M. L., and Linn, D. *Healing of Memories.* Paramus, N.J.: Paulist, 1975.
3. Seamands, David. "Love, Honor and Forgiveness." Pasadena: Tape Ministries.